C000154672

RENEE FALLS

FRANK ROSELLI

ISBN 978-1-7347132-3-7 (paperback)
ISBN 978-1-7347132-4-4 (hardcover)
ISBN 978-1-7347132-5-1 (eBook)

Copyright © 2020 by Frank Roselli

All rights reserved. No part of this publication may be reproduced, distributed, or transmitted in any form or by any means, including photocopying, recording, or other electronic or mechanical methods without the prior written permission of the publisher.

Printed in the United States of America

CHAPTER 1

Renee Falls was a quiet and peaceful town. The kind of place where everyone knew each other. It represented the stereotype example of the American dream. Violence and crime were none, existent in this tranquil setting. That was simply the work of Hollywood.

Everyone living in Renee Falls was a God-fearing Christian. It was the kind of place where folks were happy to lend a hand to someone in need, and doors were always left unlocked at night. Saint Mary's church sat in the middle of town. It was an old white church built in the early nineteenth century. It was adorned with stained glass windows displaying images of Christ nailed to his cross, and Mosses standing in the clouds. The ten commandments hoisted over his head.

On Sunday morning, it was the only place to be. Everyone was early to rise and always looked their best on the lord's day. They all gathered at the church eager to serve their loving god. 12 year- old Simon Fletcher was not as enthusiastic as the others. He found it rather boring. Often catching himself deep in a daydream while the old Irish priest went on and on with his speech about a mighty and caring, creator.

When Simon was very young his folks forced him to participate as an altar boy, which he couldn't stand. Their entire lives revolved around religion. Every choice they made had to first be approved by God. The young boy found himself being smothered by Catholicism. He felt his parents were being way to strict with him. They wanted to control every aspect of his life. It seemed as if anything enjoyable was considered a sin. It made his childhood extremely dull.

Simon often thought about running away from home to escape the constant nurturing his folks showered him with. His mother often insisted it was because they loved him so much. They wanted to make sure their only son stayed on the righteous path. They feared the devil's temptations in this world would lead them to a fiery hell for all of eternity. The bible was a manual for the way man is supposed to live. It was crucial that you follow the rules exactly.

Simon's parents believed the fate of their very souls depended on it. Stanley and Eleanor's loyalty to a cult-leader who lived almost two-thousand years ago was impenetrable. Simon often wondered in the back of his mind if everything they believed in was actually true. He feared the existence of Lucifer and his army of demons lurking in the darkness, desperate for his soul. He was also fascinated by the whole thing.

Over-all, Simon Fletcher was a good kid and did what his folks asked of him. The young boy with a creative mind would often get lost in his own imagination, isolating himself in his own thoughts right in the middle of the service, not hearing a word the priest was saying. His mother would catch him staring off in a trance, she could see he was someplace else when Father Fitzpatrick began calling people up to ingest the blood and flesh of Christ. She gave Simon a subtle warning with her eyes, reminding him where he was, and what he was there for. Eleanor explained many times to Simon how the church is only one hour out of the entire week. There was no excuse for allowing his attention to drift anyplace else during that time. Simon couldn't help himself, there was a very active brain inside that skull of his. He quietly apologized to his mother as he looked around at all the other believers surrounding him. They all seemed to be possessed by the spirit of God. It was as if he were standing right there inside the church with them.

Like all the other's Simon made his way to the altar to consume the bread and wine, before making the sign of the cross and returning to his seat. As the praising continued some of the worshippers became even more animated. They started tearing up and raising their hands toward the sky. They shouted hallelujah while reaching out for the lord's presence as if he was a tangible sequence of atoms they could literally feel. Simon wondered why he didn't share the same joy as everyone else. He assumed it was because he was too young to appreciate the power behind an all-mighty god, causing him to feel a bit insulted and left out. It felt as if god was actually present, showing himself to everyone else, while he was ignored.

Simon often wished he could be a bit more sinful when church ended. He knew his parents would be invaded by the holy spirit for the rest of the day.

Every Sunday after church they would head home in their blue and white 57 Chevy station wagon. Most of the time singing Christian songs on the way. It was enough to drive the young boy mad. Eleanor even owned a pipe organ, and sometimes she would sit and play for hours at a time. Simon did his best to stay away from the holy poison to his ears. He just wanted to escape the constant worshipping. Never seeing any evidence of this powerful being who created everything, he couldn't understand why the whole town was so devoted to nothing more than an imaginary friend.

Lucky, Simon was a gifted artist since he can remember. Drawing and painting pictures was his favorite escape from reality. Locking himself in his bedroom, he would allow his wild imagination to come out for a stroll.

For his parent's eyes, Simon would create beautiful religious portraits. The virgin Mary holding the infant Chris, Noah's Arc soaring through rough seas, as the entire world flooded, not to mention several of Jesus nailed to his wooden-cross.

Stanley and Eleanor showed how proud they were by displaying them all around the house. When no one was watching, however, Simon would scribble much darker visions into existence. Like countless other boys his age, Simon Fletcher was interested in Vampires, Ware-wolves, and exotic alien lifeforms from outer space. Being an artist allowed his inner demons to manifest themselves on paper.

Sometimes he would spend hours constructing the perfect creature, only to tear it up and dispose of it, before his parents discover his sinister passion with evil. It was his way of venting and it gave him great pleasure. Simon also spent many nights staring up at the sky, contemplating if god was really out there somewhere, watching and waiting to smite him with volts from a lightning staff for his wickedness.

God never offered him a sign and Simon continued perfecting his morbid creations.

One day while losing his temper, Simon smashed one of his mother's porcelain angels. Afterward, he felt terrible about what he had done. Simon even feared being damned to hell for his foolish actions. His mother had to convince him it was not the end of the world. She promised god would forgive him and his soul would not burn due to his foolish mistake. There were many statues and figurines of angels and saints hung and placed around the house. There were also several wooden crucifixes most of them hanging above the doorways in Fletcher's home. They even had a last-supper painting hanging in the dining room, where they sat and ate dinner together every evening, holding hands in-order to pray and give thanks before each meal.

Simon didn't truly hate god. He simply didn't understand why he had to dedicate every conscious moment to his faith. Sometimes, he wanted to place religion in a box for a while and live a little.

The young boy was also bitter about the way he looked. He wanted to be desired like the other popular kids in school. He was scrawny and sort of goofy looking. On top of it, he had to wear these thick black-framed bifocals in-order to see. Simon never really fit in with the other boys, he wasn't very popular with the girls in class either. They always seemed to ignore him, just like the god his folks worshipped so strongly.

Growing up, Simon even pondered why his parents were both blonde-haired and blue-eyed while he had jet-black hair and dark brown eyes. Of course, his father Stanley was mostly sporting a gray-colored mop on top of his head these days. It convinced Simon even more that he was a child of darkness. Maybe that was the reason he wasn't like everyone else in town. Not having many friends made it even harder on poor Simon as he grew-up under a strict but loving roof. He was a bit of a loner with not a lot of freedom. He often felt like a prisoner to the restrictions of his parent's religion.

Eleanor and Stanley feared one day he would abandon their god and commence with a life of sins. It seemed impossible to shake this dreadful feeling their only child would become the black sheep of the town. He never seemed interested in taking part in anything related to their overbearing beliefs. It was troubling and either of them could understand it.

Why would their son refuse to love the god they so revered? They couldn't comprehend the fact that Simon had another way of thinking and seeing the world and all the things in it. He often asked himself questions his folks wouldn't even think of. Questions like why did god create dinosaurs millions of years before man, and were there other intelligent beings thriving on distant planets orbiting the very stars we all stare up at on those curious nights?

Young, Simon also pondered how the universe itself could be far more ancient than the very god who created it. Or why all the other animals alive didn't have to carry the strenuous burden of a soul, that constantly had to be safeguarded from evil.

Life was short, and Simon wanted to live it his own way. He couldn't wait until he was living on his own. He knew that as long as he lived under his parent's roof, he would have to follow their rules. His mother, Eleanor owned a thriving florist shop in town. It was named after her and carried all sorts of flowers and plants. Eleanor was also known for selling religious décor in her shop. Especially around the holidays. In her spare time, the godly woman would make her own statues of angels and saints to sell to her fellow Christians in town, and even the strangers who pass through on occasion. She really enjoyed having the business and it proved to be quite profitable.

The store was always closed on the Sabbath. Sunday's were meant for god and family, not money. She and her significant other felt very strongly about that.

Her husband Stanley made a great living as an architect. He was well known in New-Jersey for creating beautiful homes and even shopping malls all across the State. He had no problem finding work outside Jersey when it dried up around him. Simon imagined he got his artistic ability from both parents. Eleanor could create angelic statues, and his old man was very artistic in his own way as well, designing buildings and fancy homes. Stanley knew everything there was to know about drawing up blueprints and then bringing the structure to life. It was only natural that he would want his son following in his footsteps.

When Simon was only 8 his father tried inspiring him with a luxurious treehouse he built in their backyard. Stanley even let his son participate slightly with the little things, like handing him the tools he needed and helping clean up the mess. Simon didn't mind though. The treehouse his father constructed was hard work and it was all for him. It was much fancier than the average treehouse and Simon was extremely proud of it. The elaborate wooden structure became his new sanctuary when he wanted to be alone. Completely detached from the main house and high up in the tree, it was much more private, allowing the troubled young boy to be himself even more. He could draw whatever his heart desired and there would be no one to stop him.

Simon knew his mother was not a fan of heights. She rarely ventured up into the treehouse to see what he was up to. As the years went on, Simon found himself spending even more time isolating himself from the rest of the world. His folks didn't think it was normal for a teenage boy to continue playing in a treehouse, but at least it kept him out of trouble.

His mother would often ask him to mind the store after school, or on a Saturday when he would much rather be doing other things. Stanley and Eleanor wanted to make sure their son understood the definition of responsibility. They were not going to let him sit up in the treehouse all day every day wasting his life away.

Simon hated working at the flower shop. It was so girly. There was nothing there that interested him. He would quickly grow bored out of his mind while waiting on happy customers. It often brought him down, never having a girlfriend of his own. He hated seeing the older boys showing off their manhood and buying roses for the women sharing their beds at night. He often imagined them having incredible sex, while he continued to be denied by every female he encountered.

Poor Simon was convinced no girl would ever love him. When it came to the opposite sex the nerdy-looking young man with thick black-framed glasses seemed invisible. He couldn't decide what was worse, sitting through church every Sunday morning? Or working at his mother's flower shop? He felt his parents were ruining his life. Most of the children living in Renee Falls grew up the same way, still, Simon felt his folks were perhaps the most religious people in the entire world. He was sick and tired of being suffocated.

Sometimes Simon would find the nerve to strike up a conversation with one of the pretty young girls who walked through the front door. Usually, they would say hello back, but he knew they were just trying to be polite. None of the attractive young customers ever showed interest in poor Simon Fletcher. Never given a second thought getting a date seemed utterly, impossible.

Most days he would stand around staring at the clock as it slowly rotated toward quitting time. He couldn't wait to go home. Most days he would bring his art supplies along. Creating new images, was the most efficient way to pass the time. Simon often did his best to paint the kind of drawings his mother would love while working behind the counter. He was afraid to express himself completely around prying eyes. That's what his treehouse was for. When he was there, Simon felt free to create whatever his twisted mind could conjure.

CHAPTER 2

As the years passed, Simon cared less about being caught in the middle of one of his grotesque drawings. There was a certain thrill that came with the possibility of getting in trouble. As he got older his lust for women also increased. Simon wanted nothing more than a girl to call his own. He thought about them all the time. Mostly the sexual things he dreamed of doing to them. Simon desperately wanted to know what it was like to touch a woman and feel her gentle kisses all over his body. Convinced he would never be so lucky as to find a young girl to give herself to him, Simon continued unleashing his anger by conjuring up morbid pictures of death and perverted destruction.

One chilly, cloudy day in Autumn, Simon found himself in the middle of a true masterpiece. He sat at the counter carefully sculpting the face of an angel much more beautiful than any his mother made-out of porcelain. She had long blonde hair and baby-blue eyes that matched a clear summer sky. Her lips were bright red in color as if they just consumed the fresh, warm blood of the living. There was a pain in the expression on her face. She was strung up in a bizarre-looking tree made of sharp flesh, digging thorns in a garden of Eden typesetting. Her arms and legs punctured with blood dripping from them. Leaving her to suffer and bleed like the mighty messiah his parents donated their entire lives to.

Simon stood there with a grin on his face, as the deranged picture gradually came to life. He was soon interrupted by a customer looking to

8

bring home a bouquet for his fiancé. He was a large handsome man with huge muscles practically, protruding through his shirt. Simon quickly stashed the devilish drawing under the counter, while wondering what the big man's bride to be looked like. He assumed she was very attractive. Men like him always seem to have beautiful women falling into their laps. Most of the time face-first, he imagined. The young man buying the flowers was everything Simon Fletcher wished he could be. He looked cool and even drove the same car Simon always dreamed of owning. A 1963 Corvette Sting Ray. It was silver like a bullet and traveled as fast as one as well. Simon pretended to be happy to see him. He greeted the young man with a fake smile and asked what he could do for him. As the bodybuilder went on talking, Simon began hating him even more. It seemed this stranger in a giant's body literally had the life he always longed for.

Making friendly conversation, the perfectly sculpted man even mentioned that his wife to be was a pretty blonde with baby-blue eyes. It was like throwing salt into an open wound, but of course, the handsome, young gentleman had no way of knowing Simon was so down on his luck with the ladies. The giant hunk was madly in love and wanted to tell the world, Simon could've done without the details, especially when the man spoke about his sex-life and how incredible it was. He wanted to reach over the counter and choke the life out of him. Unfortunately, the muscle-head could have easily crushed the four-eyed twirp with one hand. Simon wasn't even sure he could fit his tiny hands around that gigantic neck. He just wanted to hurry and get the happy fellow out of the store and out of his sight, so he could return to his drawing.

The dreary weather made him feel even more depressed about his lonely situation. It felt as if the only woman who would ever truly love him was his mother. Simon began referring to his private place up in the tree as his house of sins. It proved to be the only place where he could let loose and do whatever he wanted. That also included looking at dirty magazines and pleasuring himself in a secluded place where no one could see him. He built a secret compartment in the floor and covered it over with a dirty old area-rug with Christ face on it, and a comfortable, brown lazy-boy chair so no one would ever find it. This was the place where he could store his most vile treasures. They were like a diary of ghoulish illustrations instead of words.

Simon Fletcher was the first termite to infect the healthy, vibrant tree, as his madness slowly unraveled and spilled out into the perfect little world around him. He was gradually becoming the town's outcast with a talent for creating macabre paintings evolving alongside him, causing the portraits to become even more unholy and disturbing as time went on.

Simon couldn't help himself anything made the troubled young man feel more alive than painting and drawing demonic and crude sexual pictures behind his parents' back. Many of his illustrations involved gory, sex scenes that would send his mother to her grave, should she discover them. Including the top half of a beautiful woman with the bottom half of a serpent and a big-breasted goddess being attacked by Satan's reptile-like claws. Simon even sketched visions of Jesus nailed to his cross in the depths of hell, surrounded by fire and brimstone, while horned demons with wings circled in a feeding frenzy. They were like a vortex of dragons swarming as they tore the sacred flesh from the messiah's bones. It was the best way he knew how to vent when viciously displaying his anger and frustration towards god.

Simon still had no choice but to attend church every Sunday with his folks, as he had done his entire life. Now barely 20, he wanted desperately to move out on his own, so he could be free of god's around the clock surveillance and demands. Working at his mother's flower shop for free, and hardly earning a check from his father, it seemed they were not willing to let him grow up and be a man just yet. Perhaps it was because Stanley and Eleanor feared they might never see him again in this life or the next, convinced his soul was in jeopardy depending on how he would live in total freedom. Their only son didn't seem as interested in serving god's will as they had hoped. He was too busy drawing slutty women and praying they would come to life and fall in love with him, knowing it would never happen.

Simon would often destroy his perverted portraits in a fit of rage, savagely stabbing the pictures, even setting fire to them. The nerdy-looking young man tried his hand with women many times, always finding himself rejected for one reason or another. Life was so unfair. Even the young women who went to the same school and church with Simon every week found him a bit odd. It seemed all poor Simon Fletcher had was his paper women of art, and they were mutilated shortly after being created. Only the best pictures made their way into the dark cubby of his morbid house of sins. His hiding space was very limited and most of it was filled with Playboy magazines he had been collecting over the years. It was yet another secret he had to hide from his parents while living under their roof. They had to be stashed away with his drawings of naked angels seducing demons and Christ being ripped apart by flesh-eating cannibals in hell.

Simon often sat in his childhood treehouse scribbling madness into the world while imagining using his vulgar artwork to poison his perfect little town. Simon wanted to open a store somewhere in Renee Falls where he could sell his monstrosities inspired by his growing hatred for god. It would be the ultimate way to get even with his parents. He quickly realized he wouldn't have many customers.

Renee Falls was a place full of believers, they wouldn't approve of his unholy portraits. Simon imagined it would be worth it just to see the look on everyone's faces, especially his parents. No matter how hard he tried, Simon could never quite sculpt his perfect woman. He could see her in his mind's eye, but she never came out the same way on paper. It was frustrating often sending a title-wave of anger coursing through his bloodstream. He quickly destroyed all the pretty faces he considered failures. Usually, by stabbing them with the very pencil he created them with. He was disappointed when no blood leaked from his victims. There were no screams or added looks of terror on their already painfully constructed faces.

His satanic artwork was the only thing keeping him sane. The lonely young man didn't truly hate his parents, they have been nothing but loving to him since the day he was born. He just wanted a brief release from all the restrictions in the name of religion. Surrounded by angelic figures everywhere he went, Simon felt over-whelmed and even stalked by his parent's savior. He craved a little darkness and excitement in his mundane life. It was the driving force behind his despicable artwork.

For Simon painting mutilated angels and demons holding sickles to Jesus was exhilarating. It caused his pulse to pounce and his idling heartbeat to speed up. He knew it was extremely sinful to smash all the rules he was taught to follow carefully, but as- long as he can keep his dark-side hidden from his parents, Simon imagined everything would be alright. That didn't mean he didn't catch himself checking over his shoulder's every now and again, fearing the eyes of god or one of his angels were secretly observing him beneath a cloak of invisibility.

He silently prayed his filthy deeds wouldn't cast him into the inferno for all eternity. The constant concern for his very soul grew more potent as his sinister artistry escalated out of control.

After countless failed attempts to create his perfect dream girl with everything from pencils to paint, Simon began rummaging through all the gorgeous models posing naked in the dirty magazines he purchased behind his parents back. Slowly flipping through the pages, Simon began to examine all the sexy women and eventually discovered that one of them had the perfect pair of bright blue-eyes, but the wrong color hair or her face wasn't the one he was drooling over in his head. With a pair of scissors in hand, Simon Fletcher began dissecting his paper-whores taking only the parts he desired to construct the ideal woman. Carefully carving the eyes out of one girls head and the breast and lips from other's he was able to successfully create his own Frankenstein monster in a sense. Staring at the mutilated women's photos gave him a certain rush. It was an act of sweet revenge for the way they treated him in the real world. Simon began sweating while in the house of sins carving up his paper sluts. Eventually, he found all the right body parts and placed them together. It was a long and strenuous endeavor, but finally, he had the perfect woman with long yellow hair and baby-blue eyes that reflected the very heavens his folks prayed to.

Most people would find his master-piece repulsive and down-right disturbing. For Simon Fletcher it was a crowning achievement. He tossed the magazines with the butchered models aside and held up his prize-possession with honor. Staring at his ghoulishly, constructed dream girl the, sinister pervert never felt so much pride. He smiled wide and even gave her a passionate kiss, before cleaning up his mess.

Now that he finely crafted his perfect dream girl the rest of the magazines were worthless and needed to be disposed of. Staring out the window of his treehouse, Simon was not very far from his closest neighbor, located right next-door. It was too close for comfort he often thought while savoring his filthy delights. It was owned by an elderly couple named Robert Stone and his adoring wife Jenny. They have lived in that same house for many years. Long before Simon was born. Even before his father built the house, he was now living in. They were a wonderful, loving couple, and- also faithful patrons of St. Mary's church. Robert drove an old black Chevy pick-up truck. His wife Jenny never went forth with receiving her own driver's license. She depended on her husband of 32 years to chauffeur her around. They kept to themselves, never thinking twice about what young Simon was doing in his treehouse when no one was watching. He imagined they would be there forever, then one day poor Jenny passed away from a fatal stroke. It was sudden and tore Robert's world apart. He found it difficult picking up the pieces after her death. Never having children of their own she was all he had. Stanley and Eleanor felt pity for the old man. They often invited him over for dinner and the sake of being around others. It must be so lonely for him living by himself after sharing so many years with a wonderful companion. They would even pray with him with hopes of lifting his fragmented spirit. Simon was also forced to contribute, cutting the elderly man's lawn and handling other chores he might need help with. He simply saw it as another way for his controlling parents to prevent him from attending to his sinful and selfish pleasures.

Simon found himself busy almost all the time either working for his father in the construction field or running his mother's shitty flower-shop. It appeared as if they were deliberately keeping him from entering his demented love, nest. A grown man and still a virgin. Simon was often haunted by the reality he may never find his dream girl in the flesh. Eleanor had grown accustomed to complaints from customers pissing and moaning about his rude behavior. It was deeply upsetting, but there was nothing she could do about it. Work and religion were taking up all of Simon Fletcher's time, he had to find a way to spend more of it alone in his house of sins, he needed to release this horny demon that aggressively possessed him every waking moment.

Simon liked being able to do as he pleased in the treehouse without judgment from anyone. He was free to satisfy himself for as long as he wanted in twisted fantasies as- long as he can find the free time to indulge.

Sadly, only a few months after Jenny passed away, her husband Robert did the same. Losing the Stones was a tragedy that devastated the entire town of Renee Falls. They would be greatly missed. He died peacefully in the middle of the night from a massive heart attack. Some folks would say it was the result of a broken one. After losing the love of his life, there was no real reason for him to go on. Their house was vacant and soon put- up for sale. Simon was sad to see them go but enjoying the fact that no one lived next-door for the moment. It gave him even more privacy when adding to his disturbing gallery. His repulsive, collection continued to grow, but nothing compared to the Frankenstein woman he created with the paper body-parts of others. Simon considered her his greatest achievement. He even thought about naming her Renee. It was a pretty name and another way to take a stab at the god-fearing asylum he lived in. Simon always made sure his beauty queen was safely hidden away beneath the floor of his treehouse.

CHAPTER 3

────────── ✦✦✦✦✦ ──────────

One day while perfecting his despicable craft, a stranger drove through town. His name was Paul Price. He was a truck driver from California just passing through a joint in his mouth as he began to admire the peaceful little place called Renee Falls.

On a warm spring afternoon, a smell as alien as himself hit the air as he let the marijuana smoke escape into the Norman Rockwell type of setting. He had long black hair and usually wore a bandana on his head. Paul also had a beard and tattoos covering almost his entire body, sticking out like a two-headed freak as he passed through. His wife was a total hippie and he knew she would dig a place like this, especially since it happened to be named after her.

Paul couldn't wait to get back to the west-coast and tell her all about it. He noticed some folks giving him strange looks as he rode by, sending cannabis clouds hovering in the clean air. His big silver money symbol ornament flashing right at them in the sun's glare, blinding anyone unfortunate enough to look upon it. Paul wasn't making a bold statement about wealth, he simply liked it because it represented his family name. He drove passed St. Mary's church and Renee's hardware down the roads away. The original store had burned down in a fire over 20 years earlier. When Stanley was around his son's age, he rebuilt it from the ground up. Now it was much more modernized then when it first opened in the middle of the 19th century. It seemed like a nice place to call home, especially since he and Renee were giving lots of thought to starting a family. That meant making some babies and bringing even more joy to their lives.

Being free-spirited as possible, he imagined Renee would easily go along with his plans of moving to the opposite side of the country. Paul wanted to return with his beautiful wife and find a home they could share their lives together.

Over the next few days, all Simon could think about was spending some alone time in his treehouse where he could create horrifying images and pleasure himself to the freaky looking picture he created. Unfortunately, since spring arrived, and the weather was more inviting, work was becoming busier than he was growing used to.

Between helping his mother at the flower-shop and working with his father's crew there was literally no time for him to enjoy his raunchy sins. Simon considered a portrait of his parent's death. A bloody murder scene taking place in their bedroom. He was through being treated like a child, he was a grown man, yet his parents neglected to notice.

Simon found himself on an obnoxious time-loop of work and religion. He needed to find a way off this crazy train before it crashes and burns. It felt like forever, but eventually, Paul made it back to the west coast. It was a long trip, but thoughts of his beautiful young wife occupied his mind and helped him barrel through the seemingly endless miles ahead. They lived in a little green house with white shutters.

In the driveway was Paul's black 1968 Chevy, Camaro. Next to that was Renee's yellow Jeep Renegade. It was covered in peace signs and pot-leaves. A Beatles bumper sticker to show off her favorite band in the entire world. Like many young women at the time, she swore to love them more than any other. She even thought her husband was proof since he had the same name as one of the gods of rock n roll. It was early in the morning, and Paul just wanted to lie down and rest for a while. Those feelings were shoved aside by his shear-excitement to see Renee again. He missed her like crazy. The two lovebirds were truly meant for each other.

Sparks flooded their eyes every time they locked on one-other. When Paul entered the house there was no sign of his incredible lady. Not until he made his way into the bedroom where she was still sleeping. Paul stood in the doorway quietly watching her with a smile on his face. She looked so peaceful laying in their bed. Her long yellow hair and soft milky white skin gave her an angelic like appearance. She was wearing nothing, but a pair of pink panties when Paul quietly walked toward the bed and leaned down to kiss her. Renee instantly opened her bright blue eyes and smiled at him. She was so happy to see he had returned. It could get very lonely for her when he is on the road for weeks at a time. It was almost as if her husband was a rock star the way he traveled.

Now that he was back, Renee didn't want them to be apart for a second. She wanted to make the most of it before he hits the road again. They kissed, and Paul wasted no time telling Renee all about the wonderful place he found all the way on the far east coast. You should see this place sweetheart. It's amazing. A perfect little town in New Jersey of all places. But it's exactly like you read about in those stories you love. I mean exactly. All the houses were adorable and even the town church was amazing. I swear if you see it for yourself, you will want to pack your things and move there. Renee just smiled as she listened to her husband explain this almost magical place on the opposite side of the country. "Is it really all you say it is?" Renee asked as she pulled him closer. "Tell me, what's the name of this perfect place?" Paul replied, "that's the best part sweetie. You're going to love it. The town is called Renee Falls." The two of them started laughing as Renee questioned him, thinking Paul was making it up to really impress her. He swore on everything that he was being truthful.

The idea of living in a town named after her made Renee pretty, excited. She loved the carefree lifestyle the people of California supported. She imagined things would be different in New Jersey. It was a totally different world in her mind. There were posters of the Beatles, The Doors, and every other great musician of the time hanging around the house. John Lennon had his own spot right over Renee's bed-board. They even had a boa constrictor named Lennon. Beads hung from entrances without doors. There were, also several instruments for smoking grass laying all around the house. Paul's favorite was the giant hookah they purchased while on their honeymoon in Jamaica. It was a Buda statue with long extremities like powerful gods who ruled long ago. The two of them used it often while enjoying each other's company. Lying in bed together, Paul had Renee cuddled up in his arms as he continued teasing and convincing her about moving to this trippy little town. He promised there was something really- gnarly about it. He just couldn't put it into words. Renee confessed she was very intrigued by the idea. She also jokingly warned him that she would be the one in control once they move into the town named after her. Paul smiled. "As if you don't already have my balls in a jar", he stated humorously.

Even though Paul was a tough, manly kind of guy who drove trucks and muscle cars, they both knew Renee was in charge when it came to their relationship. Paul didn't see it as a negative, Renee was the greatest thing that ever happened to him. Moving that far from the place she grew up was a big decision. She and Paul would be leaving their whole world behind. It didn't really matter where life took them as long as they had each other. Renee kissed Paul and promised she would go with him soon and explore the town for herself. Paul asked if she was serious. While sporting the biggest smile she'd ever seen. "I think it's the perfect place for us to---"Renee smiled at him, placing her finger in front of his lips. She then instructed him to lift his arms, in order to remove his shirt.

Soon there was a small pile of clothes on the floor near their bedside, as the peace and love couple spent the morning trying again for a child. Renee wanted this to not only be the best sex either of them ever had, but she also wanted to make sure this time new life would be taking shape inside her.

Renee was so impressed with the way her husband was thinking. Starting a family in a small quiet town far from the streets of Los Angeles seemed like the right move literally. It wasn't long before, Paul took some vacation time, only to hit the open road again and show Renee the amazing little town he discovered so far from home. This time the trip would be much more enjoyable. He would be driving his Camaro instead of the huge 18 -wheeler he usually lugged across the country. His sexy bomb-shell wife at his side. He couldn't wait to see the look on her face when they got there. Paul brought a little grass with him for their journey. It certainly helped, while traveling such a great distance. Mostly they passed the time blasting the radio and sometimes even singing along.

Renee was- in charge of finding new stations as they traveled on and different towers crawled from the wreckage of static invaded ones. A bit of an old soul, Renee also enjoyed the music that was popular before the British invasion. So, did Paul. They sometimes would listen to Elvis Presley or Buddy Holly. Music's always been the best way to reach your inner spirit if indeed we humans truly do possess such an elusive yet divine thing.

Singing and listening to music is what gave Renee spirituality. When listening to her favorite songs she felt free as a bird. Especially in the Camaro at 90 miles an hour. It literally felt as if she was flying. Speed does kill, and it made her nervous, but that was part of the excitement she shared with her loving husband.

CHAPTER 4

+ + +◆+ + +

When they finally reached the new town, Renee began to see what her husband was talking about. The bright glare of the sun was almost blinding, but she could see the beautiful white church in the distance and the cute little hardware store, as they drove by. There were lots of tall green trees different looking from the ones back home, but Renee's favorite thing of all was the old wooden sign above their heads with her name on it. It almost made her feel like a princess. She couldn't take her eyes off it, as they approached.

Paul turned to witness the joy on his wife's face, he could tell she was as fascinated as he was by this perfect little town. Renee liked all the little shops lining the roadside. She couldn't wait to check all of them out. Simon was busy working at his mother's flower shop when they arrived. He was standing at the register when a shiny black Camaro pulled up in front of the store. Renee was already wide eyed and falling in love with the adorable town named after her. She turned to smile at Paul while reaching for his hand. It was everything he said it would be and more.

Renee Price was truly thinking about packing up and moving to this amazing place. Driving passed Eleanor's Florist, Paul decided to stop in and grab some roses for the love of his life. It didn't matter that she was with him at the time. He told Renee to wait in the car while he went inside to pick something out for her. She thought it was silly, but since they were romantically searching for a new place to call home, Paul thought it was the right moment to turn up the charm.

Renee just giggled and expressed how in love with him she was. Simon was busy ringing people up when he first noticed Paul approaching the door. More importantly he took notice of the young blonde sitting in the muscle car outside. She was playing with the radio as usual, and Simon couldn't get a good look at her face. All he knew is that this caveman coming toward him was much luckier than he was. Driving a fancy muscle car with a sexy blonde beside him. It was the life poor Simon Fletcher always wanted once again confronting him and tormenting his thoughts.

Paul happened to pull up right behind Simon's car, which was a shit-brown Volkswagen Thing. He hated that car and did his best to convince his folks to buy him a Corvette Sting Ray. They had the money and knew perfectly well how much he desired it. How could he ever pick up a pretty girl in that thing? It's even called a thing. That told Simon everything he needed to know about the heap he was driving. He was doing his best to pay attention to the task at hand, but the customers could see he had a wandering eye. He was clearly trying to get a better look at the stranger sitting in the Camaro out front.

Even while Paul was in the store looking at the roses for Renee Simon had an eye on her. She started messing with her hair and waving it back and forth as if she was deliberately teasing him, still Renee didn't give him a clear shot of her face. He would have to leave the rest up to his imagination as her husband approached the register with a dozen red roses for the mystery woman sitting in his car. Simon wanted a better look at her, but there was no way for him to do so. He saw his opportunity slipping away as he rang Paul up and watched him exit the store.

Simon came off a bit rude, but Paul simply brushed it off and went on his way. It was on the tip of Simon's tongue to ask the stranger what he was doing in town, but he wasn't interested in a conversation with the hairy, unkept looking man. He had no idea the loving couple were house shopping, nor that they were on their way over to the Stones old place. He didn't yet realize that the unfamiliar love birds would soon be his neighbors.

Renee smiled when she saw Paul coming out of the store with red roses in his hand. She knew he was working on getting her in the mood. Now that Renee was seeing the town for herself, Paul imagined she would be very pleased, and he would get lucky later that evening.

All Simon could do is stare out the window as the beautiful blonde finally started to reveal herself as she turned to give the hairy monster in the driver's seat a kiss. her long hair obscuring her face once again from Simon's view. Renee quickly turned forward and the fast car peeled off.

Even though Simon had no idea what the blonde woman looked like he couldn't stop thinking about her. He prayed to god that he would run into her again someday.

Moments later Paul and Renee pulled onto Madison Avenue. Renee instantly saw the for-sale sign on the front lawn, and insisted he pull the car over. They quickly exited the Camaro in-order to see what the house looked like inside. Paul and Renee went around checking in windows for a better look. From what they could see it was perfect. Just a bit dusty from sitting for several months. Renee turned to her husband with the smile of an angel on her face. They had no idea if they could even afford it, but that didn't prevent Renee from leaping into her lover's arms and locking lips. They began spinning around on the front lawn as if they were figure-skating. Renee loved it without even stepping foot inside.

Paul didn't care as- long as it made her happy. It was his sole purpose in this life. After all, this was all his idea anyway. Mrs. Anderson was the nosy neighbor always silently documenting everyone's moves. It made most of the folks living on her block agitated from time to time. Especially when she catches them doing things no one is supposed to know about. Paul and Renee Price were unknowingly being stalked at that very moment. They didn't even notice the elderly woman standing in the living-room window with a steaming hot cup of tea in her right hand.

Mrs. Anderson was curious about the young wild-looking couple checking out the house for sale. The California license plates further convinced her they were not like the rest of the town's folk. She feared the free-spirited lovers could be trouble. She stood silently sipping her tea and watching them exhibit improper, affection in broad daylight, as if they had no morals, or consideration for others. Like it or not it wouldn't be long before they went from two strange faces to friendly new neighbors.

Paul and Renee managed to buy the house they would soon call home, placing them right next-door to Simon Fletcher. The four-eyed creep with a devilish obsession for blondes. He wasn't home when the strange new couple moved in next-door. Stanley sent him off to work with the crew a couple hundred miles away in up-state New York, to a town called Apollo Springs.

A brutal winter had recently come to an end, the warm spring air was taking over his portion of the world once again. Simon had mentally prepared himself for the long journey and the enormous amount of work that would have to be done once he arrived.

There was a large shopping mall going up in the busiest part of town. It would have a total of six different stores when he and the crew were finished. Simon didn't understand why his old man would accept a job so far away from home, but there was no work in Renee Falls at the moment. He couldn't simply sit around waiting for something local to come along. Stanley had to keep the company busy or it would go under. Simon could care less it wasn't as if he was getting rich off either of the family businesses. He felt he did all the work and his folks got all the cash. It was so unfair. Simon hated his pathetic life. Even worse he saw no end to his misery in sight.

When it was time to go, Simon hopped in his ugly car and hit the road. His father said the rest of the men were there already. He didn't know why he had to go and not his old man. The one good thing Simon saw in this personal disaster was that he wouldn't have to spend any time working at the stupid flower-shop. If he was going to be forced to work, Simon would rather be doing the manlier task of helping put up a mini-mall in a town he's never even heard of. At least he wouldn't be leaving a woman behind to think about while he was gone.

Simon wasn't really going to miss his parents much either. The one thing he hated about leaving town, was deserting his house of sins, where he enjoyed his perverted fantasies. Simon wished he could just bring his box of dirty secrets and stay in Apollo Springs forever, away from his controlling, god-fearing parents. He often worried one of them would discover his raunchy little secrets when he wasn't there.

While he was away and hard at work, Simon didn't create one single drawing. He was exhausted by quieting time and just wanted to get some sleep. He couldn't wait to get home, so life could return to normal. Simon also feared being ridiculed and down-right insulted by some of his father's rough and tough employees. He didn't want them to catch him drawing naked women having orgies with demons. Simon didn't know how he would explain himself when he returned, and the word got out? Instead of letting loose with his morbid obsession of sex and death, the troubled young man cried himself to sleep every night alone in his hotel room when no one was watching. He closed his eyes and prayed even harder to his town's almighty god for a real girl to come into his life somehow. In Simon's heart he didn't believe it would ever come true, but he had to at, least give it his best try.

Simon knew attractive women never went for guys that looked like him. In- fact the only one he ever imagined got some tail was Buddy Holly and that is because he was famous. He too was a dork with glasses in Simon's distorted eyes. He didn't know that while he was gone his prayers were not exactly answered, but there would soon be reason to believe it was actually possible. The Stones, old place was no longer vacant, but recently inhabited by the bearded man with the Camaro and the sexy blonde-haired passenger. He didn't know that while he was away his neighborhood had changed forever. The way they dressed and spoke appeared alien to everyone living in Renee Falls. That didn't mean they wouldn't be welcomed with open arms.

Everyone was welcome in the Lord's house, therefore, there could be no restrictions in his most loyal coven of believers. The young hippie would do well not to admit she thought John Lennon was Jesus Christ in another time.

Renee Falls Folks would not take kindly to comparing some British rock-star to their adorned lord and savior. Such terrible statements were considered blasphemy, still everyone made the young lovebirds feel, as if they were long lost family members. The first person to introduce herself to the new faces was naturally Mrs. Anderson across the road. Always eager to know everyone's business she quickly introduced herself in-order to get to know them. They seemed kind and joyous, Mrs. Anderson also imagined they were a bit wild and crazy when no one else was paying attention. Simon's folks also introduced themselves to Paul and Renee Price. The men shook hands and started bullshitting, as the women got to know one another better as well.

The Price's seemed like a lovely young couple and totally devoted to each other. They reminded the Fletcher's of themselves, when they were young. Stanley and Eleanor already knew what their son was going to think of Renee, before he even laid eyes on her. She was everything their unfortunate son ever wanted in a woman. Eleanor feared seeing her every day might even bring him down more than usual. She and her husband knew very well that their only son was not very desirable. Now 20 years old he has never had one, single date with a girl. They dared to imagine he would be alone for the rest of his life.

The concerned parents didn't want him sleeping around with dozens of girls, but they did look forward to being grandparents someday. How was that going to happen if their son remains a virgin, up in his childhood treehouse forever? Simon needed to get out in the world and meet a woman. Stanley and Eleanor began to wonder if maybe they were being to over-protective of their only child? They feared it was the best way to keep him on the righteous path.

It was early May when Simon left to go work for his father out of state. The job was still going when Stanley called and instructed him to come home. He told Simon his men could finish the job without him. It was the greatest news in the world for Simon. He missed his dreadful house of sins. More importantly he was going through withdraw from holding back on his creativity. If Simon didn't express himself mixing sex and violence soon, he feared he would go completely mad. Every night he was away, Simon closed his eyes and fantasized about his dream woman. It was the same thing every time. There he was alone in his own comfortable bed, safely at home with a gorgeous blonde girl laying, next to him. She was completely naked and smelled better than any rose, flower or plant his mother ever sold. She was divine, like an angel with glowing flesh, and a pair of white wings covered in dinosaur, like feathers. Her yellow hair like the rays of the eternal sun sending its heat down, turning him on, causing the blood to rush out of one head and into the other.

This brainless entity he desired to feed was considered wicked by the very church he attended every Sunday. It was going against everything his world believed in. All his rational thinking would be momentarily taken over, possessed by his lustful urges. This relentless need to blast intelligent life in its purest state into the dark, cold nothingness of his right hand was uncontrollable. It was murder on a massive scale, but it happens every day.

Civilizations wiped out with one simple, repetitive motion that starts with a sexual attraction brought on by the no skulled, tiny brainless head between men's legs. It's the beginning and ending of the world we create and destroy. The balance between life and death, the survivor's and the doomed. Simon could experience this imaginary woman he dreamed up with all five senses. He might even confess other's we are unaware of, or two frightened to admit exist. Her lips were red as the fresh blood painted splatter on pretty victims in his portraits.

Simon wasn't unleashing his inner demons in the form of new-born human beings he was simply letting them ooze out into a hazardous world where life without a female partner couldn't exist. It was like sending colonies to live on Mars without food, water or even oxygen. It was a cruel and selfish act condemned by the Catholic church. The dirty deed that spawns, life has been hard-wired into our brains and there is no way to truly keep a handle on it. The sole purpose of life is to re-produce, but that's not what the four-eyed weirdo had in mind. He was simply determined to get himself off with no sexual exchange from a mutual partner what's so ever. The selfish young man was only thinking of himself, imagining she was actually lying there.

Simon used his vivid imagination to make his masturbation ritual a real-life encounter. He even heard his imaginary girlfriend moaning in pleasure as he did all the right things to get her heated, creating an alter-ego who was a stud and could get any girl he wanted. They all drooled and threw themselves at him like a padded wall in an asylum, tearing off their clothes and raping him in a forceful, yet playful way. It was as if he was the only man in the world. Although his mind was free to cheat and sleep with whoever he desired, it was always the same exact girl. The blonde-haired blue-eyed goddess he created from mutilated photos of Playboy models. The one he struggled to paint but ultimately failed. If she really was out there someplace? Whoever she was? Simon was eager to find her. He would soon learn he may not have to look very far. As he continued to please himself in the hotel room his father paid for Simon stared at the sexiest face he could fathom. Her hands pressing firmly on his chest as she moved back and forth and up and down as if she was using him like a mindless piece of meat only to please herself. It turned him on even more and he was about to explode.

Simon was so -connected with the fantasy his arms were raised in the air as if he was actually- squeezing her perky-soft breast. He was even moving around on the bed as he pictured her riding him. Simon was convinced he was being intimate with the queen his fate drove him to possess. Climaxing together as usual in his wildest, most perfect dreams, Simon and the blonde mystery woman screamed in extasy. He started to smile as the rush of extreme pleasure ran its course through his bloodstream. As he finished and teleported back to reality, Simon's anxieties began flooding in again. He started thinking about the very real possibility that he could grow old and die by himself. It didn't matter how much his parents loved him Simon knew they would be dead long before he left this dreadful world behind. Then what?

Simon needed someone else in his life, something more than an invisible spy constantly judging after drawing out your destiny in the first place. What the fuck is the point of it all? The question echoed in both ears for most of his life. How could a loving god send souls to hell for a destiny he sculped before they were even born? What could be more satanic than damning people to the fires of hell who are powerless to control their own fate? In truth souls are committing the sins instructed to be carried-out in a vivid illusion of free-will? Thinking outside the norm was considered dangerous, even down-right evil throughout the ages. While away on his work vacation Simon began to realize he was in a constant civil war with himself. He wanted to obey his parents, and his god's rules just in case it all turns out to be real in the end, on the other hand, Simon pondered the brief existence of life and wanted to get more out of it. Mainly he wanted to think for himself, please himself in whatever that statement meant at -the moment presented. He didn't want to be punished forever just to live life his own way.

In a sense Simon was a lot like Renee Price. The gorgeous young bride he had not yet learned lives right next-door. At-the moment he was busy coming down from his self-inflicted orgasmic sin. The sex goddess was already beginning to fade from his third eye as she rapidly became nothing to him now that he was through with her and preparing to get some much, needed sleep. It seemed he was no different than the handsome men he hated for having any luck with beautiful, women. What Simon really wanted was a secret sex-slave that he can take out and play with whenever he chose. Just before his angel completely absorbed back into his sub-conscious, she started to scream out in a not so pleasurable way and her flesh began decaying at an astonishing rate, while imprisoned within a solid, block of ice. This nameless young, girl was still alive somehow and chomping at the frozen walls imprisoning her. Blood-stained, sickle looking teeth gave her a terrifying appearance as she struggled to bite her way free of this icy tomb. Simon somehow found himself fighting off the very girl he was desperately seeking. as she savagely chewed her way toward him. He was frightened, as she broke free of the delicate ice structure enveloped inside a maniac's imagination. The beautiful girl smiled sinisterly, her tongue like a malnourished leach thirsty for blood.

Simon found himself under attack, watching helplessly as the girl of his dreams gorged on his flesh and spewed his blood, painting the walls red. He abruptly awakened afraid and looking for his mommy. Hiding beneath the same covers where his imaginary girlfriend appeared in-order to destroy him. Simon quickly looked around the room, but there was no sign of the frantic woman trapped inside the block of solid ice. Simon didn't know what to make of the bone, chilling nightmare, but he knew it was time to go home. When he finally made it back to Renee Falls, the first thing Simon noticed was that someone had moved in next-door. His mind began to race wondering who lived there now. He was anxious to find out, his heart skipped a beat when he noticed a black Camaro parked in the driveway, Simon also noticed it had California plates. There was also a yellow Jeep Renegade parked alongside it. He could tell by the way it was decorated they were not from around here. Simon Fletcher started wondering if perhaps this was the same Camaro he saw while working at the flower shop right before leaving town. He still hadn't seen what the pretty young blonde looked like sitting in the passenger seat, he was convinced he would soon find out. What were the odds that she would end up living right next-door to him?

If Simon sees the bearded man again, he will recognize him and know it isn't just another out of state muscle car. He quickly hopped out of his Volkswagen leaving it right in the street and ran in the house. He wanted to ask his folks all about the new people who moved in while he was away. It was the first thing he blurted out when he walked inside. It was Sunday and he knew his folks recently returned from church. He couldn't believe there were actual hippies living right next-door to him. They hadn't done much to make the place theirs yet from what Simon could see. The same ugly yellow drapes were still hanging in the living room windows. Hiding whoever was inside. Simon knew the old coffee-colored curtains in his living room had been hung since the beginning of time as well. It was even uglier against the dark and dreary wood paneling that covered the walls in most of the house. Mom! Dad! Where is everyone. Stanley and Eleanor hurried down-stairs to meet him. They had a feeling they knew why he was interested in getting their attention. He must be dying to know who moved into the Stones old place.

"Hello, welcome home son", said Stanley as he and Eleanor started giving him hugs and even a few kisses. Well from Eleanor anyway. I see someone has finally moved into the empty house next door. I was wondering if you met the new neighbors, Simon was so excited he didn't even want to talk about the long ride, or the progress made while he was on the job. His father imagined they could talk business a bit later.

Eleanor told Simon the house now belonged to a sweet young couple who came all the way from the west-coast. She said they were a little strange, but very polite. The man's name is Paul Price, his wife's name ironically happens to be Renee. She said Paul discovered their quiet little town while driving his truck across the country and fell in love with it. He mentioned stopping in my store to buy roses for his wife on the day they traveled together to have a look at the houses for sale. Wait until you see Renee sweetheart. She is a very beautiful girl. Long blonde hair and the brightest blue eyes I have ever seen. Eleanor explained. She knew how much her son lusted over the blonde girls. Simon had a huge smile on his face. He knew it was the same couple from the flower-shop, now he would find out exactly what the blonde passenger looks like. Of course, she had to be married.

Simon felt he was truly cursed by the very god he was forced to worship. Why couldn't a woman destine for him move into the empty house? Then they could fall in love and be together until the end of time. Simon didn't even know for sure how pretty she was having not seen her for himself. Still he caught a fleeting glimpse once, and even his mother found her to be a very attractive young girl. Simon couldn't wait to meet her face to face. He couldn't figure out why she would want to be with a guy like Paul, he looked like a barbarian that scratches images onto cave walls. Life is so unfair, that was Simon's most frequently used phrase. He didn't understand why no women liked him no matter who they were. His brief, moment of joy was turning to grief as he realized he would now be forced to stare at a beautiful woman every day without ever being able to touch her or kiss her lips. Renee Price would be a constant reminder of what he could never have, every time he walks out the front-door. Stanley and Eleanor would soon see their son's demeanor change as he realized this girl was not for him, much as he wanted her to be. Eleanor thought he could use some cheering up.

She explained to Simon that she and his father planned to invite the new neighbors over for dinner, so they can properly introduce themselves. She and her husband thought it would bring an instant smile to his face. They assumed he couldn't wait to meet her. Yeah. That should be fun. Simon replied without a drop of excitement in his tone. He desperately wanted to try and get the sexy new neighbor off his mind for a, while by escaping to his house of sins and creating something new and horrifying. It's been so long since he was able to express himself artistically.

Simon also wanted to spy from his hideout high above the ground at the house next-door. Unfortunately, all the curtains were down and there was no way to see inside. He would have to wait for the hot girl next door to reveal herself. Disappointed he couldn't watch her from his tower, Simon quickly changed tactics and went back to thinking of a new painting. An artist at heart he began reaching for his supplies resting on a small narrow shelf his father built along the walls of the house up in the trees. Simon was soon sitting in his lazy, boy trying to come up with something utterly repulsive. He was in no mood to draw the virgin Mary or her son who would grow up to become the greatest cult-leader who ever lived. He wanted something darker to match the mood he was in. Once again, the young nerd felt betrayed by god. His life was utterly miserable, and no one seemed to care. He thought by creating another satanic picture behind his parents back he would feel a little better. Now that he was armed and ready to scribble something morbid into existence there was nothing worth bringing to life. It was probably due to the fact he was spending all his brain power thinking about the gorgeous new neighbor right next door.

Simon didn't know that Renee was actually, in the house all by herself at- the moment. Her skeevy looking husband Paul was on the road for the next several days. It was nice to return to his hometown every- once- in a while to say hello to old-friends. He also made it a point to visit his long-term drug-dealers back in California. He didn't think he would find anything in the perfect little town he and his pretty wife just moved to. Paul usually stocked up with enough supplies to last until his next trip to the west coast. He didn't know there was a young creep living right next to the house he and his wife just bought with an eye for her. When he returned from his long voyage, Stanley and Eleanor planned to invite them both over for dinner. Simon didn't want to wait that long. He wanted to meet Renee now and see exactly what she looked like. Since it was his own parents who sheltered him to the point, he was a weirdo, Simon thought he would take his artwork out on them. He went to work penciling his folks exactly the way they looked. Only he was not going to place them in a joyous setting with shimmering angels and smiles on their faces. He wanted to make them suffer, if not in real life, at least in his depictions of them. The lonely lunatic was once again busy scribbling a new horror scene into existence. Simon wanted his folks to pay for what they've done to him, keeping him in this preserved state of innocence afraid of letting him grow up. He pitted them against the very creature they feared most, the Devil himself surrounded by the fires of hell that contained him. Their faces full of fear and sadness, as they realized it was all for nothing. It pleased him to see Satan standing before the people who refused to let him live how he wanted. Adding insult to injury, the angry young man decided to smother them with miniature demons biting and clawing at their flesh. He knew he could never harm them in real life, but he thought about killing them from time to time while trapped in his temporary bubble of anger. As he put the finishing touches on his satanic piece of art, Simon was slightly startled by the sound of music. It was nothing like his folks listened to. It was fast and aggressive. In-other words it was rock n roll. He never heard anything like it.

Simon instantly found himself drifting toward what the religious people in town call the devil's music. It was a bright, cheerful day and Renee forgot she was no longer living in the city of angels. She opened the windows but kept the drapes shut as she rocked out and un-packed the rest of their belongings. There was a band called Led Zeppelin who recently hit the scene. Renee and her husband couldn't get enough of them. They were the new meaning of flower power, Renee found herself singing along and eventually dancing to the song Whole lot of love, forcing Simon out of his chair hoping to sneak a peak of the goddess next door. He quickly noticed the mystery girl dancing sexy, shaking her ass and swinging her hair around. The way she moved her body was really turning him on, even though he couldn't see anything more than a shadow gliding behind the show-curtains it was enough to drive him wild. He was wishing and praying that she would open the drapes, so he can sneak a better peek at her private moment. While secretly spying on the sensual private dance, Simon wondered if his folks could hear the loud music blasting out of the house next-door. Everyone on the block would have to get used to the different way of life their new neighbors were bringing along with them. The quiet, peaceful little town may not be so quiet anymore? Of course, Renee would never let anyone take the place of her beloved Beatles. They were literally gods from another world according to her. Listening to their music was almost the equivalent of attending church for people like Paul and Renee Price. Simon could only imagine for now, what she actually- looked like. Coming from a place so far away, he ignorantly convinced himself she had to be exotic. Simon imagined it would be a great way to spark up a conversation when they finally met. For once in his life the four eyed, geek wanted to come off smooth. His flirting was usually bumpier than the zits exploding on his face throughout high school. Knowing her husband was a truck-driver who was away on the road a lot, Simon dared to give himself the tiniest glimmer of hope that he could somehow magically make her fall in love with him while her husband was away. It was pure wishful thinking, but that is precisely what his folks brought him up to do. Find a goal and pray to god it comes true. He imagined she must get very lonely at night when the sun goes down and there's no one to talk to.

Simon wanted nothing more than to fill that empty void in her life. He wanted to arrive out of nowhere and steel her heart away. Being so far from home must have made Renee feel even more alone and in need of human contact. This could be the girl he has always dreamed of and Paul was going to ruin everything. He continued to watch her sing and dance in front of the window as he realized he had nothing to offer her. What good was a man-child still living at home with his parents. Renee wasn't much older than him, neither was Paul, yet they had the cash and freedom to do what they wanted and live where they chose, unknowingly bringing the girl of his destiny right to his doorstep. When the peep show was over, Simon considered another drawing. This time he wanted to place her loving husband In, the presence of gruesome terror. Simon sat there thinking of all sorts of demented things he could do to express pain and suffering in a picture that isn't actually, alive. He reluctantly decided to forget about the gory portrait and head inside instead, he feared his folks might come looking for him, if he stayed up in the treehouse any longer. He knew it was only a matter of time, before meeting Renee face to face. A couple days went by and there was still no sign of her. Only the sound of music blasting out of the house as she continued getting the new place in-order. Music always helped pass the time and she felt alone without the television or radio on to keep her company, when Paul was on the road. Most of her days and nights were spent hanging pictures on the walls and decorating the house with her wild décor. She had no reason to leave the house until she had everything situated.

Renee was wishing Paul could have stayed behind and gave her a hand. It would be much better if they could suffer the burden of getting their new home fixed up together. She wasn't angry with her husband for leaving her high and dry. It wasn't his fault it was just the way the work schedule planned out. Renee tried thinking of the great memories they shared together, she wanted to pass the time quickly until he returned. One of the first things she unpacked and displayed in the living room was their wedding picture. They both looked amazing in the photo and Renee was convinced she found her one true love. Simon knew she was alone, this was the time to introduce himself, before her worthless husband returns. He wanted to see if he could steal her love and affection from Paul. One, early morning while having a much- needed smoke break, Renee noticed something next-door that caught her eye. It was a well-crafted treehouse in the Fletcher's back yard she was surprised she hadn't noticed it before. Not giving it, much thought she quickly turned her attention elsewhere. Mrs. Anderson across the street was a nice lady, but Renee didn't like how she was always staring out her window or sitting on the porch as if she was the neighborhood watchdog. Everyone else was usually gone during the day. The street was pretty-much deserted accept, for Renee and her nosy, old neighbor. Eleanor was busy running the flower shop and Simon was working with his father a few towns away in Maiden Head New Jersey. Stanley was preparing to build a small complex of apartments. It was enough work to keep him busy for a long time and it wasn't very far away. Renee was thinking about finding a job somewhere in town. She knew she wouldn't make a whole lot, but at least it would get her out of the house for a while. She enjoyed the company of others and never liked being alone for extended periods of time. Once she becomes a mother, that will be the only job she will ever need.

Mrs. Anderson soon noticed they have inherited what smelled like a skunk invasion ever since Paul and Renee moved into town. She didn't know the young couple was smoking grass in the Stones old place. The Fletcher's also took notice but didn't bother to say anything. Only they knew exactly what it was, accept, for Simon. He thought it was a skunk same as the elderly woman across the way. The young man really was sheltered from the true, nature of the world he lived in. 20 years old and he didn't even know what pot was. The sun was still shinning when Simon and his father returned from surveying the land where the new apartments would be built. It was an easy workday, which was a good thing because there wouldn't be any more for a long time. Once home, Simon quickly retreated to his house of Sins with the urge to create another drawing.

Entering the back, yard he could hear, the sound of music coming from the house next-door. He knew it had to be Renee rocking out and transforming the house into a home. One filled with cannabis smoke and British rock bands. It was driving him crazy, that he still hadn't run into her once since returning from New York. Simon started to wonder if she was ever going to leave her nest. Forgetting all about the treehouse in the yard next-door Renee went on cleaning and decorating her new home. It was a hot summer and she was never a big fan of clothing anyway.

California was a great place for someone who doesn't like bundling up. In a few months she and her husband Paul will experience their first cold, blustery winter in this new land far away from home. She wasn't sure if she was going to like it or not. She was however a little excited to witness snow for the first time. It never did such a thing in the area she grew up in. Hard at work in the nude, Renee danced and sang as if she was the only person in the world. She had no idea Simon and his father had returned from work already. She didn't know he was sitting up in his treehouse at that very moment ready to spy on her.

Once Simon heard the music playing, he forgot all about the art supplies laying around nearby. He stood inside the house of sins watching and waiting for her to show herself. Renee has yet to meet Simon Fletcher and has no idea he is a peeping Tom, his eyes dead-locked on the window upstairs leading to her bedroom. Simon was hoping this time he would get a better look then her simply shaking her shadow around in front of him. It wasn't long before Renee was dancing behind the curtains again. This time to Simon's surprise the sexy outgoing new neighbor removed the dark, ugly drapes showing off her entire body to the creeper in the treehouse. Simon did well to remain out of sight as he stared back at Renee dancing naked before him. She had no idea There was a secret admirer lurking just out of sight. Renee had the body of a Goddess, her breast, were perfect and Simon couldn't take his eyes off, of them. He didn't get a very good look at her face it was covered by her long flowing hair as she danced around in front of the window care-free. Simon wasn't paying much attention to that area of her body anyway. He was more fixated on her breast and the hairy little bush between her legs. Simon couldn't even blink as the young girl next-door showed him far more than he could 've ever dreamed. Simon wished he could go over there and dance with her, unfortunately he didn't know how to move like that. It felt like a handicap preventing him from pulling a girl onto the dancefloor and showing her the time of her life. Poor Simon didn't even go to his high school prom because it was impossible to find a date. He would really, love it if Renee Price from next-door could be his dance-partner.

Despite the fact they haven't even met yet, Simon's attraction for the young woman was already growing strong. Although he has yet to look into her bright-blue eyes or hear her soft, sensual voice, Simon couldn't believe she was standing there in the window for him to feast his eyes upon. He was soon disappointed when she turned off the bedroom light and stepped away from the window. The show was over for now, but the young pervert did his best to store that sexy image safely away inside his memory bank for the rest of his days. He climbed out of the tree in the dark and made his way inside for the rest of the night. Simon couldn't get Renee out of his mind. He had to find a way to meet her and soon. He couldn't take it anymore. She seemed so beautiful, so vibrant. Simon would give anything just to touch her skin. Or run his fingers through her long yellow hair.

Eleanor and Stanley were lying cozy in their bed watching television. There was some charismatic preacher speaking about the end of days and man's redemption before that time comes. The time to repent was now by simply offering your soul to the Lord Jesus Christ. Alone and tired, Simon decided to do the same thing. He began flipping through the channels while Renee continued to dance naked in his minds eye. Her perky tits bouncing up and down in slow-motion as he fantasized over-and over again. One of the stations had breaking news about a vicious cult leader named Charles Manson and his band of delinquent misfits. Most of them attractive women. One of his victims was named Sharon Tate, she was an actress as beautiful as the blonde bombshell, forever branded on his brain. Simon couldn't believe a short, ugly little man like Manson could make such pretty -young girls do such horrific things. The story was extremely troubling, but Simon couldn't look away. Nor could he change the channel. He wanted to know everything about this ranch of death and chaos. Simon didn't want his folks to know what he was watching. He was hoping his doting mother wouldn't enter his room any second to kiss him good night. He was still turned on by the image he witnessed from inside the treehouse. He wanted to turn off the tv and think about her some more while he pleased himself alone in the dark. A despicable obsession was rapidly taking shape inside Simon's mind. Somehow this Manson guy was able to convince a group of ordinary young men and women to follow him straight into the pits of hell, meanwhile just getting a girl to say hello to Simon was virtually impossible. The Manson family was terrifying, but he found them extraordinarily fascinating as well. He continued watching the news coverage until he eventually closed his eyes and drifted off to sleep.

CHAPTER 5

✦ ✦ ✦✦✦ ✦ ✦

The next day was hot and sunny, as it usually is during Jersey summers. Simon was busy sweating up a storm as he performed the awful chore of cutting the grass. All the while praying to himself that Renee would come out and introduce herself. He was excited to see what she was actually like. He feared she might think he was strange and turn away from him like all the other girls he has encountered in this short-miserable life. Simon was also afraid he would act weird in front of her when they finally meet. He knew so much more about Renee than she would have ever wanted him to. Her entire body revealed through a window across the way from his house of sins. His glasses looked as if it were raining outside. They were moist from all the sweat leaking through his pores. Simon even removed his shirt exposing his scrawny body to the rest of the people living on Madison Avenue. He didn't care who saw him at -the moment it was way to hot to think about anything else, accept, for Renee Price. Simon wondered what he would do if she came out and found him shirtless in the front-yard. He didn't think she would like what she sees, making him slightly embarrassed of having Renee catch him so exposed. It was strange after seeing her entire, body without even knowing she was being watched. It was an invasion of privacy, but Simon didn't see it that way. He had been dying to meet the sexy young stranger since the day she pulled up to his mother's flower-shop with her hairy, tattooed husband.

Now that Simon witnessed her breath-taking body, he wanted to see if her face matched. He wanted to know if she was truly the girl of his dreams, or just another attractive blonde he would never get close to. Simon could feel the heat of the sun beating down on him as if he was already burning in hell for his lustful urges. He was almost finished and couldn't wait to get cleaned up. Simon desperately needed a shower after all that hard, work. He also planned on imagining his wildest fantasy and getting off, since he fell asleep watching the shocking, news the night before. Simon kept the images of her body on repeat in his mind's eye since seeing it first, hand. Still unaware of what her face looks like, he was turned on simply by the rest of her soft milky white flesh. Simon imagined he would simply use the face he always dreamed of when pleasing himself. If god wasn't going to offer him a fertile destination to get his rocks off, then he would do it himself. Simon began to realize his parent's savior literally ignored every prayer he's ever asked for. What good was it having him around? His parents could never understand how he felt. They were high-school sweet-hearts who have known love and passion their entire lives.

Simon Fletcher was a dorky virgin going nowhere fast, even his vehicle was a brown heaping pile of shit. His ride was so ugly the German's couldn't even name it. They called it the thing. His parents had the funds to buy him a Corvette sting ray, yet they refused. A certain hatred crept in over the years, as Simon felt his folks loved their god even more than him. They shoveled out tens of thousands to victims in need during natural disasters and to feed and clothe the homeless, yet they couldn't afford to buy his dream car. It was so unfair. These were the things taking place inside that confused mind of his while he angrily finished chopping the grass. To his surprise Renee walked out of her house for the first time while he was taking notice. She was wearing a red sundress with yellow flowers on it. Her hair was sparkling and her skin radiant. In her hands was a large, heavy box of junk. She was doing her best to get the place feeling as close to home as possible. He froze solid as she appeared like an angel sent to earth to torment him. It wasn't long before she looked over and flashed a smile at the nerdy young man in glasses. The two locked eyes for the first time and Simon was finally able to see her perfectly sculpted features. She was looking directly at him when he assumed all the stars, moons and planets aligned perfectly in the heavens. He began thinking about the girl he always dreamed of, while mentally placing the morbid Frankenstein's monster collage of severed women over her face and they melted together perfectly. She was precisely sculpted to all -of his grueling specifications. The most flawless woman god has ever created in his eyes. Suddenly she was standing right in front of him, and he had no idea what to say. All he could do is stare and compare her to the picture of mutilated models he selfishly constructed in-order to bring her to life. It was as if god had finally come through for him, after all this time. The ultimate deity finally decided to show itself. Overwhelmed he wanted to get down on his knees right there in front of her and thank his lucky stars. He wanted to sing songs about the Lord and praise his name from the highest rooftop. The goddess who had been locked inside his mind finally manifested into the real world She was even named after the town he grew up in. It had to be his fate to end up with the woman he had always dreamed of. Maybe his life was, destine to suck until this very moment. Fuck Paul, he selfishly thought. Simon was going to find a way to win Renee over.

Now that he finally felt god was on his side, Simon began praying that something awful would happen to her husband. He honestly didn't care who answered, that being God, or his rival angel Lucifer. A servant of light cast into the darkness after the extra-terrestrial fall-out. All Simon cared about was getting Renee next-door to fall in love with him. He dreamed about her his entire life, now there she was standing right in front of him, a tangible being, something he could see, touch, even taste if he was really, lucky. Thinking with his little head the horny virgin sent all the blood away from his brain and into the careless, sexual deviant between his legs. He wanted to be the man who pleased her with his average sized tool. Unfortunately, he's never done it before and being with the girl of his dreams after all these years of wanting and waiting, Simon expected to spoil the moment by ejaculating much too soon. He feared he would get off the very moment Renee touched his penis, getting her, all worked up for a giant let down. How would he face her after that? Knowing he would have no choice but to see her every day he lived under his parent's roof. He would feel like a complete failure every time he walked out his front-door and forced to admit Paul was the better man. How could he keep the girl of his dreams if he couldn't even last more than two seconds under the covers. That was the reason he wanted her around in the first place. There was no point in possessing his princess if he couldn't even fuck her good. Simon didn't give much thought to what they would do together when they weren't satisfying his selfish needs. He didn't actually- love Renee or care about her feelings. He just wanted to insert his throbbing stiffy into her warm, wet pleasure zone. Renee didn't know what was going on inside his head, but he gave her a strange vibe. She smiled and waved at him, careful to be polite in a new town far from home. There was something in his eyes that gave her an unsettling feeling, sort of like the Manson Fella on television. He seemed different from the rest of the friendly folks in town, as if he was hiding something.

Renee gave him the benefit of the doubt knowing who his parents were. She ignorantly assumed he was just tired and a bit moody after working so hard in the sun. When she smiled and waved at him, it was as if he was watching the second coming of Christ right there on his very own street. Simon couldn't believe his eyes. The most beautiful woman he has ever witnessed was saying hello to him. Simon smiled and waved back at her, but it was a goofy looking smile, unlike hers that literally took his breath away. Renee casually placed the trash down on the curb and turned to go back inside, she appeared to have no interest in him, as he watched her turn and walk away. Simon angrily went about his business mowing the front lawn after discovering the girl who's haunted his every conscious, thought was now, living right next-door. He couldn't believe how much she resembled the Frankenstein version he created before they even met. Simon had to admit, he found it a bit chilling, almost believing he had the power to bend reality to his will and bring his queen into the physical world, without the help of the Christian

God. When the lawn was finished Simon started trimming the hedges and plucking the weeds. It was back-breaking work, especially under the bright burning sun. The only thing that motivated Simon was watching, as Renee came out several more times to throw away useless trash left behind. He thought about asking her if she needed any help. The bags looked awfully heavy and he wanted to seem like a gentleman by offering her a hand. Simon imagined he would appear as her knight in shining armor if he helped her clean out all the trash in her new home, instead he chickened out and did his best to stare at her in crossing without being caught. Dirty images flooded his mind as he imagined all the unspeakable things, he wanted to do to her. Things so filthy and wrong he even feared his parents would disown him for it. He wanted to fuck her like a wild animal in his bedroom right down the hall from his folks while they slept. Her sweaty body was doing things to him mentally and it was getting harder for Simon to control himself. He was struggling to keep his thoughts focused on the task at hand. The desperate young man had to find a way into the girl next door's heart and panties. He loved the Stones growing up like everyone else in Renee Falls, but he was much happier to have this beauty queen living there instead. She disappeared back into the house and hadn't come out for a while. Simon assumed that was the last he would see of her today. He was busy picking weeds when he was startled by the presence of someone sneaking up behind him. Simon smiled when he turned and saw it was Renee coming to formally introduce herself, although there was something off about the timid looking young man, she knew they were going to be seeing a lot of each other, it seemed rational to be friendly. Simon was nervous as hell, he was shaking like a leaf on a dying, tree when Renee engaged in conversation with him. He could barely get it out, but he said Hi my name is Simon Fletcher. My name is Renee Price. It's very nice to meet you Simon Fletcher. I already introduced myself to your parents. They seem really, nice. Simon stood up, while rubbing his hands together, desperate to clean the dirt off before shaking hands with an angel. Renee didn't seem to mind the dirt, although she didn't have a spec on her, she seemed as if things like that didn't bother her much. The stunningly, beautiful young girl may look like a royal princess, but she didn't behave like one. As she reached out her hand, Simon gently squeezed it. It was so soft and smooth. Her perfume smelled incredible and her eyes were like portals into a heavenly like realm. Simon found himself in a sort of daze. It was a little awkward meeting her face to face, now that it was really, happening. Simon silently hoped she didn't know he had been spying on her from the treehouse. He couldn't face the humiliation if she was to bring it up right now. Lucky for him, she had no idea he was a peeper just yet. As Renee continued talking to him, Simon started undressing her with his eyes. He already knew what she looked like under that sexy sundress. Even her voice was exactly the way he heard it in his head. The nervous young man did his best to pretend he was hanging onto her every word. He quickly agreed with her that his folks were very loving and caring people. He wanted to invite her over for dinner tonight while her husband was still on the road but didn't have the nerve to ask. He just kept the conversation basic as he day-dreamed of tearing off that dress and jumping on top of her. Simon admitted his folks often go out of their way to help others, usually by donating money when some catastrophe occurs somewhere in the world.

"My mother owns the flower shop in town as I'm sure you already know, and my father is an architect.", said Simon.

"I know they were telling me all about it when me and my husband Paul first moved in. You will have the chance to meet him when he returns from his long voyage across the country. I think the two of you will get along just fine." Renee replied.

Simon did his best to pretend he was excited to meet her husband, but inside he was still wishing ill will on him. He apologized for not coming over and introducing himself sooner. He said he has been home for days now and should've properly, welcomed her to the neighborhood when he first returned. Renee smiled, insisting it was no big deal. She confessed she has been stuck inside trying her best to get the new house in shape. She was glad to say she was almost finished. Her smile was more beautiful than anything Simon had ever seen, and she was flashing it right at him. He started telling her how he sometimes hated his parent's for being so hard on him. He admitted between work and religion he had no time for himself. Renee tried to help, insisting they just want what's best for him. Simon's worst fear was that his folks would eventually do something to humiliate the shit out of him in front of her. Yeah, I know what you mean, but I think god is pretty, gnarly. You should be happy to have parents who care for you so much, not everyone is so lucky. All Simon could do is stare into her dreamy- blue eyes, they seemed so familiar to him. The longer he stood on his front-lawn talking to Renee, the quicker he began falling in love with the forbidden, fruit. Simon assumed the friendly chat she mercifully offered him would end any second. He wanted to keep her talking as, long as possible. Nervous and unsure what to say next? His fears were replaced by a slightly embarrassing moment when Renee asked him about his ugly shit box car. So, is that your Volkswagen Thing I saw you driving the other day?

"Yes," Simon reluctantly confessed. He smiled at her while having a hard time believing she actually liked it. Renee said it was a great car for a hippie like herself. She even confessed she recently traded in her Volkswagen Bug for the Jeep Renegade. She swore she loved his car and thought it was really- far out. You really think so? He nervously questioned. Absolutely she confessed. Simon wanted to press his luck and ask her to take a drive with him, he would even put the top down so the whole town could see him driving around with the sexiest girl in the world. When the moment came, Simon chickened out again. He was far too frightened of being rejected. As many times as, it's happened in his short pathetic life, the four eyed lonely, boy never got used to it. Renee never considered herself a religious person, but her hippie lifestyle did cause her to believe in love, peace and happiness. Which in a way are the same thing minus the church and all the nonsense rules and regulations enforced to condemn pleasures of the flesh. Simon was glad to hear that Renee liked his car. Deep down he assumed she was just being polite. He was sure to let her know the car he really wanted was a Corvette Sting

Ray. Maybe that would convince the eye-popping wonderous creature to find him cool or even slightly attractive. His folks said it was too expensive and a waste of hard- earned money. Simon swore he would have one someday when he was out on his own. Renee flashed another smile at him, she agreed Corvettes are very nice cars. Simon imagined if he had one in the garage, he'd have a much better chance at taking her for a ride in it. Renee asked him where the car was now? He explained he usually keeps it parked in the garage. Simon enjoyed the way Renee was staring at him, he started thinking about the beautiful blonde bringing up his shit-brown car. She must have actually been paying attention to him. How else would she know what kind of car he drove? It made his heart pound faster and sent a small tsunami of blood coursing through his body, then Simon began to realize he was foolishly getting his hopes up. He knew it was simply a matter of time before she was going to see the ugly thing coming down the street. Simon wished he could be that important to such a beautiful girl. Renee could see the innocence in his eyes. It was obvious how sheltered he was growing up. Simon was taking in the precious moment that his finest, creation had not only come to life but was actually- standing there before him, talking to him and even gracing him with her gorgeous smile. Simon was going to have to find a way to control his demons if he is to spend any more time with the sexy young blonde next-door. He didn't want Renee to discover what a creep he truly was. There was something about her that drove him completely wild. Even the sound of her laugh turned him on in a way no other woman could. It was almost as if Renee brought on some infectious disease, a crippling disorder overwhelming the brain with extreme sexual desires.

The severely frustrated virgin found himself utterly consumed by dirty thoughts when Renee occupied the space inside his head. Running out of things to say, Simon felt the conversation dwindling fast. He failed at making a grand impression exactly the way he feared he would. Standing there in an awkward moment of silence Renee ended the encounter buy jokingly suggesting they get back to work. Simon agreed although he didn't want to see her go, and quickly went back to plucking weeds, but not before watching her walk away. He saw that the back end was just as miraculous as the front. Simon kept an un-healthy hope that this simple friendship would blossom into something romantic. Consumed by lustful thoughts day and night proved stronger than the devil's possession. Renee was constantly invading his mind, clogging his judgement and causing his rage to flair, up often. Simon simply, didn't want to feel lonely anymore and found himself falling in love at first sight. Unfortunately for him it was one sided. It was a debilitating sickness from which there was no cure. No doctor or Priest could heal Simon Fletcher's shattered heart.

As the days passed his parents also noticed a drastic change in him. Simon hadn't been eating much and forcing a smile out of him was virtually impossible. They were growing concerned for their son's wellbeing. He became distant, always wanting to be alone, mostly in his house of sins. He would sit up there every waking moment he wasn't working for one of his parents, thinking about Renee and drawing sinister portraits that would shock the town he lived in. There was even one with Satan's hand punching through Father Fitzpatrick's chest, sending his ribs crashing into the lake of fire below, while squeezing the remaining blood from his heart. Simon also kept a close eye on the house next-door. He was waiting for his luscious goddess to un-knowingly show herself again. He couldn't wait to get another look at that incredible body. Simon began to feel like he was her personal zombie, after-all she controlled every single thought flashing through the neurons inside his head. It was like an ongoing nightmare he couldn't awaken from. Renee's face was the last thing he saw every night even after closing his eyes. She was also the first thing he thought of when he awakened the next, morning. This cycle of chaos and depression had to stop, or Simon was going to lose it. The only cure he could think of was winning her over. How the hell was he supposed to do that? It was impossible, and the deteriorating young man continued falling to pieces inside. Even his dreams were haunted by sex-fueled urges placing him in the same bed as the queen he so desired. He could touch her soft skin and smell her fresh breath gently blowing in his face. Sometimes they would last until the sun rudely interrupted the following morning. Bringing an unwanted end to his intense fantasies. He tried many times but always failed when it came too falling back to sleep and entering the same dream. It was often enough to spoil his entire day. It was as if he worshipped the attractive hippie the same way his parents did their god. Simon didn't want to know what the Lord thought of him now. There was no excuse for his wicked, behavior. He was too in love with another man's woman to think about anyone or anything else. Stanley and Eleanor knew it had to do with the pretty young blonde living next-door. There was simply nothing they could do. It wasn't Renee's fault she hadn't done anything intentional to draw this type of attention to herself. The stressed- out parents didn't want to admit their son was slightly demented all they could do is cry out for Jesus to save him.

The following Sunday was a warm and bright one. Still, Simon Fletcher felt as if a cold, dark rain cloud was lingering above his head, even while he sat in church with his folks, as he had done since the day he was born. For some reason he felt even worse today, despite the priest going on about god's love and how everyone has their own purpose in life. It was clear to the four-eyed pervert he must have been forgotten. It felt as if god created him, but never quite got around to developing the rest of his story. His mind continued to unravel as he sat in church with lewd visions contaminating his imagination. It was wrong of Simon to imagine Renee giving him a blow job while sitting in the house of god, the old Irish man preaching his heart out. His strong accent from the old country helped lure the souls who wanted to be saved from damnation.

Most people who met Father Fitzpatrick found him very warm and easy to talk to. It was no wonder why he was a representative of the good Lord here on earth. As angelic as he may be? Father Johnathan Fitzpatrick had no way of knowing about the demon infestation growing inside the mind of one of his youngest followers. He was blind to the depravity the young man would eventually sink to. It was as if minions from the deepest depths of hell were reaching out to grab him. Simon knew it was wrong, he just couldn't help himself. Not even this holy temple could protect him from his sexual impulses. All he could see was his blonde angel with her face in his crotch during the service. Simon did his best to ignore it, but the filthy vision refused to evaporate. He noticed people crying out with their hands stretched toward the sky. Ever since he was a young boy Simon felt left out when it came too experiencing the Lord's presence. He was always the one who couldn't see what everyone else saw. It wasn't fair, making him resent god even more.

Simon wondered why the Lord never showed himself to him. He felt remorseful for his sins but couldn't find a way to control them. He blamed it on god for creating him this way. He must have intended on him being such a lustful, sinner. Simon felt he had no choice but to keep this sick obsession with sex bottled, up inside. There's no way he could admit to it while sitting in the confession booth. That would be more humiliating than anything the disturbed young man could fathom. How could he swing his serpent tongue around in the presence of such a pure and wonderful instrument of the almighty? He knew it was confidential, still this raunchy behavior was nothing like the people in town are used to. Simon feared it may be too much for the old-man's ticker to handle. He had no choice but to suffer in silence. Slowly drowning in his own misery, the best antidote for Simon's condition was another woman. For someone like him that meant there was no cure. Even if some other girl found it in her heart to give him a chance, Simon wasn't interested in anyone else. Sitting just in front of him was a pretty- young girl about his age named Jennifer Collins. She was very pretty with brown eyes and dark brown hair. Simon knew her his entire life but sparks never flew between them even after numerous encounters over the years. He used to find her kind of attractive, but no one compared to the blonde he envisioned for as long as he could remember. Now that she was real and lived right next-door no other woman even existed. One way or the other he was going to find a way to make Renee his own. Simon always hated Sundays because he was forced to praise a god, he cared little to nothing about. He didn't have the same mind set as everyone else living in Renee Falls. Simon wanted to live a carefree life like the girl he obsessed over 24/7, he wanted to share the same nature loving beliefs. He still felt like a little boy riding home from church every Sunday in the back of his father's family cruiser.

This particular Sunday was going to prove even more devastating for the young lovesick psychopath. Pulling up to his house, Simon immediately noticed Paul Price's black Camaro parked in the driveway next door alongside Renee's jeep. His stomach started to turn as he got all worked up thinking about the two of them happy together in the house where the Stone's used to live. He knew Renee would be excited to see Paul, and anxiously willing to give her body to him. Simon knew now that her husband was back for a little while, he would once again become the invisible man. Renee was going to be all over Paul showing him love and affection, and there was nothing he could do about it. Simon had an evil look in his eyes as he created situations in his head causing a hatred to brew beneath the surface of a weak and fragile looking young man. No one knew just how bad he had it over this woman. His attraction was slowly mutating into something truly dark and twisted. He pictured the two lovebirds being intimate while wishing he was in Paul's shoes. He wondered how he could ever leave such a wonderful piece of ass behind for so long. If Renee was his girl, Simon felt they would never be apart.

Like most insane people, Simon was convinced no one could ever love her the way he does. The truth was if she really was his someday? Renee would probably find herself locked in a cage like a bird as his around the clock sex slave. He would be too jealous and afraid to let her out roaming around on her own. Simon had no confidence in himself what's so ever. He would always feel as if some other guy would come along and snatch her up. He desperately wanted to be the one who comes home to her every night, showering her with kisses and smothering affection. In his twisted mind, Paul didn't deserve her. He wanted to believe Renee would be much happier with him. It was a bias judgement since Simon knew nothing about her loving husband. He hated Paul for no good reason at all. Stanley and Eleanor saw the change in him when he noticed the muscle car in the driveway, they hated what was happening. Renee seemed to have a tight hold on him like nothing ever experienced before.

The strikingly gorgeous, young woman made the most terrible mistake by moving there, she had their son acting as if the world was coming to an end. How was Renee supposed to know the nerdy young man would grow dangerously attracted to her? Ever since she moved in next door it was as if nothing else existed. Stanley and Eleanor missed the Stone's. They couldn't help but wish they were still alive and well, living in the same house they had for decades. Now they were both in a better place and a completely different breed of human beings were calling their old place home. The young couple seemed to be a bit strange but pleasant. It was just this powerful crush their son had with Renee that troubled them. It wasn't healthy, and they've never seen him act that way before. Now that Paul had returned, he and Renee were supposed to come by for dinner later that evening. At the moment Stanley and Eleanor weren't sure if that was the best idea. After all their son looked as if his best-friend just died. Since Renee was the cause of it all, they weren't sure if inviting her and her husband over was a good idea. They would have to talk it over with Simon once they get inside the house. Simon was also starting to miss the elderly couple who used to live next-door. At least back then his heart wasn't being pierced by tiny arrowheads every second of his pathetic life.

Unfortunately, there was no way to set things back to the way they were. Simon would have to find a way to forget about the ultimate girl next-door and somehow move on with his mundane life of unwanted celibacy. Simon headed straight to his room once he was out of the family wagon. He didn't want to be bothered by anyone. His mother offered to make him a delicious ham and cheese sandwich with mayo and tomatoes, just the way he liked it. Simon refused the delicious lunch swearing he wasn't hungry. He may have been too depressed to eat, but his father Stanley always seemed to be starving. Unlike his son, he had no intensions on turning down a yummy sandwich. Stanley did his best to convince himself his son would eventually snap out of this constant funk he was in. Simon loved the fact that Renee had finally removed those ugly drapes hanging from the bedroom windows, he was praying they would never be replaced, but soon found himself a bit disappointed when they were. Their replacement was a deep purple colored pair of drapes, but they were much thinner than the old school ones hanging prior. Simon imagined even if she was undressed behind them, he would still be able to see her glamorous body through the fragile vail. Below him, Simon's parents were still trying to decide if they should continue with the dinner plans? The loving parents were afraid of the way their son might behave if they place him in a room with the husband of the girl he was clearly infatuated with. The last thing they needed was their grieving son to attack their new neighbor. They didn't want to have to send Simon to his room in front of company. He already resented them for treating him like a child. If they do it while Renee's watching? Stanley and Eleanor feared their son might never forgive them. Simon sat alone in his room wondering how long it would be before Paul hit the road again, leaving his sexy little wife behind. He seemed to be forever trapped in this vast blackhole of depression with no escape. Simon felt as if his very own sanity was spiraling out of control.

Right next-door the young woman he was losing his mind over didn't seem to care about his emotions in the least. In fact, she wasn't thinking about him at all. Renee was far too, excited to have her lover back in her arms again. She missed him so much, it felt as if he had been gone for a thousand years. Paul felt the same way, squeezing her tight, and bathing her in soft, kisses. Perhaps his job traveling the open road separating the two is the very fuel that kept the fire burning. The young lovers never had time to grow tired of each other, proving it was healthy to miss one another from time to time. That didn't mean Paul liked leaving his gorgeous wife behind for even a second. He always looked forward to returning home, so he can see her breath-taking smile and enjoy the company of her incredible spirit again. For Paul the, amazing little hippie, chick made life worth living, getting back to Renee is how he coped with the long miles he faced while cruising across the U. S. A. It seemed as if they just moved when he had to turn around and hit the open road again.

Looking around Paul loved what his baby did with the place. He felt bad about not being there to help her get things in-order, but he was responsible for keeping a roof over their heads. Leaving Renee behind and suffering the torment of loneliness on the road was just part of the game of life. He gave Renee a kiss, thanking her for all the hard-work she has done while he was away. Long gone were all the old-fashion decorations the Stone's had lying around the place. It was feeling more and more like home to them. Renee smiled and jumped in his arms. They spun around in the middle of the living room, while staring into each other's eyes, completely in love with one another. While in their moment of bliss, Paul showed Renee the small forest of cannabis he purchased while back home. It gave her another reason to smile. She was almost dry by the time he returned. Doing all that housework makes you want to get stoned, she jokingly explained. Renee found it kind of ironic that the last people to live there were the Stones and she and her husband were stoners. Glad to have him home, Renee demanded that he rolls up a fat joint the two of them can share. Paul couldn't agree more and got right to it. He was planning on listening to music while getting baked and having much needed sex with her later that evening.

While Paul went to work breaking up the weed and rolling up a perfect dooby, Renee explained how amazing it would be if John Lennon and Janis Joplin did a song together. They were her two- favorite music-artist from both sexes. It would be the most- groovy song ever recorded she imagined. Paul agreed, but wasn't as much of a hippie as his gorgeous wife. Whenever Paul returned from a long trip all the lovebirds wanted was each-others company. Renee walked over to the radio and turned on some music, now that her man was back, she wanted to sing and dance with him. Renee wanted his full un-divided attention until he was on the rode once again. Day-dream believer was playing from the monkeys.

Renee loved that song and once Paul was through rolling the joint, she reached out grabbing his hand as if she was the home coming queen and he was her king. Paul could do nothing but smile and take his lover by the hand. He used the other to place the moist joint in his mouth, since Renee snatched him before he could dry it properly. They smoked and slow danced through that song and the one after called Turn, Turn, Turn from The Byrds while looking into each- other's eyes as the marijuana started taking affect. The song really made sense to them since they were in the middle of starting a very new season of their own.

While dancing around the house and sharing a joint the two kindred, souls fell madly in love all over again. It seemed what they had was special and Paul Price was a very lucky man. There was nothing in the world Simon could do to tear them apart. When a commercial break ended the moment, they separated, and Renee walked over to lower the volume. Turning to glance out the window she saw a beautiful blue-bird siting on a branch staring back at her. She felt like this really was the place they were meant to be. Renee was so excited to start her life over again with the man she utterly adored. It was only after Paul was completely baked that she mentioned going to have dinner with the Fletcher's later, that evening, practically destroying his high. Paul's eyes widened, he started to panic, he was stoned and didn't want to be around anyone in that condition, especially nice religious folks like the Fletcher's. He suggested she reschedules. Renee told him there was plenty of time to sober up, before they have- to go over there. She confessed she was really- high as well. Renee further enticed him by saying there would be plenty of delicious food to munch on. That was enough to change Paul's indecisive mind. He knew there was nothing like devouring good food during a major case of the munchies.

With the joint hanging from his lips, Paul turned to look at the clock while asking Renee what time they were expected to be there. Renee told him she wasn't exactly sure. She was thinking around 5 or so, but she would check in with Mrs. Fletcher to be certain. Carefully observing how Renee transformed the place to look like their pad back in California, Paul joked about what the old people would think of their house if they saw it now. Renee insisted they get cleaned up by taking a shower together and washing the weed scent away. Paul loved the idea it was the best way to get their clothes off. He was thinking about doing filthy things to her while getting clean. Renee knew what was on his mind by the smile on his face, and the look in his eyes. She smiled as she grabbed the joint from him and took another hit, blowing the smoke in his face. They both began choking and laughing together. I guess this means no L-S-D trips for me today huh, Renee just laughed unable to even make a comment. She was enjoying her life as she always had while Simon sat in his room wasting away over a girl who was never his. It was pathetic, and he knew it. For some reason he just couldn't shake these feelings. He was so down he didn't even have the imagination to draw something obscene in order to feel better. Instead, Simon sat on his bed staring out the window at his true, loves house. He suffered in misery thinking about the way he wanted life to be, with no hope of it ever coming true. Simon Fletcher knew nothing about Paul Price, yet hated his guts, all because he had the disillusion of a woman fated to be with him. He continued wishing and praying for something terrible to happen to the luckiest man alive.

Maybe someday he won't make it home? He kept saying to himself. A bright, cheerful summer was passing young, Simon by, as he voluntarily dragged himself through the cold, dark, murky depths of hell. He should have moved on and tried finding another girl to take Renee's place. He may have done just that, had it not been for the cut and pasted version of her he created before she even came into his life. He was convinced it was fate that brought them together. He stared out that bedroom window with demons fluttering around in his eyes. Paul and Renee were too busy getting ready for dinner that evening to notice him staring at their house. Paul hopped in the shower while Renee phoned Eleanor from next-door. It appeared everything was a go.

The Fletcher's were going to stick to their plans, even if it made their grown son pout in his bedroom like a child. Eleanor thought it would be rude of them to cancel now. Renee started heading toward the shower, removing her clothing along the way. She was so happy to have her man back and couldn't wait any longer to be intimate with him. Paul smiled when Renee joined him in the shower completely naked. A glow in her eyes. She told him their dinner date was on for tonight. He hugged Renee and gave her a kiss, while she grabbed the soap and started washing him with it. They had plenty of time to do whatever they wanted with each-other before it was time to head next-door. Eleanor decided to break the news to Simon that they were going through with the dinner plans. She fixed him a sandwich, despite the fact he insisted he wasn't hungry. She was hoping he would eat it eventually. Simon wasn't happy about the arrangements he told his mother that he really liked Renee and that it was awkward to sit and have dinner with a girl he can never have. He added the fact that it would be even more difficult sitting across from her husband, forced to watch as they kiss and hold hands all evening. It was enough to spoil his appetite all over again just thinking about it.

Annoyed by her son's selfish behavior, Eleanor told him to stay in his room if he couldn't act like a grown-up. She was having the new neighbors over whether he liked it or not. She went on to tell him it was wrong to look at females the way he did. A woman that's married under god cannot be looked upon as a suitable mate for other men. She angrily insisted that he gets over it. Simon told his mother she was probably going to frighten Renee away with all her creepy religious artifacts. There were saints and angels positioned like soldier's all-over the house. Simon pointed to the wooden crucifix over his door, reminding her that there was one above every single room in the house. That included some of the closets as well. Simon tried blaming his parents for his ludicrous actions Looking around the house it was obvious, she and Stanley got carried away with their beliefs in god. Maybe her son was right, but It was no excuse for his sinful behavior. Simon turned to look at the clock, counting down the hours before his goddess arrived. He forced himself to eat the sandwich after his mother left the room and spent the rest of the day grooming himself. He knew it was all for nothing, but he wanted to look his best when Renee finally arrived to have dinner in his dining room, before the last-supper portrait hanging on the wall.

Stanley and Eleanor did their best to make sure the house was perfect when their guest arrived. Since cleanliness was next to godliness, they didn't have much work to do getting it in order. Eleanor always kept up with the dusting and vacuuming. She and her husband didn't like a dirty, unkept house, especially with new faces stepping through their doors for the first time. Unlike their love, sick miserable son, they were looking forward to spending the evening with the kind young couple recently joining their neck of the woods. Paul and Renee Price seemed a bit different, but that was all the reason for the loving Christians to understand and embrace their way of life to a limited extent and possibly even show them the way to the Lord's light as time goes on. Eleanor and Stanley lived to save souls from damnation, Paul and Renee were the perfect converts for them. Simon finally cleaned that wax out of his ears and trimmed his fingernails. He even trimmed his nose hairs and took an extra-long shower. After shaving the scruff from his baby-face, Simon drown himself in after-shave and cologne. He then dressed in one of his best collar-shirts and slacks.

After sex and showering, Renee tore apart the closet she just organized to find something nice to wear. Paul was more of a rock t-shirt kind of guy. Renee wanted to dress a little more formal. It would be another disappointment for Simon if he was expecting her to show-up in something revealing, assisting him later with his bedroom fantasy. Renee slipped into a little black dress that didn't give too much of her curvature or cleavage away. She didn't want to look like a cheap whore in such a religious home. Paul was even more nervous about going over there for dinner, still feeling a bit stoned from the joint they shared earlier. The way he traveled Paul didn't think he would have much time to get to know them anyhow. What was the point? He pondered. Renee just wanted to be accepted in this new place, giving the appearance of two completely different worlds colliding. Paul agreed to go if it would make his wife happy. He just prayed they wouldn't have to do the same thing with everyone living on their street. A crumby fruit-cake worthy of the trashcan would do just fine. Paul had no idea the young kid living next-door was madly in love with his wife. That would surely change his decision to march her over there like a piece of meat.

When the time finally came, Simon felt his heart starting to pound as he couldn't help but wonder what she was wearing and what she would smell like. He prepared to join the party, even though he knew it was going to be a miserable time. His mother smiled as she opened the front-door, greeting her company and doing her best to make them feel welcome. Renee was holding a delicious salad she prepared, while Paul had dessert. A delicious fudge cake she sent him to the bakery for earlier, feeling it would be rude to show up empty handed. They both noticed the house smelled delicious.

"Come on in", Eleanor insisted, excited to get the evening under way. She also called out for her husband and Simon to join them. "Smells lovely Mrs. Fletcher", said Renee. "Please sweetheart. Call me Eleanor." Renee smiled as they followed her to the dining room where dinner was waiting. They were soon joined by Stanley and the ever- creepy Simon Fletcher. The two older men shook hands first to get acquainted. Paul then reached out for Simon's hand as well. He could sense some resentment in his eyes and body-language. Still Paul did his best to remain friendly with the new neighbors. It didn't take a rocket-scientist to figure out why the nerdy looking young man wasn't fond of him. It seemed clear already that Simon was interested in his beautiful wife.

Turning his eyes back to Renee, Simon couldn't figure out why this angel would want to be with a man who looks like he should be part of the Manson family. As far as he was concerned Paul wasn't welcome in his house. Paul knew Renee was incredibly sexy and he was very lucky to have her. How could any man not look twice at his beautiful wife? Stanley was lucky enough to get away with giving Renee a kiss on the cheek. Simon imagined if he tried doing that fist would be flying. He did his best to hide his hatred for Paul or let him know just how desperate he was to be in his skin. It wasn't hard to miss the ominous vibe he cast off. Even Renee could see there was something troubling Simon by the look in his eyes. With a very subtle tension accumulating in the air, Eleanor took Renee by the hand and lured her closer to the dining room. She asked how she and Paul liked it here so far? Renee smiled as Paul explained how he hadn't even been around to enjoy it, since they moved in. He felt as if he has been on the road the entire time but told them how he first came upon this perfect little town. He said it reminded him of the cards you find during the holidays. Everything about it was perfect. Especially the fact that it was named after his gorgeous, young wife. He said it was destiny that brought them to this amazing place. Simon kept a watchful eye on Renee, while listening to her husband speak. The conversation continued as they gathered in front of the table to feast. Stanley and Paul hit it off right away. Stanley respected the younger man for working so hard to support the woman he loves. It was the way things are supposed to be in his book. All that driving can be a real burden on a family. Stanley wondered if he would still want to pursue that career after bringing children into the world? It would make it even harder for him to say goodbye when it was time to leave. Paul insisted he loved his job, traveling across the country was the definition of freedom to him. He reached for Renee's hand while explaining how hard it was leaving her behind. Paul mentioned the romantic trips they've taken together in the past.

Renee squeezed his hand and said "I too, enjoyed traveling to new places and meeting new faces." Sort of like what was going on at-the moment, she jokingly brought to light. The only one at the table who seemed to be quiet was Simon. He seemed distant. As if he wasn't interested in any of their conversations. Everyone else was getting along just fine and having a nice time. It was driving him crazy every time Paul would turn and kiss his woman at the dinner table. It seemed like perfectly acceptable behavior for a young couple eager to start a family of their own. Simon was hoping his parents would disapprove and throw them out. He couldn't bear to watch this insufferable act continue any longer. He wanted it to be him that Renee was all cuddled up with while eating his mother's delicious meal.

Everyone's eyes soon migrated to the food in the middle of the table, it looked scrumptious. Paul and Renee thanked the Fletcher's again for having them over. Now that the food was ready to eat, Eleanor insisted that everyone holds hands as she says Grace and gives thanks to her god for their countless blessings. As they did so Paul's wondering eyes noticed the last-supper painting hanging before him. As he reached out taking Renee's hand and Eleanor's. Eleanor then reached out for Simon who was holding his father's hand. Stanley in turn was the lucky one who got to gently squeeze Renee's other hand. Simon hated being the only man left out of the direct connection with the beautiful and vibrant young woman sitting at his dinner table. Once again, he found himself being held by his overbearing parents. When the prayer was over everyone dug into the delicious home-cooked meal Eleanor prepared. She made chicken with mashed potatoes, along with corn and broccoli. There was plenty enough to go around. Simon couldn't find his way into either of the conversations taking place during dinner. His father seemed to be more interested in what Paul had to say. They were discussing Paul's job as a long, distance trucker, while Renee started asking his mother all about her flower-shop. She confessed she has yet to go inside and have a look around, while insisting she couldn't wait to check out the place. Paul overheard and joined the conversation, saying he wanted to stop in earlier and grab some roses for Renee, but they were closed. Eleanor apologized for that, explaining it was the sabbath, and that no money should be made on a day of rest and worship. Renee smiled at her husband for thinking of her. She couldn't help herself and gave him another loving kiss at the dinner table. Simon's parents found it romantic, but it was making him want to tear his brains out of his skull and stomp down on them, as hard as he could. It almost seemed as if she was doing it on purpose, showing extra affection to her husband right there in front of him. Simon felt he needed to engage in conversation soon before he really makes everyone uncomfortable. He didn't mind pissing off his parents, but he didn't want to look like a complete ass in front of the girl he was so desperate to impress. Paul said the store was lovely and that he would be back soon, obviously to butter up Renee and get between her legs.

Simon thought to himself how he couldn't wait for the time to pass, as everyone enjoyed themselves, accept, for him. His mother and father knew exactly how he felt. They wanted to have a word with him once their company was gone. He was acting very rude to the warm, friendly guest. Things would flow so much better if it was just Renee sitting at the family table. Simon couldn't stand the sight of Paul anymore, especially as he watched him drink out of one of their glasses and place one of their forks in his filthy mouth. Simon even hated the fact that Paul was enjoying his mother's cooking. Mercifully Renee found a way to get the angry heart-broken young man to speak. She asked Simon what he liked to do for fun? He finally cracked a genuine smile and began to explain that he was a pretty talented artist. Looking around the house she and Paul both noticed a few pictures still hanging up in frames from the time when he was still a young boy. Simon insisted as he watched them take notice that those were ancient, relics and that he was much better now. Renee swore she wanted to see some of his finest, work one day. Her husband Paul also acted as if he was enthused to see the strange young-man's portraits. It seemed to be the only other thing besides Renee that brought some color and life back into his complexion.

Eleanor smiled, glad to see all the food disappearing as she had hoped it would. Even Simon was beginning to empty his plate like a good little boy. He started thinking maybe he was being a little hard on his parents, they were just trying to be nice as usual. Always wanting to be around others, it was just their way. Simon became more alive the more they talked about his incredible drawings. Renee turned and smiled at her husband letting him know she was pleased with the way things were going. It was her way of saying thank-you without a single word being spoken. Simon was soon forced to listen as his mother changed the subject and began talking up a storm with Renee about women stuff, losing his interest. He was now forced to get involved in the boring chat between his father and worst enemy, at least in his mind. As the salad and dinner vanished from sight, everyone, besides Simon was thinking about dessert. Even though they were all stuffed, no one could resist trying a slice of the delicious looking fudge cake Paul and Renee brought. Eleanor started clearing the dirty dishes to make room. Renee quickly got up to give her a hand. Eleanor really liked Renee. She seemed like a very sweet girl. The kind of girl she wouldn't mind seeing her only son ending up with. Renee didn't mind helping clear the table, or washing dishes, while Eleanor made a pot of coffee for everyone. Even Paul had to admit he was glad he listened to his beautiful wife. That is why she was the one in charge of their healthy and loving relationship. He continued chatting with Simon and his father about California and what life is like on the west coast.

The Fletcher's have been on plenty of vacations together over the years, ironically none of them included the most western parts of this great nation. They usually ventured to tropical islands that mimicked heaven on earth. Stanley said he was sure it was a wonderful place to live. He asked why they would leave the city of angels for a small town in the middle of nowhere. Paul laughed and again confessed this place was just so perfect. Simon was wishing he never ventured to his perfect little town. Things would've been better if he stayed the hell away. Paul feared the cult followers as he also saw religious groups would've been more judge, mental. They seemed to accept him and his wife just the way they were. Renee did convince him to leave his bandana at home and simply comb his long hair. As usual he did what his woman commanded. The coffee smelled delicious and Paul couldn't wait for a cup, he also couldn't wait to get home and light up another joint. After a meal this good that was all he could really think about. Simon was beginning to understand why he was the oddball at the table. Seeing how even his parents could keep a steady conversation going with the new neighbors made him realize he was a boring person. When he had her one on one in the front yard, Simon quickly ran out of things to say. All he wanted was Renee's attention, but had no idea how to get it. He began to admit maybe Paul was the better man after all. Soon the coffee was ready, and Eleanor began serving it while Renee cut the cake into slices for everyone, as they remained gathered around for dessert.

Paul asked anyone willing to answer, what happened to the people who used to live in their house? He was curious to know why it was up for sale in the first place. Before Eleanor or Stanley could utter a word, Simon blurted out they're dead. They were pretty- old. I guess we all have- to go sometime huh. It was a cold way to put it giving Renee the creeps, she didn't like knowing someone died in her house. She began to wonder if it could be haunted. Stanley and Eleanor shifted their eyes toward their son and then at poor Renee. They were horrified and Eleanor wanted to send her twenty, year old son to his room in front of their company like she wished she wouldn't have to. It was too late now to take back what he said. Paul was also a bit discouraged, even troubled by not only the news he was hearing, but the way it was being presented. No one ever told him the past owners perished inside the home he bought. Paul quickly regretted bringing up the dreadful subject. Although Renee had been practically living in the home by herself, with no signs of the past owner's, she still couldn't get the idea out of her head. Just knowing someone died in the same room she sleeps in was a bit unsettling. If Simon was trying to impress the girl of his dreams, he was doing a terrible job of it. He was proving to everyone at the table that he was a real party popper and a bit of a weirdo. Paul was just happy the Fletcher's didn't bring out the good book and start preaching verse to them. He knows how religious people can be, wanting to push their god onto other's because for some reason they are the true and only god. Paul was content with the life he had without a divine being in it. He already had the most beautiful woman in the world, what else could he ask for? Luckily, they didn't come off that way.

Eleanor and Stanley were just very kind, hearted people who held god in high regards. Simon hated the way his father praised Paul for working so hard to provide for himself and Renee. He imagined he would leave the country, possibly even the entire planet, if it made the woman of his dreams happy. The love Simon was experiencing for the pretty young girl next-door was not the same as Paul. His was a dark, obsession, the creepy kind women should always stay away from. In truth Simon didn't love Renee, he simply wanted to possess her for his own selfish sexual desires. As the hands slowly orbited the face of the clock Simon knew he wouldn't have to stare at Paul's mug much longer. He wore out his welcome, before even stepping foot into his home. Unfortunately, that also meant Renee would be gone from his sight as well. It's always upsetting to see her go, but Simon knew she would forever hold a place in his imagination. He knew every inch of her face and could see her whenever he wanted.

He was beginning to drift off in his head as Renee asked in a sweet voice if he wanted a piece of the cake they brought over. How could he resist. He smiled brightly. Thanking her for the delicious looking dessert. Paul was busy talking to Stanley, but he did notice the way Simon looked at his girl over the course of the evening. He was not going to say anything about the young man's horny gaze. Paul didn't want to start a fight with his new neighbors over it. His wife wanted to make friends in this new world, even if they are old religious freaks. Besides, Paul wasn't afraid of losing his girl to someone like Simon Fletcher. He felt no need for jealousy or hate. Lots of men stare at Renee. She is very attractive, and he has grown used to the constant attention. Paul has even seen other pretty women hitting on Renee because of her flawless features. Renee smiled at Simon as she handed him a piece of fudge cake. If he could Simon would have saved it forever, just for the sake it was given to him by the one and only Renee Price. He knew the critters would devour it eventually, and instead chose to enjoy it.

The room got quiet once everyone started digging into their delicious, dessert. Stanley was enjoying it so much, he feared it may actually be a sin. Finishing his coffee as dessert came to an end, Paul looked at the time and suggested they get going. It was getting late, and he was growing tired from his long trip, he just wanted to get stoned and watch television with Renee by his side, but not before thanking the

Fletchers again for a lovely evening. Renee asked Eleanor if she needed a hand cleaning the rest of the dirty dishes, Eleanor told her not to worry, and that she had everything under-control. She insisted Simon could give her a hand as he finished his last few bites of cake. Paul reached over to shake his hand and say goodbye. Simon forced a smile on his face and insisted it was a pleasure to meet him. Renee said goodbye to Simon with so much joy, and life in her voice. She was everything he ever wanted. Now she was going, home to be alone with the man she'd fallen in love with. Simon acted as though it didn't bother him, but he hated to see her go. His parents walked the happy-young lovers to the front-door, Renee insisted they get together again soon. Stanley and Eleanor agreed, they thought it was a fantastic idea. As she was preparing to leave, Renee began looking around at all the statues and angels guarding the house. She thought they were creepy and comforting at the same time. She then exited the front-door as Paul and Stanley sad their goodbye's.

Closing the door behind them, Stanley turned to look at his wife. They were both happy with the way the evening turned out accept, for some of their son's screw-ball behavior. They were really worried about him. Once their company was gone, Stanley and Eleanor went back into the kitchen to finish cleaning up, with lots of concern for their boy. There was something slowly eating away at him from the inside. If Simon didn't do something to stop its rampant progression soon it would eventually devour him. Eleanor wanted to go comfort her son like she did when he was a child. Stanley suggested she leaves him be for the night. It was obvious he was suffering from a broken heart, but this was like nothing his parents have ever seen, especially since it was over a girl he never dated and hardly knew. Their son was deeply in love with another man's wife and it could not continue. They had to find a way to conquer this demon before it claims their only son. Eleanor had a feeling inviting Renee and Paul over was a bad idea. Now she can see she was absolutely-right. She felt guilty as if she teased him all evening with something he could never have. She listened to her husband's advice, leaving Simon alone to wallow in the sorrow he created for himself. He ran up the stairs stomping his feet along the way, slamming the bedroom door behind him searching for pity. His window open, Simon could hear laughter coming from outside, it was a combination of Paul and the most amazing woman he's ever laid eyes on. Simon started watching them, wondering why they were standing there all cuddled up instead of hurrying inside, since they were in such a hurry to get going. Simon started to wonder if perhaps he did something wrong, something that turned Renee off? Maybe she didn't want to be around him any longer? It was horrifying to think about.

Simon could hear their lips smacking in the dark, as they warmed up for the erotic evening to come. There was an evil expression on Simon's face and his eyes were dimming into black, bottomless pits, as Paul and Renee decided to enjoy the night air for a while, before heading inside. Simon slammed the window shut and turned on the radio to block out the sweet sounds of passion in the night. He turned to glance at the wooden crucifix hung over his door and wondered if the figure was secretly watching him, as he was confronted by The Left Bank and their hit, song, walk away Renee. He returned to the window to try and see his beauty queen in the shadows of darkness and streetlights, while listening to the eerie lyrics. Just walk away Renee, you won't see me follow you back home. The empty sidewalks on my block are not the same, you're not to blame. From deep inside the tears that I'm forced to cry, From, deep inside the pain that I chose to hide. Tears began forming in Simon's eyes as he found himself relating to the musician singing his sorrows away, while watching the love of his life kissing another man.

Simon could no longer take it and soon found himself lying in bed, curled up in a ball crying like a child. All he could think about was Renee's smiling face as she reached over and handed him a piece of chocolate fudge cake. He could hear her soft sexy voice speaking kind words to him and wanted nothing more than to be lying beside her. It felt as if his brain was swelling or being compressed from a foreign object in his cranium. The pressure built as he imagined Paul and Renee having sex in the house right next-door. The thought of Paul putting his nasty hands all over his queen drove Simon crazy. He desperately needed a way to prevent the walls from closing in any further, as he tried crying himself to sleep. The demented virgin had to get those disabling thoughts out of his head before it spontaneously combusted. All he could picture in his mind's eye was Renee lying there making funny faces as she moaned in extasy. Simon wanted so badly for it to be his hands all over her body. Paul was fucking her harder and harder in his mind, until he couldn't take it anymore. Finally, Simon opened his eyes and turned on the tv, hoping for some relief. Again, the evening news was all over the Manson murders like flies on shit. It was rancidly captivating. He imagined it was probably the only thing that could possibly keep his mind off Renee, until he can pass out from exhaustion. Simon was wishing Paul next door really was part of the Manson Family, or at the very least one of their victims. Then Renee would be all his forever.

Sexually frustrated as he was, Simon began finding Charlies angels pretty- attractive, especially Leslie Van Houten. He started undressing them with his eyes. Stripping away their prison uniforms to see what lies beneath. It was turning him on a little, but none of them compared to Renee Price. Not even their famous, victim Sharon Tate. It did sparsely redirect some of his thoughts when it came to the girl next-door. He thought about having all the Manson girls to himself at the same time. It was a degrading and worthless endeavor to forget about the girl he was so crazy about. Simon knew his parents would shit Easter eggs if they knew he was watching that trash in their house. As far as Eleanor and Stanley were concerned, Charles Manson was the devil incarnate, and his follower's demons from the deepest depths of hell. Simon didn't care what they thought. He was trapped inside his own hell every moment of every day, ever since his dream girl moved in next-door. Watching the story about the dark cult proved to be the best distraction Simon could find, to shield his thoughts from Renee, he eventually did fall asleep with the vile news story playing.

He was awakened sometime later by the sound of someone entering his room. Simon reached for his glasses, assuming it was his mother coming to check up on him in the middle of the night as if he was still a baby. When he turned to see who it was, Simon was shocked to find Renee standing in his doorway. She was wearing white, lacey lingerie, as she slowly walked towards him. The smell of her perfume made her even more edible, as Simon thought about all the perverted things, he wanted to do to her. With his eyes bulging out of his head and his tongue practically flapping around on the floor, Simon couldn't believe what he was seeing. Renee smiled at him with lust in her eyes. She started dancing sexy, moving her hips and showing off her perfect breast with no music to speak of. It didn't matter as far as Simon was concerned. For all he knew there was music blasting and he just couldn't hear it. He imagined too much blood went to his penis for his ears to work properly. It was impossible to blink even for a second, unwilling to miss any of the free show she was presenting. As Renee danced closer, she proceeded to get in bed next to him. Simon didn't know what to do when she cuddled up close and stuck her tongue down his throat. His eyes widened even further as she slid one of her hands down his pants. It felt so good, Simon couldn't enjoy it. He kept worrying that he would cum to quickly destroying the entire fantasy come to life. He did his best to focus on her eyes and the taste of her lips. She helped him out of his shirt and started kissing his right ear. He could feel her warm breath gently blowing into it as he became further aroused. Soon his pants were lying by his bedside, and Renee was slowly slipping out of her enticing choice of bedwear. It was almost too good to be true that she was there with him. He wondered if his folks heard her sneaking into the house to be with him. Simon also began to wonder how she let herself in, then he remembered no one ever locked their doors in Renee Falls. His heart was beating like a humming, bird during a stroke as he stared at Renee's magnificent, body, she pushed Simon down on the bed gently and climbed on-top of him. Confused, the horny virgin didn't know what to do, or what body part of hers he should grab. Everything looked so inviting. He started feeling on her breast, squeezing them softly as Renee sat on-top of him and began doing all the work. It was instantly clear that the beautiful young woman was far more experienced in this department than he was. What did Simon know about sex? He was still a virgin up until the moment Renee grabbed his penis and slid it up inside her. Full of energy she began moving around slowly to get things warmed up, while locking eyes with the sex craved lunatic. Not wanting the sexual encounter to end quickly, Simon took his eyes off, of her and began looking around the room, trying his hardest not to spoil the greatest moment of his life. Renee started moaning louder and louder as she continued using the four-eyed virgin to please herself.

Simon never felt so lucky in his whole life. All he could do is lay there and enjoy the ride, inevitably, gluing his eyes to Renee's fuck faces as she went to town on him, until finally awakening from his wet dream with seamen still gushing out in the real world. He watched in horror as Renee slowly disappeared- from view. It left him extremely angry and even more upset inside, especially knowing Paul was able to have the real thing whenever he wanted. All Simon ended up with was dirty bed sheets. His mind was playing some rotten tricks on him, tormenting his thoughts as he slept. Maybe his parents were right? Maybe he should forget about the girl next-door and find someone else who might actually- feel the same way about him in return. It seemed impossible now that Renee was real. The dream was so incredibly vivid, all the sensations were as realistic as anything else he has experienced in life. Renee Price was literally driving him insane.

Sitting up in his bed he turned to looked out the window at the house she was sleeping in. Her dirtbag looking husband by her side. Anger and sadness had exhaustingly, tight grips on him, each pulling in their own delusional directions. Simon had to find a way to cure himself from this life-draining love, sickness. He just stared at Renee's bedroom window praying for another glimpse before closing his eyes again and struggling to fall back to sleep. Simon turned off the tv, disappointed as usual and closed his eyes. He couldn't help, but wonder if his morbid, creation somehow brought Renee to life? The brain-clogged virgin wasn't sure if he wanted to be with her again that night? Or if he just wanted to be left alone to dream about puppies or something. Anything besides Renee Price next-door. No matter what Simon did there was nothing that could change the way he felt about her. In his mind's eye he kept placing her face next to the mutilated model he carefully constructed, the two always fused together flawlessly. Fate was the reason he couldn't let her go. One way or the other Renee Price would prove to be his destiny. As days and weeks began to pass, Simon kept repeating this to himself in his head. Someone's voice was talking to him from deep within, who knows who it really was bathing him in false hope? His folks would say it was the work of the devil. Simon was beginning to come to terms with the fact he might actually- be insane.

Instead of getting better, Simon's obsession continued to grow even more potent. He would sit in his treehouse for hours watching her walk around practically nude all the time. Once- in a while the drapes were closed, but other times they were wide open granting him the power to see everything. Especially on nice, sunny days, Renee loved to have the windows open inviting all that fresh, air inside. From his watch-tower high up in the trees, Simon could watch her dance around in her bra and panties. Sometimes nothing at all. He would catch Renee singing along to her favorite songs and fall even deeper in love with her. Simon had become infatuated with the girl next-door. He continued stealing her private moments and it was completely wrong of him. He knew it was bad, but it didn't matter, his impulses were too great. It was almost as if his body was being operated by a mind not of his own. Simon was unable to control himself he also loved the rush of possibly being caught. Renee had no idea he was hiding up there spying on her every move. She glanced at the treehouse now and then but didn't think much of it. Even after Simon came off as a bit of a creep at dinner that one evening. Renee was too full of life to think about the ugliness lurking just out of view. She didn't want to concern herself with the darkness and the horrible things that might be thriving in its shadows. Often being alone in the house while her husband was away, Renee refused to think about such things. She did her best to fill her mind with positive, happy thoughts.

One of Simon's favorite things is when she takes a shower and eventually loses the towel while he is peeping from the tree like a bird. As more time passed Simon also noticed when Paul would leave and return from a trip. He liked it much better when he was away. Simon knew he was never going to get in Renee's pants, but while Paul was on the road, he couldn't have her either. It was enough to give him a minute sense of joy. Simon always did his best to be present while her husband was gone, often spending less time in the trees and more of it in the front yard. Out in the open where Renee could easily see him and engage in conversation if she chose to. Most of the time, she would give a quick smile or a wave just to be polite, while doing yardwork, or simply in passing. She never really felt an urge to go have a long conversation with him. Simon didn't seem like a man of many words. Renee felt bad about pretending to be interested in his art. She never asked him to show her any of his current drawings. Knowing how much that meant to him, she was aware of the excitement he would feel to display his craft and talk about what he likes to do best with her. One day when she has time, she promised herself she would do the right thing and ask to see his work. Simon couldn't stand seeing how happy Renee was whenever her man would return. He would see them hugging and kissing on the front-lawn, until Paul carried her in his arms into the house. The two locking lips the entire time. Why couldn't he have a life like that. No matter how friendly and kind Renee was to Simon, he knew he meant nothing to her, placing his heart in constant agony. He didn't notice, but Mrs. Anderson across the street who keeps tabs on everything going on in her neighborhood payed close attention to some of his stalker-like actions. She has seen him checking Renee out from behind the thick vegetation or peeking from around the corner of his house careful not to let her know he was there. The nosy old woman also saw him climbing into his treehouse to sit and watch Renee from the high, grounds more than once. She couldn't prove what he was doing up there, but she had a pretty good idea. She knew he had his eye for the pretty young blonde next-door. The question was should she say something to Renee about her secret admirer? Or keep this troubling information to herself. Mrs. Anderson was also considering telling Simon's folks what he's been up to. In a way she felt maybe they wouldn't believe her. Even more she felt she was sort of doing the same thing by spying on Simon, who was in-turn spying on Renee. Still Mrs. Anderson didn't think it was the same thing. What Simon was doing was really- wrong. He was obsessed with that young girl and invading her privacy. It- seemed as though whenever Renee would step foot out of her house, Simon would somehow be right there to greet her. As if he was watching her from inside and hurrying out the front door to make it look like a coincidence. She felt something ought to be done about it. Simon's behavior gave Mrs. Anderson the creeps and she was slowly becoming afraid of him. She got the chills whenever she noticed him hiding behind some bushes out of sight while watching Renee bend over doing yardwork. Simon continued to have dreams about Renee sneaking into his room and stripping out of all her clothes to seduce him. Every time she wore something sleezy and looked amazing, and every time he would wake up just before getting his rocks off, leaving him high and dry at the last minute. It was the worst part about the sexually driven dreams. It, annoyed Simon Fletcher even more to know it was his very own mother's flower shop that provided the perfect entrance between Renee's legs. Paul could simply buy a couple of red roses and have her all night long. Eleanor and Stanley continued to notice his behavior darkening even further whenever Paul was back in town. Something terrible had a tight grip on their son and neither of them knew how to stop it. Even when Paul was on the road Simon sat around depressed, there seemed to be no way out of this hell that binds him. Making matters even worse, one day while working at his mother's store he had to deal with the customer he hated most of all. Paul was returning from another one of his long trips. He wanted to surprise Renee with more flowers. Simon had no choice but to be polite and sell the man what he came for. Paul couldn't resist he explained with a smile on his face, as he passed the store, he said he just had to stop. He knows how bringing home flowers always puts a big smile on Renee's face. He was speaking to the wrong man when it came to mentioning Renee's sex life. If Simon could, he would brutally, murder her husband in cold blood and take his place, as if he never existed. Paul didn't think much about his dorky neighbor having the hots for his girl. He didn't know how depraved Simon Fletcher truly was, or that the young man was constantly praying for his demise. Listening to Paul's words and knowing he was bringing those flowers home to his dream girl was like being hit in the groin by a sledgehammer. Simon wanted to take the bouquet and shove it down the truck-driver's throat. He wanted to watch as he slowly choked to death on them. After Simon rang him up with a fake smile on his face, he said goodbye and watched as Paul hopped into his black Camaro and drove off. Even his car was better than Simon's He and Renee didn't even believe in god, yet they seemed to have everything in the world they could ever want.

Simon wondered why god hated him so much. He was surrounded by angels and crucifixes, yet his life was completely empty. Simon didn't think he was that bad of a person, he may have drawn some demonic pictures once in a while to vent, and he may be a bit of a horn-dog, but it was no reason to burn in the fires of hell he imagined. It seemed god was really testing the young man Simon wasn't sure how much more he could stand? Whenever the time presented itself, Simon usually retreated to his house of sins. It was the place he felt most alone, and he could indulge in his sinful acts without any witnesses. That included Mrs. Anderson across the street. He had even gone as far as purchasing a pair of binoculars, so he could make it easier to watch her without being seen. Now it was like being in the same room with Renee, instead of all the way across the yard. There were a few occasions when Renee felt that tingly, sensation that someone was watching her. She grew used to brushing it off since she knew she was home all by herself, unless it was the ghost of the old couple who once lived in her house, she joked to herself from time to time. Every now and again Renee would turn and look out the window but see no one, flashing her tits right at Simon who was no doubt watching her from the wooden structure up in the trees. Sometimes she would wonder if Simon still used the old treehouse, or has it been abandoned since he was a child? It gave her an uneasy feeling after a while to know he could possibly be hiding up there, watching her every move? The little bit of time Simon did get to spend with Renee, which was usually a brief conversation before heading in the house or out for some errands, was sacred to him. He cherished every moment he had with the beautiful blonde girl next-door. He had an equal sadness for when the friendly chats ended. Simon couldn't decide if he was more miserable when he was in front of Renee? Or when she wasn't around? Somehow no matter what he found himself in a constant state of mourning. Simon began to see his encounters with Renee as a spiteful tease sent from his wrathful creator. He must be punishing Simon Fletcher for all his nasty sins. One afternoon while sitting up in his treehouse thinking about Renee, Simon began drawing a very angelic picture of her. Her eyes even brighter than reality and her hair glowing yellow like bars of gold dangling from her scalp. Her flesh was radiant, as the stars twinkling in the night sky Simon even went as far as adorning her with a pair of pearl-white feathered wings. When he was through, Simon couldn't stop staring at his wonderous creation. His portraits of Paul were not so kind and spiritual. Simon would place him in torturous situations, often he is being stabbed or beaten to death with whatever weapon came to mind. It made him feel a little better, but the empty joy never lasted long. Not even when he set fire to them, pretending his intended victim could feel the heat of the scorching flames as he watched their face melt away into a drizzle of raining ashes.

CHAPTER 6

❖ ❖ ❖ ❖ ❖

The hot summer days had passed, and Autumn was creeping in on the small peaceful town of Renee Falls. Seasons no longer mattered to Simon. His life was carelessly drifting by without a shred of happiness or ambition. With Renee being so close, yet so far, he didn't know how to think about anything else. He would soon find he was going to have a couple of days without her lingering so close to his heart and home.

On Monday, Paul would be hitting the road again. He wanted to make the most of the weekend before parting with his beautiful wife. He thought it would be a great idea to plan a spontaneous, camping trip in the woods. Food beer, water and some other treats would make it a wonderful get away. They were going to travel to the nearby State of Pennsylvania and find the perfect spot to party in the middle of nowhere. Simon was forced to watch from his bedroom window as they packed up Renee's jeep and prepared to hit the road together. As usual, the two lovers were all over each other, kissing and holding one another as if one of them was going to die. It made Simon sick to his stomach, in his mind it should be he and Renee spending a romantic, getaway together involving plenty of sex in the woods surrounded by other, wild beast. He wouldn't see his princess again for days, but out of sight, out of mind wasn't going to work this time, he thought to himself. In- fact it made him even angrier knowing they would be alone for who knows how long? Having a wonderful time, enjoying, all the sex and drugs they could handle.

While Simon was forced to work at his mother's flower shop, selling fancy vegetation and worthless relics of a false god. Without being able to spy on her whenever he wanted, Simon imagined he would be bored to pieces until they returned. He remembered how happy Renee sounded when she told him about the trip a few days earlier. She could see there was something behind those eyes, something odd that she couldn't quite put her finger on. The four eyed young man wasn't like anyone she's ever met before. Simon did his best not to cry as he watched her, and Paul drive off. on such a cloudy, dreary day. With nothing better to do Simon continued staring out the window and listening to the radio while watching as the rain started to fall outside. It was lonely and miserable, as he sat around thinking about a girl that would never be his, especially as one particular song came over the airwaves. Simon felt as if the lyricist was in his head and knew exactly what he was going through, his words painfully describing his unfortunate life story. Paul Anka sang, I'm just a lonely boy, lonely and blue. I'm all alone with nothing to do. I've got everything you could think of, but all I want is someone to love. Someone to kiss, someone to hold at a moment like this. I'd like to hear somebody say, I'll give you my love each night and day. Somebody please, send her to me, I'll make her happy, just wait and see. I've prayed so hard to the heavens above, that I'm going to find someone to love.

Simon Fletcher felt the same way as the famous musician, only this was real life for the four eyed, virgin. He experienced the sadness the depressing, melody was offering, as he watched the raindrops beating against his window, pane. Paul and Renee were enjoying their brief journey into another state they've never been to. The two looked at each other and smiled when they heard the Beach-Boys singing Surfing USA. They found it a bit funny since they were headed toward the mountains in the opposite direction. Still it was a great song, causing Renee to reach for the dial and turn it up. They both enjoyed the song as they drove down the highway. When it was over Paul turned down the radio to ask Renee how she feels since the move. He wanted to know she was truly happy with their decision to relocate across the country. He asked Renee if she ever felt home sick? Or if she regretted leaving California behind? With a big smile on her face, Renee told her loving husband it was the best choice he ever made, besides choosing her for his bride she humorously added. She then leaned over to kiss him while he was driving. Paul removed one hand from the steering wheel and reached out for hers. He gave it a kiss as well, telling Renee how much he loved her. Paul felt good knowing he made the right choice moving so far from where they both grew up. If Renee loved it as much as he did, then there could be no regrets. Renee couldn't wait any longer for a buzz, she asked Paul for his cigarette pack and grabbed the joint already rolled up inside. She loved being high on a highway. There was something about it that made her feel truly, alive. Paul could not object, he wanted to take a few puffs while making the few hour- hike as well. He didn't want to go to some popular campground where there would be dozens of other people partying alongside them. Paul's plan was to find a beautiful spot off the beaten path so it could be just the two of them. They were enjoying the ride as much as they planned to enjoy the camping trip. Leaving the gray skies behind as they traveled west it turned out to be a perfect day for a drive. Music helped make the miles seem much shorter. The sun was shining brightly above them and there were hardly any clouds in the sky. Renee stood up to give herself the illusion she was literally flying down the highway and it was incredible. Paul could see his carefree beauty queen being the free spirit he fell head over heels in love with. He cranked up the radio again as James Brown sang and watched as Renee shook her ass and sang along.

While the happy lover's put distance between themselves and Renee Falls, Eleanor and Stanley were stuck dealing with their severely troubled son. He seemed even worse while Renee was out of town. His folks assumed it was because she was on a romantic getaway with her husband, leaving him behind to suffer. They also knew the young couple was trying for a baby. It was the process needed to make them that really, had Simon coming unglued. All he would do is mope around the house or sit up in his tree thinking about Renee and drawing sexy pictures of her. Only to destroy them later.

He often tuned into her favorite rock station, imagining they were listening together. Simon's heart started to beat faster, when he heard a song from the Beatles, since it was his queen's favorite band. He found it was even more significant since it was titled Eleanor Rigby, sharing the first name with his very own mother. He did his best to sketch away, as the song played. Paul and Renee eventually found the seclusion they had been searching for. They were in the middle of nowhere in a town called Sparrows Grove. They absorbed the beautiful new scenery as they found the ideal place to set up camp. Paul was hitting a joint and drinking a beer before even getting the fire started. Renee was also enjoying the alcohol and marijuana. It wouldn't be long before the munchies took over their minds. Luckily, they came prepared. They were going to melt smores like children and they also had hot dogs and burgers for the fire. There was plenty of grub for them to satisfy their ravenous appetites due to smoking all that pot. As the fire crackled and they passed the joint back and forth, Renee started paying attention to the other life-forms sharing the great, outdoors with them, a little spooked, she didn't want to meet any wild creatures face to face, especially insects and snakes. Paul reminded her that they were surrounded by nature, but also that they have a tent if need be? There was nothing to worry about. He really wanted to sleep outside beneath the bright twinkling stars shining down on them. Renee was turned on by the idea at first, she wanted to make love to him right there in the middle of the woods like a feral creature in heat. Although Fall was in the air, it was a very warm evening. Drinking and enjoying each, others company in front of a fire, beneath the stars was exactly what the young lovers needed. They felt free to do whatever they wished, with no one else around to judge them. Renee tried not to think about him leaving in a couple days. She wanted to remain as close to him as possible while it lasted. The sounds of wild, life continued to screw with Renee slightly, she was afraid of something leaping out at her any minute. Finally, she came up with a genius way to forget about the many creatures sharing the night with them.

She got up for a moment and went to the jeep to collect the portable radio. She imagined listening to music was the perfect way to really relax in the wild. Paul thought it was a great idea. He was also in the mood for some tunes. It would surely liven up the dark deserted woods they were camping in. No longer would Renee be forced to listen to all the things that go bump in the night. They turned on the radio and heard Led-Zeppelin playing Stairway to heaven. They both found it peaceful instantly. It was a great time that Paul and especially Renee were wishing would never end. They smoked another joint and went on emptying beer cans as the music played on. Renee suggested Paul puts up the tent. She wasn't willing to sleep on the ground with no shelter. Paul had a feeling that would happen, especially because of all the mosquitoes flying around like mini vampires in search of blood. As usual Paul realized the woman was right. He listened as always and went to work on the tent, taking a hit off the joint and passing it back to Renee for the moment. Once Paul was through setting up, they found themselves even closer.

They started making out by the fire, and slowly removing their clothing. Renee leaned over to change the station to something more romantic. She stopped when she heard Elvis Presley singing it's now or never. Come hold me tight. Kiss me my darling be mine tonight. Tomorrow will be too late. It's now or never my love won't wait. They soon found themselves inside the tent making love. The music playing at a comfortable volume nearby. It was obvious how much love the two young people had for each-other just by the intense look in their eyes as they stared into one another's. Renee was lying on the ground while her husband pleased her. Soft kisses between her legs led to oral and eventually penetration. After a few minutes, Renee gently pushed Paul off, of her and got on top taking control of their intimate moment. Renee was hoping to get pregnant, so there was no need to worry about protection. She wanted every drip of his baby-batter inside of her. Renee felt a little safer in the tent and out of the watchful eye of potential predators. It was such a turn on doing it in nature where the rest of the world's creatures lived and bread. As Paul laid there staring up at his beautiful wife, he also tried his best not to think about deserting her again soon. His goal was to make the most of the night and meet all her expectations for the rest of the weekend.

They both felt moving to Renee Falls was the best decision they ever made, especially after seeing the Manson Murder's all over tv. Renee felt they got out of there just in time. It didn't seem like the right place for her to raise children. They had some trouble making friends back home she knew they could do without. Renee also planned on cleaning up her act, once life starts growing inside her, it was all the reason to live it up for the moment. Neither of them knew what was brewing inside the mind of the love-sick maniac hell-bent on taking over Paul's life. Simon wanted what he had and didn't care about how it might affect others. Renee was the only thing he could think about. Simon felt as if his brain had somehow been poisoned? Or taken over by a demonic force, as if he was re-programmed for misery. No matter what he did his heart ached for the beautiful girl-next-door. As many times as he master-bated while thinking of her as his sexual partner, it did nothing to make him happy, especially once the brief -moment of pleasure was over. Getting his nut off did nothing to distract his thoughts from Renee Price. She remained the main, attraction in the center of his mind. Usually, men are momentarily relieved of their dirty thoughts once they drain the vital juices, but not Simon Fletcher. He was instantly lusting over her again as if he had been building his sperm-count for decades. This was not the way he expected his life to turn out. He thought it was bad before, now he was experiencing hell on a level he didn't even know existed. Simon Fletcher had been viciously stricken by constant grief that showed no signs of letting up. He hated god and even his parents thinking it was their fault for raising him like such a sissy his whole life. Simon hated himself more than anyone. He couldn't explain why he was torturing himself over a girl who could care less about him. She was living it up with her husband without a care in the world. She had no feelings for Simon in return, giving her no reason to dwell on the four-eyed weirdo. It was all a waste of time. He was putting himself through hell for no reason at all. Simon needed to accept the fact that she belonged to another man. He despised himself for voluntarily bringing this chaos into his life. For the rest of the weekend, Paul and Renee partied. Doing drugs and having wild sex most of the time.

They left early Sunday morning to head home, but not before stopping in a groovy little town called Intercourse Pennsylvania. They wanted to find souvenirs they could bring home with the town's name on them. It would be a perfect way to remember this little getaway for the rest of their lives. Walking around and stopping in different stores they found a few things that caught their eyes. Paul and Renee each bought a white t-shirt that said I love Intercourse Pennsylvania. They also found shot-glasses, coffee mugs, and refrigerator magnets. They thought it was great and decided to stack up on trinkets. Renee ought to be very wary of wearing a t-shirt that says I love intercourse on it in front of her next-door neighbor. That could very well be the sign he was waiting to make his move. For Paul, the long trip home was simply a warm, up for his grueling voyage ahead. Renee wanted to hang onto the precious memories, knowing the loneliness and boredom she would once again be facing, while he was away. At least she could sit around thinking about the amazing weekend they shared. In many ways Renee couldn't be happier with the life she was given, everything seemed to be perfect. Simon on the other hand wanted to crash his car into a still, standing tree at 100 miles per hour with hopes of killing himself instantly.

Then he wondered if his crappy car could even go that fast. He imagined he would probably just hurt himself really- bad or damage his already undesirable face, making him even more unattractive to the opposite sex. He may end up with some sympathy from Renee for the tragic accident, long as she didn't find out it was a suicide attempt. That would be humiliating and would probably make his Goddess lose any respect she might have for him. Simon soon realized she wouldn't be that broken up about it. Renee didn't care for him like she did her mangy looking husband. Simon assumed it would all be for nothing, like almost every moment of his natural, life. A few days after Paul left, Renee was sitting around the house feeling pretty -glum. She had been savoring the fresh memories of their wonderful camping trip together and couldn't wait for him to return. Later that afternoon Simon watching from his treehouse high above the ground noticed that Renee was dragging Halloween decorations out to spice-up the Stones old place and be festive. He quickly ran out of the house of sins and toward the front yard to see if maybe she needed a hand. Simon's parents didn't care much for the dark Holiday. They never decorated their godly home with Witches and demons. Eleanor especially believed it was a way to invite evil into their home. She and Stanley did have candy for the children going around trick-or-treating, but it wasn't something they enjoyed celebrating.

Simon was desperate to escape his god-fearing parents, they were ruining his life and contributing to his madness. Renee had been at it for a little while and the house was already looking spooky, Simon was hoping he could use it as an excuse to get closer to his gorgeous next-door neighbor. If he was, lucky, he might even be invited into her house for once. He assumed that would never happen, not even in a million years. What Simon was unaware of as he made his way out front to join her, was that Renee had gotten completely stoned before attempting to get artistic with the front-lawn. She planned to get baked and enjoy the nice cool Autumn air. Getting high helped Renee zone out into whatever task she was facing. Mainly it was something to keep her mind occupied while her husband was away. She didn't even notice Simon sneaking up on her as she continued decorating. Wow, this looks fantastic so far, he stated with a big smile on his face. Renee a bit startled from being sucked out of her little world turned to thank him. She said she wanted it to look nice and scary for the neighborhood kids when they hit the streets in search of candy. Well, I think you're doing a great job, this is sure to be the best- looking house in town.

Renee assumed he was just being nice, probably because he was using this opportunity to flirt with her, but living in such a holy town, she imagined no one spent too much time dressing up the place for the devil's invitation. I guess I won't be so lucky when it comes to Christmas huh? Renee jokingly stated. She could only imagine what his folks, let alone the rest of the town did to celebrate the birth of their messiah. Renee assumed there would be more saints and angels swarming the streets of Renee Falls than the heavens themselves. She wasn't even going to try and compete with the Jesus Freaks surrounding her. She seemed, busy as if she didn't have time to talk to him. Simon wanted to invite himself to give her a hand, but as usual, when it came to girls, he lost his nerve. Feeling unwelcomed, Simon turned to head back home, after taking a couple of steps, Renee felt bad for him. She turned and kindly asked where he was going. She insisted he hangs out a while and gives her a hand with the rest of the decorations. Simon couldn't believe his ears. He was incredibly excited about her offer. Now he could spend time with his queen and do something he was never allowed to as a child, putting up decorations for the ghoulish holiday. Simon was lucky his folks even let him go around trick or treating when he was younger. Are you sure? Simon asked wondering if this was simply an act of mercy. He didn't want to be there because she pitied him. Renee insisted she could use the company, confessing she was pretty, lonely since. Paul wasn't around, especially late at night when the world is asleep. Simon smiled and got to work. He could tell something was different about her this afternoon, her eyes were red and glassy, and she didn't seem quite like herself. Simon didn't know she was high as a kite in the spring air. He insisted that Renee keep this between them, he didn't want his folks to know he was touching the Satanic decorations. Renee laughed and told him his secret was safe with her. The worst part about hanging out with his dream girl was having to listen to her talk about Paul and how much she loves and misses him. It was poison to Simon's ears, he hated knowing how much Renee cared for her husband. Telling, him how she ached for his return was not the words Simon wanted to hear. She couldn't wait for Paul to see how wonderful the house looked. The night before, she got baked and carved some scary-looking pumpkins to spread out on her front, lawn. Even though Simon was right there helping decorate for the coming Holiday, it felt as if Renee didn't even know he existed.

Everything was about her perfect, husband. The depressed lunatic was slowly unraveling, he was beginning to wonder if he should stick around? Or return to his house and sulk over her like a baby again, until his parents come home. Simon was lucky enough to have a day off from both jobs and should be taking advantage of it. He continued to secretly imagine what life would be like if Paul Price was no longer around. In his heart, Simon knew he wasn't a killer, he would never be able to claim his enemies, life with his own two hands. What would his folks think if they ever found out? How could he ever explain himself? Simon also knew it would earn him a place in hell for all of eternity. It was obvious he wasn't a tough guy. Just another broken-hearted fool unable to get the girl. Simon was too naïve to even realize Renee was high on marijuana, he had never even taken a sip of cold, beer. He was a virgin to everything fun and exciting and it was all his parent's fault.

As the front of the house came alive with Renee's decorations, Simon knew his time with her was running out. He was not much for conversation, especially when she was around Simon assumed, he would be back in his house alone in the next couple of minutes. He was wishing he was one of those guys who always knew just what to say to get the girl he desired into his bed. When they were finally through, Renee grabbed Simon by the hand, dragging him into the street so they could have a good, look at how her house would appear to people passing by. Simon couldn't believe she was actually- touching him. It was only handed, but for Simon it was monumental. He did his best not to show how excited he was and prayed she wouldn't notice his growing erection. Renee seemed so happy, we did it, look how gnarly it is Simon. I think the kids around here are going to love it. Simon agreed, but he knew their folks would not be so impressed. It was almost demonic to dress up your front-lawn that way. Mrs. Anderson had been keeping an eye on them here and there, as they continued to pollute the neighborhood with filth. She wasn't a fan of Halloween either. She wished it would be banned from American culture. Mrs. Anderson also noticed Simon checking out Renee more than she was aware of. His eyes were usually on her ass or breast whenever it wasn't obvious. The elderly lady was becoming aware of what a pervert he truly was. Simon and Renee had no idea the nosy neighbor was secretly watching them. It was as if this whole street is filled with peeping Tom's.

This quiet little town was turning out to be even stranger than Los Angeles. Simon agreed that the house looked amazing, he could tell it was the end of the road when it came to spending time with Renee. With nothing interesting to say he quickly assumed she was getting ready to slip back in the house. Thank you for helping me, Simon. I sure needed the company. Paul is going to love it when he gets back. Once again, he had to hear that fucking name. He didn't want to stick around if they were going to talk about Mr. Wonderful all day long. He would rather escape to his house of sins and draw his enemy bathing in blood. Simon's heart was beating a million miles an hour until Renee released his hand again, he wanted to remain attached to her forever. His hand was all warm now from squeezing against hers. It was disappointing that their encounter ended so soon. Simon day-dreamed of touching her even more, in places he knew she would never allow.

He soon noticed Renee reaching into her pocket for a cigarette, she even invited him to stick around until she was through. Simon didn't care about breathing in her second-hand smoke. Taking seconds off his life was worth the risk, to gain a few extra ones with the girl he was dangerously obsessed with. Renee jokingly suggested they decorate his house next with ghosts and goblins. It was a perfect excuse to spend more time with her, unfortunately, his parents fucked that up without even knowing it. Simon laughed, insisting he would love to see the expressions on their faces if they were to find the house demonized with vampires and other hellish spooks. It would be such a wonderful way to piss them off. Renee told Simon she hopes they don't hate her for her evil display of monsters and ghouls. As they talked, Simon started looking at Renee's cancer-stick as an hourglass counting down the time until they go their separate ways. Knowing how he would feel when he was alone, Simon started thinking of it as more of a dynamite stick counting down to an explosion.

Every drag turned more of the clean white paper into a black withering, ash. Simon did his best to take at the moment while it lasted. He explained that he went Trick or Treating when he was younger, but his parents never really liked the Pagan holiday. He did warn her about Christmas, however, admitting. they decked the place out as if Christ was going to show up for cake on his birthday. Simon was proud of himself when Renee started laughing really, hard. He didn't think what he said was that funny. Since Renee was a bit stoned, she had an enhanced sense of humor. Looking at her cigarette again he noticed it was much smaller this time. It was down to seconds as she took another drag. Simon watched in horror, he wanted to tell her to stop but had no good reason to interfere with her nicotine fit. Renee had an old bucket on the porch to place her butts in. She soon excused herself to throw it away. Simon's time was up, he would have to wait impatiently until she felt like speaking to him again. A wave of depression came over him as they said their goodbyes and parted ways. He wanted a hug from her but didn't get one. She just flashed a smile at him and turned to head back inside. Simon spent the rest of the day sitting around watching tv and daydreaming about the girl-next-door. The more time he spent around her, the further in love he fell. Simon could feel his brain growing and compressing in his skull again as anxiety and misery caused it to feel as if it were swelling.

He did his best to re-watch Star-Trek episodes but found it really, hard to concentrate. Renee was taking up all the space his finite mind had to offer. Later -on, when his mother returned from the florist, the first thing she noticed was Renee's house and all the devilish decorations morbidly displayed. If only the deceased couple could see what their house looked like now? She thought. Eleanor was also wondering what her husband would think when he saw what the young hippie girl did to the house next door? It wasn't enough to get her down. Eleanor wasn't fond of the dark holiday, but she knew soon enough all the Ware wolves and Jack O Lanterns would be replaced by holy relics that represented the god. She didn't waste too much time dwelling on it and quickly made her way into the house. She wanted to say hello to Simon and see what he was up to. As usual, he seemed to be in the same crumby mood. Eleanor found him sitting on the couch watching tv with a blank stare on his face. It was almost as if he wasn't really -there. She continued growing concerned for his well-being. Simon was lucky Renee was also a bit naïve. She simply didn't take him for the crazy stalker type.

After growing up in the city of angels she has encountered some pretty- bizarre people during her life. Simon seemed slightly off, but she imagined he was like every other geek with glasses who wanted to bed a beautiful woman. He hated having to pretend he was content with their platonic relationship. Simon knew in his heart he wanted much more. It was just as painful being around Renee as it was when they were apart. Whenever he was fortunate enough to share a few fleeting moments with Renee, Simon found it more and more difficult to hide his feelings from her. Often it took everything he had not to kiss her or hold her hand again. It was as if there was a higher power manipulating his mind to continue torturing itself. Perhaps it was the cruel god the whole town is so crazy about? Eleanor had things to do like get dinner started. She didn't have time to sit with her son and talk about his unhealthy obsession with the girl-next-door. She and her husband would do well to keep a close eye on him during his time of sorrow.

A couple of days later, Simon was working at the flower shop and as usual, he was bored out of his mind. There had been a few customers and not a whole lot to do. For Simon that meant flooding his thoughts with the girl he feared he couldn't live without. He was thinking about getting to work on one of his disturbing drawings when suddenly the door opened. Simon wasn't paying attention to who was entering his mother's store at- the moment. His eyes were focused on the art instruments lying around as he searched for inspiration. With nothing to do he was anxious to get busy on something truly grotesque until he looked up and saw the one and only Renee standing there before him. She looked amazing as always in her hippie styled clothing. Simon wanted to say hello, but he was momentarily frozen by her beauty. Staring into those bright blue-eyes the young lover found himself lost in them. Renee smiled as she noticed he was someplace else at- the moment. He apologized as Renee asked him what he was up to? Simon told her he was thinking about creating another cool drawing. Looking around the store, she could see why he was considering it. There was not much else to do. Renee also wanted to know if he had any of his masterpieces to show off, Simon disappointingly insisted he did not, saying he never brought pictures from home to work with him. Aw. That's a shame. I want to see some of your more recent work, although the pictures of Mary and Jesus hanging around the house since you were a kid are pretty -darn good as well. Renee insisted. Her charming words caused his heart to beat a little faster inside his chest. Simon couldn't believe she was actually- interested in his artwork. He promised to show her something very soon. All he had to do is spend a little time on something normal.

These days his folks would be lucky to get a drawing or two a year from him. Most of the stuff he does ends up being disposed of soon after. Renee smiled and told Simon she was going to hold him to it. He promised to paint a beauty specifically for her. Simon then asked Renee her reason for coming to his mother's crappy store, usually, Paul is the one who comes in to buy things. He was also trying to figure out exactly what he should draw-up for Renee, so he's prepared the next time they meet. As thoughts raced through his head, Renee jokingly answered his question. She suggested he draws a picture of her. It took Simon by surprise, especially since he could never quite get her the way he wanted.

He had been feverishly trying even before they met. Simon smiled back at her saying her wish is his command. He promised to have it ready for her to feast her eyes on soon. Renee assumed she would have to be present for him to get it right. He began wishing she would come over to his place and posse in the nude for him. Like everything else he dreamed of in this miserable life, it would never happen. Simon often wondered why negative things always seemed to materialize easier than positive ones. He saw himself living in a cruel world. A world full of hate, greed, and great disappointment. Renee seemed very excited to see the self-portrait the young man next-door would come up with. She reminded Simon that she's never been to the flower shop and wanted to check it out. She looked around with joy on her face, there were beautiful flowers and plants everywhere. Renee also saw the homemade saints and angels, just like the ones at Fletcher's home. She found it interesting that Simon's mother made all of them herself. Her work was also quite impressive. I can see where you get your talent. Said Renee with her eyes still wondering the room. Yeah, my mother is something, isn't she? Is she here now? I would love to say hello and let her know what I think of the place. No, she's actually- home today, making more porcelain statues I'd imagine. They shared a chuckle as Simon stared into her magical eyes, it was another moment he didn't want to end.

When did he ask if she was interested in anything? Or just looking around? Renee wasn't sure how to respond? Being it was her first time in the store, and the Fletcher's seemed like nice people, Renee felt obligated to buy something. She could always use a pretty plant around the house. Rolling her wondering eyes around the store, eventually something caught her attention. It was a pretty- purple plant called a Saintpaulia ionantha that she could leave on her windowsill in the living room. It was cheap and would dress the place up a bit. Wanting to get home she cut the conversation short, paying Simon for the plant and reminding him of the picture he owed her. She turned to leave-taking her sweet smell along with her. Simon was still holding the money Renee gave him in his hand, as he turned his attention to her walking toward her yellow jeep parked out front. He watched carefully as she hopped inside and drove off. It was only then he remembered he was still holding the two dollars Renee gave him for the plant. He smiled realizing how precious these two -dollar bills were. He quickly reached into his pocket and replaced them with money he already had on him. Simon was going to stash the cash away forever as a precious relic of sorts. Now he had something tangible that once belonged to his goddess. Knowing she touched it made the small amount of money almost priceless to him. It was sitting in her tight jeans just a couple of minutes ago. He put it in a separate pocket for the moment and quickly went back to what Renee said about drawing a decent picture of her. He didn't care to paint her with clothes on, but this time he would have no choice. Since the store was still silent as the grave, Simon grabbed his supplies and went to work. He sat behind the counter praying no one would come in and disturb him from his masterpiece. Seeing Renee in his mind's eye, as if she was standing right in front of him, it wasn't long before the pencil was moving across the paper.

Slowly she came together, each feature of her face precisely sketched to perfection. He drew her wearing the dress she had on when they first met. It was a red sundress with yellow flowers on it. This time it was simply shades of gray from his led pencil still when he was finished, she was incredibly life-like. Simon stared at it for a few seconds, proud of what he had done. He also felt a sense of relief knowing Renee was aware of this particular drawing. For once it wasn't for his selfish lust and he couldn't wait to show it off. Simon couldn't believe he was lucky enough to finish the entire drawing without interruption. Soon after he was through, the folks of Renee Falls started to appear again. For once he was actually, glad to see other faces. Now that he got his creativity out, the lovesick young man needed something else to keep him busy. No matter how many people came to shop that day? No one would compare to the one sale he made earlier that afternoon. If there had been a video camera in the flower-shop, Simon certainly would have been watching the tape over and over until it wore-out from so much usage. He found himself hanging onto that picture for more than a week. He had been working around the clock without a day off accept, for Sundays when he was forced to stay home and listen to his mother play the stupid organ and sing about god all day. He had not seen Renee since she walked out of the flower shop. It seemed strange since she lived right next door, but it happens that way sometimes. Busy schedules cause chance encounters only when the timings right. Finally, not long before Paul was due to return from the west-coast it actually- happened. Simon found himself home all alone as he wanted in the middle of the week. Eleanor was working at the store, and Stanley was busy building a shopping mall with his crew out in Maiden Head. Renee spent most of her morning cleaning the house. She wanted It to look nice when her hubby returned.

It was a warm sunny day for the middle of October, Renee almost forgot how close she was to experience her first winter in a new land. In a way, she was kind of excited. She dared to daydream about a white Christmas this year. It was something she had never done before. Living in LA, the odds were stacked against her. As she swept, mopped and dusted the new house, she started to feel really at home there. Even though it's been a few months since she and her husband first moved in, Renee was still a little home-sick in the back of her mind, but she didn't want Paul to know. She wanted him to believe she was just as spontaneous and free-spirited as he was, especially since that's what she always claimed to be. Everything and everyone seemed so nice here. Renee was really- proud of her husband for finding this perfect little paradise. As her thoughts continued to involve Paul, while straightening up the living room, her eyes were soon fixated on their wedding picture, sitting on a small end-table with a brown and yellow lamp sharing the same space. Renee smiled and told Paul she loved him.

The young hippie woman felt extremely lucky for finding her true soulmate. She knew there was no one else for her in the world. That was terrible news for poor Simon still holding on to hope that he will steal her heart some, lucky day. Renee enjoyed the music playing in the background It helped pass the time while Paul was so far away. It also reminded her of the wonderful times they shared. She eventually turned away and went on freshening up the place. This morning when she rolled out of bed, Renee didn't feel like getting herself all done-up, instead, she put her hair in a ponytail and threw on a pair of sweat-pants and one of Paul's T-shirts. It was black and had a picture of Jim Morrison on the front. Simon noticed the way she dressed when her husband was away. It was the only time he would catch her dressed in his clothes. He found it a bit odd, but It didn't matter to Simon what she wore. Renee Price was the sexiest woman he has ever laid eyes on. Part of her chores for the day was getting the dirty laundry clean. She had been neglecting

Paul's things since he wouldn't be home to wear them anyway. Knowing he would return soon, she finished folding a load and prepared to put it away for him.

When she got to the bedroom and opened his top draw wear all his favorite t-shirts were usually stored Renee found her loving husband left a little surprise behind. Inside the draw not hidden but placed right on top of other clean shirts was a cigarette-pack. Renee knew it was meant for her to see. When she opened the small box, she found a surprise stash of joints for her to enjoy while he was away. Renee smiled when she rediscovered how amazing her husband truly was. It was such a perfect day outside and she knew there wouldn't be many more. Soon the cold would be trapping everyone in their homes until the spring thaw. She had nothing important to do now that the house was practically spotless. Alone and absent of any dire plans, Renee decided to smoke a joint. She grabbed one out of the pack and took it with her. Paul, she said quietly with joy on her face. If only she would have found his present sooner? She felt like a bit of an ass for neglecting his dirty clothes for so long. Paul was the greatest husband ever. She knew it was his way of saying thank-you for holding-down the fort while he was away. Renee wasted no time reaching into her pocket for the book of matches, so she could spark the surprise joint and enjoy herself. Heading down the stairs with the intensions of adding a splash of vodka to her glass of orange juice she wanted to sit outside for a little while and enjoy the gorgeous day, forgetting she was no longer in California, Renee went and had a seat on the front porch, the grass burning in one hand and the screwdriver in the other.

CHAPTER 7

Simon had been carrying the picture he drew for Renee around the house with him like a trophy. He wondered if she would not only keep his work of art but cherish it even half as much as he did the two singles she used to pay for the purple plant. He was home all day waiting for her to come outside so he could catch her and show off his masterpiece. Simon was sitting around watching some old western movie, but his eyes kept wandering toward the window leading to Renee's place. Finally, right in the middle of a gunfight, it happened. Simon turned his head again, and this time he spotted Renee sitting on her porch. He imagined she was smoking a cigarette like always, he had to hurry, before she goes back inside. Simon quickly shifted his eyes toward the drawing resting on the couch beside him. He snatched it up and headed for the door. A virgin not only to sex but also drugs Simon began searching everywhere for the filthy skunk wandering the neighborhood. She was in the middle of smoking a joint when Simon approached, he was clueless about what she was doing. Renee didn't even notice him coming closer until it was too late. Hey. Said Simon with a smile on his face, noticing the joint in her hand, he was still under the impression she was enjoying a cigarette. Renee jumped for a second startled by his presence. Simon felt bad and quickly apologized, saying he didn't mean to scare her. She swore it was no big deal, as she noticed him rotating his eyes in all directions. It was as if they were about to be mauled, by a wild animal. What are you looking for? Renee asked while exhaling, spraying Simon with her skunk spray.

You're telling me you don't smell that? Playing along Renee asked him to explain what he was talking about. She claimed ignorance for a good laugh.

There's a damn skunk around here someplace, probably has rabies. I thought they were nocturnal creatures, Simon innocently stated. A rabid- skunk huh? Renee questioned while taking another hit off the joint in her mouth. She realized that Simon had no clue what she was doing. She started laughing as she blew a cannabis cloud right in his face. It was at that moment he realized she was smoking grass. Of course, marijuana that's what you're smoking, Simon stated for anyone with ears to hear. Shh. Are you crazy? You're going to get me busted. Sit down and try some. How could Simon resist? He immediately had a seat on the porch next to Renee as she continued to get stoned. Of course, hippie, pot. I get it now. I'm guessing you have never taken part. Simon started laughing. Yeah right, me smoking grass, now that's funny. You've met my parents. Simon was never exposed to such things growing up in a strict, religious home. Again, Renee asked if he wanted to indulge. Simon was really- nervous to try the so-called gateway drug. What would his parents say if they found out? He was terrified to think of their reaction. Simon was also afraid of the way it would make him feel, but Renee continued to assure him it was perfectly safe. She said he will mostly feel happy and eventually hungry. Being drunk and stoned, Renee knew all Simon needed was a few drags to catch up to her. He was after all a virgin with virgin lungs. Mrs. Anderson was silently watching them from across the street. It was as if she was taking note of the citizen's sins and good deeds, similar to an angel working for god. Simon was extremely nervous, and Renee could see it all over his face. She started laughing again, insisting he didn't have to if he didn't want to, she was just offering. If he wasn't interested so be it, more for her she figured. Simon didn't want to look like a total geek in front of the goddess presenting harmless drugs to him. If he didn't take a drag off the weed cigarette as he saw it, Renee would think he was a child in a slightly older child's body.

Even though there was no pressure, Simon felt it growing tighter by the second, twisting his intestines into knots. He was worried his folks would smell it on him, or they would notice the change in his behavior. Renee continued hitting the joint, as he struggled to make up his mind. Finally, with his hand noticeably, shaking, Simon reached over and grabbed the grass from Renee sitting beside him. She was surprised as he placed it to his lips and took a hit much bigger than necessary. Renee watched and tried not to laugh, as he began coughing his brains out, adding momentum to his first high. Renee told him to take it easy as giant cannabis clouds came pouring out of his nose and mouth. She felt bad and quickly started apologizing. Simon couldn't stop coughing from the thick mass of smoke invading his lungs. Are you ok? Renee asked as he finally slowed down. Wow, I guess I hit it a little too hard huh. Simon asked with a smile growing on his face. Renee took it away from him and placed it to her lips showing him how to do it right. At that moment Simon felt as if he almost kissed the girl of his dreams. She had her moist lips on the same piece of rolled-up paper as him. It was a kiss in a very distant sense, but a kiss never, the less. He watched carefully as she gently, breathe in hardly even brightening the cherry at the burning end.

When she was through, Renee didn't cough, not even a little. Simon was impressed, the beauty-queen was a pro at this. He remained anxious to know what it would feel like to be stoned. Since Simon was such a sheltered young man, Renee assumed he also thought she was drinking ordinary orange-juice. She thought about offering him a screwdriver as well, then realized it might send him right over the edge.

The glass of orange-juice looked completely innocent to Simon. He had no idea she was getting drunk right in front of him. Renee decided to keep it to herself. Now that Simon seemed alright, Renee asked if he wanted to try again. Simon had gone too far to back out now. He had to indulge a little further and see what it felt like when the burning grass took effect. He smirked at her, as she handed it back to him. Remember this time take a very small breath, no cowboy stuff. The sound of her voice drove Simon wild, especially when she was talking to him. He couldn't believe they were sharing a joint. Simon knew Paul would be home soon and Renee would have no time for him, as usual. It was depressing to know he meant nothing in her world.

This time when he raised the joint to his lips, Simon pretended he was kissing her. The paper was slightly damp from her saliva. He was sure not to make a fool of himself again, taking a much smaller breath this time while inhaling. He still managed to cough a little after, but it wasn't as bad as the first time, so he was thankful for that at least. Simon's first experience with the confidence only instigated him to take a few more harmless, drags from the weed cigarette. He quickly began to feel different after the extra hits. It was as if the air had been sucked out of his head, appearing much lighter. It also felt as if he used all his bodily fluids to water the cannabis plant, he ingested, his mouth drier than death-valley. Renee soon felt she made a terrible mistake inviting her innocent neighbor to get high with her, it's just that she missed Paul so much and couldn't stand the loneliness. Renee soon started to panic as she realized her loving husband laced it with a little something special. It was the only rational explanation for why John Lennon was sitting up in the tree on her front lawn, strumming his guitar and singing, while staring into her eyes, as a hemorrhaging bullet wound slowly opened in his head. His eyes rolled back into his skull while dropping his precious instrument and falling to the ground, bringing her face to face with the divine musician's future demise.

There was no sign of his assassin, as Renee wondered what the fuck was going on? She turned to look at Simon wondering if he could see what she was seeing at that exact moment. Renee quickly saw that he was much more interested in keeping his eyes glued to her with an item resting close to his side. She assumed it was very important that the mystery baggage was evaluated as soon as possible. Renee started looking around, realizing that the image of one of her beloved Beatles being killed was only in her distorted mind, even though she could still hear his voice faintly singing to her. Confident her loving husband laced the joint with a kick Renee aggressively snatched it out of Simon's hand and told him he wasn't allowed to have anymore. Simon didn't understand why she was being so selfish all, of a sudden with the pot. He has yet to discover that he had just taken something much more thrilling, and potentially terrifying. Simon's heart started to beat faster as he became nervous about Renee's sudden panic. He didn't know why she was acting so strange.

At the same time, Renee didn't know if she wanted to come clean about accidentally slipping him a demon of a drug that can hijack the mind and drive it to insanity, fearful of his reaction. She also knew he would soon feel as if he's not in Kansas anymore. Once he starts losing his grip on reality, Renee knew she was in for a long day, she was going to have to play co-pilot and coach him out of the madness. Experienced, with drugs Renee knew how to think to maintain a positive trip. She didn't want Simon to propel himself into shear, terror. Keeping the vibe positive was key while experiencing psychedelic drugs. Everyone is -capable of creating their heaven or hell within the confines of their minds. Where you end up depends greatly on your positive verse's negative energies at the subconscious level. Simon was starting to freak out and it was all Renee's fault. Now he was going to start seeing shit that doesn't even exist. Renee felt terrible for instigating the drug intake. She sat frozen on the porch staring at Simon for a change, it was so often the other way around while realizing she couldn't get completely lost in her head this time. With all senses thrust into turmoil and the chaos it created, Renee played it cool as Simon shrunk and grew gigantic before her eyes. She told him he had enough since he was such a virgin at this. It was the wrong choice of words, but she was far too shit-faced to care. Renee didn't want to smoke anymore either. She was treating the heavily laced joint as if it were just grass. She accidentally sent poor Simon down a rabbit-hole with no warning or instructions. Renee hoped her guilt wouldn't trigger a bad trip for herself as well. She had no choice, but to make sure the four-eyed dork next-door remains calm. She didn't want to have to explain to Fletcher's how their precious son ended up that way. It looked as though Simon finally had his wish. He would be spending a horrifically exciting day with the beautiful girl next door. She put the joint out and placed it back inside her cigarette-pack.

Hopefully, Simon didn't absorb too much, and his thrill-ride would be spine-tingling but brief. It seemed to be Renee's punishment for having a good time. She didn't feel like playing babysitter as they sat on the porch in awkward silence, Simon also felt the urge, to get going. Renee lit a smoke, inviting him to stay with her a while longer, it wasn't very hard to convince him. All Simon Fletcher wanted to do is spend time with the woman he constantly obsessed over. The desperate love-sick puppy would lay at her feet until doomsday if she so demanded it of him. Buzzed off the joint, he was becoming too nervous to go anywhere else. Simon asked Renee when her husband was due back? Very soon, I hope. Renee replied. While in the middle of the conversation, Renee remembered the picture sitting next to Simon on the porch. she smiled and asked if that was the portrait he promised? Simon was excited and a bit nervous as well to show it off. He feared it may not be good enough and she wouldn't like it. Reluctant to hand it over with a pathetic, grin on his face, Simon gave Renee the picture he worked so hard on and awaited her opinion. She was soon smiling ear to ear, insisting it was like staring at her reflection. Renee was extremely impressed with his work, until the mirror image suddenly came to life, forcing her to watch helplessly as her youthful face quickly aged into dust. Soft skin wrinkling and peeling from the decaying bones beneath, sending a shockwave of terror through her entire body. Placing her fear aside, Renee did her best to remain calm. She swore the portrait was incredible and that she loved it. Renee's words made Simon feel as if he was finally signed in this hateful, world he found himself trapped in. He could finally be proud of something he's done. He told Renee she could keep the picture if she liked it. There is no way you're getting this back, Renee threatened in a friendly way, although it, sort of freaked her out. I can't believe it? it looks exactly like me. Renee said as she stared at the portrait smiling. She continued to drink liquor on top of the hallucinogens and weed, making her brain border-line insane. Soon she might not be able to control her state of mind.

Let alone the poor bastard from next-door. Renee knew the only way to soothe her troubled mind was to listen to music. She told Simon she would be right back while heading in the house to play some tunes., as the colors of the world around her began to change. As fate would have it, the end from the Doors was playing, while she was wearing a black t-shirt with Jim Morrison's face on it. Foolishly, Renee spilled a little extra vodka into her glass of orange juice, while an unexpected trip was taking flight. When she returned to the porch, Simon found himself staring at her breast, but for the first time, it wasn't because he was being a pervert. It was because he could have sworn Jim Morrison winked at him momentarily from her t-shirt. It even appeared as though his hair was blowing in a gust of wind that wasn't there? Renee's gorgeous breast just added certain gigantism to his face. Somehow the painted image had come to life. His eyes were animated, not fixated forever sculpted into place by the photographer.

The gifted musician appeared to be watching Simon's every move. He shifted his attention away from Renee's chest and just as expected, the portrait of Jim moved his painted eyes, eerily following the stalker. How was he going to explain that to Renee, especially if she catches him staring at her tits? He found the music a bit trippy and fun, as if he was at one of the Doors concerts, performing in his imagination. The image remained still, but the band played on until suddenly it completely changed to a much darker, demonic sounding melody of horror spewed directly from the pits of hell. It was as if the devil himself was the composer of these demonic tones. Guitars were screaming and screeching as he had never heard before, way beyond the music Renee listened to. The sound of the beating drums gave Simon the impression of demons cracking skulls and snatching souls while coming his way. He imagined the falling angels would be clashing with gods on the streets of Renee Falls, an apocalyptic battle taking place right before his eyes.

It was the loudest and most disturbing sound he had ever experienced, yet ear-shattering as the satanic music seemed to be, Simon managed to hear, the sound of rowdy voices mixed within it. It was as if a large group of punks from who knows where just showed up uninvited, seeking trouble and possibly the only thing that could draw his attention away from Renee's breast hidden beneath her rock band t-shirt. When he turned to look across the street to see who was causing all the ruckus, Simon was confronted by a group of terrifying looking teenagers who appeared as if they just came from a seance in the local graveyard, either that or they crawled from the mouth of hell itself.

One of them had a blue mohawk made of sharp spikes that appeared capable of impaling anyone who gets too close. He also had a silver chain running from his right ear to his lip. Simon couldn't make out exactly what his shirt said, but it was something like metallic or metal. They were mostly dressed in black and had tattoos of Lucifer and fire breathing dragons on their flesh. One of the young men was short and very stocky with a black, beard. He had a spiked collar around his neck and bracelets to match around his wrist. One of the other men was tall and creepy, looking with long black hair and wearing a trench coat, even the girls appeared as dark angels. One of them was heavy set with red hair, tattoos and lots of piercings decorating her face, but the other was kind of cute, Simon knew he could never see himself with such a devilish looking woman, although he couldn't deny his strange attraction to her. She was pale-skinned with long purple hair covered in ink and wearing a black leather corset with a black mini skirt covered in little white skulls.

There were a lot of intimidating looking teenagers standing around across the street, and Simon wondered what they were doing there. The sound of their sinister laughter and demonic music echoed through the quiet neighborhood, as the tall kid with the mohawk looked directly at Simon while taking a hit from a thick joint and tossing it into the road. He then began acting like an idiot with his friends by doing flips around the roof bar of his piece of shit Volts wagon thing, only now it was even more repulsive, gradually turning into rust bucked on wheels. The rebellious teenagers appeared satanic and Simon wanted them to go away. It began to feel as if time itself was slowing down, as Simon watched the delinquents continuing to act up, blasting the most, vile, music he ever heard and treating his car like it now belonged to one of them. It was as if somehow, he stepped into another place and time.

This was some far, out shit Renee has given him, but he wanted to get back to reality immediately. Unfortunately, it doesn't work like that. Simon turned his attention away from the satanic kids and toward the brightly burning sun and as it scorched his fragile eye's he could 've sworn there were two giants, beast fighting each other on the surface. They had large sharp claws and spines like a dinosaur from what he could make out. Rings of fire danced around them elegantly, until the duel ended and both opponents melted back into the raging star burning high above the earth. His eyes were being blinded by the intense brightness of the sun and his ears were ready to explode as the horrific music continued playing from his very own car. it was Metallica's trapped under ice screaming out at him and Simon was desperate to make it stop, he even considered retrieving the family bible for protection. Turning his head away from the light source, Simon discovered it was almost impossible to see anything.

When he glanced over at where the scary-looking kids were, he saw them moving toward him with weapons drawn. They were armed with large knives, spiked bats and even pitchforks made from wooden branches sharpened to penetrating points. One of the boys even had contacts that made his eyes appear as if they belonged in the skull of a wolf. They were bright yellow with a blank expression on them. As the murderous gang of demonic-looking teens slowly approached Simon while taunting him, one of the misfits opened his mouth, spilling out blood staining his chin red, as it dripped from vampire fangs inside his mouth.

The pretty girl began self, mutilating her body right before Simon's eyes, carving into her arms to release some of the torment she was suffering during this thing called life. He even noticed a ghostly appearance of the moon dimly glowing in the blue sky, during the sun's hours. Simon could see that it too was burning and there were gigantic claw marks with glowing red lava gushing out onto the surface. There were even silver shaped chariots flying from behind the moon toward him. It was as if the gods were returning just as promised in holy scriptures around the world. He was convinced this was the end of everything. It meant he wouldn't have much time with Renee Price while present in this universe. The gods were coming to invade and soon everyone would be judged, the rapture, it seems was finally upon the world of man. Simon never believed his mom and dad when it came to the gospels, but now he was beginning to doubt his denial, as he witnessed alien battles in the skies above him. He wondered how Renee didn't notice what was going on, as the skies began to burn. his entire neighborhood was going to be incinerated, as gods and demons went to war above Renee Falls.

It was frightening for Simon to envision Armageddon, but he was going to use this petrifying hallucination, to his advantage when constructing his next masterpiece. The strangest thing to Simon was that the gods and demons didn't appear as they were described in the holy bible. He watched as two dueling space crafts landed and when the pilots stepped out, they were unlike anything he had ever witnessed before. One side was short gray skin beings with elongated skulls and big, black eyes, the other appeared more reptilian, like the dark angel in the holy book They were much taller and muscular, with long tails and red glowing eyes. It also reminded Simon of the depictions he eerily, created while expressing himself vulgarly with his disturbing portraits. Simon was overcome by fear regret and denial, as he listened to the sound of church bells ringing out. The world invasion was finally at hand, all he could do is watch as the gods from outer space descended onto his world, fulfilling the promise of their return. Renee did her best to keep it together asking Simon what was wrong with him. She struggled to keep one hemisphere of her brain in- reality and the other in the lucid visions she was encountering. Simon pulled back frantically while letting out a blood-curdling scream, that was sure to get Mrs. Anderson's attention across the street as she watched I Love Lucy. When she looked out the window, she saw Simon still sitting there with Renee Price. She didn't think he had any business over there, especially while her husband was out of town.

Old fashion and religious as she was, Mrs. Anderson found almost everything to be a sin. When Simon turned to look at the beautiful voice calling to him, he was overwhelmed by horror. Renee was no longer the beautiful, vibrant goddess he often praised. Her skin was dry and bluish, gray like the dead, and the gloomy, emotionless visitors from the sky. There were black-holes where her baby-blue eyes should be, and her teeth were yellow and filed to ice picks as she reached for him, shaking the frightened young man to get his attention. Renee returned to normal before Simon could blink. She said she was sorry and insisted he clears his head of bad thoughts, swearing it was the best way to control the visions that appear in one's imagination. Simon couldn't believe pot could produce such a wild ride. Renee said it only made you happy, and hungry. She never mentioned the horrifying reason for the strange sightings he was experiencing. Renee could see the fear in his eyes as she did her best to steer his mind away from a bad trip. It was getting harder as she continued seeing fucked up shit as well.

Taking a sip of her vodka and orange juice, Renee noticed there was something alive and moving in it. A fat multi, colored insect with a large orange head and two sets of purple wings flapping rapidly, but going nowhere, it was unlike any creature she had encountered before. The bizarre insect also had four large green eyes with a centered black pupil in the shape of a ridged flint knife blade and a flesh piercing stinger at its back. Renee could even see the jagged mandibles in the monster's jaws. When she placed her hand over the top of the glass to show Simon, it started aggressively gnawing its fangs against the transparent walls while flapping its wings rapidly to free itself from captivity. The alien insect appeared hostile leaving Renee both fascinated and terrified. She went in for a closer look, as the grotesque creature broke free, shattering the glass and splashing orange juice in her face, as Simon confessed, he was seeing strange and scary things that weren't there. Lizard like locus with gold armored chest plates and dagger-like tails aerodynamically pinpointed themselves in his direction as he tried to speak. Confident they were indeed venomous Simon was convinced he would be meeting his maker very soon.

As they changed course and flew away, he asked if this is how most people reacted off -of weed? Forcing Renee to confess that they smoked something else as, well. Watching the fear grow in Simon's eyes she promised she didn't know. Renee confessed the joint was already rolled and waiting for her. As she did her best to explain what happened, Renee could see the panic growing inside the severely sheltered young man sitting on her porch. She assured him that the things he was witnessing were only in his head. That's why they all vanish when he stops focusing on them. He couldn't believe the drugs could change the physical world around him so vividly. Confused and terrified, Simon didn't even want to explain the crazy shit he had been experiencing in detail. It's bad enough he felt as though he was losing his mind. Renee suggested, they go inside for a while, so the neighbors don't witness the extreme behavior they were liable to display. Simon agreed to stare at her ass as he followed her inside. He couldn't believe he was actually- being invited into Renee's house. Simon had been there many times before, but he was curious to see what Renee has done with the place, knowing it would be completely different than the last time he was invited inside.

As Simon shifted his eyes in all directions, he felt being in the house might turn out to be even more of a terrifying experience. He was already bugging at the wild-colored tapestry's hanging from the walls, as they swayed in a phantom breeze. Simon was seeing disfigured faces in them imagining they were trying to reach out and grab him. He did his best to stay clear of the ghouls trapped on the decretive fabric. Simon then started paying attention to all the posters hanging on the walls surrounding him. Most of them were of the Beatles, especially John Lennon. It was obvious he was her favorite. Stoned out of his mind, Simon felt nervous again, as colors began peeling off items and transforming into new ones while floating around unattached to anything tangible. His brain was on a roller-coaster ride through hell and beyond with no exit.

Simon nervously asked Renee how long this feeling was going to last. Renee was desperate to change the subject. She didn't want to stress him out anymore, then he already was. Simon wondered around the living-room until something he was convinced was real and interesting caught his eye. Renee turned and noticed what he was staring at. Oh, I'm sorry Simon. I should've mentioned him sooner. This is our pet boa-constrictor, his name is Lennon. They both smiled, knowing what a die-hard fan she was. He's cool, my folks would never let me have anything like that in our house. They still believe such creatures are not made by god's hands but by the fallen angel. Pretty out there huh? I would love to see him eat something one day. Maybe you can invite me over when its feeding time again? Simon's words were a bit chilling, but Renee remembered most men are interested in that sort of disgusting shit. She told him that was the worst part about having a snake for a pet. Renee then confessed he belonged to her husband. She never enjoyed feeding adorable mice and rabbits to the ugly, serpent. With a sinister look in his eyes, Simon insisted he would be willing to do it for her next time the snake feeds, therefore lifting her disgusting burden and enjoying it at the same time. He felt reluctant to admit there was something else he had in common with the man he despised, aside from the flawless Renee Price. Simon's thoughts quickly shifted in another direction, when he noticed what seemed to be a live snake crawling from the mouth of the dead one. The beast was shedding its skin and taking on a new identity, a black forked tongue hissing with aggression.

Simon could also see and hear the giant rat clawing and biting its way out of the slithering predator that swallowed it alive. The emerging snake was pure white with the reddest of eyes. As the devil's pet was being eaten from the inside out and bleeding internally, Simon watched as blood poured and began to gather in its tank. The snake jumped around in agonizing pain, as it was separated into two wiggling ends. Blood, a stained rat with a chunk of meat in its teeth still gorging on its surprised victim acted as if Simon wasn't standing there dumbfounded and staring at him. Simon kept all four eyes glued to the repulsive sight until Renee tapped him on the shoulder asking if he was alright. Simon almost leaped out of his skin as a result of overwhelming fear. Before he could answer

Renee, Simon Fletcher had to find the courage to glance back at Lennon to see if he was still savagely torn in two.

He was delighted to find everything was back to normal, as the beautiful girl next door looked him in the eyes concerned for his well, being. Simon lied saying he was totally fine and ready to rock and roll as if he knew what he was talking about. Renee turned and made her way over to the record player. She found the perfect album to go along with their drug-induced minds. It was very relaxing and usually brought fascination out of the nightmarish things that manifest in the mind while on drugs that harshly alter the brain. She reached for a record called A Saucer full of secrets, by Pink Floyd. The trippy sounds of the music instantly placed Simon Fletcher in a deeper trance. Renee insisted he has a seat on the ugly orange colored couch and relaxes for a while, taking her advice it felt as if he landed on a cloud drifting calmly through the heavens. Looking around he couldn't believe he was sitting in her living room any more than he could believe the waring aliens were real or that the chameleon, lizard man changing from dark brown to bright green standing behind Mic Jagger in the poster was real, reaching out its long reptilian arms with three extended fingers. Simon watched with fearful excitement, his very own creation was alive and performing before his eyes.

The music playing in the background made Simon feel even more as if he entered some hidden dimension of reality. The creatures, claws were draped around the rock stars' shoulders, its red glowing eyes peering deep into Simon Fletcher's soul. He sat there trembling, as the scene continued to unfold. The demon's flesh abruptly changed from green to bright red mimicking the holy bible's impression of the devil, as goat horns pierced through the top of his skull. The entire painting was soon saturated in blood, as the demon dug its long pointy fingernails into Mic Jagger's shoulders and the two of them began melting together. Their faces becoming one, giving the satanic vision of the rock star a pair of wicked horns while providing the reptilian man with bizarre features in return.

The hideous face was screaming high notes, making the situation even more hectic, as the locust with razor, sharp weapons crashed through windows invading the house. They were coming from every direction and swarming around Simon like a tornado constructed of carnivorous scavengers gnawing at his face. Simon tried swatting them away, but there were too many. He could also hear the devil laughing at him as he vanished back into the macabre painting. It felt as if he had fallen into a hidden portal, as Renee returned with a couple of glasses of water for them to drink. Simon appeared to be petrified of her Mic Jagger poster.

Dumping the rest of her mixed drink down the drain seemed to be the right move, she wasn't expecting to trip out all day. Renee knew three other joints were waiting for her in the cigarette pack, she didn't know how many were laced. it was clear her unexperienced neighbor was losing it and would need her undivided attention. Simon felt as if his brain was melting slowly inside his skull. Wasted, as she may have been, Renee still had her wits about her. She was going to try her best to keep Simon calm, as she struggled to sober-up. Eventually, the music did start to calm him and the hideous-looking monsters popping out of Renee's walls took a much -needed intermission. Renee told him again how much she liked the picture he drew of her. Simon was too afraid to look at it now. He felt it might shape-shift into one of his secret drawings while Renee is watching allowing her naked and blood-covered image to step off the page and introduce herself to the woman she was gruesomely based off, of. What if she could see what he sees and discovers something truly, twisted and perverted hiding not so deep inside.

It was enough to get Simon's heart racing again. He stared into Renee's eyes as she continued speaking softly to him, asking if he dug the music she was playing. Simon confessed his parents never let him listen to Rock N Roll. They say it's the devil's music. He said he liked it and wanted to hear more, he also admitted he wasn't as religious as his folks. Mostly he was trying to look cool and impress her. Slowly opening -up to his dream-girl, Simon nervously looked around waiting for the demons to slither out of the shadows and drag him into the cold, murky abyss. He was struggling to keep his composure as the walls seemed to be closing in on him, and then retreating again. The fact he was with her excited Simon enough to remain somewhat sane. For a while it felt as if they were actually- a couple, their conversations finally flowed naturally. Simon couldn't believe he was finding all the right words to say for a change, even as his mind continued to play tricks on him, Simon didn't miss a beat expressing himself.

He was convinced it was the drugs that were controlling his tongue. Was that even possible? Or maybe it was because he finally felt free to say whatever he liked. For once he didn't care if his confessions got back to the ears of his folks. He told Renee that he believed in aliens from outer space and time travel, Simon even went as far as saying he's witnessed them with his very own eyes. Finally, Renee was finding him a bit interesting. Maybe she should offer him drugs more often? He was coming alive as if it finally rained on a micro-organism lying dormant for ions. Now that he was enjoying the strange topic taking place, he couldn't shut up. The quiet, timid nerd was coming out of his shell. As band members on the wall came to life and began performing to the song playing in the background Simon reminded himself that none of it was real. Paranoid or not he was determined to enjoy this valuable time with the girl he always wanted. In his mind's eye, he again started placing the play-boy model he fashioned with the body parts of others against Renee's actual face. It was easy since she was looking right at him.

They melted together, as if he was placing the soul back into the bag of flesh and bones from which it came, her eyes slowly dripped back together making Simon's water, only these were no teardrops, but the proof he needed to assure himself It was his destiny to end up with this woman someday. Maybe this is the start of it? He desperately hoped. Simon wanted to make a move on her, but he felt it was too soon. Sitting close on the couch, Renee mentioned the fact that most talented artists perform their best beneath the influence of drugs. Seeing the things, he was seeing at- the moment Renee appeared to be right, Simon found himself intoxicated by excitement and terror. Thinking of the paintings he could create while on whatever Renee had rolled up in that white piece of paper, Simon imagined he would have a whole new style of art. If only he could smoke with Renee more often? She was right, creativity comes much easier when the brain is altered by certain foreign chemicals.

He also knew it was a slippery, slope to becoming an addict. Renee knew she had to keep him talking and interested in her, to prevent him from freaking the fuck out again. So, your folks are really, religious huh? I noticed they keep saints and angels everywhere. Yup. I guess I'm the safest person in the world when it comes to being possessed? I think It would be utterly impossible for a demon to enter someone in my house. They shared a much, needed laugh as Renee decided to get up and find something else to listen to, she turned off the Pink Floyd album and switched on the radio, she came across a song from Jimmy Hendrix called if 6 was 9 and started shaking her ass and making these weird movements, swinging her arms around, while reaching to the sky. Simon had never seen anyone move like that and couldn't deny how much it was turning him on. She moved in a slithery motion and looked incredibly sexy in her black t-shirt and blue jeans. Simon wasn't entirely sure if it was happening or if he was imagining it like all the other bizarre things he was seeing?

It felt as if they had an audience as all the famous musicians hanging on the walls watched Renee dance around the room. He was forced to sit on the couch, motionless and carefully, observe her every move. Renee felt responsible for Simon until the drugs wore off. She had to keep him calm or he could very well end up in the loony-bin, forever stuck on a hellish trip. The music appeared to be getting louder, even though no one was touching the radio several feet away from where Renee was raising Simon Fletcher's temperature with her seductive moves. The only other thing he paid slight attention to, were the plants and flowers displayed around Renee's house. They stood out since they came from his mother's flower shop, reminding him that god is always watching and keeping tabs, like the nosy neighbor across the road.

He was being very naughty and wondered if the angels would punish him for his raunchy behavior, especially as the vegetation began to stretch out and reach for him as if they had become carnivorous meat eaters in search of a tasty meal. The small branches seemed more like tentacles from a creature visiting from some other world. Thorns from the blood-red roses started piercing Simon's flesh, causing him to bleed, as the gigantic, armor-plated locus swarm filled the air. The red roses luscious, pedals stretched forward, puckering up to him, with the wasp, chasing killer bees from their volcanic center spewing flames, with stingers large enough to poke Simon's dimwitted brains out. He was so petrified, he even forgot that Renee was dancing dirty right in front of him.

Voyaging on a negative trip, all he could see now were the plant life forms viciously, attacking him, wrapping themselves around his arms and legs, tightly tying him to the couch. Renee noticed her strange and extremely, a sheltered neighbor was beginning to lose his mind again, she had to find a way to draw him out of misery and escort him to a much more, positive place. Without even taking the time to ask Simon what he was seeing, as his body reacted in complete terror to the imaginary vision being dredged up in the darkest corners of his mind, Renee did the only thing she could do under the circumstances.

She took off her t-shirt and dropped it to the floor. She wanted to throw it at Simon in a playful way, but she was afraid it might freak him out even more. He might imagine a giant stone or a dismembered, human head coming toward him, with hateful, none blinking eyes. When that didn't get his attention, Renee placed her right hand between his legs and began gently messaging his balls, teleporting him back into the reality from which he strayed. The vision instantly vanished, and Simon just sat there staring at Renee's incredible, breasts.

He fantasized about all the things, he wanted to do to her. Renee's plan was working, her paranoid neighbor from next door escaped the vicious plant attack, but she didn't know how to stop the collapsing avalanche from falling any further., Renee knew sex was the one thing that would surely hold his attention. The room got even hotter when she felt pressured to slowly remove her pants, as well. Simon was convinced this was not his imagination. Or was it? The murderous, coward was too frightened to act as he sat there, motionless, staring at her naked body. Renee continued dancing hoping to turn him on, shielding him from the abstract, terrors of the mind. She knew she was going to regret her decision, but for the moment it felt like the right thing to do, even though it meant smashing her sacred vows. Simon was imagining what his parents would say if they saw him right now. He kept praying this was real and not another hallucination. It would be embarrassing if she discovers the stiff log bulging through his pants. Renee moved closer to Simon who was impatiently waiting for her. The moment he had always dreamed of was finally happening. Simon feared having sex with her convinced he wouldn't be able to last more than a couple of seconds.

To actually -touch her flesh and feel it against his was almost too much to handle. He couldn't believe he was actually- going to lose his virginity to the girl he had been fantasizing about his entire life. Yet there she was standing completely naked before him. He couldn't wait to taste her lips as she started helping him out of his clothes. Simon soon found himself kissing the gorgeous blonde with intensity. Maybe Renee was actually- into Simon and didn't care about cheating on her husband? Or perhaps she didn't even realize it was the neighbor next door. Simon was seeing all kinds of bizarre things. He wondered if Renee thought he was Paul the whole time she was coming on to him. Whatever it was that had her shoving her tongue down his throat? Simon sure wasn't going to interrupt and start asking questions, it was best to just go with it, especially when he was going to get lucky right there on Renee's couch. Pulling away from his lips, Renee began gently sucking and nibbling on his ear. It was turning him on, especially as she reached for his hands and gently placed them on her breast. Not sure what to do, he squeezed them softly and hoped for the best.

Before he knew it, Renee had her hand down his pants. It felt so good he almost leaped out of his skin. She was still kissing on him and making sexy sounds as she sat on top of Simon, helping place himself inside her. It was so tight and wet. Simon didn't know how long this ecstasy moment would last. He feared it was simply another hallucination from the drugs she offered him. It was either that or this whole thing was a dream. Simon assumed he would be waking up in his bedroom alone any second.

Renee asked him if it felt good as she moved up and down, and even side to side. The four-eyed virgin couldn't speak a word, he was actually-there in the flesh, making love to the girl he always wanted. The music playing in the background added to the excitement. Renee placed her hands on Simon's head and started moving even more aggressively. Her long yellow hair in his face as she used him like a chunk of meat for her pleasure. To Simon's surprise, he was actually- able to stay afloat during the incredible experience. It seemed like Renee didn't even notice he was there with her, as she continued using him to please herself. Simon could care less, that she was no longer paying attention to him, now the horny, pervert could spend all the time he wanted staring at her while she made a man out of him. They were in the middle of having sex and it felt like the only time where it wasn't wrong or filthy to be observing every inch of her body in such a way.

Simon just laid there on the couch watching as Renee used him to get herself off. He was soon distracted by the eerie sensation of someone watching him. Knowing things are not what they seem at -the moment, Simon did his best to ignore the tingling on the back of his neck. He pretended it had something to do with the remarkable sensations he was experiencing during the world's greatest sexual encounter. Renee started to moan louder and louder as she inched closer to climaxing. Simon's eyes were glued to her fuck faces as she rode him in a place like a mechanical, bull. When he finally took his eyes off, of her for a moment to distract himself from exploding, Simon noticed the musicians were still playing, the songs were blissful, but the animated portraits seemed to have a darkness to them. Simon couldn't turn away, as John Lennon and the rest of the Beatles began transforming, shedding their human physiology into their natural insect form. He watched in terror, as sharp thin wiggling, legs first pierced through their eyes and then the rest of their bodies, causing blood to spill from the poster. The metamorphosis appeared agonizing, but Simon couldn't hear their cries, over the loud music and Renee screaming in ecstasy.

The hideous-looking bugs continued tearing themselves free from the inside out, savagely ripping the infamous band members to shreds. Simon remained fixated on the ghoulish vision, as the half man half insects began sprouting wings and flapping them, outside the two, dimensional paper they were placed on. Simon saw that each was re-emerging in a different color. John Lennon had short legs and was red and black, he even had six black dots on his thorax, two larger ones in the middle, and four smaller ones in groups of two at the sides. Ringo star appeared to be green, yellow, and even a reddish-gold, while George Harris was terrifyingly similar, to a yellow jacket bee-like none he had never seen before. It had long legs and massive antenna protruding from the sides of its head. Simon imagined he was going to be stung if the deadly insect left the picture completely. He could feel its huge black eyes staring back, presenting an even more disturbing feeling, to fester in his mind and the pits of his stomach.

The paranoid young man didn't know how to make this horrifying image go away, as he was soon drawn to Paul McCartney's transformation into the most, trippy, looking beetle of them all. It was green with thin stripes of red and blue running down its side, resembling the strange-looking clothing some musicians of the day would have been seen wearing. He watched as the huge insects flapped their wings as fast as they could and began flying out of the picture. Simon was forced to look away from the outrageous scene, only to discover that some of the other posters of band members hanging on the walls were also beginning to change the form, only this time their flesh began flaking off their bones almost in a Mars-like dust-cyclone. It was peeling away in huge chunks and dropping to the floor until their skeletons were visible beneath. Simon saw the misery in their tormented eyes.

This time, he even heard their ear-piercing screams as they burst into flames and melted away. He forgot all about Renee riding him so intently and when he turned his attention to her sexy body, Simon found she too was nothing but bones with some rotting flesh hanging from them. She still had her long blonde hair and she was still very much in the mood for love, holding Simon down and boning him. He freaked out, shoving his lover to the floor, frantically hurried into his clothes, and ran for the front door. He simply couldn't be there anymore. Simon felt as if he was being attacked by a rotting corpse and desperately needed fresh air, and some time to calm down. He didn't even stop to see if Renee was alright, or if she was a zombie from beyond the grave. He just wanted to get away from her. Renee lay there on the living room floor wondering what the fuck just happened. She was in the middle of getting off when suddenly her partner threw her off him and ran for the front door. Renee wondered what she did wrong, then she remembered he was not only having sex for the first time, he was also tripping, while he did it. She imagined it was too much for him, still what could have sent him running out of the house the way he did? Something about it, troubled Renee. She wanted to know what he saw that terrified him so badly. Naked and alone on the living room floor Renee felt like a complete fool, she was not going to go running after him. If Simon wanted to go, she would not stop him. Renee thought she was giving her a strange neighbor exactly what he wanted. She began feeling guilty for cheating on her loving husband Paul. How could she do this to him?

It was so wrong and there was no way to take it back now. In a way, Renee was glad Simon jumped up and ran off. She realized it was probably for the best. It was a huge mistake and never should've happened. Now Simon's damaged mind was going to be all alone, in the middle of a chaotic, thrill ride through hells gates. Renee was praying he would be alright by himself. She needed a nice long shower to wipe both the stink and the sin off her body.

Even if Paul never found out about it? Renee knew she would always carry the dreadful, memory of her meaningless betrayal. It was something she would simply have to learn to live with. Renee couldn't shake that look in Simon's eyes right before he shoved her off, of him. What would make him behave that way? Since he wasn't there to ask in person, she would be forced to spend the rest of the day alone thinking about it. Turning off the music Renee wanted silence for once, so she could try and get her head together. Like Simon next-door, she would have to wait until the drugs ran their course.

Once back in his own house, Simon began thinking about his boneheaded actions. He actually, pushed Renee off, of him because of an image that wasn't even there and took off with-out saying he was sorry. He thought about going back, but he was too embarrassed to face her at -the moment, proving why Paul was the better man for her. He would never do something so mean and stupid. Simon Fletcher was finally having sex with the most beautiful girl in the world and somehow blew it at the last minute. He realized they were about to get off at the same time when he freaked and ran away, spoiling both their chances at a mind-blowing, orgasm. How could he ever face her again? That was the biggest question on his mind. Simon knew Renee was a sweet girl and she would not only understand but forgive him. After all, it was her fault for giving him the hard drugs. Savoring the image in his head of Renee dancing sexy, while stripping and taking advantage sent a smile soaring across his face. No matter how it ended he still had her. So, what if it never happens again, he struggled to convince himself. Renee was a married woman, she may never find the desire to cheat on her adoring, husband again. Simon didn't know if he was happy or sad that the once in a lifetime fantasy was over?

Or that it actually- happened in the first place. Regardless of how events unfold in the future, Simon knew he would have these vivid memories imbedded in his brain for as long as he lives. What he needed to be thinking about was his parents returning. Simon didn't want to see demons and aliens roaming the house when they were present. If he didn't sober up by then? He would have to find a way to hide it. Simon planned on staying in his room and keeping to himself for the rest of the evening, it was the best way to avoid trouble. Making his way up the stairs, Simon noticed his mother's porcelain angels were cracking at the seams, he stood frozen, watching as the infant faced deities flapped their bird feathered wings and began flying around the house.

They gathered, together and went after Simon, as he attempted to hurry down the stairs and towards the back, door with a weak feeling in the legs that carried him. Unable to think Simon headed for the treehouse with the bizarre-looking angels giving chase. When he made it to his house of sins some of the angels were already waiting for him. Their humanoid faces changing into elongated monstrous-looking creatures, with fangs in their jaws and eyes black as a universe void of stars. The sound of flapping wings grew louder as Simon looked around and saw the fires from the damned surrounding his wooden hideout. All the trees were burning as the inferno hitched a ride on the fierce winds rushing past. Simon saw giant monsters roaming around in the shadows, as the intense heat began melting his flesh. It was a scene of utter chaos, hell on earth with souls running around as flames danced on them, some were even crawling from beneath the scorched dirt only to escape into a blistering world above. It terrified Simon to the core as he collapsed into the fetal position in the middle of his sanctuary begging god to order his watcher's away and to remove this disturbing image of hell from his sight, while visions of Renee dancing naked played vividly in his head. Simon didn't understand why he was so terrified of the benign creatures but felt the angels his mother molded to resemble those in the good book appeared no different than hell's demons. Her decorations had come to life and he was under attack. The troubled young man imagined it was for all the dreadful sinning he had been doing in his dark perverted mind, seeing females as filthy sex objects he can use and discard at his pleasure. When he finally lifted his head and looked around, Simon saw that the world was back to normal but the drugs he had taken were still in control of his mind, body, and even soul.

After making sure all the angels and devils had vanished from his reality, Simon turned his attention back to Renee's place next door. He watched her prance around naked, as she prepared to rinse away her biggest mistake. Simon prayed it would be enough to occupy his frantic, mind from the bad trip he'd been forced to embark on. He hadn't finished what he started even after coming so close. Simon was still extremely horny and desperate to get off while carrying Renee's scent and the erotic memories fresh in his mind. He watched her intensely, as she fixed herself a bath, hoping and praying she was still in the mood as well and would finish herself off in the tub while he was spying. Soap never felt so good, as Renee did her best to scrub away the guilt.

The melting bar of cleanliness appeared as a slow-moving slug being smooshed slowly against her arms legs and breast., it even took the time to gaze upon her beautiful face through its black, soulless eyes, bubbles came in the shape of dome-like structures that would shelter astronauts on other planets. With the gentle gust of her breath, tiny battleships would form and take flight around the bathroom. Renee wasn't frightened but fascinated by the astonishing, creativity her brain was capable of. She was doing her best to enjoy this unstable trip, knowing it could go bad any minute. Positive thoughts were key, as she smiled back at the slug, watching carefully as the slimy creatures, eyes turned blue, and the bar of soap gradually returned to normal.

The soothing sound of the Beatles played softly in her head, but to Renee, it echoed vibrantly through every room in the house. Just as Simon was doing his best to go back and relive the precious moment, his imaginary lover was trying her best to forget. Renee tried not to think about how close she came to climaxing with Simon Fletcher from next door. Picturing her loving husband's face, she shoved the bar of soap between her legs and began cleaning away her deepest regret, turning herself on again in the process. Simon was right, she still wanted an orgasm, only not with him, even worse he wouldn't be able to see it. Renee imagined Paul entering the room, as she slowly dropped the soap and started pleasing herself using only her fingers.

It was as if her husband was there making passionate love to her, she could feel every sensation as her toes curled with extreme pleasure.

Her eyes rolled back in her head, as a wave of mind-numbing ecstasy was about to explode between her legs. Paul peered into her eyes and although they were both about to erupt with joy, there was a certain look in them clinging desperately to the troubling vibe he was transmitting. It was as if somehow, he knew what she had done, making Renee's blood run cold. Her mind was playing harsh tricks on her which is what she was struggling to avoid. Once again, she had been disrupted from her special moment.

It was still tingling a certain group of neurological cells, but the feeling had passed. Simon was being patient reframing from touching himself until his love goddess reveals herself to him again. Eventually, Renee came strutting out of the bathroom with a white towel wrapped tight enough to show off her magnificent figure. Simon didn't want to lose the moment and immediately began touching himself, while her glistening flesh was visible, showing. Renee put on the perfect display for him, as she turned on the radio and began dancing around looking for something to wear.

He began sniffing his fingers to remind himself of the way his princess smelled, it was a scent he would never forget. Renee slowly removed the towel that covered her, while moving around as if she was the invisible man's private dancer. Simon continued to remain excited, knowing he had his scrawny nerve twitching worm inside her and it managed to hold on for dear life, almost until she was satisfied. It helped further convince the perv they were meant to be together. He could still hear the way she moans and visualizes the awkward faces she made while giving herself to him.

As she continued moving around the room, unaware she was teasing him, Simon finally got off and for the next thirty seconds, sex wouldn't be the most dominating thing on his mind. He strongly regretted his cowardly decision to run away while in the middle of completing his most intimate fantasy. He would never forgive himself for it, but Renee's house was simply too much for him to handle, everything was new and way beyond what he was taught to believe.

The wild décor blew his artistic mind, causing his imagination to get yanked in all sorts of dark places. Still, how could he be such a chicken shit he actually- ran out on Renee Price. If he ever did have another chance with her? Simon was convinced he surely blew it, naturally he blamed it on Renee for giving him the hallucinogens without a fair warning. Even if she did drugs and take advantage of him?

How on earth could he be upset with her, he finally got what he always wanted. Hoping to get some of the drugs out of his system sooner than later, Simon exited the treehouse and stuck his fingers down his throat to vomit up the volatile, substance hoping it would make him feel better. After yacking up whatever he could in the backyard, Simon returned to his bedroom. When his folks returned later that evening, he simply told them he didn't feel well.

His mother wanted to cater to him as always, asking Simon if he wanted her to fix him some soup while suggesting he go see the doctor the next morning. Simon agreed knowing he was completely fine. He just didn't want his mother turning into a purple elephant or something while he was looking at her.

CHAPTER 8

········◆◆◆◆◆········

Paul had been traveling across the country and was now almost at the end of his journey. He was exhausted but eager to get home and see the love of his life. He felt almost home-free, once he shed the ginormous truck and hopped into his little Chevy Camaro. He kept thinking of Renee's pretty face, as he pressed on, counting down the miles. The only other thing that helped him stay awake was the music on the radio. Led Zeppelin Trampled

Under Foot was playing and he had the volume- cranked. With his eyes growing heavy and nothing but black pavement ahead and trees of the deep forest surrounding him, Paul thought about lighting the joint resting on his right ear, with wonderful memories of himself and Renee flashing through his mind. Imagining it will help him pass out as soon as his head hits the pillow, Paul grabbed the joint and placed it in his mouth, carefully watching the road while digging into his pocket for his book of matches. Soon the whole car was full of smoke, and Paul decided to open the window, letting some of the cool fall air inside. He couldn't wait to get home, kiss Renee, and get some much, needed sleep. For the moment he was enjoying the song playing on the radio and the pot he was smoking, exhaling, a dark cloud, and using his steering wheel like a pair of drums as if he was John Bonham.

Paul accidentally dropped the joint on the floor, he panicked knowing it was lit. With the music blasting, he began looking around in search of it, taking his eyes off the road ahead and placing his life in grave danger. Reaching around with his hands and searching with his eyes it was nowhere to be found, his foot growing heavier on the accelerator, as the burning torch of cannabis continued to elude him. Normally a calm laid back guy, Paul began losing his cool and swearing up a tornado inside the vehicle. Fearing the wondering joint might set the car on fire he was in a bit of a panic, when finally, there it was, the burning torch he had been searching for. Paul smirked before turning his attention back to the road, he had just enough time to realize he was on a collision course with death, as he sped toward the trees. Before he had time to react Paul and his Camaro smashed head-on into a huge ancient tree, killing him almost instantly. His body, as well as his pride and joy, were demolished beyond recognition, blood and guts painted the Camaros interior red. His head was split open revealing part of his brains oozing out of the fractured skull, his eyes staring off with no emotion in them. The radio fell silent in the fatal collision, leaving a gruesome horror scene of unspeakable carnage.

The eerie silence was soon interrupted by the hollering sirens screaming in the distance, Renee was half asleep and didn't think much about it, she opened her eyes for a moment looking around the bedroom, before going back to sleep. She felt a bit uneasy since Paul hadn't returned yet. When help finally arrived several minutes later police and paramedics found themselves facing the grizzliest sight any of them ever experienced. One look at Paul and they knew there was no chance of saving him. Instead, they called for a coroner to take away the mangled body.

The next morning Renee was sound asleep dreaming about her loving husband. She was locked within a vision of her true-love walking through the front door for the first time in what seemed like an eternity. She was so happy to see him again. They smiled with lust in their eyes, as they ran toward each other and embraced one-another with open-arms. They hugged and kissed passionately, as they spun around like figure skaters going for the gold. Renee held a smile on her actual face as the most wonderful dream she ever experienced continued.

It would be the last time the full of life, beauty-queen would smile so joyously. She was soon interrupted, rudely awakened by a loud pounding at the front door. Renee quickly began to panic as she turned to look for her husband who's, whose side of the bed was still void of his presence. She was expecting him to return in the middle of the night and slide into their bed beside her while she slept. A bad feeling began forming in Renee's gut, she felt sick to her stomach, as she hopped out of bed and quickly headed for the front door. Wearing nothing but a pair of purple panties she grabbed the first thing she saw to cover herself up with, which was the "I love Intercourse-shirt", sitting at the top of the clean clothes pile resting on her dresser, she had neglected to put away. She nervously, threw it on wondering who could be at her house unexpectedly so early in the morning? Neglecting to throw on any pants, Renee rushed down the stairs to the front door.

There was a bad feeling brewing that something may have happened to her soul mate Paul, but she also assumed it could very well be Simon Fletcher from next-door. She began remembering the terrible truth that she slept with him, just so he wouldn't lose his mind, after accidentally slipping him L-S-D. Renee imagined he took things a bit more seriously and invited himself over as if he was taking her husband's place. She froze there for a moment now sober and fully aware of the dreadful actions, she made the day before. Guilt and regret were already preparing to bring on the tears. How could she do this to Paul? She adored him and he in return adored her. Renee didn't know if she should confess like Simon's folks on Sunday for her unforgivable sin while growing more upset as she continued down the stairs half-dressed. If it was the four-eyed nerd from next-door? Renee was going to politely ask him to leave, Simon's face was the last one she wanted to see since he reminded her of the worst mistake she ever made. Renee felt overwhelmed with emotions, as she neared the bottom of the stairs. she turned toward the front door and noticed the flashing lights curbed on her property. Her heart raced as she nervously answered the door. Standing there were two young police officers.

The taller of the two asked if she had a husband named Paul Price? Already a bit shook she confirmed that she was his wife while trying to hide behind the door since she was half-dressed. Renee desperately wanted to somehow avoid the horrible news that was inevitably on its way. I'm very sorry to report to you that your husband is dead. That can't be? She insisted while in a state of denial as she began crying hysterically. The police officer strongly confirmed her lover and best friend was gone. Wiping the tears from her eyes, the distraught widow asked the nice policeman what happened? She demanded to know how her entire world ended in the blink of an eye. I'm sorry to tell you this ma'am, but your husband was involved in a horrific traffic accident late last night. Renee couldn't believe it, thinking that was impossible. Paul was a great driver. She explained how he drove 18 wheelers across the country for a living. Renee continued to break-down as the policeman explained what happened.

The tragedy became even harder to accept when she realized it was his stupid fault. She didn't know how she would manage without her other half. The lawmen could tell she was heart-broken, they were desperate to relieve themselves from her property so she can mourn in peace. Poor Renee was un-consolable, she collapsed right there in the doorway and continued to cry her eyes out, knowing she would never see her loving companion again. The naive young beauty-queen had yet to notice the predator next-door, secretly watching and deviously hoping something truly awful happened to his ultimate rival. In his twisted mind, Simon always imagined he would be able to take her husband's place. Early to rise and looking out his bedroom window toward Renee's house, as he did every morning, Simon quickly noticed the flashing police cars parked out front.

At first, he was afraid something might have happened to Renee, but it didn't take long for Simon to dare dream that his darkest fantasy had finally come true. When he didn't see Paul's Camaro in the driveway a sinister smile rapidly crept across his face. Simon's heart started to beat faster with a certain excitement building up inside him. At last, he thought, they could finally be together. He was praying for the worst and preparing for the truth. So far there was no sign of the beautiful Renee. With her jeep in the driveway, he assumed she was home and perfectly safe. Simon wanted nothing more than to run next door and comfort her.

He was overcome by joy as he continued convincing himself it happened. Did his most vulgar prayer ever ask, finally come true? If Paul Price was dead? Simon knew it was his fate to be with the woman who's haunted him for as long as he can remember. He couldn't get the thought out of his head about the moment she took off her clothes and sat on his miniature throbbing rocket. It was more than just a dream come true, for Simon Fletcher it was the shedding of one life and the beginning of another. Simon's happiness soon turned to anxiety as he thought about his parent's reaction to the tragic news. He also dipped his feet in paranoia to splash around even more chaos, imagining what god would have to say for his selfish and most heinous thoughts. Simon Fletcher cringed at the punishment awaiting him on the other side. Especially when his filthy imagination began to take over his rational thoughts as if there was a microscopic army of demons conducting a mind-control operation deep within his physical brain. Secretly coordinating every electronic impulse coursing through his energetic, neurons. He was momentarily free to venture into the depravity of his imagination as a man lying dead in the morgue. Simon's wishes came true, and although he didn't yet know it for a fact, the deranged artist felt it in his bones. Simon experienced a tidal, wave of electronic pulses as if temporarily operated by god.

He knew in his heart that Paul was dead, and Renee was his for the taking. He desperately wanted to run over there with open arms, cradling her in her time of need. She knew no one in this strange new place and would feel all alone. It was the vulnerability Simon was counting on. Since she had no one, he imagined it wouldn't be long before Renee came to him for a shoulder to cry on. If so, Simon would gladly give the devil his soul, as- long as that meant he could possess his queen for an instant in this puny, insignificant life. He began having images in his head of the two of them together sexually, as Renee too found herself cast into the flames of damnation. They began sweating as the fire grew more intense, melting them together like twin wax candles placed side by side and set at a slow burn. When he finally snapped out of it, Simon decided it was best to give her some space for now and let her grieve in peace

. He was torn between smiling and crying for his reward and punishment in this life and the next, according to the god his tiny world worshipped. That's if he even existed at all. Simon was going to do as he pleased and that meant his gorgeous beauty queen could end up paying the ultimate price for his lustful sins. How could he be so lucky was the only thing going through his warped mind for several minutes as he watched like a hawk while the policemen spoke to whom he assumed was sexy little Renee standing just out of view.

Could his darkest of prayers have finally been answered? Only time would tell as he waited ever so rambunctiously to discover the terrible news. The sex-craved lunatic was lying in wait for the right moment to strike. Sooner or later he knew she would need a friend and he would be there for her. Deep down he wanted to be far more than that. He was hoping and praying to be Paul's replacement. That is in fact if something awful did happen to him. Simon would never forget the taste of her lips as well as her sweet, delicious scent.

He relived that brief -moment of bliss over- and over again inside his head, almost continuously since it happened. Picturing her fuck faces perfectly he even considered putting them down on paper, making sure he never forgets them. This was the perfect opportunity to get closer to the prey he had been desperately chasing. Shifting his eyes, Simon noticed that Mrs. Anderson was also watching the action from her front porch, curious to know what happened? He quickly vanished behind the moving curtains as he did his best to get out of sight before the old woman saw him spying on the pretty neighbor's house.

If she asked? Simon would simply say he was curious why the police were there, same as her. He didn't know Mrs. Anderson had been watching him watch Renee for quite some time now. She was on the verge of walking over there and spilling the beans. Simon didn't give it too much thought. He was basking in the reality that he was one step closer to fulfilling his destiny. Assuming Paul was officially out of the picture? Simon saw everything falling into place, perhaps god had been listening to his prayers all along? All he knew is that he had to possess her. Not even the ghoulish recreation, he constructed with various body-parts of several women could satisfy his insatiable desires now. Renee was not only made of flesh and blood she was also closer than ever to being, his sex slave.

While sitting on his bed digesting the potentially, refreshing information Simon was interrupted by his mother knocking on the door. She also noticed the police outside Paul and Renee's place. Simon acted as if he was still completely unaware. He pretended to be shocked and upset at the potentially tragic news. He did his best to keep his internal excitement from reaching the surface. What he was waiting for was to hear the fatal news from Renee's lips. Eleanor had no idea what happened, but like Simon, she assumed it had something to do with Paul. I hope everything's alright. She said while nervously praying for the best. Me too, said Simon as he walked toward her, a coldness in his eyes, as he struggled to appear sympathetic.

He reached out and hugged his mother. All they could do for the moment is wait, to find out what happened. Looking out the window Eleanor saw the police car riding off. Renee was still trying to comprehend the heart-wrenching news slowly settling in. She couldn't accept it as fact, not just yet. He was supposed to be there with her that morning. She had been waiting impatiently for several days for her hubby's return. Renee sat there against the wall in the doorway her head in her hands crying hysterically over the loss. Wiping the tears from her eyes, she eventually found the strength to stand up and make her way over to the couch in the living room. She sat curled up in a ball staring at their wedding picture. She was imagining all the wonderful memories they shared.

It seemed unthinkable to face the fact that she would never see him again. Her eyes were red and full of tears as she stared at the happiest moment of their lives. It didn't take long before Renee started to realize how alone she was. She abandoned her entire life back in California to start over with her other half, now he was gone, giving Renee the impression, she had no one. The walls were closing in, as she continued sinking deeper in despair. The world around her was no longer the safe, innocent place she had always seen it to be. It was a vicious killing field.

A graveyard full of rotting flesh and bones. She started thinking about the dreaded funeral. The love of her life all alone in a tiny box left to decay underground. Renee knew how badly he hated tight spaces. It was the main reason he loved his job so much. Being able to travel the country and take in the gorgeous sights as he moved along. Paul may not have been as much of a hippie as his beautiful wife, but he loved the concept of total freedom just the same.

The young beautiful widow wasn't just struggling with her husband's untimely demise, but how it happened. Renee knew it would be a closed casket and that she wouldn't have the opportunity to kiss Paul goodbye since he was mangled in the crash. The only people she knew in this strange new world were Fletcher's next, door. It was a constant reminder of her worst mistake ever, sleeping with the strange young man who lived there. Now with her husband deceased, it was even harder for Renee to cope with. She blamed herself for lacking the knowledge of the ramifications that followed. Renee was also unaware just how infatuated her oddball neighbor truly was? She thought if he ever came on to her again, she could simply blame it on the drugs. Simon would never accept that it was a mistake. He felt fated to be with her forever. It seems Renee's actions were coming back to bite her in the ass. She wasn't attracted to Simon Fletcher in any way, yet she found it in the depths of her heart to sleep with him.

How could she ever forgive herself? She wanted to somehow scrape that blemish away from her body and soul. Renee also had to face the troubling task of informing all their friends and family back home of his sudden death. Those, phone, calls were going to be very difficult to make. Renee had to get her mind straight, and the best way she saw to do that was by raiding the liquor cabinet and drowning her pain in a bottle.

Although it was early in the morning, Renee felt she desperately needed a drink. She had to do something to calm her twitching nerves after receiving the worst news possible. All her dreams of the future were violently obliterated in an instant. She would never have his baby and grow old with him as a happy family. Renee didn't want to take her eyes off the wedding photo, but she had to if she was going to fix herself a stiff concoction to numb the pain. She reluctantly left the couch behind for a moment to grab the bottle of vodka out of the kitchen cabinet. She didn't need a glass. Renee was going to simply chug the liquor straight from the bottle for the rest of the day.

As she made her way back into the living room, Renee passed a mirror hanging on the wall and realized it wasn't her t-shirt she was wearing, but her husband's. She sniffed it hoping since it belonged to Paul his scent would still linger. Taking in a deep breath, Renee quickly discovered it did, causing tears to flood her eyes all over again. Before collapsing back on the couch with her bottle in hand, Renee slowly made her way over to the record player. She put on the new Beatles album called Abbey Road hoping it would ease her mind a little, she planned to sit alone and reminisce over the good times.

As a small buzz began to seep in, Renee realized the liquor wasn't making her feel any, better, she was becoming even more depressed with every sip. It wasn't going to detour her from continuing down that dark path. Focusing her attention on the wedding photo. Renee imagined the two of them dancing in the middle of the floor as if they were the only two people on earth. The world she knew was no more without him in it, and she didn't know how to go on? Renee had no way of knowing her nerdy neighbor had diabolical plans in store for her. She didn't know he was planning to possess her, even if it was against her will.

As she sat there getting drunk and listening to the Beatles the beautiful young hippie girl was giving lots of thought to moving back to the west coast. Now that she had nothing here, there was no real reason to stay. It seemed like a wonderful and refreshing idea. Getting as far away from Simon Fletcher was a brilliant plan. Renee wanted to move back to the city of angels where she had friends and family that cared about her. She could find no reason to stay in this quiet little town so far from everyone and everything she knows. Simon was still wondering what could've happened to Paul. He wanted to knock on Renee's door to check in and see if she was alright. Simon wanted to witness her pain and sorrow, even if from a distance. He ventured into his house of sins to scope out her place more efficiently. He had his trusty binoculars to see into windows better should she happen by. He quickly discovered all the curtains were drawn and there was no way to see inside. It, angered Simon as he too began to wonder if she was going to move back to California now that her loving, husband was dead. He knew if that were the case?

He would never see her again. He was determined not to let that happen. Simon saw his parent's faith in a powerful god differently that day. He suddenly understood why they were so devoted to his every command. At last, Simon imagined? Finally, he had witnessed his first miracle taking formation. He prayed for Paul to be gone and now it appears he was. The great lord had done it for him, without the need of getting his hands dirty. For that Simon was eternally grateful. He does work in mysterious ways after all. Simon wanted nothing more than to scoop up the fair-maiden and ride off into the sunset. First, he would have to find a way to convince her to fall in love with him. Ultimately, he had to make certain that she doesn't move back to the west coast. Simon wanted to be her knight in shining armor. Deep down he knew it was virtually impossible. Just because she slept with him out of pity once, didn't mean she had any feelings for him, especially at- the moment. Simon understood that a terrible, tragedy had befallen on her. He was simply waiting to hear the news from the unicorn's mouth. His folks also wanted to go over and see what happened, but they too decided to give her some space for the moment.

They knew she would need time to get her head on straight if Paul was dead? After enduring such a long and fruitful marriage themselves the Fletcher couldn't even imagine what the poor, young girl was going through. They also knew how alone she must feel being in a new town so far away from home. They couldn't fathom the thought of life without one another. It was so tragic knowing they had their whole lives ahead of them. Eleanor and Stanley would speak to father Fitzpatrick and make sure he holds a lovely ceremony for the poor man. They were willing to help Renee any way they can. Eleanor would start by providing all the flowers necessary for the funeral free of charge. She knew it would do little to ease the young widow's suffering, but it was the least she could do. Renee was a sweet young girl and didn't deserve this awful hand she was dealt with.

Stanley agreed, he too had a kind and giving heart. It was the reason she fell in love with him so long ago. Helping others in need is what life was all about. Renee continued getting shitfaced drowning herself in a bottle of vodka. It was probably best that everyone let her be for the moment. She just wanted to be left alone to wallow in her sorrows. She was even thinking about smoking another one of Paul's magic joints. Then she feared it might sinisterly antagonize her darkest thoughts even more. Renee could do nothing but sit on the couch and cry consumed by grief. The only other thing on her mind was getting the hell out of this town. It was so cute of Paul to leave everything behind and move to a perfect little place named after her. It didn't seem quite so charming and magical without him. Renee was distraught over his death and needed to be around loved ones. She was going to put the house up for sale and get out of Jersey as soon as possible.

As the hours passed, the sky darkened, bringing on another chilly October night, Simon crawled out of his house of sins and joined his parent's for dinner. Renee staggered to her bedroom and drank until she passed out with tears in her eyes and agony in her heart and mind. She hadn't eaten a single thing all day, losing her appetite after receiving the heart-wrenching news. Renee knew she would be sleeping in this bed for the rest of her days without Paul by her side, he was never coming home. She turned and stared at the empty pillow and the vacant space next to her. She wanted nothing more than to cuddle up next to him and fall asleep, but that was impossible now.

The next morning Eleanor decided to go to Renee's house and find out exactly what happened to Paul? She held out hope that maybe she was exaggerating the situation. Maybe it was something less serious? Still, she felt in her heart that was not the case. Renee answered the door wearing the same t-shirt from the day before. Her hair was a mess and she appeared as if she just crawled out of bed. I'm sorry sweetheart. Did I wake you? Eleanor asked sympathetically. Yeah. It's alright. I suppose I have, to get out of bed some time huh. I'm sorry to bother you, but I- I know why you're here. Renee replied cutting Mrs. Fletcher off. I don't quite know how to say this, but Paul passed away the other night. Renee broke-down crying as she began to explain what happened. Eleanor placed her hand in front of her face, horrified at the tragic news. She discovered that poor Paul was involved in a terrible accident. At first, Eleanor thought Paul was driving the large truck. Renee explained he was in his Camaro and only a few miles from home. Eleanor reached out to hug the young widow as Renee wiped the tears from her eyes. I don't know what I'm going to do without him. Eleanor did her best to comfort her neighbor in distress. She insisted she would speak to their priest and make sure the funeral is promptly arranged. She also offered to supply all the flowers to decorate the church. Renee thanked her as she continued crying over her loss, letting Mrs. Fletcher know how much she appreciated everything she was doing to help. Eleanor would see to it that there would be a wonderful ceremony prepared. She felt awful for the pretty young girl and knew nothing she could say would take the pain away.

Later that afternoon when she met her son at the flower shop, Eleanor explained to Simon what happened to Paul. It was difficult to keep the rolling smile off his face. It was the greatest news he'd ever received. Simon had no choice but to put on an act, pretending to be sad and devastated over the tragedy. Inside he was jumping for joy. Eleanor was disturbed by her son's curiosity, as she went on in detail explaining what happened to his biggest rival. Simon basked in the violent ending of a man he hated for no good reason. In his mind, Simon began to imagine Paul's violent death. Now he knew for sure that God had been listening to all his prayers. It was either that? Or the Devil had taken interest in his morbid wish.

All that mattered now was that Paul was out of the picture and soon Renee would belong to him. It was obvious to Eleanor that her son wasn't very broken-up about the terrible news. She knew how much he liked Renee, but she didn't know how badly he obsessed over her. He smiled on the inside knowing Paul's body was too destroyed to display in a casket. He was delighted to have his prayers answered but was afraid to thank god for them. What happened to Paul was gruesome. He wasn't entirely sure the lord would perform such a horrific act.

Did he continue to wonder in the back of his mind if it was all his fault? He could be punished forever if he was responsible for commanding god or even the devil to carry out such a ghastly sin. Since he had nothing to do with the innocent man's death literally, Simon assumed he was off the hook. After all who was he to force god's hand to murder one of his own? Knowing Renee would always be home alone sent a chill of sinister delight up his twisted spine. Simon went on working for the rest of the day in a better mood than he had experienced in a very long time.

CHAPTER 9

A few days later was Paul's funeral and to Renee's surprise, the church was packed. She couldn't believe how many folks from the town showed up to pay their respects. Most of them didn't even know the newcomers to their town. She quickly realized once a part of Renee falls, always a part of Renee Falls. In between shedding tears, the heart-broken young girl went around thanking everyone for showing respect to her beloved husband, especially the Fletcher's. Eleanor personally decorated the place to Resemble the mythical garden of Eden. Renee was impressed and couldn't feel more, humble. Simon was sure to look his best. He wanted to impress Renee at her husband's funeral.

There was an ice-cold heart beating inside his chest, as he offered his condolences to Renee and gave his best performance to seem broken up about the terrible, tragedy, but there was this negative vibe surrounding him. A creepy feeling came over Renee, that she never experienced before around Simon Fletcher. Almost as if she knew his sadness was nothing more than a thin shell covering his joy. She did her best to ignore it and hugged the four-eyed weirdo, thanking him and his family for attending the funeral and helping with the flower arrangements. Simon did his best to briefly take in her scent and feel her warm body against his. Renee looked stunning in her black dress fit for a funeral. She finally had a reason to get dressed up and leave the house for a while.

As they separated and parted ways, Renee could feel this emptiness in the air. She didn't have time to give it much thought, there were lots of other people to greet and thank for showing up. That was especially true for some of their friends from back home who traveled from California to be there. It was the one thing that managed to put a temporary smile on Renee's face. Even Paul's father attempted the journey, although he wasn't in the best health himself at the time. Renee loved him, especially since he looked so much like the man she cherished.

His wife had passed away a few years earlier from cancer, and now he was struggling with the beginning stages of the same sickness. He was happy to see Renee, there was a huge smile on his face as they began chatting about the wonderful Paul Price. He was perfectly aware of how much she cared for his son. To lose him so terribly, so sudden? It seemed like a never-ending nightmare. Simon was watching from the other side of the room, as Renee hugged Paul's father and even a few young, handsome men from the city of angels.

He silently feared one of them would take Paul's place. Particularly the tall, skinny gentleman with long blonde hair. He looked like a girl, but the way he and Renee gazed at each-other gave Simon a bad impression. Father Fitzpatrick and other folks from Renee-Falls couldn't help but stare at some of the strangers who ventured here from the west coast. Some of them wore suits and dresses like everyone else. Others however appeared as if they just arrived from outer space. They had long straggly beards, and tie-dye t-shirts on. Some of the men were even wearing bandanas on their heads. For Paul's father and Renee, it was no big deal. He, of course, did dress the part in a black suit and tie. They were a bunch of strange-looking individuals, but everyone accepted them for the way they were. After all, they were here to say goodbye to a very kind and loving man.

Their vagabond appearance was completely irrelevant. Most of them were covered in tattoos and odd-looking jewelry. Their rough exterior may have seemed intimidating, but it was just a façade. Inside they were all about peace, love, and happiness. They just saw things in a different way than the cult followers and their religion. Father Fitzpatrick went on with the service, ignoring their repulsive fashion statements. They were all teary-eyed and doing their best to comfort their friend in need. They had come a long way to be there for her. Renee felt incredibly loved and appreciated. She was too busy to notice Simon standing there watching her from across the room. He couldn't hear her friend's conversation, convincing her to move back across the country as soon as possible.

They insisted it would be easier for her if she was around loved ones. She confessed she was giving it some thought herself. Renee knew there would be painful memories wherever she wound up. Staying here by herself seemed like a bad decision. She didn't want to suffer the loneliness in total isolation. They all insisted there was no reason to stay in New Jersey, now that Paul was gone. Even though Simon couldn't hear the words being exchanged, he knew what they were talking about. He knew she was going to heed their advice and move back to the city of angels where she belonged.

These were people who she had known her entire life. Why would she want to stay behind and be with him? He understood that soon Renee would be gone forever, and a new set of faces would be moving in next door. Life seemed so much simpler when the Stones lived there. Their demise spun his mundane world into chaos by inviting his dream girl to move in next door, leaving the troubled young man to fantasize and drive himself mad with obsession. It was much different when the women weren't real. Faced with a living, breathing person the twisted, stalker wasn't sure what to do? He was dangerously obsessed with the beautiful young woman and had no choice, but to keep his sinful lust to himself. Simon feared if he confessed his filthy thoughts to Father Fitzpatrick the town would never see him the same way again, even though his confession would be confidential. If word ever did get out? It would destroy his family, reputation for good. There was a dark cloud spreading across his mind, effortlessly consuming his sanity.

As the service came to an end, everyone made their way over to the sealed casket with Paul's remains inside. Renee refused to cremate him and place his ashes in an urn somewhere inside the house, it was a little too morbid for her liking, she wanted him to be buried in a coffin as if his body was still perfectly in-tact. She kneeled, down for a moment, and did her best to say her final goodbye to the man she loved. When it was all, over Renee was surrounded by loved ones outside. She was doing her best to keep it together, as sorrow consumed her. Renee struggled to take her mind off the grief by giving lots of thought to what all her friends from back home were saying. Some of them went as far as suggesting she comes back to California immediately, leaving the house behind to sell on its own. She had plenty of places to crash until she can buy another home and return for the rest of her belongings. That way she wouldn't have to suffer alone. It was very tempting, and Renee appreciated everyone coming together in her time of need. She wanted to cry for the sake of their kindness, but there were not many tears left. Moving back home seemed like a no brainer, but leaving Paul's remains buried in New Jersey meant she would never even be able to visit his grave, who would leave flowers and hold endless conversations with thin air. She felt as though she was abandoning him.

Renee wanted to be able to visit his grave-sight and possibly have a few one- way drinks with him. It was the only thing holding her back. She knew he was gone, and it would only make things harder if she stays. Renee also knew it was best to surround herself with the living. She had to summon the strength to go on without her husband. It would be foolish to stick around, only to visit a body buried and left to decay in the earth. Before taking off with his folks, Simon walked up to Renee one more time while talking to her friends and expressed his sadness, praying she buys it. He was hoping for a hug or even a little kiss from his yellow-haired princess. He would receive neither. Simon Fletcher was the last man she was interested in seeing at -the moment. In truth, it brought back the guilt she was feeling for cheating on Paul. She also saw Simon as another good reason to head back across the country.

She was beginning to fear he might try taking things to the next level since he managed to have her once already. Staring into his eyes beneath the thick black-framed bifocals, Renee sensed something troubling about his demeanor. She didn't want to be around him anymore. As tears filled her eyes, Renee was forced to introduce Simon to some of her friends from California. Most of whom were heading back right after the funeral. Some on the other hand would remain behind to look after their poor friend. Simon did his best to act like a gentleman greeting all her friends with a smile on his face. He even went into his pocket to remove the handkerchief, so he could gently wipe the tears away from her eyes. Renee smiled and thanked him for his kindness. What choice did she have? She felt obligated to keep the peace since his parents were so kind and helpful. Renee could always tell when someone was lusting over her, it was scripted in their body language. She was yet to discover her drug-induced mistake would prove to be far more catastrophic than she could 've ever imagined. Sleeping with her was the most incredible experience of his entire life.

Of all the strange-looking friends who came from California the one Simon truly didn't want to be friendly with was the handsome man with long blonde hair. He felt he was staring at Paul's replacement and the biggest threat to his delusional plans. He did his best to remain polite and respectful to the man who smiled and introduced himself as Travis Oakridge. Simon wanted to keep the conversation brief with the new man he was rapidly growing to despise. In his imagination, he was thinking of gruesome ways to draw his death when the next current of creativity strikes. Renee went around saying her goodbyes and thanking everyone for showing up to pay their respects to Paul. She was wishing they could've all gotten together under better circumstances. Still, it was nice to see so many familiar faces again. Renee told a few of her friends that she would be seeing them soon enough.

Once she has time to clear her head and get the house up for sale, she was planning to return to her home state on the opposite side of the country. Travis smiled and told her not to take too long. They all wanted to see her back where she belongs as soon as possible. Simon couldn't ignore the closeness between Renee and Travis. It seemed, as though they were already lovers in his eyes. He didn't know they grew up together since they were children.

Despite his dashing good looks, Travis and Renee were more like brother and sister. It became even more convincing to Simon when he realized Travis was one of the few friends staying behind. He imagined the two of them sleeping together and it made his stomach twist and turn. It didn't take long for Simon to start wishing him dead as well. It worked once before. Simon thought it couldn't hurt to try again. With any luck, he would be accompanying Renee to another man's funeral in the near future. Simon was becoming extremely jealous as he observed the chemistry between the two young, attractive people. He pictured the two of them having sex on the couch where he was taken to heaven and back again.

The fictional thoughts had his blood melting with fury, the obsessed maniac was getting himself all worked up over nothing. It would be a long while before Renee considered sleeping with any other man. She was going to be grieving over her dead husband for quite some time. Renee was happy to know her good friend Karen and her fiancé Bobby would also be crashing at her place. She was so thankful that she wouldn't have to go back to an empty house and sleep alone tonight. Poor Renee was in desperate need of a company. Karen and Bobby Coleman were of the wilder bunch, he was wearing a tie-dye t-shirt and a red bandanna on his head.

Karen was dressed in her hippie clothing, the stench of cannabis boldly pronounced. They thought it would be a good idea to get completely stoned before the funeral. Renee could care less as- long as they were there for her and her dead husband. She imagined the pot buffered them from Paul's death. She wanted to get wasted herself in-order to numb the pain. They drove a lime-green Volkswagen Bug, graffitied with blue, yellow, and purple peace signs and pot leaves. It was one heck of an eye-sore for most people who saw it, but for Karen and Bobby, it was far-out. They could care less, what people thought.

Most of the time they were too baked to realize what was going on around them anyway. They were sure to pack the bug full of feel-good narcotics that would momentarily take Renee's mind off her troubles.

Losing a good friend, the hippie stoners didn't want to mourn his death but instead celebrate his life. Simon was thinking about all the new victims he would soon paint in terrifying situations. He wanted to continue celebrating with the princess he was convinced was sent by god to be his forever, but he knew Renee wasn't going to invite him over for the after-party. He also knew his parents wouldn't allow him to spend time with her tree-hugging, pot-smoking hippie friends. They didn't want their son exposed to drugs and alcohol. Renee noticed Simon standing off to the side alone. He seemed to have a lot on his mind.

Even more than herself, which seemed utterly impossible. She knew he and Paul hardly knew each other. She also assumed he was not fond of the man being buried today. Renee began to wonder what was going on inside that head of his. Travis took Renee by the hand and walked away, just as Simon felt her eyes upon him and turned to look at her. He was outraged to see the two of them holding hands and walking off together. He was convinced they were going to fall in love and eventually get hitched.

He was not going to allow that to happen. Simon was going to do everything in his power to make sure Renee stays right there with him, where she belongs. He didn't want to see her go back to California when the rest of her friends departed. Simon became further annoyed when he heard his mother's voice calling for him to get in the car. It made him feel like a little boy all over again. Simon was forced to watch his destiny wander off with another man. He found himself livid and ashamed getting into the family wagon to head home.

Later that evening Simon found himself sitting alone in his room, while Renee was smothered by affection from her good friends who traveled from so far away. Renee was still plenty upset as she did her best to cope with her loss. Karen and Bobby continued to offer her drugs and booze, insisting it would make her feel better. All she wanted was to see her lovers face again. She wanted to tell Paul how much she worshipped him once. Karen handed the joint to Bobby and put her arm around Renee, while Travis took charge of the music. Again, Renee thanked her good friends for the long trip, and the support she was in desperate need of. Under My Thumb from The, rolling Stones played on the radio as Karen suggested Renee get out of her goth-funeral clothes and slip into something more comfortable. It sounded like a great idea. The two men engaged in conversation as the women went off to see what else Renee could wear for the night. She didn't care much about how she looked. She simply wanted to throw on one of her husband's old t-shirts, especially the ones that still carried his scent on them.

Besides, she was not exactly looking for a date. Karen went rummaging through her closet, finding all sorts of cute little girly outfits. Renee wanted nothing to do with any of them. Ignoring her good, friend's advice, she grabbed the I love intercourse t-shirt that she'd been wearing for days and put it back on. It reminded her of Paul and the last great weekend they spent together. She then threw on a pair of gray sweatpants in-order to be comfortable. Karen looked at Renee and told her she looked stunning in the t-shirt and sweats and she was right.

The sexy blonde looked amazing no matter what she was wearing. Renee forced a smile on her face as she thanked Karen for being there for her. Karen got a kick out of the t-shirt she was wearing. I love intercourse huh. I bet you do tramp. She said jokingly. I bet the boys are going to love it as much as I do. Renee forced another smile as she turned to exit the bedroom, so they could re-join the men downstairs. Renee insisted on drinking more and indulging in whatever drugs they had to offer. Karen smirked at her heart-broken friend. That's what I was waiting to hear. She replied with a joyous grin on her face. It didn't take long for Travis and Bobby to notice them and begin reading the naughty, a billboard on Renee's t-shirt.

The women were almost ready to place a bet, who would make the crudest comment. They also wondered who would make the first remark. It came from crazy Bobby as he shouted out me too! Everyone got a good chuckle even Renee. Travis stared at his sexy friend unsure if he should act like a dog? Or keep him pretend electric collar from zapping him silly. A million jokes raced through his head, yet he remained silent. He told Renee she looked ravishing as always, he then strongly insisted she needed another drink. Using the corniest of jokes, he came up with while staring at her he laughed saying he would grab her a stiff one.

It was delayed but everyone laughed anyway. As Renee looked around the room and saw people she might not see again for a while she did her best to put on a happy face. No matter how hard she tried to pretend to be un-effected, Renee felt empty inside. She couldn't stop thinking about Paul. None of them could. He was the talk of the night, bringing up old times as the drugs and liquor were quickly consumed. It just wasn't the same without him. If he was with them right now, he would be, in charge of the laughter in the room. Paul was always the life of the party. He had a magnetic way of drawing people toward him. Renee felt a little weird when Travis placed his arm around her while sitting on the couch with a drink in her hand.

She couldn't help but wonder if Paul was up there somewhere looking down on her? The grieving widow didn't want to give him the wrong impression that she was ready to move on. She made it very clear to Travis in a kind and subtle way that she was only interested in a friendship right now, just in case he had other ideas in mind. Travis insisted he was just trying to comfort her, he had always been a great friend to the two of them, never once crossing the line. Renee felt bad, she apologized blaming it on her chaotic mind-frame under the influence, it was completely understandable. As the music played and the party continued, Renee started thinking about the young man next-door. She couldn't put her finger on it, but there was something very peculiar about him.

Something almost animalistic in nature. A troubled soul was hiding behind those dark brown, windows leading to the soul. She just didn't feel comfortable around him anymore. Something about the way he looked at her didn't feel right. She began wondering if it was wrong not inviting him over. Simon was turning into a creep but, Renee felt she owed his parents and had to remain polite and friendly to the weirdo after they had been so generous to her. As Renee day-dreamed in her head, her friends carried on a conversation without her. When she finally snapped out of it, she turned to Travis and gave him a wet kiss on the cheek. She then smiled and thanked him for being such a wonderful friend. They hugged each other as the house continued filling with smoke and fond memories from the past. With the music continuing to be background noise Renee and her closest friends did their best to celebrate their loved one's life. Karen reminded everyone of the way Paul used to dance. Once she mentioned it the room erupted in laughter.

They all shared the same hilarious image in their heads. It was impossible to forget because he was so terrible at it. It was one of the things that made Renee fall in love with him. He was the worst dancer she'd ever seen, yet he was brave enough to summon the courage to ask her to be his partner. Although he failed miserably on the dancefloor, he still managed to win her heart. It felt good to share those precious moments out loud with others. Doing her best to enjoy the evening with friends, Renee couldn't help thinking about the loneliness to come when they take off for the west coast. She wanted to leave everything behind and go with them, especially when Travis mentioned it again, suggesting she had plenty of places to lay her head until she finds a place of her own. Renee knew she needed to be around loved ones, but she couldn't run away just yet. Karen and Bobby also offered to take her in until she finds a new home. None of them wanted to leave their dear friend behind. They feared she might fall into a deep depression alone and do something foolish. Renee promised she would meet them out there very shortly.

They could all celebrate and get completely wasted again. It'll be the biggest welcome home party ever, Karen promised. As Renee sat there drinking with her friends, she was thinking about sharing one of the remaining joints with them. It would be very special for everyone knowing it was prepared by their now deceased friend. There were a few left and Renee knew she had to keep at least one forever in the memory of him. She didn't know if they were all laced with L.S.D. or not? Renee wasn't even, sure she wanted to go on an even more exotic, ride then she was already on. She was already feeling it from the vodka, shrooms, and cocaine they've ingested. As Renee played ping-pong in her mind deciding whether, or not to smoke a sacred joint with her pals? Karen started channel surfing for something a bit slower to listen to. She came across a song called Since I don't have you, by the Sky Liners. Travis asked Renee for her hand, wanting to dance with her. Karen and Bobby also locked hands and eyes as they began gliding across the floor. Renee finished her drink and placed the empty glass down on the coffee table in front of her. She then smiled and reached up to take Travis by the hand. They began slow dancing, but Renee started feeling a little strange. She was far from over Paul and they were just joking about his incredibly awkward moves. She hoped she wasn't doing anything wrong by having this dance. Travis could tell as he looked into her troubled eyes, she was someplace else in her mind. The lyrics to the song seemed fitting after losing the man she was so in love with. Renee did her best to keep her tears from falling.

What are you thinking about? Travis asked. I- Wow, look at you two. Looking, good sweetheart. Said Karen severing her friend's sentence before it could even begin. Renee smiled at her and continued her conversation with Travis. Assuming she was going to mention her dead husband, Travis was shocked when Renee mentioned the special joints she had left from Paul. His face lit up with joy, especially when she confessed, they may be spiked with L-S-D. Renee admitted she didn't know for sure if all of them were, but the one she tried certainly was. It could've been the lucky ones, and all the others are ordinary pots. It didn't matter either way she had his undivided attention. It was inevitable that one of them gets sparked, especially once Karen and Bobby catch wind of the magical joints.

So far, the secret was quietly being discussed by the two of them, as she whispered in his right ear. Travis insisted none of the joints were ordinary since they've been rolled by such a special, friend who was no longer with them. Renee dared not tell any of her friends about the wretched mistake she made sleeping with the geek, next-door. It was bad enough she lost her husband, but Renee also had to deal with the guilt of cheating on him right before it happened. So, where's that joint? Travis wanted to know. As Renee went to speak, he announced Karen and Bobby dancing only feet away. Renee here just told me she has a very special joint for us to smoke. That was all it took to get the pot-heads attention

. What's so special about it? Bobby wanted to know. It may or may not be laced with L-S-D? Travis replied, causing the room to brighten with enthusiastic, excitement. How do you not know if it's laced or not? Don't you remember if you added a little something extra to it? Karen asked Renee, who found herself forced to fill them in on the other little surprise. Well, you see. I didn't roll the joint Paul did. Renee replied. That's what makes it so magical. Travis added. Well shit. What the hell are we waiting for? Where's this joint? Karen demanded to know. She insisted they spark it up and enjoy it in Paul's honor. It was a symbolic way for them to celebrate with their lost friend one final time. Renee left her friends on the dancefloor and headed to her bedroom to retrieve the pot. The three stoners waited patiently for her to return.

As Renee grabbed the cigarette-pack off the dresser she imagined Paul in her head sitting there on the bed rolling the joints for her with a smile on his face. She could hear his voice calling out her name as if he was standing beside her. Renee didn't care if he haunted her. She would give anything to see him again. Taking a joint out of the pack, she could 've sworn she felt his presence in the room. When she turned to the sound of his voice, Renee was startled and joyous to find Paul standing in the doorway staring at her. Holding the joint in her hand, she told Paul she loved him with all her heart and that she missed him terribly. I hope you don't mind me sharing one of these with our friends downstairs, and don't worry Travis and I are only friends. I have no intention of being with anyone now that you're gone. Paul just smiled at her without saying a word. It was enough to know he wasn't angry with her for her actions. Walking toward him, the image vanished as suddenly as it appeared. Renee smiled with tears forming in her eyes.

She was so happy to see him again, even if only for a moment. She assumed he was never really- there and that it was her un-stable, heavily intoxicated mind playing tricks on her. Renee did her best to forget the vision and head down-stairs to join her friends. They were all happy to see she had returned with the sacred joint. Renee also noticed she missed the rest of the slow song, and her opportunity to dance with an old friend.

After what she just saw in the bedroom, she imagined it was for the best. Renee wanted to convince herself Paul was in-fact keeping an eye on her from the great beyond. It made her feel safe as if he was her guardian angel. Standing in the middle of the staircase, Renee smiled and held the weed up high for everyone to see. They all cheered anticipating a hit from a joint rolled by a friend who passed on. It was as sentimental as it was up-lifting for Paul's lover and close friends. Making her way over to them, Renee held the joint in her hand for everyone to feast their eyes on. She explained how she discovered them by accident while putting Paul's clean clothes away. It was very kind of him to display his affection for her so thoughtfully. Karen insisted Renee lights the joint since she was married to their fallen loved one.

The men agreed, and Renee placed the joint to her lips for ignition, sharing a kiss at a distance with her lost lover. Smoke filled the room as they passed it around and continued talking about the good old times. Everyone felt as if Paul was actually -with them as they enjoyed his final gift. Being burned by the lungs of four people it didn't take long for the joint to shrink into a smoldering roach. Renee was the first and last with cannabis. She placed the remains in the nearby ashtray for the moment, but she would be careful to put it someplace safe for the rest of her days. It was even more valuable to her now that it was shared with the grooviest friends anyone could ever ask for. They all noticed sooner than later that it was a regular joint. Renee was kind of happy it didn't send her spiraling off even further into darkness without a tether.

As much as she wanted to escape her reality. As the night wore on and Renee did her best to enjoy the company of her friends, Simon was grieving next-door and filling his head with jealousy and rage. Staring at the house next door, he could only imagine what was taking place inside. He knew Renee was in there with the handsome young man who had to be just as ambitious as he was to get in her pants. If she was willing to do drugs and have sex with him? It seemed obvious she would be willing to do the same with a much better-looking man. It angered Simon to imagine the two of them excusing themselves from the rest of the guest and disappearing to Renee's bedroom where they had the privacy to be all over each other. Simon's head felt like it was going to explode as sexual thoughts of the two consumed his imagination. He wanted to invite himself over, so he could get in between the new lovers as he saw them. In truth, it was all in his crazy mind. Simon Fletcher was becoming more and more unstable, he wanted to create one of his sinister drawings, but he was far to agitated to concentrate. He was seeing red with false visions of Travis laying on Renee's bed, as she stripped naked and got on top of him.

This time picturing his princess having sex didn't turn him on. It created fury in his soul. Simon wanted to be the one who had her moaning and making goofy faces during the passionate lovemaking. The thought of someone else pleasuring Renee sent Simon into a blind, rage. Life was an on-going misery with no happiness in sight. He didn't want to do it anymore. Huffing and puffing in his room while contemplating suicide, Simon feared he would draw his mother's attention. He didn't want her barging in on him during one of his mental breakdowns. Simon was also overwhelmed with the concept she may be going back to California with her friends when they leave town.

There was that nagging possibility that he would never see her again, ever so slowly digging its claws in and doing its best to invade his every thought. A dark and hopeless future without Renee in it was a place he didn't care to venture. Thinking back to the eerie image he once created from mutilating models in magazines, Simon knew he could never allow his queen to desert him. Somehow god would find a way for the two of them to be together forever. Simon fully believed she was his destiny. He decided to wait until he was calmer to pulverize his new enemy monstrously on paper. Simon eventually drifted off to sleep with negative thoughts hammering away at the very neurons that made him tick.

The next morning Simon was getting ready to head to his mother's flower shop when he noticed a hung-over Renee outside saying goodbye to her friends. They decided to head home sooner than Renee had hoped. They were supposed to stick around for a few more days, but Bobby had to get back to work and their plans were destroyed. Simon stared at them as Renee gave everyone a hug and a kiss. That included the handsome man he was growing an intense hatred for. Simon watched as anger boiled inside him. He wanted to walk over there and start swinging wildly at Travis but had to keep himself together if he wanted Renee to believe he was a good guy. Simon reluctantly shifted his thoughts in a more positive direction. Travis may have Renee in his arms at- the moment, but at least Simon knew she was staying behind and would remain close to him.

The pretty boy would be hitting the road without her. Simon felt as if he won knowing he still had her living right next door. He could still see her beautiful face every single day. It brought a sliver of happiness to him, though he knew it was only temporary. He smiled as he watched them drive off in their ugly bug on four-wheels. Renee hadn't even noticed him standing there watching the whole thing. She lit a cigarette and had a seat on the front-porch oblivious of his presence until Simon casually walked over inviting himself by saying hello. Renee wasn't sure if she was glad to see him? But the bad company seemed better than no company for the moment. She unsurely asked him to have a seat for a minute while she finishes her smoke. Simon could tell she had been partying heavily the night before. She looked like a mess, but still beautiful in his eyes.

He wanted to ask her about her wild night and any sexual encounters she may have experienced. He decided it would be a terrible idea and ignored the troublemaking voices whispering in his head. Renee was still wearing Paul's I love intercourse t-shirt with a black and red, lumberjack looking flannel over it, but it didn't hide the perverted message from

Simon's hawk eyes. He immediately stared at it while thinking of the right thing to say. So, you love intercourse too huh? Was the best he could come up with on the spot. It was weak and pathetic, and Simon knew it. He should have just kept his mouth shut. Renee thought it was kind of funny how the men never noticed it says Pennsylvania at the bottom.

To them, it simply screams I love sex. It's the words all males want to hear, especially when coming from such an attractive, young woman. Renee was hoping to be rid of Simon when the cigarette was finished. She couldn't wait to get out of Renee Falls and back to Sunny California. She wanted to make her exit soon to escape her first cold winter in the northeast part of the country. Renee's thoughts of returning home to be around loved ones were the only thing that gave her the strength she needed to go on. Simon was doing his best to pretend he had a heavy heart for Paul's unexpected demise. He wanted Renee to think he was as kind and caring as his folks. As Renee continued sucking down the cigarette, Simon knew his time with her was running out. He decided to ask her if she was going to stay here in Renee Falls? Or move back to California where she is from now that Paul's gone. Simon had his suspicions and he felt they were right

. He just wanted to hear it from her luscious lips. Renee informed him that she was planning to put the house up for sale and move back across the country as soon as possible. She insisted there was no reason to stick around, now that her husband was dead. Renee explained, she needed to be around friends right now. Her words were hurtful to Simon. They made him feel as if he was nothing to her, even though they 've been intimate, with one another. Simon found it difficult to hide his true feelings and Renee could see the anger and disappointment scribbled on his face. It was a strange reaction she thought being they hadn't known each other that long. Renee didn't understand why he was so attached.

Then she realized her mistake. She was far more attractive than any other girl Simon had probably ever even spoke two words with. She took his virginity knowing he had a crush on her. What did she expect to happen? The most troubling thing about the whole situation was that Simon was obsessed with her long before they ever slept together. He was infatuated with Renee Price before he even laid eyes on her. Renee couldn't believe how quickly his demeanor changed as she confessed, she wanted to return to the city of angels. She could see the wheels turning in his head. They appeared to be off course and barreling toward a brick wall with no intention of stopping.

The look in his eyes, even the tone of his voice changed slightly, as his world came crashing down all around him. So, your saying I'm not important enough for you to stick around? That I'm not your friend? It was a weird thing to say. Renee wasn't sure how to answer him at first. She just stared at him with those beautiful blue eyes of hers. Look Simon I hardly even know you. You're a nice guy and I love your parents to death, they're wonderful people. I can never thank them enough for everything they 've done for me and Paul. But I can't stay here in this little town where everything reminds me of him. What happened between us was a mistake. I shouldn't have stolen your virginity and I'm sorry. That should 've been saved for when the right girl comes along. I fucked up and I feel awful about it. So, then I was right. You don't give a shit about me. Simon replied as his temper continued to flare. I want you to stay with me. I think you'll learn to love it here. Not to mention my parents adore you. They would love it if you stayed. Who knows what crazy person will take your place when you're gone? I can't imagine seeing you again.

The more Simon tried convincing her to stay, the further he was pushing her away. She was getting seriously freaked out by his darkening behavior. Even if Renee wanted to stay there? Simon was doing his best to convince her to run like hell. She tried keeping the peace, insinuating she would keep in touch with him by writing or talking on the phone. Simon was no fool, he knew once she was gone, he would never see nor hear from her again. Observing Renee's disturbed reaction to his behavior, Simon did his best to back-pedal and pretend it didn't bother him so much, asking Renee how long she thought it would be before she was back on the sunny west-coast? Renee confessed she wanted to get out of there as soon as possible. Will you be gone before the holidays? Or do you think you might stick around until they're through? I mean you've already decorated for Halloween. It would be a pity to take everything down and pack it in now. Wouldn't you agree? Besides you're about to experience your first winter in the cold north-east. Don't you want to at least witness a sample of old man winter dumping his beautiful-white snow on-top of us? Trust me, Renee, there is nothing groovier than being snowed inside your house for a couple of days. If you leave now? You will surely miss out. Simon even tried telling Renee that his mother would hire her at the flower-shop if she needed a job. She smiled and thanked him, but as expected politely declined the offer. It was clear he was doing everything in his power to convince Renee to change her mind. It was never going to work she didn't love him.

Now that the cigarette was finished and placed in the ashtray, Renee saw her escape. Simon also saw that his time had run out. Renee confessed she imagined it would be extremely lonely trapped in the house all by herself, with nothing to do and no one to talk to. Simon wanted to invite himself to be that fill in. He chose to remain quiet, knowing he had done enough damage already. As Renee exhaled a nicotine cloud, she stood up hoping Simon would take the hint that their brief encounter was through. Doing his best to keep the conversation going to buy himself more time with his beauty-queen the four-eyed stalker spilled out another bunch of foolish words further condemning him to a forgettable chapter in the gorgeous young woman's life.

He was never good at communicating with females, especially the one he could never again live without. Now he was making an even bigger mess of things by blurting out, So, are you and the man with long blonde hair going to start a new life together? I can see the way you two look at each other. His rude accusations were making Renee angry, which was pretty- hard to do. She wanted nothing to do with the boy-next-door and boldly told him it was none of his business. She insisted she and Travis were only friends. She swore he was more like a big brother to her, still, Simon couldn't accept it. Look, Simon, it was nice talking to you, but I've got to get back inside I have a lot of thinking to do. I'll talk to you later ok. Simon had no choice, but to suck it up and turn away a ball of mush. He was completely crushed inside.

The love-sick puppy knew for sure that he and Renee would never be together with the way he had hoped. It wasn't long before the demons in his head began taking hold of the angels. As he got in his car and headed to the florist to work, Simon's hatred for his parents, god returned in a whirlwind of madness. He felt betrayed for the last time. He hated Paul with a passion, even though he was the only reason Renee ever existed in his world. The twisted lover didn't realize by losing one he would have to give up the other. If the lord did answer his prayer? It completely backfired on him. Thoughts of throwing his car off the road on the way to work crossed Simon's mind as well as other diluted fantasies popping in and out of existence like the tiniest particles in the universe. It, infuriated Simon to know Renee could care less about him. She was just another shallow bitch like all the other women he has ever met.

Allowing his anger to stir itself into a frenzy, Simon began growing hatred for the sexy blonde next door. He wanted to get back at her for treating him as if he was nothing. He even thought about stopping at the cemetery after work to dig up her dead husband and place him on her front-lawn with the rest of the ghoulish decorations for spite. Simon could only imagine the look on her face the following morning when she is confronted by her dead lover back from the grave. He eventually realized it would be much safer if he painted his dismay into the world as he had always done. Rather than digging up a corpse and giving it a lift back to Renee's place.

The joy would be far richer if it was the real thing, but the punishment could be just as severe as the reward. All Simon could do is obsess over the number of days he had left before his beauty-queen is gone forever. Now that she was finally real, he couldn't imagine going back to the crude image of her created from the dirty magazines. It felt as if god had given sight to a blind man long enough to witness the miraculous world around him only to take it away suddenly, plunging him back into the dark abyss from which he came. Simon wanted to die. He wanted to scream on top of his lungs so the whole world could hear his pain. Visions of Renee and Travis having sex played over and over in his mind as if it was a recording with no end.

He was relentlessly trying to convince himself that it was real, even though it was simply his vivid imagination, almost as if he was enjoying the suffering brought on by his demented thoughts. Purposely adding fuel to the firestorm already burning inside his head, He wondered if his madness would somehow enlighten him with the right course of action needed to win over the girl of his dreams. Simon felt lucky to be in his car at- the moment of his break-down. If he was home? He feared he would 've smashed all his mother's false idles, egging on the god he despised and daring him and his angels to show themselves.

As if the porcelain statues were going to fray at the seams and feathered wings of angelic beings would fly out of them, shedding their fragile casings like the time they chased him out of the house while on drugs. Or the Wooden statues of Jesus would tear themselves from their crosses and announce their presence. How would he explain that when his parents returned home? He had to calm down before walking into his mother's establishment. If he throws his temper around in front of the customers, he will have to hear about it later.

Arriving tardy as usual, Simon was fortunate to find no customers standing around waiting for him this morning. Dealing with blissful lovers was the last thing in the world he wanted to do. Simon's mind was at war with itself as he stood around with nothing to occupy his turbulent thoughts. Eventually, he even considered the option of kidnapping Renee. It was a preposterous idea he knew would never work. How can it when he lives right next door with his parents? Not even his sacred house of sins would be desolate enough to mask her screams from all the potential witnesses sharing the block with him. Simon desired Renee Price to be his permanent sex slave and do whatever he says. It was a dark fantasy he desperately wanted to bring to life. Renee was in the middle of a much-needed shower. She felt dirty from all the partying the night before. Her thoughts soon shifted to what Simon said to her earlier. His behavior was troubling, to say the least. Renee felt it was none of his business who she kisses or hangs out with. She's had guy friends her entire life. Who was he to comment her pal, Travis? If she wanted to fuck his brains out, she could and no one had the right to stop her, especially not the four-eyed geek from next-door. Behind the soft-spoken shy façade, a monster was lurking. Renee finished washing up, trying to make sense of the way he acted when she told him she was leaving town. He sped off in his car as if he was going to harm himself or someone else. Simon's actions revealed a side of him Renee had never seen before. In some ways, she wished he hadn't. It was a definite warning sign of things to come.

After her shower, Renee planned to go to the store and pick up some boxes. She wanted to get started on the packing at least the stuff she didn't need at, the moment, in case things get further out of control with her naughty four, eyed neighbor? She was almost ready to get in her jeep and make the journey back to Los Angeles right there and then. With concern for her safety growing, Renee imagined she would rather sleep on her friend's couch, than next-door to this potential, psychopath. Losing Paul and being stalked was enough reason to get the hell out of that cursed little town immediately. She felt terrible about leaving his remains behind, all alone in a place they never got to call home, still, Renee knew it was in her best interest to get the fuck away from Simon Fletcher. She was planning to be long gone by the middle of November. She didn't want to spend Thanks-Giving all alone, or even more disturbing with the Fletcher family next, door. She wanted to spend the coming holidays with trusted loved ones. Not interested in saying goodbye, Renee imagined driving off in the middle of the night when no one was watching, never to look back.

The following Sunday Simon had returned from church and since he finally had off from work, he was excited to retreat to his house of sins and work on one of his morbid creations. Simon Fletcher quickly gathered his supplies and settled in for a new painting. He decided to sculpt a torturous portrait involving himself as the killer, chasing down

Renee in the nude. Wielding a large blade, tightly gripped in his left hand, Simon went out of his way to express the terror in her eyes. Her naked body covered in blood as she ran for her life.

Her face was carefully carved open with knives, leaving deep gashes across her once flawless surface. His heart started beating faster, as Simon the artist began feeling as if he was literally, inside the painting. Scorching sweat dripped down his face as he scribbled chaos into existence. He found himself distracted from time to time, staring at the house next door waiting to catch a glimpse of the young woman who unknowingly had full control of his every thought. The living zombie spent every conscious moment fixated on a girl who would never feel the same about him.

This wicked obsession was plunging him deeper and deeper into the black hole he willingly slipped into. Simon was so addicted to his lustful fantasy, he hadn't even tried crawling out of the consuming depths, in which he was falling balls first. He couldn't wait for Renee to remove the drapes, so he can spy on her again if she didn't already figure out what a pervert he truly was. Simon continued working on his painting placing himself back into the gory, heart-pounding situation he was creating without the spilling of real blood, but how long would it be before the graphic artwork isn't enough? Simon wanted to know what Renee's screams sounded like and how it might feel to kill someone.

That would anger the god he struggled to believe in. The god who always managed to let him down. Simon noticed he was running low on red paint as usual. He needed enough to not only paint this portrait but the ones he would create shortly. Having her once already, there was no way Simon Fletcher wasn't going to receive the same mind, blowing experience he once shared with her. He wanted to taste and feel Renee's warm body against his. Her moaning grew louder in his head, as he tried concentrating on the final touches of the picture. Snapping out of it by simply checking her house again, particularly her bedroom window. Simon got the feeling she was secluding herself from him, due to his unsavory behavior, and quickly went back to his violent drawing. It was perfect and worthy of being preserved beneath the floorboards.

Somewhere buried deep, was the chilling truth that Renee Price would have to die in, order for Simon Fletcher to get what he wants. The dark unavoidable concept tormented him more than he wanted to admit. Worried it would consume the rest of the day if he spent one more second on it., Simon took a final look, before placing the morbid portrait in his secret hiding place, with the rest of his macabre collection. He thought it was almost dire to specify her long yellow hair drenched in blood, Simon wanted to destroy Renee so she wouldn't be so gorgeous anymore. He began toying with that famous notion if I can't have her no one can. Treacherous thoughts knowing most of the time they end in tragedy. He couldn't wait to draw even more hellish scenes involving the two men he hated most. If he couldn't kill them in real life, Simon Fletcher was going to torture them in his paintings, as horribly as possible

Already worked up over the illusion that Renee was running off to be with Travis, it wasn't hard for Simon to step willingly off the deep end. It reminded him of being a coward who still rode in the back of the family station wagon on the way to church every Sunday. He was still that same weak little boy afraid to make a stand no matter how much it counts. Incredible as his paintings were, he knew his enemies were out of harm's way, long as he was too frightened to make a crucial move. Fate removed Paul from the picture, but he was instantly replaced by another man in his eyes. Renee's husband was no longer a problem, but Travis was threatening to move her to the other side of the country.

The more Simon thought about her returning to California to be with her new, prince-charming, the more convoluted his thoughts became. Simon wasn't entirely sure he could go through with the murder of the woman he claimed to love. It didn't prevent him from fantasizing about it. As he sat there with malevolent thoughts stampeding through his cranium, Renee was doing her best to get on with her life. The bright sun was shining in the sky and as she wondered the house naked, she began opening the windows to let the light and fresh air inside. Renee suddenly didn't feel comfortable walking around the house so freely showing herself off to the pervert next-door. She no longer felt completely safe around him, uncertain If he was watching from a distance? Renee was in no way flattered by her peeping, Tom. Just the thought of it made her skin crawl.

Giving herself to him continued to prove itself as the worst thing she ever did. Renee was never going to admit that numb-skull decision to anyone. It would silently follow her to the grave. Glancing out the bedroom window she reached for a t-shirt with John Lennon on it to cover herself up with, just in case he happened to be watching. She soon became fixated with Simon's treehouse built high above the ground in Fletcher's back yard. Simon neglected to mention it to her, and she couldn't help but wonder why? Why would a grown man want to hang out alone in a treehouse in his parent's backyard? Renee stared at it asking herself if he was up there right now? Staring back at her from the dark wooden structure. It was disturbing when she realized its proximity to her bedroom window. It provided the perfect view for Simon to hide in the tiny house and watch her in secret. She would never be able to look at it the same way again. Simon was watching her from the house of sins hidden up in the trees.

He was disappointed when she covered herself up. He could still see her long sexy legs sticking out of the bottom of her black t-shirt with John Lennon's face planted on it. Simon wondered if she was on to him, or if she could see him hiding up in the treehouse keeping a watchful eye on her. Renee dared to imagine how many times he may have spied on her while parading around the house in the nude. She had no proof but strongly felt her privacy had been invaded without her knowledge of it. Renee was growing more disturbed and curious every second. She wanted to sneak into the treehouse when no one was around and see what it was like up there. She was curious to know what Simon did when no one was keeping an eye on him.

Perhaps she could expose a demon before heading back to the city of angels. For now, all Renee could do is pull down the shades and try to forget about the little creep next door. She wanted to get back to packing a few things she was able to live without. It felt so strange boxing her possessions so soon after moving into this lovely little home in the middle of small-town America. She felt as though they were still getting settled in when her world was torn apart. Renee was not expecting the wicked curve-ball life planned to throw at her. It was a cruel joke taking away the love of her life so suddenly. Renee tried convincing herself things would get better once she's back home, but there were even more precious memories there waiting for her. She put on a Beatles album and got to work with compassionate memories and startling terrors floating around in her head. When Stanley and Eleanor found out their sweet young neighbor was moving back to California, they too felt bad. They would miss her but understood why she wanted to leave.

After seeing the way her presence affected their son, they assumed it was probably for the best that she' s removed from his sight. Perhaps that will help distance her from his mind as well? Although they liked Renee, they felt the sooner she was gone the better. Eleanor was growing tired of his attitude at home, but she was really- angry with him for the way he was treating her loyal customers. He was often making rude comments to anyone who dared to enter the store in a positive mood. Simon Fletcher was miserable and wanted to see others as miserable as himself. What he wanted was to be the kind of guy who women fall head over heels in love with.

Unfortunately, he would never be one of those guys. Whenever Simon was home, he noticed there weren't a lot of Renee sightings. She had been keeping her curtains drawn and staying to herself. She spent most of her day thinking about the future and getting things ready for the big move. Usually, Simon would get lucky and catch her sitting on the porch enjoying a cigarette. Over the last several days there was no sign of her. Renee was doing her best to stay away from Simon and his weird behavior. She felt he was obsessed with her and it made her really- uncomfortable. The one thing she would save until last to pack was their wedding picture. Renee felt she needed it around to make it through her day.

On the rare occasions when Simon did spot Renee out of her house for a few minutes, he would always try to seek her attention. It made her even more cautious of him. How did he always know exactly when she would be outside? Was he watching her house every second he was home to catch a fleeting glimpse of the girl he had been obsessively stalking? Renee stayed inside as much as possible to reduce her chances of having an encounter with Simon Fletcher. She considered talking to his parents, but she was afraid they wouldn't believe her. She also feared Simon would retaliate if he discovered she was a snitch. She didn't want to start anything knowing she would be gone soon anyway. It was best to suck it up and keep the peace. Renee was a free-spirit and not used to living in such a confined environment. She always had her windows wide open for the fresh air to enter and make the house more cheerful.

Now she had everything locked and shut-down tight. It seemed a bit bizarre since she once thought this was the most peaceful place on earth. She actually- felt safer in L A then she did around one four-eyed creep.

CHAPTER 10

❖ ❖ ❖ ❖ ❖ ❖

As Halloween night rapidly approached so did the first real sign of the coming winter. The temperature had dropped significantly, and thick gray clouds filled the sky. The last thing Renee needed was a creepy night of unexpected guests dressed up as ghouls and goblins. No matter what the children decided to wear as they brazenly hit the streets in search of candy? Nothing would freak her out more than answering the door and finding Simon Fletcher on the other side. Flipping through the channels she began watching Dr. Jekyll and Mr. Hyde.

After a few seconds, she decided it was a little too scary for her, considering a crazy man was living right next-door who's possibly out to get her? Renee continued channel surfing until she came upon a much better movie to help pass the time. It was the Wizard of Oz, one of her favorite movies. She was hoping it would cheer her up a little and even cause her to forget about Simon Fletcher and his compelling desire to be with her.

Every time she heard a dreaded knock at the door, she imagined it was Simon coming to prevent her from leaving Renee Falls. Luckily it was always a group of little, brats seeking candy. It didn't stop her from jumping every time the stupid bell rang. Even though it was expected the sound sent a shiver up her spine. She imagined if Simon Fletcher did dress up for the evil holiday, it would be fitting for him to masquerade as an escaped mental, patient with red horns stabbing through his skull. Renee would never forget that crazy look in his eyes when he discovered she was moving back across the country.

As she answered the door and handed out treats, she noticed it started raining lightly. She had a feeling it would soon grow worse, putting an end to the trick or treating taking place. It felt cold and damp, and she just wanted to stay in the house where it was warm and dry. The dreary weather was adding to her growing depression and anxiety of the strange young man living only feet away. The storm that was moving in had the same negative effect on Simon. Looking out his bedroom window, he watched as the rain splattered against the glass distorting Renee's house as he stared at it thinking of a way, he could prevent her from vanishing from his life. He rightfully assumed she figured him out since the house appeared to be on lockdown ever since he begged her not to go. In a way, he blamed himself for chasing her away with his odd attachment.

Then he convinced himself she was going to leave Renee Falls either way. He still wanted to place the blame on Travis for persuading her to relocate, so they could be together. It was his strongest attempt to shield himself from taking the blame. The rain started falling heavier and a gust of wind sped through the streets tossing around anything to light to withstand its strength. Now it felt like Halloween, but Renee wasn't enjoying it. She couldn't wait for the burning sun to rise the following morning. The first thing she was going to do is take down all the scary decorations and pack them up for travel. Renee wasn't used to, nor did she like being on edge.

Constantly anticipating a surprise visit from the boy next, door, she started thinking about the remaining joints Paul left for her. She was tempted to smoke one, but there were only two left, and she didn't know if they were laced. The last thing she needed was an unexpected trip during the raging storm. Instead, she poured herself a screwdriver and continued watching The Wizard of Oz. Renee needed something to ease her vibrating nerves, she was also hoping it would help her sleep like a baby. She knew if she remained sober, she would be tossing and turning all night long. She took a giant gulp as Dorothy and the others came across the cowardly lion.

He was her favorite character in the film since she was a little girl. Renee was doing anything to keep her spirit in a positive place. She had always lived a carefree life, now she was barricading herself indoors and living in fear. So far Simon hadn't done anything extreme to make her feel so anxious for a violent confrontation. She couldn't explain why? She just couldn't ignore the gut instinct taking over her mind. It was as if Renee had finally awakened and instantaneously became street-smart. Simon eventually gave up staring at her house and turned on the tv to occupy his troubled mind. Unlike Renee, he didn't choose to watch something from his childhood to lighten his soul.

He instead chose to continue watching the Manson murders and finding it more and more fascinating with every savage detail. The media had been dragging this story through the muds of hell and back because of twisted viewers like Simon Fletcher. It should 've been old news long ago, but the whole country seemed to want to know more. Ratings were climbing to the blues of the sky, it appeared not even the heavens were out of reach of such a devilish cult. To Simon, Christ was simply a peaceful version of Charles Manson thousands of years in the past. The more they showed off the bloody murder scenes, the more they desensitized Simon Fletcher.

He began wondering if he too could pull off something so dark, so repulsive that the entire world would tune in to hear his story. They might be put to death, but their names and gruesome tales would live on forever. Simon did his best to convince himself that he was also capable of such a Satanic act against both god and man. In his warped mind, Simon was foolish, thinking about murdering the girl he loved more than anything in the world, if it meant he could possess her always If these attractive young girls could go through with it and even smile about it afterward, how hard can it be? Still, he didn't want to kill Renee. What good was she to him dead. He wanted her soft warm, wet body to satisfy his perverted needs in the bedroom. If she was cold and stiff? She would be no use to him. Simon found himself being drawn deeper into the demonic influence presented before him.

The strictly raised Christian was voluntarily being led astray. With the storm taking place over his town, Simon became even more consumed by the grizzly tale that took place in the same state Renee Price was from. He was glad she didn't become one of Manson's victims, that didn't guarantee she wouldn't become his. As the old classic came to an end, Renee felt her eyes growing heavy. The room was starting to spin, and she knew it was time for bed.

As Dorothy watched the wicked witch burn under the presence of water, she turned off the tv and made her way to the bedroom to sleep alone. It was something she was going to have to get used to, still dressed, Renee hit the pillow pulling the blanket on top of her. The liquor knocked her out cold as intended. Simon had other ideas in mind. He waited until his folks were sound asleep, before getting dressed to venture out into the storm. He was immediately soaked as he went around Renee's house trying to find a way inside. He knew that house better than she did. Simon imagined it would be a piece of cake to gain entry. He was surprised to discover every door and window was shut tight and locked from the inside. as if she was waiting for him to arrive.

Growing frustrated, he was not going to give up. Simon was determined to get in Renee's house and watch her while she slept. He had no intention of using it, but he did hock a knife from the kitchen, on the way out just in case. What if Renee was awake when he arrived? What if she attacked him to save her skin? Simon didn't want to hurt her, but he was prepared to, should something go wrong. Almost ready to call it quits, he remembered one entrance Renee may have over-looked while safe, guarding the house. He headed for the door leading into the basement, drenched and starting to shiver from the cold, praying for the best. With his fingers crossed, on one hand, he used the other to enter the house. To his surprise when he yanked on the handle the door opened.

Now he just had to hope the door leading to the rest of the house was open as well. Slowly Simon crept up the basement stairs leading to the room where his princess was sleeping soundly. He was tracking in mud and staining her floors along the way, leaving wet footprints announcing his presence.

As Simon quietly crept through Renee's house toward her bedroom, he imagined the look on her face, should she wake up and catch him standing over her bedside. It would be the most bone-chilling scare she could ever receive on the demonic holiday. His rage grew darker when he looked around the house and noticed boxes were lying around filled with her belongings.

It was the evidence he needed to know she was planning on leaving him behind. His rage grew even darker realizing why he hadn't seen her around the past several days. Simon was convinced Renee was trying to avoid him. The truth he discovered was even worse. She was getting the hell out of town and never looking back. Simon noticed the wedding picture proudly displayed on the small table. It enraged him further inside, making him want to smash the reminder that he could never be Paul. He wanted to take the photo home and separate the lovebirds, preserving Renee and slicing Paul's half into tiny slivers with a pair of rusty, old scissors.

Overcoming his urge for destruction, Simon left the wedding photo behind and paid a quick visit to Renee's snake, Lennon. He was silently slithering around waiting for a live rodent to drop out of the sky. Lennon didn't care for Simon's company, but he was the wrong, animal for the job when it came to- protecting the house. He minded his own business, as Simon stood there staring down at him with four-troublesome eyes. He then turned his attention to the stairs leading to the master bedroom. That was the real reason he was there. He hoped the storm wasn't keeping his love awake. If she catches him in her house uninvited in the middle of the night? He would be in serious trouble. Making his way up the stairs, Simon could feel his heart beating like a battle-drum.

He was nervous and excited to see what she would be wearing when he walked in on her. Since she was no longer willing to show herself to him, Simon was going to find a way to do it himself. He couldn't accept the fact that he would never get the opportunity to sleep with her again, now that she was moving thousands of miles away. When he walked into the bedroom, Simon found his beloved Renee out like a light. She was lying naked on the bed before him. He looked down at her a smile on his face. She looked so peaceful, he wanted to crawl up in bed and lay next to her while she dreamed of happy things. Simon was also thinking about removing his pants, but he felt it was too risky. He could feel his erection growing as he stared at Renee in the nude.

He was getting turned on and didn't know what to do about it. Simon stood there watching her sleep as he struggled with his menacing thoughts. He wasn't sure if he wanted to reach out and touch her? Or himself while he had a visual of his goddess laid out before him. The heavy rain and strong winds continued to thrash around outside as Simon completely violated his sexy neighbor's privacy in the most disturbing way. Poor Renee had no idea her peeper was standing right at her bedside as she slept. It gave the nerd with the mundane life a chance to feel his blood course with excitement. The thrill of lusting over Renee without her knowledge of it made his heart do cartwheels in his chest. Simon never felt so alive, it was almost more thrilling than actually having sex with her. Simon no longer cared if he joined the fallen angel's army after this life was through.

He wanted to feel joy and excitement and doing what was considered forbidden filled that empty void in his life. Pushing himself further, he gently ran his fingers through her long yellow hair. Thunder was crashing, and lightning brightened the room, revealing an even clearer image, adding to the nightlight Renee had plugged in to feel safe. He placed his nose against her face and smelled her flesh, before very gently kissing her on the cheek. With that Renee started to stir slightly, causing Simon to jump back and leave her be for the moment.

His eyes were fixated on her breast which was staring him right in the face. Renee could 've sworn she felt someone touching her but brushed it off as her imagination, all the while Simon was standing only feet away carefully observing her every move. He didn't know whether to run for it or stand perfectly still, hoping she will remain asleep. A few seconds later, Renee opened her eyes and quickly surveyed the bedroom. There was no sign of Simon or anyone else for that matter. Thinking it was her mind playing tricks on her, she just wanted to go back to sleep. She knew she would be long gone very soon and would never have to see Simon Fletcher again, still, she couldn't shake that nerve-tingling sensation on the back of her neck.

That extra sense of letting you know there is something else living and breathing nearby. Hard as she tried, Renee just couldn't shake it. A penetrating gaze seemed to be set upon her from an unknown source. Renee kept telling herself she was simply afraid to sleep in the dark house all alone, especially during a violent thunderstorm. Her thoughts quickly turned to her neighbor Simon Fletcher. If anyone was lurking in her home? It had to be him. She remembered the phantom touch and it freaked her out. Did Simon touch her while she lay there sleeping peacefully? It was almost too horrifying for her to imagine. As she thought about getting out of bed to explore, before attempting to go back to sleep, Renee was sure to thank god for the lovely storm he sent her way sarcastically. Severely troubled, Renee felt she had to get out of bed and have a look around, to make sure the house was safe. She couldn't rest with the thought of that creep hiding somewhere in the shadows lying in wait to attack her. Renee hopped out of bed, placing her feet right on the damp carpet below. They felt an instant chill as she reached for the nearby lamp.

Looking around there was no sign of anyone. It was enough to convince the frightened young woman she was right. She felt like a little girl again as she bent down to have a look under the bed. She was relieved to find there was no one under there. The next place for a monster to hide was naturally the closet. Had Simon slipped in there at the last second? She could feel more of the floor was moist as she slowly walked toward the closet, terrified to see who or what was waiting on the other side. Reaching for the knob, a loud crash of thunder startled her even more as she anticipated the worst. Was Simon going to jump out at her a weapon in his hand? Ready to fight for her life she quickly opened the door and had a look inside. Again, to Renee's surprise, no one was there. She was beginning to question her sanity. Maybe it was all in her head? Or maybe something even grander was taking place? The heartbroken widow dared to question if perhaps her dead husband was coming back from the other side to visit? If Renee was being haunted, she demanded he shows himself immediately. She asked Paul out loud to appear before her but got no reply. Renee turned to look out her bedroom window as a bolt of lightning flashed, illuminating Simon's house of sins, reminding her that she wanted to go there and scope it out.

The eerie hide away quickly faded back under the cover of darkness. With the fear of a predator still lurking about in the shadows, Renee asked herself how he might have gotten inside. She had been very careful to make sure all the doors and windows were locked uptight. It had to be her imagination toying with her paranoid mind. Realizing she was still walking around naked Renee threw on a tie-dye t-shirt and prepared to check the rest of the house just to be sure. She didn't even have a weapon to defend herself, god forbid there was someone out there waiting for her. Renee gathered her strength and prepared to brave the rest of her home.

As she walked out of the bedroom, she was faced with a dark shadow holding a bright shiny knife. Before she could turn to get away, Simon stepped forward and began stabbing her. Renee looked up at him while he plunged the knife deep into her flesh, stabbing her again and again. With an evil grin of satisfaction on his face, the weirdo from next-door proceeded to claim her life. Renee fell to the floor, as she felt the sharp stabbing sensation from the knife carving through her beautiful flesh. She stared at the satisfaction in her killer's eyes as she bled out all over the bedroom floor. Pulling the sharp blade from her gut, Simon raised it over his head again ready to strike. She asked why he was doing this? As she gasped for air. If I can't have you no one can. With that, he heaved the blade down toward Renee as she awoke in a puddle of ice-cold sweat.

She leaped up, turning on the lights and checking around the room for any sign of her sexually, a perverted intruder. Renee quickly noticed even if Simon's invasion wasn't real, the storm certainly was. She could hear it making a statement outside her window. She looked right at Simon's house imagining this was his fault somehow. How could she have been so stupid to have slept with him? She should 've known a guy like that would take things to the extreme. Now it was too late, and she was being visited in her dreams, not by an angel, but a demon.

Once she convinced herself it was only a dream, Renee abandoned her attempt to search the house and turned on the tv, so she wouldn't feel so alone. It may be nothing more than an animated picture tube? But it helped Renee's mind settle. She needed something cheerful to forget her troubles and eventually passed out watching the Honeymooners. The next morning the storm had passed leaving a bright orange flame burning in the middle of a beautiful blue sky. It was cheerful enough for Renee to rise out of bed and begin her day, but she was unable to completely shake the dream she had the night before. Chilly from the drop -in temperature she put on a red and black flannel and a pair of tight blue jeans. Giving herself a glance in the mirror, Renee moved the hair out of her face and stared into her own beautiful sky-blue eyes. The once carefree hippie wanted to be happy and naïve like before but found she was still reeling from the sudden death of her husband and the guy-next-door who gave her the willies. Before hopping in the shower and properly grooming herself, Renee's first task was to go outside and take down all the Halloween decorations. She didn't want to see anything remotely frightening for another 365 days.

The fresh nightmare was enough to scare her for the rest of the year. Stepping out into the cool autumn air Renee was anxious to finish before Simon noticed her. Why couldn't Stanley send him out on a long job far away? Buying her some time to get things together and move back to the west coast. Never really believing in god, she swore to give him a fighting chance as- long as he rescued her with divine -intervention just this once.

She was hoping Simon was already off to the flower-shop to work for his mother. Since he always parked his shit-brown heap in the garage, there was no telling if he was home or not. With her fingers crossed, Renee began taking down the scary décor she set up not so long ago. She even disposed of the pumpkins, tossing them in the trash, before they start to rot. She was almost finished when she nearly jumped out of her skin from the sudden touch on her left shoulder. Hello Renee. Sorry if I frightened you. I'm also really, sorry for the way I acted when you told me you were moving back to California to be with your friends. I can't say I blame you. If I were in your shoes? I'm sure I would do the same thing. Renee didn't even want to look at him the sound of his voice was like jagged nails on a chalkboard. She decided to play it cool, hoping he would go away. It gave her goosebumps to know he was working for neither of his parents. She wondered how long he might have been keeping an eye on her from inside his house.

Without him noticing, Renee quickly glanced up at Simon's treehouse reminding herself of the mysteries that must lie within its tiny walls. If it was such a special place, why hasn't he invited her up there to check it out? If there was ever a neat way to start a conversation that was it. Knowing how desperate Simon was to keep her attention once he has it, Renee found it odd that he never mentioned the old wooden box hiding up in the trees, every day becoming more noticeable with the dying leaves. Renee told him his reaction was understandable and not to worry about it. Simon thanked her for her generous nature, although he wasn't quite sure she truly forgave him. For now, it would have to do. Mrs. Anderson was watching the two of them from her living room window while enjoying a hot cup of tea.

It reminded her that she wanted to have a little talk with the pretty young girl concerning the very person she was engaged with. Something about him didn't sit right with her either when it came to Simon's behavior ever since Renee moved in next door. Usually, she keeps most of the dirt in the neighborhood to herself, she just liked having the advantage of knowing everyone's deepest secrets. It might just save a life one day. Once Simon was out of sight she was going to walk over there and have a friendly chat with the heartbroken widow.

The two have talked here and there, but mostly a simple hello in the street while getting the mail or doing yardwork. The elderly woman was afraid Simon would be spying on them and become suspicious of their conversation, on the other hand, she felt it was time for something to be said. Mrs. Anderson had been watching Simon watch Renee for a while now. She felt there was something very troubling about it. Renee did her best to remain polite to Simon, but she made it very clear that she would be moving back home where her friends and family were waiting. She crushed Simon's heart even further with her careless words, insisting there was no reason for her to remain in his world. It made him feel as if he was worthless. Renee said it felt strange being there now that the love of her life was no longer with her. I understand why you want to leave, but I don't want to see you go. As you can see, I don't have many friends.

It gets lonely living here with no one to talk to besides my parents. You're the kindest and most beautiful girl I 've ever laid eyes on. I still can't believe you found it in your heart to even say two words to me. Renee was praying Simon wouldn't bring up her worst mistake ever while spewing his true feelings to her, she needed no reminder. It's alright if you never want to again. I'm sure you think I'm strange or something, but I do like you a lot. Renee was waiting for him to start crying right there in front of her. I truly am sorry about Paul. He was a great man, much better than I could ever hope to be. It's just awful what happened to him.

If I were you, I'd probably get the hell away from this place as well. Simon chose his words wisely, careful not to freak her out again. Still, Renee wasn't fooled. She could see the manipulative mind at work, and the jealousy in his eyes as if it were tangible enough to smell and touch. She wasn't fond of her neighbor any longer and couldn't wait to be rid of him for good.

So how far along are you now? Simon questioned causing a strange look to come over Renee's face. As if she was expecting. Simon quickly explained himself better by simply saying I meant packing. Do you still have a lot of packing to do inside? His words instantly reminded Renee of the nightmare she had the night before. She wondered if he had been inside her house while she was sleeping. It seemed like a wacky kind of question to ask her.

Renee began to assume maybe he wanted to know how much longer he would be able to torment her with his perverted presence. He laughed slightly for his innocent mistake. Renee also flashed a smile for his silly words. Deep down it gave her a hollow feeling. She was wishing to get pregnant by her loving husband, now he was gone and that would never happen. Renee told him she would be around for a little while longer.

She confessed she wanted to be back in L A before Thanks -Giving. That gave him a couple of weeks at best before never seeing her again. How on earth was Simon going to convince her to stay behind? He could tell things weren't the same between them. Renee didn't seem to have that same glow around her when they spoke. He was doing his best to keep his warped thoughts to himself as he stood beside Renee on her front lawn.

He could tell she didn't want him there. In some ways, she was used to being annoyed by men she wasn't interested in. It was one of the curses she had to endure for her beauty. Attractive people attract attention, and she was the most beautiful of them all, especially in Simon Fletcher's eyes. Renee was trying to find a good excuse to get away from him. She asked why he wasn't at work? It wasn't like him to run this late. Simon simply told her he demanded to have a day off. He seemed proud of himself as he explained how he finally stood up to his sweet Christian parents. Every time her eyes caught a glimpse of the treehouse high above the ground, she remembered wanting to go investigate when the opportunity presented itself. Simon felt tormented whether they were together or apart. He didn't know which was worse, but he loved nothing more than to see her beautiful face with his own two eyes. Being without her was surely the crueler fate. That's why he had to prevent her from leaving him behind. Once Renee was gone, he would never see her again. He was not going to let her run off with the handsome boy who looks like a girl. Renee felt relieved from the mounting pressure when Simon told her he was just kidding about defeating his mother.

He smirked admitting he had to head over there in a few minutes. Eleanor did allow him to sleep in a little for a change, she was early to rise and wanted to open the flower shop. Renee couldn't be happier when Simon said goodbye for now and turned to fetch his car. It was chilly outside, and she was anxious to get into the house where it's warm. First, she had to lug all the Halloween decorations inside. Renee planned on leaving them near the front-door since she wouldn't be there much longer anyway. As she stacked the boxes in the corner, Renee gave more thought to Simon's treehouse. She needed to have a look inside. She had a feeling there would be something of great interest awaiting her. As Renee came outside to retrieve the last box, she was greeted by Mrs. Anderson. She had the look of urgency on her face, as she crossed the street. She felt safe talking to the young woman now that she was sure Simon had gone. Renee immediately asked the elderly woman what was wrong? Mrs. Anderson wasted no time spilling the beans about Simon always watching her when she doesn't know he's around. It sent a shiver up Renee's spine when she heard it from someone else that Simon Fletcher was completely obsessed with her. Mrs. Anderson explained how she noticed him spying from his treehouse and behind the walls of his parent's home.

He even stared at her from around corners, as she did yard work in skimpy clothing over the summer. It gave Renee the creeps since she was also beginning -to notice what kind of man Simon Fletcher was. The old woman next-door confessed she was worried about Renee's safety and didn't want to wait until it was too late to say something. She felt the pretty young girl deserved a warning. Renee never liked the elderly woman's nosy, behavior. now she was thankful for it. Renee knew she wasn't crazy for thinking suspiciously about the young man next-door. She thanked Mrs. Anderson for letting her know what she discovered about Simon.

They both knew there was no way to convince his parents that he was a major pervert. They were far too invested in their god for such horror to invade their blessed and perfect little lives. I think you should do your best to stay clear of that boy Renee. If you see him try to avoid him. I'm afraid he has it bad for you. Mrs. Anderson was correct, but she hadn't known everything. She didn't know Renee made the fatal mistake of having sex with the troubled maniac. When Renee explained that she was planning to move back to Los Angeles, Mrs. Anderson smiled insisting that it was a wonderful idea, although she didn't want to see her go.

She was also very sorry to hear about what happened to her husband Paul. She made that known by attending the funeral but decided to remind the unfortunate young widow. She knew it was the best way to steer clear of Simon and whatever terrible things he might have in-store for her. Renee told Mrs. Anderson, she appreciated her concern disregarding the fact that the elderly woman was a bit of a stalker herself, keeping a watchful eye on everyone. Mrs. Anderson simply wanted to feel safe among the other human's surrounding her.

She loved god and man, but she didn't always trust her fellow man. In Renee, she saw a kindred spirit, a loving, peaceful soul that deserved the fruits of heaven in the hereafter. She didn't want to live with it on her conscience if god-forbid something happened to Renee. Knowing she was preparing to pick up the pieces almost three thousand miles away, made Mrs. Anderson feel better. She always knew there was something off about the boy across the street. It wasn't hard to see, he was nothing like his parents, there was something dark hiding inside him. It took the beauty queen living next-door to propel it towards the surface.

As Simon headed to the flower shop to give his mother a hand, he listened to the radio. He was turned into a station playing the devil's music, according to his folks. Since Renee listened to it, he imagined that wasn't the least bit true. She was the beauty and he was the beast after-all. As fate would have it the Beatles were playing on the radio. Can't buy me love was being blasted by the love-sick lunatic as he continued forward with sadness and anger confiscating his heart and mind. The message in the song was so true. Money could never buy Renee's love. No matter how much of it, Simon had to offer. He often feared no girl would ever love him. As he approached his mother's flower-shop, Simon turned the radio down. He didn't want to announce that he was intentional, misbehaving god. He knew his mother would be able to hear it clear as day.

She noticed the pathetic look in his eyes the moment he entered the store. His heart began to race, as she asked what was wrong with him. Simon lied swearing he was fine, but Eleanor knew better. She assumed it had something to do with Renee as usual. What's the matter? Thinking about Renee again? Going against everything she believed in, Eleanor suggested he bring her some flowers. All girls love flowers, usually from someone they already love or have an interest in loving. She knew it was a bad idea, but she was desperate to cheer him up.

Simon knew it would never work he could never win her love. It was an impossible task, yet he still adored her with every ounce of his being. The mutilated model image he created convinced him he was on a crash-course with destiny. Simon sadly told his mother there was no point.

Renee would know the flowers didn't even cost him anything, no matter how exotic and expensive they were. Simon also knew in his heart that Renee wanted nothing to do with him. He was going to have to either kill her? Or accept the fact that she was ready to move on with her life without him in it. Falling in love and starting over with her good friend Travis wasn't in the cards, but in Simon's imagination, it was a scientific fact. Losing his cool, Simon raised his voice, blaming his mother and father for his countless failures in life.

If they hadn't sheltered him and treated him like a baby all the time? Things would be different. He wanted to make his hatred known, as he watched Renee slip effortlessly through his fingers. He was desperate to get far away from his smothering parents, pleading his case that he was old enough to move out and live on his own, his mother observed his outburst with worry in her eyes. He wanted to be rid of their strict, religious ways. Simon wanted to live alone in a big fancy house, Renee as his obedient sex-slave whenever he wanted her. He continued to lash-out, blaming his mother for ruining his life. He worked his ass off and was hardly paid.

He called Eleanor out saying it was her way of trapping him under her roof. He was also quick to place blame on his father for going along with the plan. How was he to start a life of his own, when they continued treating him like a child? Eager to abandon his parent's strict rules, Simon wanted to convert to a lifestyle of despicable sins.

A world surrounded by sex and perversion in the most potent form. He imagined Renee being restrained in some sadistic way, so she couldn't escape. Since she refused to be with him willingly, Simon imagined he would simply keep her caged. It was not considered punishment since that's exactly the way his guardians treated him from the day he was born. His mother insisted they had always done what's best for him. Simon didn't see it that way. He always felt they controlled every single aspect of his life.

He 'd grown tired of being the prisoner. It was time to take charge of his worthless life. Simon Fletcher was going to find a way to possess the girl of his destiny. He wanted her more than anything in life and failure wasn't an option. One way or another in his head, Renee Price would be his. Simon would never forget that one chance encounters they experienced drugged out in her living room. He would never stop until he satisfies himself at the expense of her flesh, not just one more time, but for the rest of her life. He planned to capture Renee and keep her alive to full fill his most demented sexual desires. His biggest dilemma was finding a safe place to store her, where his folks wouldn't find out. It was impossible as- long as he lived under their roof. Simon needed someplace desolate enough to mask her screams and desperate cries for help.

He even thought about buying sexy lingerie, so he can dress her the way he wants when in the mood for love. Simon's blood was almost a slushy type of texture running cold and hot through his noxious, veins He was angry, excited and most of all sexually, frustrated. He had Renee once and he would have her again, no matter the consequences.

The memory was so vividly detailed, to the point he imagined it was buried deep enough to follow him into the afterlife. Eleanor was a very patient person, but Simon was now dangling, from her last and final nerve. She was sick and tired of hearing him complain about the wonderfully spoiled life she and her husband had offered him.

He had some nerve throwing their love in her face. She and Stanley did everything they could to bring him upright, turning a blind eye to the devil's temptations and following the righteous path. She told Simon they only wanted what's best for him. His mother could see he wasn't only entirely ungrateful, but a bit mad as well. Why was he in such a hurry to move out and be on his own? That was the most troubling question running through her mind.

She imagined he would be extremely lonely and take his own life. Knowing he never mingled well with the opposite sex, she and her husband doted on him, so he would feel important. They thought they were doing a good job of it and that their misfit son needed them to feel as if he had a purpose. An only child, Simon felt they were the only ones who loved and cared for him. As he continued to scold her, Eleanor was thankful there were no customers in the store at the time. It would look really- bad for business if the town-folk witnessed the family feud taking place. Knowing she may be placing Renee's life in danger, she sent her son home to cool off for a while. She couldn't allow that hostility around her establishment.

That ticked Simon off, he went so far as to threaten he might crash his car off the road and end it all. Eleanor felt her heart moving around in her chest as if it wasn't fixated in one place but bouncing freely around her entire body. The look in her son's eyes was darker than anything she had ever seen before. Something inside him was changing. Eleanor knew Renee had something to do with it, she also understood the pretty blonde did nothing to deserve this. What her son was doing was wrong, he had no business falling in love with the married woman next-door in the first place.

The grip on his obsession was tightening as he wished his mother dead with a menacing, stare, and stormed out of the flower-shop. Enraged as he peeled off, Simon even blasted the rock n roll station, while rolling his windows down so the whole town could hear. Including his mother as she watched with concern from the front window. I Can't Get No Satisfaction from the Rolling Stones was screaming through the otherwise peaceful, silent air. Eleanor felt a growth forming in her gut, as she thought about calling Renee to warn her of her son's aggressive arrival.

She didn't know if he was going to pay her a visit with the same level of hostility. Her only child was coming apart at the seams and there was nothing she could do to stop it. As he drove off like a bat out of hell, Eleanor started thinking about the vacation she and her husband had planned next weekend. She wasn't sure if leaving Simon behind was such a good idea. The way he's been behaving lately, the doting mother felt like he needed her to be around.

She was going to have to discuss it with her husband later that evening and get his opinion on the subject. She was praying that once Renee is gone her son will eventually return to normal. She had no idea how deep, and dark his poisonous, obsession was. Renee was all he could think about. When he finally made it home, he stormed in the house and turned on the television in the living room. He was furious and had to find a way to calm his nerves. If not? Simon feared he might do something he regretted. He wanted to walk next-door and drag Renee out of her house, to claim her. Again, he turned to the news of the Manson Murders to take his mind off, of Renee. Even if only for a little bit. She was always in his mind's eye. Usually naked or wearing something she would never offer in real life. Not since he realized he was a complete basket case. Simon didn't know about the friendly little chat Mrs. Anderson had with her earlier that day. It was sure to create even more distance between them until she is on the road back to California. Simon sat there wondering how many more times he would see her before she is gone forever.

She seemed to be avoiding him as much as possible, and he knew exactly why. Later that evening when his parents returned from work and got dinner ready, they all sat around the table, holding hands as Stanley gave thanks to the lord. The last supper painting watching over them. Simon sat there with a blank expression on his face. He hardly ate anything, as his parents struggled for a solution to their son's problem. They didn't know how to fix a broken, heart. Not when it's as damaged as Simon's was. The thing they couldn't understand was why he was so in love with a girl that didn't belong to him. They were unaware of the fact, the two shared a sexual encounter.

They imagined he was still a virgin. That missing information would surely add substance to why he was losing his mind over Renee moving back across the country. He felt like god brought her here only to torment him. There was nothing his folks could do or say to lift his spirits. They would have to let the hornet's nest of emotions run its course. A few hours later Eleanor and Stanley were lying in bed, watching some colorful preacher speaking about the end of days and the second coming of Christ. Eleanor thought it was a good time to talk to her husband about their upcoming getaway. Ever since Simon was born, they doted on him.

All the vacations throughout his childhood had been kid-friendly places. They lived to make their only son happy. Now that he was an adult, they felt it was time for them to live for themselves. At least just a little. The loving and nurturing parents didn't care how long Simon lived with them? They just needed some time to share as a couple. Romance had dwindled from their relationship since parenthood took the driver's seat. Going to Bermuda together was exactly what they needed and deserved after raising their special boy. Stanley understood where his wife was coming from, he was also concerned about his son's increasingly negative behavior.

He turned to Eleanor and told her he didn't want to go if she wasn't going to enjoy it. What would be the point? He reached out for her hand and held it softly. Stanley lowered the volume on the television as they continued their discussion. As Stanley agreed to cancel the trip and stay with Simon who needed them, Eleanor began having a change of heart. She told Stanley he was a big boy and maybe he was right about the way they 've been treating him? Maybe they did shelter him too much? We deserve this vacation and he is going to have to accept it. Eleanor even wondered if that was the reason, he was throwing this hissy-fit. Perhaps he was jealous of them going away without him. Stanley let go of his wife's hand and placed it around her waist squeezing her tight. You're right, sweetheart. Let's go enjoy ourselves and when we return, we will do something wonderful for Simon to cheer him up.

Maybe even a nice new car? Eleanor smiled at her husband as she could see the love and compassion dancing in his eyes. She thought it was a great idea. They both realized it would come in the form of an apology for leaving him behind in his darkest hour. Hard as it is to admit, Simon's a man now Eleanor. He can survive for a week by himself. He has, to run the flower shop every day, which should keep him busy until we return. Simon hates working there, you and I both know it. He would much rather be in the field with your crew.

As you said, he's a man, being around flowers and lovebirds all day must be awful for him? As she spoke, Eleanor began to realize how badly she had been punishing her son. Unfortunately, Stanley was right though, someone would have to mind the store while she was away. She considered paying Renee for a couple of days, but she knew the young widow was in a hurry to get out of town. Eleanor also knew her son would probably hang around all day driving the pretty girl nuts.

Agreeing to go-forth with the plans for a getaway, the loving couple kissed goodnight and the conflict was settled. What they didn't know was that Simon wasn't in the least sad or angry about them leaving him behind for a week. It was a dream come true. He would have the entire house to himself and all the freedom he could stand. Simon couldn't wait for them to leave.

He imagined doing whatever he wanted, with no one to stop him. The timing couldn't be better. With no supervision, he could certainly find a way to prevent Renee from ever leaving him. A diabolical plan was forming, and it was heading straight for Renee Falls. His insatiable appetite was growing inside, how long before it surfaced and operated his every function?

One good thing about having a misfit son was no threat of wild parties taking place while they were away. Who would poor Simon invite? Besides they knew Mrs. Anderson was around the clock surveillance. Sometimes seeing things, she wished she hadn't, especially Fletcher's creepy son stalking another neighbor. Stanley didn't trust Simon to be completely alone for an entire week. He told Eleanor he would see to it that Father Fitzpatrick stops in every so often unannounced. Simply to check on Simon and his mental state. Eleanor agreed, she also imagined calling him often to talk on the phone.

She prayed the threat of the priest showing up would detour him from doing anything he might later regret. Neither of them considered the fact they were placing Renee's life in the line of fire by leaving their mentally disabled son behind. Or maybe it was just well hidden? Buried deep in the depths of their minds where they dare not venture. The truth was just to bone-chilling to accept. The god, fearing parents simply couldn't fathom their child being capable of harming or even killing another human being.

Over the next few days, Eleanor gave Simon a much -needed break from the flower shop. Since he would be trapped there all next week, she decided to run the store, open to close. She would sculpt statues when no one was around. The holidays were fast approaching, and she counted on the followers of her god to come out and spend their money on the angelic pieces. She saw this as the perfect time to get a head-start. Simon was happy to be working with his father's men on a local job right in the heart of Renee Falls. They were going to be busy putting up another strip mall in town. It made everyone in Renee Falls feel as though they were slowly, spilling into the world at large.

They enjoyed the quietness, but wouldn't mind more places to shop, especially the women. For Stanley, it was a paycheck for his men and most importantly his family. More people more money he imagined, although he and his wife were not greedy for cash. Sitting, quite comfortable, they imagined more work was good for others trying to make their way through the game of life. As the days passed on Renee didn't see much of Simon.

He was leaving early in the morning and returning long after dark. It was a relief to her, but a punishment for Simon. She could be leaving any day now, and he couldn't catch a single glimpse of her. Renee had been keeping her place practically boarded up, especially after speaking to Mrs. Anderson. It made Renee's blood run cold as she imagined him standing there watching her. Before leaving town, she was going to have a look around that treehouse. She had to know what was inside. She knew she would be placing her life in grave danger, but she didn't care.

Every time she saw it, the wooden structure up in the trees gave her an eerie, feeling. The still-grieving widow continued getting phone calls from her good friends back in California. They kept promising the grandest party ever to be thrown by the man when she returned. It was going to have more drugs and sex than wood-stock. Renee couldn't wait to get back home, especially as November continued to settle in, making itself comfortable. The west coast hippie girl was getting her first taste of a frigid winter on the way.

Now she had to bundle up whenever she left the house. At least she had a jeep to get around in when the snow finally falls. She was glad to know she would be long gone before the real chill of old man winter arrived. She would soon be back in sunny California surrounded by great friends and fond memories.

CHAPTER 11

+ + + + + +

A few nights later Renee was in the middle of watching television when she noticed it was snowing outside, the strong wind whistling passed as her eyes lit up and a smile streaked across her face. As much as she was dreading the cold weather, Renee was extremely happy to see snow for the first time. She grabbed her coat and went outside for a smoke and some cold fresh air.

She wanted to get a better look at the snow as it fell majestically from the sky. Renee wanted to taste it on her tongue and feel it on her skin. Her attention was soon drawn to the red roses resting ominously on her front porch. It was not a first-time. She quickly turned to look at Simon's house next-door, knowing they were from him as if the two of them were in love. It was starting to freak her out. Renee wondered if his mother knew he was stealing all those red roses, only to contribute to filling her garbage can? She kept telling herself she would be gone soon. She would never have to see Simon Fletcher again. The poor widow was still struggling to forgive herself for cheating on Paul. It weighed even heavier on her mind since he tragically passed away soon after.

She would never get the chance to see him again or say she was sorry for her behavior. Renee stayed on the porch, close to the front door, wanting to be ready to dart back inside, should Simon appear and try to dwell sinisterly in her presence. She was hoping to get out of there without ever seeing him again. Renee wanted to warn his parents about the strange behavior he was displaying. She knew they would be going on vacation in a few days, leaving their crazy son behind. She wanted to be gone before they departed. Renee didn't know how Simon would behave when his folks weren't around to keep an eye on him. Standing on the porch as the cold wet snow slowly covered her, Renee was growing more afraid of her peeping, obsessed neighbor.

The storm made it even more terrifying as she did her best to ignore her increasing fears. She finished her cigarette and turned to go back inside. Now that it was coming down, Renee had no interest in watching the show she had on. Instead, she fixed herself a drink and watched the storm outside. It seemed strange to receive snow so early, but Renee wasn't from around here and didn't know the weather in Jersey can be just as unstable as some of its inhabitants.

It felt so cozy, but she was wishing Paul was there to share the moment with her, she still missed him terribly and imagined she would never get over his death. Renee thought about picking up the phone and calling her best-friend Travis but didn't want to burden him with her stupid problems. She chose instead to suffer in silence. Ready for another round, Renee made it to the kitchen for a re-fill. She felt a little on edge as if Simon was going to come crashing through the door any second. She made a pit stop on the way back to the chair near the window to say hello to Lennon who didn't seem to care that she was acknowledging him.

He looked hungry. Renee was going to have to venture to the store soon to get him some grub. She hated feeding the snake. It was the one reason she didn't want Paul to own one. Feeding it live mice and even rabbits seemed wrong, not to mention disgusting. Renee found them to be adorable and more soothing for pets than the long serpent that fed on them. She wanted to exchange Lennon at the store and bring home something that would offer more companionship now that Paul was gone. If she was going to get a dog or a cat? Renee would rather wait until she's back across the country. It was a long ride to deal with an energetic animal that goes to the bathroom often.

As much as Renee wanted to, she could never get rid of Paul's snake. That was his obnoxious pet and she refused to part with it. That meant she would have to continue doing the dirty work now that he's gone. Sipping her vodka and orange juice, she left Lennon behind and went back to looking out at the storm. Renee decided to pass the time the same way she always had. Listening to music as she drank her way toward a buzz and stared out at the first snow, storm she has ever experienced. On the radio, there was a song playing from mama's and Papa's. California dreaming on such a winters day was exactly what Renee was doing at -the moment. She felt it was the appropriate song to be playing right now. Almost as if the d j was sending it out to her unintentionally. The song brought back memories of her and Paul when they were still together and naively blissful. Completely unaware of the cruel fate their story had in store for them.

She continued sipping her drink and daydreaming of better times while the song played on. Renee was experiencing flashbacks from a joyous past. The warm sun beating on her face, while locking eyes with her only soulmate. It was as if their entire relationship flashed before her eyes as she listened to the song play and reminisced of a perfect life cut tragically short for no reason at all. The beautiful-falling snow was almost breath-taking, and as she sipped her booze Renee wondered how people could remain so devoted to god when life is so, cruel and unfair. She began wishing they never left the west coast.

Perhaps her husband would still be alive? Simon was used to snow and the storm outside did little to piqued, his interest or draw his attention from the task at hand. He was giving a lot of thought to the fact his folks won't be around to supervise him for a whole week. The realization it was happening so close to Renee's departure back to the city of angels seemed to perfect to believe, yet it was happening. He hadn't spoken to Renee and had no idea when she would be stepping out of the front door for the last time. He assumed she wanted nothing to do with the red roses he had been leaving her. She hadn't made any attempts to swing by and thank him for his romantic gesture.

He should 've known she would freak out if he acted this way. As he sat in his room thinking about her running back to Travis on the opposite side of the country, Simon constructed one of his most disturbing portraits of them all. It was a picture of Renee being brutally strangled, by his very own hands, squeezing tightly around her throat. Renee's eyes were bulging out of her head, as she fought for her life in a still portrait. It was so realistic it almost gave Simon the creeps. He had to make sure no one ever found the troubling image, especially Renee herself. He was compelled to keep the picture since he worked so hard on it, and because it took on a life all its own. It was difficult for Simon to take his eyes off of her.

He feared the chilling image might come to life if he loses his temper while in Renee's presence. How would he explain that to his folks? It seemed the only solution to prevent her from running away. As the days ticked down to Stanley and Eleanor's vacation. Renee couldn't help fearing Simon would do something crazy while they were away. She felt there was nobody to protect her, should he decide to put his ghoulish plans into action.

Living alone was not something Renee felt comfortable with, especially so far from home with an obsessed maniac living just feet away. Paul might have been on the road often, but he was there most of the time to protect her, now she felt completely vulnerable to the dangers of the word. By Thursday, Renee was really on edge, knowing the Fletcher's would be heading out of town the next morning. They wouldn't be back for an entire week. Renee was angry with herself for not getting the hell out of there before her stalker is left all alone to do as he wishes with his free time. The frightened young woman planned to make sure the house was sealed up tighter than ever.

After that disturbing dream she suffered recently, Renee even made sure to lock the basement doors leading to the world outside, although she hadn't been down there since the day, they moved in. It was a dark and harrowing abyss. The dungeon looking cellar was the last place Renee wanted to be. She just needed a few more days to get everything packed and ready then she was going to take what she needed and hit the road, leaving Simon to believe he still had a few more weeks with her. She would have a moving truck pick up the rest of her belongings and meet her in California once she finds a new place of her own. Renee began to stress how she would pay the bills, now that Paul was dead.

He was responsible for bringing home the paychecks, she was going to have to find work as soon as she gets back to L. A. Renee was thankful, she had friends who cared about her and were not only willing but anxious to take her in. Just a few more days she continued repeating to herself. It did little to make her feel better. She knew after tonight she would feel completely alone. Who was going to protect her from the monster when his guardians were out of town? As the hours slowly ticked by, Renee struggled to fall asleep. Like so many nights before, she was watching repeats of the honeymooners. Hard as she tried? Renee couldn't seem to set her mind at ease. It was a clear and chilly night, but Renee felt in need of some air.

She was also wondering what her creepy neighbor was up to. Dressing for the brief adventure onto the front-porch, Renee threw on a warm jacket. She just wanted a quick smoke and a breath of fresh air to counteract the poison being self-distributed into her lungs. Once she made it outside the cool autumn air smacked her in the face like an open hand lying in wait. Lighting the cigarette and doing her best to keep warm, Renee once again turned her attention to the foreboding treehouse, she was going to have a look around, before leaving this strange little place forever. It was almost midnight, and Renee wondered if this was the perfect time to be sneaking into Fletcher's back yard in search of god knows what, it might be the only chance she has.

The next morning Eleanor and Stanley were leaving for a romantic getaway in paradise. She was happy for the two of them, the son they left behind was a different story. She feared how he would react to being left all alone. Having Mrs. Anderson across the street did little to make her feel safe. She needed a man, or at the very least a dog to protect her from monsters in human form. The old wooden house built up in the trees had an ominous vibe about it even during the day, but it was much more sinister after dark. Renee was getting goosebumps under her thick sleeves just looking at it. She feared this to be her last opportunity to go rummaging through the four-eyed weirdo's secret belongings.

Once his folks were gone, she would have to pray he went to work at the flower shop and stayed there for as many hours as possible. If he decided to come home for some strange reason while she was inside? Renee feared it would be the death of her. Standing on the porch, hurrying to finish her cigarette, Renee wanted to get back in the house and out of Simon Fletcher's sight. She stood frozen as the garage door opened and Simon's Volkswagen appeared like the grim reaper's chariot awaiting her demise. He turned right and floored it so quickly, Renee wasn't even sure if he noticed her standing there or not? As he flew by a piece of paper was spotted blowing by in the wind. Renee got this unsettling feeling in her gut, about what it might say. Now that Simon was gone, Renee saw her chance to sneak into his treehouse and expose him for whatever the fuck he was? She was still ignorant of his complete depravity. Renee wanted to run out into the street and retrieve the litter, she had to make certain, Simon was out of sight. She didn't want to be caught snatching the paper he tossed in front of her house. Renee's curiosity was eating away at her as she stared at the wrinkled-up piece of paper. She wondered what in the world it might say.

Once she was confident Simon wasn't in a hurry to return, Renee hurried into the street to retrieve the piece of paper he tossed out the window, as he sped by. She assumed it was meant for her and was nervous to see what was written on it. When she opened it up, Renee quickly discovered it was a suicide letter. Simon Fletcher was threatening to kill himself. The way he sped off into the night, Renee had no reason to doubt him. He swore that he was going to crash his car into a tree at high speed, eerily similar, to her husband, Paul, in- an attempt to kill himself instantly. Renee wasn't sure if he would go through with it? Or if he was just trying to get her full undivided, attention morbidly? She was shaking and unsure of what to do with this crucial knowledge. Renee thought about running next-door and warning his parents, she knew they were scheduled to leave early the next morning and that they would be sleeping. She didn't want to wake them but imagined what it would be like landing and getting the terrible news that their son had taken his own life.

Struggling with the angel and devil on her shoulders, she listened to them both whispering in her ears. Renee wasn't fond of her four-eyed stalker, but she didn't want to be responsible for his death. Then she began thinking about him waiting until the exact moment she was standing on the porch having a smoke to drive away and toss the paper virtually at her feet. He wanted her to find and read his shameful and desperate cry for help. The skin-crawling question was how he knew she would be outside at that very moment? Renee assumed he must have been watching her house for countless hours. Waiting for the right moment to strike. She remembered the dangers of his folks leaving the next day, feeling her life was still in danger, Renee thought about the treehouse in the backyard. She paid closer attention to the devil in her ear as he convinced her to go exploring.

It was indeed the perfect opportunity, the one she had been waiting for. Renee also felt it was her last chance to expose the troubled young man living next-door for what he truly is. She was planning to be long gone before the Fletcher's returned from their much, needed vacation. Renee also realized if he truly was hell-bent on destroying himself, his parents would receive the terrible news early the following morning. Just like she did when her loving husband tragically passed away without warning.

Turning her attention back to the sinister-looking treehouse, Renee got a bad feeling in the pit of her stomach. Her biggest fear was Simon returning and catching her red-handed. What if he wasn't going to kill himself? What if this was a precisely calculated plot to snare the woman he loves into a deadly trap? For Renee, it was worth the risk, besides she imagined she would see him coming down the road, from high up in the treehouse. She would have to take that chance if she wanted to learn the dark, truth he was withholding from everyone.

As she stood there shivering slightly from the cold, Renee finished her cigarette and contemplated whether, or not she should sneak into her neighbor's hideaway and have a look around. Her heart was racing with adrenaline and fear. She didn't want Simon to catch her going through his most personal things. Renee frightfully, imagined he would murder her if she knew his darkest secrets. Once the cig was finished, she threw it in the small bucket she used as an ashtray and turned her attention in the direction Simon drove off in. Renee did her best to convince herself this was the right thing to do. There was no sign of Simon or any other cars coming down the quiet street. Renee couldn't help feeling like he was parked nearby watching her every move, despite the fact it was all in her head. Simon was still speeding in the opposite direction on his date with death.

Renee quickly and quietly headed to Fletcher's home. She was simply going to walk through the fence door and climb into his disturbing house of sinful mysteries. She kept an eye on her surroundings as she made her way onto their property, waiting for the lights to turn on inside the house, letting her know someone was awake. So far, everything remained dark, and there was no sign of Simon anywhere. Renee walked cautiously to the four-walled loony bins up in the nearby trees.

As she approached it and started climbing the stairs, Renee could feel the fear intensifying throughout her body. She didn't know what she would find. Or how twisted her stalker would turn out to be? Unless she explored forbidden territory. Slowly making her way up the steps, Renee could see a great distance, in case Simon decided to return. Now that she found herself standing outside the treehouse door, Renee hesitated for a second or two. The night appeared to be dark and silent, as she took a much- needed a deep breath and entered Simon's house of sins. She didn't feel safe even though she had high grounds. Once inside Renee realized it didn't seem like the secret-lair of some sex-crazed maniac. She was expecting to find dirty pictures hung all over the interior of the grown man's treehouse. Instead, the only thing she found naked were the walls surrounding her. There was a lazy, boy chair with an area-rug below it.

The old, beaten up cloth had a fading portrait of Jesus displayed on it. Renee also noticed a box in the corner, but as she started looking through it, she realized it was nothing more than his art-supplies. It seemed logical since he was an artist, and that seemed to be his favorite workplace. Renee was a little surprised to find the small room so ordinary at first.

Then she realized he wouldn't be foolish enough to leave his dirty work lying around for all to see. Scratching her head, she began to wonder where his secret stash of perverted artifacts could be? With nothing in plain-sight, Renee took a moment to look out the window leading to her bedroom upstairs. It was the perfect place to spy on her when she wasn't paying attention. Being there made Renee feel violated and foolish for allowing him to watch her in secret for so long. It appears a carefree lifestyle was about to catch up with the gorgeous young hippie.

As she continued staring out the window of Simon's treehouse, the suicidal young man continued barreling through town to end his own life. It seems he was desperate to even the score with his parents, choosing to take his own life on the night before they were scheduled to go away together. It was a selfish and spiteful move, but Simon only cared about himself. He wanted to die and put an end to this unlimited source of misery. His life felt worthless, consumed by heartache and pain. He simply didn't want to deal with it anymore.

He knew Renee was leaving soon and that he would never see her again. She was unlike any other girl he's, ever met and it would be utterly impossible to get over her. Simon feared death was the only way to bring peace to his tormented and crumbling mind. He started thinking about the morbid collection of art he had hidden in the floor beneath the torn-up area rug in the treehouse. He wondered if it was a safe enough hiding place. Once he's dead and gone, all his dark pieces would be vulnerable to discovery.

He couldn't imagine what his religious folks would think of him if they happened upon his unholy stash. He began considering- the fact that he was too young to die. Renee was still living next door to him for a little while longer. He still had time to figure out a way to prevent her from leaving him behind. Simon knew once his parents were gone there would be no stopping him. He feared in the back of his mind, that if he didn't go through with his pathetic plans to off himself, eventually it would lead to the death of the woman he swore to love above all else in this world

. It was the only way to prevent her from moving on without him. With his brain racing a million miles an hour, Simon slammed on the brakes in the middle of the road and turned the car around to head home. He decided not to end his tragic story just yet. Renee unaware of his change of heart, sat in the chair in the middle of the treehouse. She was trying to figure out where he could be hiding his secret world? That's when she turned her attention to the area rug below her. The religious old piece of fabric. appeared to have seen better days. Renee couldn't help but wonder if there was a secret door beneath the old shaggy looking rug. She quickly hopped out of the chair and moved it aside, so she could have a look under there. Renee didn't know if she was prepared for what she was about to see. She looked down at the small area rug anxious to know what? If anything was hiding below it. Before lifting the filthy old, worn-out rug, Renee looked around to make sure no one was coming.

Luckily there was no sign of anyone. She had no idea Simon had changed his mind and was heading right toward her. She felt the urge to light up a cigarette but imagined it added insult to injury, after breaking an, entering in-search of his darkest secrets. Instead, she got on with it bending down and rolling the tiny carpet into a jointly shaped time-loop of filthy fabric. Low and behold-there was what looked like a trapdoor of some sort just waiting to be revealed. Renee smiled brightly as the most, fearsome of fears began to overcome her.

Simon had the radio blasting as he sped home consoled by the reality that he would finally be left alone with Renee, to do as he wished. When no one was watching, he would make his move pushing his way into Renee's house, shoving her to the floor, binding her, and eventually reliving his fantasy of having sex with his princess all over again. It was the only inspiration he had left to go on. He was going to spare himself and take his love life instead. Simon wasn't entirely sure if he could go through with it? Nor did he know if he would be able to live with himself after the dirty deed was done? He started zoning out to the music of The Rolling Stones. He couldn't get any satisfaction either. Simon imagined he knew just how Mick Jagger was feeling.

The music further inspired him to take what was his. Simon couldn't wait for his folks to leave the next morning. He had enormous plans, ahead. He needed to work up the nerve to claim the life of his beauty if he wanted to be with her always. The only problem with his plan was that he could only be with his love in death. On the positive side, if Renee decided to have him one last time before moving back to the city of angels where she belonged with handsome young Travis? Perhaps he could spare her life? Allowing Renee to leave with a thimble of satisfaction somewhere slowly dissolving within his puny lifespan that he, sort of succeeded. Simon headed toward home with deadly intentions on his mind. The angel of good had been cast-out in the name of jealousy and the need to fulfill his insatiable sexual desires. Only the fallen ones could have his ear from now until the end.

They effortlessly whispered the words of death and ecstasy. He began to lose some of his better judgment as blood abandoned one head for the other at an alarming rate. Leaving the soft-tissue numb-skull without a brain in charge. He was basing his decisions on the little head with no real comprehension to speak of. Simon pressed on with a hideous grin upon his face. He couldn't wait until it was time for his sinister plan to spring into action. Back at the treehouse, Renee was in the middle of lifting the lid to have a look inside. She was fully prepared to expose him for the monster he truly was. She just had to hurry before Simon returned from his failed suicide attempt. Having one last peek around the neighborhood, she removed the lid and found a large wooden box within its narrow walls. She was afraid, yet extremely curious to open it up and have a look inside. The first thing she noticed when she opened the mystery-box was a pair of expensive, binoculars. It sent a chill up her spine, but there was far worst to come. Renee imagined he used those as an extension of his already poor vision to spy on her when she wasn't paying attention.

Knowing how many times she walked around the house practically nude, she assumed he must have been watching her from the very beginning. It was, creepy, making Renee feel kind of dirty about the whole thing. She wasn't very surprised by the alarming discovery. She imagined he would possess such a tool, being the- pervert he was? After speaking to Mrs. Anderson, Renee was even more convinced he was dangerous. She was afraid of his behavior once his folks boarded the airplane the next morning. Nervously, she placed the binoculars down on the floor and proceeded to go through Simon's things. There was a thin piece of wood beneath the binoculars, concealing even darker secrets below It was Simon's last attempt at preventing the world from discovering his true nature. It did nothing to fool Renee. She knew there had to be more than just eye-equipment stashed in his sacred-temple.

When she lifted the final veil, everything she wanted to know about her stalker was displayed in plain sight. Shining her flashlight into the shallow abyss Renee wondered what she might find, inside the hideous treasure-trove she discovered in the treehouse of a madman. She quickly found herself upon much darker drawings. She saw strenuous detail encoded in these elaborate depictions of Jesus being crucified in hell, while demons poke and carve at his burning flesh with pitchforks and swords. They looked like they should be displayed inside some demonic church. Angels were falling from burning skies, while the virgin Mary gave birth to a snake-like creature. The images were repulsive and started shaking slightly in her nervous hands. These pictures were nothing like the ones hanging around the house for all to see. They were the secret portraits, displaying who the real Simon Fletcher was. It was urgent, she gets out of Renee Falls immediately.

The scrawny four-eyed neighbor was severely demented and now she had proof. Renee took a moment to have a look around, making sure it was safe to carry on. Disturbing as it was, she had to keep digging, unaware that Simon was racing toward her. She couldn't comprehend why anyone would want to create these horrific images. Simon Fletcher was a monster hiding among the god, fearing residents of this perfect little town. Renee wanted to expose him, before leaving for good, afraid of what he might do someday. Rummaging through the rest of his macabre works of art, the terrified young hippie, came across an ancient Goddess being torn to shreds inside a cave, by a tall muscular lizard man, not of this world.

There was agony on her face, as blood dripped down her breast. Renee found it eerie that the creature's eyes possessed this penetrating ability that somehow saw through to her soul, she wondered how he could get any more vulgar than the paintings she has already discovered until she came upon pictures of herself and her husband Paul. They were gruesome depictions of Simon Chasing her down with an evil smirk on his face. She saw herself naked and covered in blood, running down a dark road. Her- dead husband, chopped up and laying at her feet. She began shaking and frantically looking around as she kept the flashlight facing the ground, careful not to give up her position.

There was no sign of Simon or anyone else for that matter, but soon his headlights would be visible as he approached the neighborhood. She best is gone by the time Simon arrives. He was doing his best to summon the courage he needed to commit the hideous murder. He didn't know his victim was already waiting for him inside his house of sins. If he catches her there? It will be another visible sign that this is the fate he was destined for. One picture from Simon's morbid collection made the hair on the back of Renee's neck stand up. It was a troubling image of her attacker's hands placed firmly around her throat. It -appeared as though he was choking the life out of her.

The terror in her eyes was so realistic, it was almost as if Renee was witnessing her death. It was beyond chilling and seemed as if the deranged artist took great delight in its sadistic construction. Renee didn't want to look at it anymore, yet she was compelled to do so. For some unexplainable reason, she couldn't look away. It was fascinatingly horrifying. It felt as though the picture was alive and could feel her killer's wrath. Simon's headlights were about to become visible from the treehouse, if in fact, Renee remembered to look out for them.

After going through all the alarming pictures Simon had drawn of Renee and her dead husband, she realized how potent and deadly his obsession was. Renee was terrified and felt she needed to get out of there. If Simon had taken his own life? The police were going to find him sooner than later. They will be informing his parents, waking them from their sleep, and preventing her from leaving without being noticed. She knew it was time to go, but as she was about to start putting everything back where she found it, the frightened young girl noticed there was a very- unique and disturbing image at the bottom of the Devil's graveyard nestled up in an innocuous treehouse. Renee stared at the bizarre picture of a beautiful woman, unlike all the rest. It lacked violence, even though a combination of body parts were pasted together to create it.

She noticed how Simon Fletcher methodically sliced up women from dirty magazines to create this spine, tingling version of the perfect female. As she looked closer, Renee realized the crudely constructed woman looking back at her was a repulsive attempt at recreating her. She assumed he designed the hideous image after meeting her, but when Renee observed how aged the paper was, she knew they all came from magazines dating back before they even met. Renee fearfully began to imagine Simon Fletcher was some sort of prophet or future visionary. How else could he know exactly what she looked like? It was utter, madness. Renee was convinced her strange neighbor somehow knew of her coming before she arrived.

It sent crawling sensations creeping under her skin. She just wanted to hurry and get out of there. Taking a good look at the monstrous version of herself sculpted by Satan's hand, Renee noticed a dim light briefly illuminating nearby, in a panic she quickly got to work placing everything back in the box the way she found it. She wanted to cover her tracks, so Simoon would never know she was there. Renee moved as quickly as she could, so did Simon who was coming around the corner at that very moment. Simon angrily got out of his car and made a beeline dash for the treehouse. Renee would never get that fused version of herself cut from other women out of her head. She did her best to clean the mess in a panicked hurry, placing the thin board of wood down with the binoculars on top of it. She then covered it with the dingy area-rug and slid the chair back in place

. As she turned off the flashlight and headed down the stairs, Renee was frozen by the sight of Simon standing there at the bottom looking up at her. Her heart was beating so fast she feared it was going to break free from its restraints and leap out of her mouth. There was no place to go. Simon had the look of evil in his eyes as if he was possessed, racing up the stairs toward her. Renee looked at him with terror on her face, while backing up slowly.

The same kind of terror he vividly captured in his portraits. Simon almost felt as if he finally brought them to life. As he glanced over at the chair Renee knew what her attacker was getting at. He wanted to know if she found his secret hiding place. You, sick bastard. I know what you are. I'm going to tell your parents what a monster they have for a son. I'm going to tell the world about you, Simon Fletcher. You saw my drawings, Simon questioned with sweat beading up on his forehead and veins bulging from his neck, as he stepped forward. I can't imagine what you think of me now, he said as he came at Renee pinning her up against the wall. Don't you see Renee? I knew you were my destiny before we even met. I especially like the work I did on that hairy, dirtbag husband of yours. I prayed day and night, that the lord would remove him from this paradise of ours. I had almost lost my faith in god completely until I saw the police at your house that morning. That's when I knew my prayers had been answered. Renee was frozen stiff.

Too scared to move or even say anything, she just stared into his volcanic eyes as hellish eruptions took place deep within. Now you're here with me, in my holy temple. Can't you see Renee? You're my destiny. Renee finally regaining control of her body was able to speak. She threatened to scream as loud as she can to wake up the neighborhood if he doesn't take a step back and allow her to leave. I can never let you leave Renee. Didn't you hear what I just said? You're my destiny. Simon wrapped his hands around her throat and started squeezing, but not enough to kill her. He just wanted to shut her up. Renee realized she was going to die exactly, the same way Simon depicted in his hair, raising portrait. She started kicking and fighting for her life as a flash, backs of herself, and Paul came flooding back into her current memory. She imagined it was her brain trying to calm itself and prepare for the end. I can't let you go. You're the love of my life, and you were going to just leave me behind like a piece of trash. When I first saw you, I knew all my prayers would eventually be answered.

Then you gave yourself to me, that was the greatest moment of my life, even though things ended kind of poorly, due to you drugging me. Don't worry Renee, I think that's really, sexy. I mean I would have done the same to you if given the chance. You're the hottest girl I've ever seen Renee, a matter of fact why, don't you take off that jacket for me, at least for starters? Please, Simon, it's freezing out here, just let me go home. With a certain coldness in his eyes, he demanded that she shows off that ravishing body. I will keep you warm Renee, just remove your jacket before I tear it off you. Lord knows what else I might sink my teeth into during my ravines attack. With oxygen clouds spilling during every breath, Renee did what she was told, slowly removing her jacket subjecting herself to the unfamiliar chill of northeast autumn. Simon let go of her throat and in the most, slimiest of ways wrapped himself around Renee to keep her warm.

Even if it was a thousand degrees, she would still have the chills in his presence. He could see she was afraid of him and admitted to himself that he kind of liked it. For the first time, he had real, power over her, while dangerously wondering how she could betray him like that, breaking into his holiest place and invading his most private things. Simon felt there was no choice left, but to kill her now. First, he wanted to feel her warm insides, before they slowly turned cold. Chilly as it was Simon wanted Renee to remove far more clothing, than just her jacket, so he could see her flawless body, as he fucked her one last time.

The angelic bird was in his nest, just like the vision he had when his mind was controlled by higher forces and feathered angels chased him out of his godly, dwelling. Simon watched carefully and thrived on Renee's fear. He knew if he let her go now, she would tell everyone about his horrific collection of sinful trophies. What would the town think of him then? Simon didn't want to be remembered as a sexual predator or a perverted stalker. Death was the only way he could safely silence her forever. More importantly, he could never allow her to run off with Travis and live happily-ever-after. Simon stared into her frantic eyes as he reached for her soft, trembling flesh and squeezed it tightly with his bony hands. It was the most gorgeous flesh ever stretched over muscle and bone. For the first time, he felt like more than a man.

He had the same power over life and death as the god everyone prayed to. It made his blood pressure soar with excitement. Now he would be in control of how much time they spend together, and even how they spent it. So many things were racing through the young, maniacs head as he placed his hands around Renee's throat again and started squeezing hard enough to control her, but not enough to completely asphyxiate his victim. Renee continued to struggle with false- hopes of being set free, as Simon told her he wanted her to be with him always. She was gasping as Simon forcefully, pinned her to the wall, using his legs to push hers open. Too terrified to fight back, Renee complied with his grotesque demands. Simon stared into her eyes while removing one hand from her throat to take off his bottoms, expecting his beauty queen to do the same.

He kicked them over toward her jacket, before lowering his eyes, signifying his demand without saying a word. No. Renee fought to say choking and sweating in the cold. You drugged and raped me once, now it's my turn bitch. Simon punched her in the face, hard as he could, knocking her to the ground, dazed and confused. He immediately pounced on his gorgeous and distraught victim and started tearing off her clothes so he could have sex with Renee against her will. Simon placed one finger over his lips warning his princess to keep quiet or he would kill her for sure. Wearing nothing but her pants around her ankles, Renee kicked Simon in the face, trying to get him away. It was enough to toss him clear across the tiny confines but angered him even more.

This was the way destiny ended her story and soon she would be in heaven with her dead and mangled husband. Renee rushed to her feet and tried to get away, but it was hopeless, she could easily trip and fall down the entire flight, leaving a broken and battered corpse in Simon's backyard. He charged at her, smashing Renee into the tree wall. You're fucking crazy, Renee Hollard for the whole world to hear, praying it would keep the madman at bay. Simon momentarily found himself distracted by her sexy body. He so vividly remembered what it felt like to be inside her and he wanted nothing more than to feel it again. In a fit of rage, Simon wrapped his hands around Renee's throat again and brought her to the floor. He placed himself inside her as she struggled and squirmed to getaway. The fear in her eyes turned him on, even more, knowing he was finally the one in control. All, of his life Simon felt his folks were in the driver's seat.

For the first time, he felt like a man. He never felt so alive before. Renee could feel her attacker penetrating her like a wild animal, while slowly strangling her to death. Simon stared into those wondrous blue eyes while having his way with his princess. The terror in them was glorious to the madman, as her soul fought relentlessly to remain inside the body. He warned Renee to shut her pretty little mouth, as she did her best to cry out with the limited amount of air she had left. Simon started smashing the back of her head on the floor to quiet his dying victim, but then he remembered he didn't want to leave a bloody and damaged corpse. Simon planned on keeping his gorgeous queen after death so he could still enjoy her flesh.

A clean kill was best, saving him from cleaning a gruesome mess. It was a terrible way to die, but Simon lacked empathy, even when it came to the girl he swore to adore. He was more interested in fulfilling his atrocious needs. The expression on Renee's face, as she died by his hands was a bit creepy, but it was even more troubling for Simon Fletcher as he listened to her final words. Renee told him how he would be caught and spend the rest of his life in prison if she didn't get to him first. Staring into her killer's eyes, Renee threatened to return from the other side, if it existed to seek vengeance. It sent an icy chill down his spine, as he began squeezing hard as he could until she passed away in his house of sins. Simon watched carefully as the light faded from her eyes, while he continued to penetrate her. He was too close to the finish line to quit now and couldn't stop himself from fucking the fresh corpse. He was fully aroused with his hands still tightly gripped around her throat.

Several minutes after Renee was deceased, Simon slowly removed his hands from around her neck, while staring into her lifeless eyes. They stared back at him in an eerie emotionless gaze. Finding it to be a morbid distraction, Simon turned away from her death stare and focused on her beautiful firm breast. He began touching them and gently caressing the rest of her body, it was still warm to the touch, but it was cold inside the treehouse, making it harder to perform. From a distance the wooden house up in the large tree appeared serein, hiding the ugly event taking place inside its walls. Simon Fletcher screamed out with delight as he achieved the most thrilling orgasm of his life with a dead body. He was so lost in the moment he wasn't even sure if she was really, dead? In a way, he didn't want her to be. As he called her name, there was no response.

The blankness in her eyes and the stiffness of her body as it lay there on the floor of his treehouse asylum convinced Simon she was gone. He smacked her across the face and cried out her name, but she didn't flinch, nor did she say anything about the assault he was carrying out on her after death. He was in shock that it actually- happened. This time he did it. Sobbing softly, Simon could feel the guilt trickling in slowly, realizing what he had done. He claimed the life of the woman he loved most in this world, and there was nothing he could do to bring her back. It was almost impossible to accept. Renee was there with him one moment and vanished into thin air the next. Simon continued to sob and apologize to Renee as she lay there dead on the floor next to him, knowing he would never be forgiven. Simon couldn't help but admit that she still looked beautiful and turned him on even after death. He began thinking back to memories of Renee when she was so full of life and flashing the most incredible smile the world has ever seen. He also thought about running out on her in the middle of having sex while drugged. Sadness and grief soon turned into panic, as Simon got up to have a quick look outside the treehouse windows, he had no idea what he was going to do next. He wasn't even sure how to get her out of the tree, never mind what he would do with her remains when he was through with them. A joyous fear came over Simon as he was extremely happy on one hand and wanted to die on the other. He knew he wouldn't be able to keep her corpse around forever.

Eventually, he would have to find a safe place to dispose of it. First, he was going to enjoy her company, even though she would no longer be the life of the party. At least he knew she would never leave him now. Simon wondered what her friends back home would think when they discovered she was missing. His interpretation of love was the wrong kind. It was the possessive, jealously obsessed kind. Now an innocent life has been taken and he was the cause of it. Simon had to make sure no one would ever find the body and figure him out.

She was cooling off by the second, as Simon moved some of the hair away from her face. She was still so sexy, he almost forgot she was dead. He wanted to have sex with her again and planned to sneak her into his bedroom with his parents sleeping only a few feet away while doing his best to forget the look of hatred on her face as she violently slipped away.

He was also trying hard to forget the threat she made to come-back from beyond the grave if there was such a way, to get even with him. As Simon put his pants back on and redressed his victim head to toe, he found his victory bitter-sweet. He finally had Renee Price and could do whatever he wanted with her, she couldn't get away now, but it cost the beauty queen her life and he would never again be able to enjoy her animated company.

He snuggled up to her for a few minutes in, an effort to warm her cooling corpse, but you just can't warm up a dead person no matter how hard you try. He kissed her cheek, once again claiming his boundless love for her, yet there she lay dead on the dirty old floor of his treehouse. He committed a murder which was the worst sin in the entire bible. Simon was free to do as he wished, convinced he would be burning in hell for eternity for his earthly pleasures. Staring at his prize, the punishment didn't seem to bother him. He was anxious to get her into his bed and continue having sex with the dead woman, while she was still fresh. If caught? He would be cursed with the humiliating title of a necrophiliac. If he couldn't find a living volunteer? The desperate sexually frustrated lunatic was going to sleep with a deceased one. First, he had to find a way to smuggle her through the house without his parents knowing. How would Simon explain himself is his mother saw him dragging Renee through the living room at 1 o clock in the morning? He could just see the look on her face now. God has already proven to be on his side. Either that or it was the devil granting all his wishes, pretending to be the lord's work? Whichever deity was lending a hand, Simon would have to thank them later. Right now, he felt he needed assistance from the divine more than ever before. He needed an invisible lookout until Renee's corpse is safely in his bedroom.

The easiest way to get Renee out of the tree was to simply throw her out. She was already dead and wouldn't feel a thing. Ignorantly, he lifted Renee to her feet, and as she fell forward toward him, he shoved her out the door. He watched as she hit the ground and landed staring up at him. He took another quick look around, before racing down the stairs to retrieve her. The easy part was done.

Now came the difficult one, dragging her through the house without his parents discovering what he had done. It felt like an arduous journey even though it was only through the living room and up to one flight of stairs.

Once Simon is in his own room, he can lock the door and keep her hidden until his parents leave the following morning. He would have the house and the fresh corpse all to himself. Careful not to track dirt in from dragging her across the yard, Simon threw her over his shoulder and carried her into his god-fearing parent's house while they slept. What he was doing went beyond anything holy. He took a few moments to question his madness, knowing he was about to anger god and all his angels even further with the disgraceful actions he was preparing to make. Simon brushed it off as nothing more than paranoid thoughts. He was going to go through with this heartless act and nobody could stop him. Simon listened carefully for his folks. Any kind of movement and he would have to stash her in the linen closet nearby. Lucky for him the house remained silent as the morgue. Only the sound of his foot, steps tracking through the house a corpse dangling over his shoulder could be heard.

Simon couldn't wait to get her naked again and under the covers with him. First, he had to make sure he didn't get caught. Every little sound seemed magnified as he slowly crept up the stairs. His night had turned out completely different than he expected. Instead of taking his own life, he decided to take that of the woman he adored. His heart seemed to be louder than a drum-solo at a concert in the summer, time.

As Simon reached the top of the stairs, he felt the brief walk down the hall lasted forever. Simon could hear the tv in his parent's bedroom. He was hoping it would be loud enough to mask any unwanted sounds he might create as he hurried toward his room. Stanley was beginning to toss and turn in his sleep, as his son slowly walked past his door. Renee's fresh remains over his shoulder like a hunting prize. He felt the need to get up and go to the bathroom. Eleanor had her arm draped over the top of him, and -also awoke as he moved around getting ready to get up and take a piss just down the hall from where his son was hiding a dead body. He sat up as Eleanor reached out her hand and asked where he was going? He kindly explained that he had to use the potty, she insisted he hurries back. It didn't seem like a favor, but she was buying her son the extra seconds he needed to get his dead lover's corpse hidden away. Simon was doing his best to open his bedroom door with Renee hanging over him. He pushed his way inside as his father came walking out of the bedroom and turned to walk in the same direction. Renee's long blonde hair was still sticking out of the doorway, but he wasn't paying attention to Simon's room at that particular moment. He thought he heard Simon's door close and took a glance but saw and heard nothing else. Stanley thought about going to check in on his son when he was through peeing. Tomorrow he and his wife would be leaving him behind for an entire week. In some ways, they almost felt as if they were abandoning him.

As he went about his business, Simon was breathing a much-needed sigh of relief. He made it into his room with Renee and no one saw him. Knowing his father was out in the hallway just as he closed the door, Simon felt a huge surge, of adrenaline electrocuting his body with excitement. He couldn't believe he had gotten away with it by the skin of his teeth. Had he entered the house a few seconds before or after? He would 've been caught red-handed. For the very first time, Simon felt like he was the luckiest man alive. He did his best to calm down and turned his attention to the beautiful Renee as she lay there peacefully and fully clothed, but not for long. Simon was careful to lock the door, before indulging in his most despicable fantasy. He didn't like the fact that she was stiff, he wanted very much for her to be alive. Since she no longer was, Simon would have to simply pretend. He would take her for one of those lazy women who just lay there and let the men do all the work. His mind ran wild with rancid concepts of what hell was going to be like. He stared at the fresh, corpse while taking off his shirt when he heard the toilet flush. His heart started to beat louder and faster when he heard his old man's feet walking in his direction. Simon started to panic. He didn't know what to do. Did his father actually- see him lugging the pretty young neighbor into his bedroom? Simon assumed his dad would hold off on his urine disposal if he saw his son carrying a dead body through the house. He imagined his mother would 've been informed and she would be screaming right now. Instead, everything seemed calm as usual. Everything besides his behavior that is. Simon was a nervous wreck.

There she was laying, dead in his very own bed, his father coming his way. The terrified killer didn't know what to do with Renee's corpse. He was about to stick her under the bed when he heard his mother calling, and the footsteps stop. Simon listened carefully to what she said next. His hand on Renee's arm the whole time ready to stash her out of sight and open the door as if everything was just honkey dory. Simon's mother became his savior as she called her husband back to bed.

She asked him what the heck he was doing out there? He didn't want to tell her the truth, then she would want to get out of bed and smother their only son with hugs and kisses. They had a long day tomorrow and needed their rest. Stanley told her he was coming. He couldn't help feeling troubled about leaving Simon on his own for a whole week, he was surely right to do so. They hadn't even left yet, and already he murdered the neighbor and carried her into his cave-like barbarian. His poor parents had no idea their child would soon be having sex with a dead girl just down the hall. Simon turned on the tv, not only for a way to dimly light up Renee's still lustful body but to make a little natural noise so his folks don't hear him going to town on the fresh carcass. It's too bad she was no longer alive he thought to himself. He was so desperate it didn't even matter if his partner could breathe or not. Simon laid next to her for a few minutes making sure his parents were settled in. Then he began stripping Renee of all her clothes and tossing them underneath his bed. He had no interest in covering her up tonight.

Finally, he could admire her flesh without fear of being caught or thought of as a pervert. Making sure she was comfortable Simon prompted her head upon his pillows and began kissing her and fondling her still warm enough breast. Her lips still tasted fresh and he was quickly succumbing to his darkest fantasies. He continually professed his love for her as he kissed her up and down and finally placed himself inside her again. With her eyes still wide-open he started penetrating Renee as she watched with a blank expression on her face. It felt so good and no matter how aggressive Simon was Renee remained silent. She lay still letting him do whatever he pleased. Lifting her legs and wrapping them around his head, Simon was truly making the most out of his first necrophiliac experience. It didn't matter how long he lasted since his unwilful partner couldn't feel anything anyway, still, Simon wanted to go all night for his own sick and twisted pleasure.

He knew he wouldn't be able to pull it off once she gets cold and starts to stiffen. Even the following evening, he assumed it would be too late to sleep with her again. He had to get it out of his system tonight and figure out what to do with her in the long run. He also needed a safe place to store her until it was time to get rid of the human remains. The for-the moment Simon was having the time of his life, with a dead woman. He got a rush knowing he finally had the girl he felt destine to be with.

It was sort of thrilling knowing his parents were sleeping in the room right down the hall, having no clue what he was up to, and it brought a sinister smile to his face as he continued to please himself using the fresh corpse. Simon had no remorse, nor did he seem to be ashamed of what he's done. He wanted to take things slow with his goddess and make it last all night.

At long last, Renee Price was lying naked in his bed, yet Simon had no desire to turn and acknowledge the wooden crucifix of his savior hanging above his doorway. He was too busy eying the fresh kill with his dick between her legs. He was desperate to relive the biggest mistake he ever made, by cutting their orgasms short and running for the hills.

Now she would never get off, no matter how long his pencil lasted between her stiffening, dried up thighs. Simon told Renee how excited he was to be spending an entire week together while trying to keep quiet so his folks don't hear him grunting with pleasure in the night. With his dead lover lying stiff as a board, Simon had to do all the work, including memorizing the nut-busting faces Renee made when she was getting hot. It was the antidote Simon needed to get himself off during all those lonely times in his bed or up in his house of sins. With the subtle scent of death creeping into fine for the human sense of smell to pick up, Simon began sniffing her still fresh body as he slowly fucked the cooling corpse. He's already gotten off once tonight, but Simon Fletcher was the horniest, most sex depraved man on the planet and planned to satisfy himself until the morning light. He could vaguely hear the dark prince snarling quietly in the shadows as if he was ominously vindicating the unofficial deal never quite made.

All Simon cared about tonight was getting his nut off over and over again with the girl he loved to death. He softly caressed Renee's remains as if she was somehow getting pleasure out of it, as he continued to violate her even after death. Simon could hear the news vaguely and the squeaking of the bed, as he ignored his conscience and celebrated his morbid victory.

When he was finished, Simon rolled over and kissed her. He lay next to Renee all cuddled up as if she was still alive, staring at her beautiful face imagining his wildest dream had finally come true. He was staring right at the ghoulish proof.

CHAPTER 12

＊＋＋◆＋＋＊

The sun rose early the next morning, and Stanley and Eleanor were already on the go. They wanted to get an early start packing up the family wagon and heading for the airport. When Simon eventually came around, he assumed the whole thing was just a dream, until he turned and saw Renee's dead-body sharing the bed with him. He was horrified at what he had done. She was really- there with him. To make matters worse, he could hear his mother walking toward his room calling out his name. His heart was beating a million miles a minute as he panicked lying in bed next to a corpse. Eleanor wanted to let him know breakfast was ready. Simon threw the blankets over Renee as if no one would notice the shape of a body underneath. He yelled to his mother, letting her know he was getting dressed. Simon told her he would be down in a minute. He hurried to get into some clothes and meet his folks for beacon and eggs.

All the while pretending everything was perfectly normal. He had to act as if he didn't rape and murder the young girl-next-door, or that he had her remains lying in his bed upstairs. If one of his parents go into his room, it will be the end of the world as he knows it. Simon couldn't wait for them to leave the house, so he could be alone with Renee for a while. He felt they were going to enjoy a romantic week of their own. In a macabre sort of way. As Simon sat there chowing down and thinking of the wonderful day he was going to spend with his dead lover, Eleanor reminded him that he had to open the store this morning. He did his best to pretend he didn't care, but his mother noticed the rage manifesting in his eyes. She knew he hated that store and never wanted anything to do with it. She didn't want to start an argument right before boarding a plane. She unknowingly furthered his stress when she mentioned Renee's name. She suggested stopping over there real fast before they leave so they can say goodbye. Odds were, she would already be gone before they returned. Simon had to find a way to prevent that from happening.

He could see his father also thought it was a good idea. He didn't want them to be suspicious of her disappearance before they even take to the skies. The jeep was in the driveway, so it was obvious she was home. She is such a lovely girl. I still can't believe what happened to poor Paul. It makes me sick. Eleanor stated. She and Stanley confessed they would miss having her around. They were only glad she was leaving so their son could forget about her and get on with his life. Now that he killed Renee in cold blood that will never happen. Simon wanted his parents to go on their vacation with happy feelings in their hearts and minds.

He swore to let Renee know when he sees her that they said goodbye. Simon insisted she was probably sleeping anyway. It was so early in the morning, it seemed rude to wake her. He kept his fingers crossed as his mother relented and agreed with him. Give her our love sweetheart Eleanor suggested. Looking at the time, Stanley suggested they get going. They didn't want to get held up in traffic and miss their flight. Simon insisted he would take care of the dishes before going to the flower-shop. Thank you, honey. Said Eleanor as she and Stanley got up to head out the front door.

Before doing so, Stanley landed a sucker-punch informing his son that Father Fitzpatrick would be stopping by now and then to check in on him. Once again Simon did his best to explain that he was a big boy now, he didn't need a baby-sitter. He knew it was their way of controlling him from a distance. Simon hated them sometimes for the way they treated him, he felt they were trying to restrict him from having the freedom to do as he pleases. Simon knew he would never be able to talk them out of it. He would just have to keep his eyes open for the uninvited guest.

There would be no reason for the priest to go snooping around in his bedroom. He would just have to give him the impression there was nothing out of the ordinary taking place while his folks were away. Simon imagined if the priest did discover his darkest secret, he would have to join Renee in death. Simon was not going to let it spoil his good time. He imagined spending late nights with her anyhow. He didn't expect the old-timer to show up at his door at the stroke of midnight. He walked his parents out to the old wagon and helped them with their heavy luggage.

After the exchanging of several hugs and kisses, they were off. Simon turned to go inside with many jumbled thoughts racing through his mind. He pointed his eyes toward the top of the house knowing that's where his deceased lover was waiting for him. Doing the dishes as promised, Simon realized he couldn't leave her out all day long while he was at work. Renee was now a decaying piece of meat. If he wanted her to maintain her beauty a while longer? He was going to have to keep her on ice. Simon scrubbed the dishes clean as he feared to leave her out at room temperature all day. He was afraid she would start stinking up the house with the stench of death.

It was at that very moment that he experienced a eureka moment. Simon would simply keep Renee in the freezer down in his basement while he was gone. It would act like a frozen casket in a sense. It was genius and Simon, was quite proud of himself for thinking of it. When he was through with the dishes, he was going to hurry down there and see how much dead meat is already stored.

The basement was a dreary kind of place. Dark and damp, it was nothing like the bright sunny state of California. Renee hated gloomy places like this. It would anger her spirit even more if she knew how he was treating her remains. Simon didn't seem to care much. He was more concerned with his own selfish, needs. Walking down the old wooden steps, Simon came upon the white freezer that did look sort of like a coffin. When he opened it up and looked inside, he discovered there wasn't a whole lot of meat stashed away. Luckily his parents hadn't restocked it for winter yet. He assumed they would when they returned in a week. Simon quickly went to work emptying the freezer and tossing the packaged meat on the floor nearby. He would move what he could to the smaller freezer upstairs and do his best to eat the rest. Once it was empty, Simon hurried to his bedroom to retrieve the human carcass. He wanted to store her away, so she doesn't decompose so easily. When he entered his bedroom to remove the cover's he saw Renee lying there naked and waiting for him.

He was overcome by the temptation to jump back in the sack and have sex with the stiff. Convinced music would enhance the vile experience, even more, Simon turned on the radio to fittingly find a song playing from the zombies, while wishing his dead lover could come back from her one, way trip to oblivion. But its too late to say you're sorry. How would I know, why should I care? Please don't bother trying to find her. She's not there. Well, let me tell you bout, the way she looked. The way she acts and the color of her hair. Her voice was soft and cool, her eyes were clear and bright. But she's not there.

As the song played, Simon removed his clothes and crawled beside the still somewhat attractive corpse. He stared into her motionless eyes and gently ran his fingers through her long yellow hair. He then leaned forward and kissed her cold lips, as if she was still alive. It seemed to have no real effect on him that her skin was changing color slightly, or that it was cold to the touch, as he caressed it. Simon started fondling her breast and sliding his tongue further down the dead girl's throat. The twisted pervert did his best to ignore the horrendous behavior he was displaying.

This act of complete lunacy could never be mentioned to the old Irish priest. It was almost too heinous for Simon Fletcher himself to accept. He understood how wrong it was, but simply didn't care, falling victim to the sins of the flesh. As Simon placed himself inside her, staring at her cold stiff body, he pretended she was still alive and willingly having sex with him. In his mind's eye, Simon placed himself back in the memory, when the two of them were intimate. Her skin felt soft and warm and he could even hear that sexy moan she couldn't control as she used his penis to please herself. He gazed into her heavenly blue eyes while trying his hardest not to blow it too soon.

He found her even more beautiful than ever before. As Simon continued using his victim as a sex object, Renee started to lose her appeal and change back into the cold stiff corpse she truly was. Her moans of pleasure turned into bone-chilling screams for help. The disgusting bugs from deep within the earth began to pour from her mouth, as he pulled away from her cold lips in terror. Renee then began peering into his eyes with the blankest expression on her face, it was the look of a dead woman staring back at him. Simon was soon impacted by the gruesome reality which he brought upon himself. He was appalled and sickeningly satisfied in a strange way with what he has done.

He looked deep into Renee's dead eyes while touching her chilly flesh as the song played on. Simon began to wonder if he was capable of living with this dark secret for the rest of his life, yet still found himself sexually attracted to the rape victim he continued to assault even after death. After ejaculating, Simon carried Renee's corpse in his arms down toward her new resting place. All the while praying his folks don't return because they forgot something. He could still smell her perfume, but her body was no longer soft and warm.

She was cold to the touch and stiff as aboard. Simon looked as though he was hugging her as he moved through the house. Her blank stare facing him the entire time. Even though she was dead, Simon found her incredibly attractive. He was truly proving to be sick in the head. Thinking about the time, Simon knew he had to get going. He was in no mood to deal with angry customers so early in the morning, he feared if they pressed his buttons under the amount of stress he was already under, he would have to dispose of a couple more bodies before his folks returned.

Struggling to get a grip on his fears and the grizzly task at hand, Simon dragged the beautiful, slow decaying corpse down the creepy basement steps toward the icebox. He gently placed her naked body down and gave her another kiss, before closing the lid and saying goodbye for now. Making his way through the house, Simon started to feel a little strange around all the religious décor surrounding him. He felt as though they were all watching and. Judging his every move. After what he has already done, Simon imagined they were keeping a close eye on him. How could he ever get away with what he did? He just wanted to get the hell out of there for a while, so his head would stop spinning.

Once at his mother's store, Simon felt the paranoia sinking in. He was surrounded by angels and saints there as well, but he did his best to ignore them. All Simon could think about was returning to Renee later that evening. He even planned to bring home some really, nice flowers for her. It was a little too late to play gentleman now. The only flowers Renee should be receiving should be from loved ones at her funeral. It appeared Simon wasn't going to grant her that right.

She would never have a funeral like her poor husband Paul. Simon wanted to keep her on ice forever, but it was impossible. Especially while he is living under his parent's roof. What was he going to say? Sorry, dad but I need the freezer space to store Renee's corpse, so I can continue having sex with her? His life was spiraling out of control and he hadn't even fully realized it yet. Lots of old women came into the store to have a look around, with no intension of buying anything. For Simon Fletcher, it was much more discouraging when a handsome young man walked in with a smile on his face and hearts floating in his eyes. Simon wished he could order Cupid to shoot fiery arrows at them, putting an end to their happiness. He couldn't stand the fact that he would never be like those men.

As the hours slowly ticked on, Simon stared at the clock and counted down to quitting time. He couldn't wait to see Renee. He was so excited that she was at his house patiently waiting for him to return. It was especially slow he assumed because his mother was going to be out of town for the week. Anyone who knew of her plans would probably think better than to come shopping when Simon was in charge. Most folks in town would rather wait until she returns from vacation. Simon could be pretty- rude at times and difficult to deal with. His temper seemed to flare up more often since Renee came into the picture. When there was no one in the store Simon put together a nice bouquet for his dead lover.

He planned to surprise her with them when he gets home. Simon was doing his best to pretend his actions were completely normal. As if he was simply going home to spend time with his girlfriend. He was so excited they would be spending another night together. When the workday finally ground down to a grueling end, Simon wasted no time grabbing the flowers and closing, up the shop. He hopped in his car and sped off. Hitting the liquor store for a bottle of vodka on the way, he wanted to have a few drinks to celebrate. With flowers and a fresh bottle of booze on the passenger seat, Simon almost felt like a normal man. The kind of man who attracted the ladies and even caused some of them to fight over his affection. He never drank before, but Simon felt he could use a few to relax with the dead woman resting in the family freezer.

The closest his folks ever got to drinking was sipping the blood of Christ served in church on Sunday morning. He was going to get completely drunk and spend the evening with the girl he loved to death. When he got home, Simon backed his car into the garage as he usually had done. He was also sure to close the door behind him. Simon didn't want his nosy neighbor across the street to know what he was doing. He didn't want her to see him smuggling a big bottle of the devil's poison into the holy sanctuary. He feared it would get back to his folks that he was drinking. In truth that was the least of his problems. He would be in far more trouble if anyone discovers he has a corpse in the basement freezer. How long? He wondered before someone notices Renee is missing and reports it, especially Mrs. Anderson across the street. She watches everything. How the hell was he going to sneak Renee out of the house when the time came?

The deranged killer didn't want her around, should the law come digging for answers. Living so close to his victim, he knew it was a matter of time before there was a knock at the door. He also knew how suspicious he would look if Mrs. Anderson saw him entering the house with liquor and flowers. She knew perfectly well he was incapable of getting a date.

Once inside, Simon opened the new bottle and stuck it in the freezer for a few minutes to cool off. He then went into the living room with the big bouquet and set them up nicely in a purple vase, so Renee would be surprised when she sees them as if she was still alive and well. When everything was ready, Simon ventured back into the basement toward the icebox where his love was being stored. When he opened it, Simon noticed she was ice-cold to the touch, but she still looked like the beauty-queen he was destined to be with. She looked so at peace as if she was merely sleeping. Simon couldn't wait to get her out of there and warm her up. He wasn't sure if he would be able to have sex with her again.

She was stiff and hard from rigor mortis settling in. If he was crazy enough to give it a try? He would not be pleased with the results. He at least wanted to pretend she was still alive, so he would have someone to keep him company while his folks were away. He was planning on having a romantic week at home. Since Renee still looked pretty, fresh, it was easy for him to forget she was dead. It wouldn't last forever now that her body was vacant of a soul. You look so cold, sweetheart. Let me get you out of there and warm you up a little. She had an eerie look in her blank white eyes as Simon briefly stared into them. He couldn't help but wonder what if anything they were seeing now? He also began wondering if she was watching him from some other place outside the three -dimensions we living are confined to?

If so, was she growing angry with him, not only for causing her death but disrespecting her remains afterward? He stood there in the basement by the freezer speaking to her as if she was at a normal funeral. Even though the twinkle in her eyes no longer existed, Simon still found himself lost in them. He was preparing to pull her out of the icebox and invite her into the living room to sit on the couch and watch tv with him like an ordinary couple. In the back of his mind, he thought about the priest showing up unannounced.

How was he going to explain himself when caught red-handed with his tongue down the throat of a corpse? Considering the time, he assumed the old man was probably getting ready for bed. He didn't think he would show up so late in the evening, but one can never be too sure. It was a chance he was willing to take. Tonight, Simon Fletcher was going to live it up and pretend he is completely free to do whatever he wishes, no matter how grotesque. After removing Renee from the frigid coffin, Simon carried her upstairs in the nude and laid her on the couch. He told her to wait a moment as he poured himself a drink and asked if she liked the flowers, he brought home for her. She laid there silently as if she wasn't interested in anything he had to say.

The vodka was going down smooth and traveling right to his head. When the glass was empty, Simon placed it down on the table in front of him. He wanted to get closer to Renee. Leaning over her he began squeezing on her rock-solid breast. She no longer felt the way she did when he first slept with her in her house while she was alive. He kissed her icy-lips and gently moved some of the hair away from her face, as the phone rang loudly, startling Simon and causing him to freak out momentarily. He felt his heart starting to pound, as he left Renee on the family couch and ran to see who was calling? Hello. He said to the person on the other line as he picked up the receiver and placed it to his ear. Simon sweetheart it's your mother. How's everything going? She questioned loudly. Simon moved the phone away, so he didn't go deaf, as his mother appeared to be very excited about speaking to him. It was as if they hadn't spoken in weeks. Everything's fine here mom. Where's dad? He's right here if you want to speak with him.

She explained that she meant to call earlier, but they were busy getting settled in. Eleanor could tell there was something off about the tone of her son's voice. It was because he had been drinking without their knowledge. She asked if everything was alright again? Causing Simon to slightly lose his temper. He was so tired of being treated like a baby. He wanted to tell his mother what he was doing, to spoil her vacation. Simon wanted to confess he was drinking vodka with the neighbor from next door. He also wanted her and his father to know she was dead, and that he was the cause of it. He chose to keep his cool and allow them to have a good time without him, most of all he didn't want them returning so quickly.

As Simon waited for his mother to hand the phone over to his father, he turned his attention to Renee resting motionlessly on the couch in the living room. Hello son. Are you holding down the fort as I asked you? Stanley asked with excitement in his tone. You are the man of the house now so enjoy it. Not too much of course. He warned in a joking yet stern sort of way. I know dad. Stanley also noticed the change in his son's voice. He too assumed Simon might be indulging in some drinks while they were away. It wasn't anything to spoil their vacation over.

After all, he was a grown man. What Stanley didn't know was that Simon murdered the girl-next-door and was preserving her remains in the family freezer. He insisted Eleanor wanted to check in and let him know they touched down safely. Simon told him not to worry and to enjoy themselves. He said everything will be fine until they return. With that, they said their goodbye's and Simon quickly turned his attention back to Renee. He was feeling buzzed as he continued pouring the liquor down his throat. Once again, he found himself leaning over the couch staring at her cold, beautiful dead face. After another swig, he placed the bottle down on the table and started kissing her again.

He began feeling on her cold, stiff breast, and acting as if she was still alive. Simon wanted to be her prince and snuggle up to keep her warm. He knew that was impossible with his ice-queen. Heating a corpse is the worst thing he could do. Once she starts to decay, Renee will not only lose her angelic features, she will also release the stench of death into the breathable air. He didn't want to stain his parent's furniture with decomposition. Simon was also growing tired of the deafening silence.

He wanted to liven up the place a little by playing some music. Money can't buy me love from the Beatles was playing again when he switched it on. Simon thought the message couldn't be more- true. He knew perfectly well, that even if he was the richest man in the world? Renee would never be his. Yet there she was lying on the family sofa.

Simon turned with a smile on his face, asking if she wanted to dance with him? Renee just laid there staring off into oblivion.

The last thing she heard on this earth was her killer professing his love to her with his hands gripped tightly around her throat. I suppose you couldn't dance with me even if you wanted too huh sweetheart. He wanted to dress Renee up and make her look new again. He also imagined it would be decent if he put some clothing over her. It was wrong to have her dead, decaying flesh spread out on his parent's sofa. Looking around the living room he again took notice of all the saints and angels watching over him. As well as a replica of Christ above every doorway.

He was giving his divine audience one hell of a show if indeed they were somehow watching through their carefully sculpted or painted eyes. Simon knew how wrong it was of him to be performing these incredibly sinful acts, still, he thought about sneaking into Renee's house and searching her closet for something nice for her to wear. He would use some of his mother's make-up to doll her up a little. First, he had to take care of business in the bathroom.

All that liquor was going right through him. As he stood there pissing and staring out the window, Simon noticed it was snowing outside. It added to the romantic evening he was delightfully sharing with a corpse. For Simon, it even helped solidify his fate with Renee somehow. He couldn't deny that god himself placed her in his hands for a reason. His wish was granted, and he should be rejoiceful of her awful passing. Still, there was a small part of Simon that felt really, bad for what he has done. Apologizing to her was not going to make a difference. He understood his crooked fantasies lead to her ultimate nightmare. If he was going to break into Renee's house for some sexy supplies? He was going to have to do it in the middle of the snowstorm. He wanted to make her look as alive as possible. The coloring of her skin was changing as the process of death and decay gradually started taking over.

There was nothing he could do to make Renee appear as gorgeous as she was when there was still air in her lungs and light in her eyes. Simon was now in love with a rotting piece of meat. An empty vessel lacking a source of energy. He thought of the conversations they had about experiencing her first cold winter in the northeast. He selfishly took that away from her. The happy couple never expected things to turn out so tragically when they packed-up their lives and moved to a perfect little town called Renee Falls. Who knew they would both be dead within months? Simon washed his hands and dressed warmly for the stroll next-door. He was eager to raid her closet and find a few things for her to wear in-order to please him. Simon felt as if every statue in the room was shifting its eyes and looking at him as he walked over to Renee and told her he would be right back. I'm going to fetch you something elegant to wear my darling. Renee continued to stare off blankly, as Simon headed for the door.

He was praying Mrs. Anderson across the street wasn't keeping watch as he darted from his house to the one next door. Finding a way in was easy as pie. Renee forgot to lock the front door as she went searching through Simon's house of sins. A decision that would cost her life. Simon slipped inside and went straight to her bedroom. The house seemed so different without her smiling face in it. It also felt empty because most of her things were already packed away. He took a glance at the wedding picture still being displayed as he headed up the stairs. Simon knew she was saving that for last. Ignoring it for now, He continued to Renee's room and started tearing it apart. Tossing clothes on the floor that he had no interest in. Finally, he came to a sexy red dress. It was tight-fitting and he was sure Renee would look ravishing in it, dead or alive.

Before leaving he went through some of the draws hoping to find some sleazy lingerie he could dress her up in as well. He was growing angry as he kept opening draws and finding Paul's things in them. Worthless items as far as he was concerned. Trashing the room as he frantically went through the other bureau hoping it was Renee's he eventually found what he was looking for. At the bottom of the bottom draw, he found hot pink lingerie.

It was perfect, and Simon couldn't wait to see her in it. He was in a hurry to get out of there before someone finds him out. Taking the dress and the lingerie, Simon headed down the stairs toward the front door. Before leaving the house, Simon entered the living room and took one last look at the wedding photo of Paul and Renee on the happiest day of their lives. She looked so amazing. Simon imagined what life would be like if he could make girls like that fall in love with him. The only reason the beautiful blonde wasn't running away from him is that she was dead. Simon grew angry staring at Paul's face smiling back at him. He smashed the picture frame against the little end table it sat on and took the picture home with him. Simon was completely unhinged and didn't give a fuck about the consequences. It was as if his brain had been set on autopilot ever since he placed his hands around his loves throat and strangled the life out of her. He felt a strong urgency to get out of there, it didn't feel right without Renee's presence.

As he headed for the front door, a gust of wind whipped passed. Simon could have sworn he heard Renee's voice calling his name from within it. Assuming his mind was playing tricks on him, due to his intoxication and guilt? Simon did his best to brush it off, but not before having a quick look around. He even went as far as to call out her name, but there was no one there. With the wedding photo and clothing in hand, Simon stormed out of the house, slamming the door behind him.

He felt a little uneasy about the gentle voice calling out his name, reminding him of the threatening words Renee spoke with her dying breath. Was she going to return from the dead and torment him for ending her life? He tried distracting himself from the troubling thoughts by imagining what Renee was going to look like when he got her all dressed up. He placed the clothing and the photo down on a nearby chair. The cold snowy night convinced him to get a fire started. Once it was burning hot, he ventured to his mother's room to retrieve some of her finest cosmetics. He intended to make sure Renee looked beautiful as ever, as he took what he needed. He hurried back to the living room where his stiff as a board date was waiting for him.

With an unnerving smile on his face, he placed everything down on the coffee table and took his glass to the kitchen for another refill.

He wanted to pour one for his charming date, but he knew she was no longer cable of enjoying the simple trappings of this mortal world. Simon would be forced to drink alone. At least he hoped he wouldn't have to dance alone. He began sipping his drink as he had a seat next to Renee and started freshening her up, when a song called Graveyard Poem from the doors caught his attention with its trancey lyrics, disturbingly serenaded him with rhyme. It was the greatest night of my life

. Although I still had not found a wife, I had my friends right there beside me. We were close together. We tripped the wall and we scaled the graveyard. Ancient shapes were all around us. The wet dew felt fresh beside the fog. Two made love in an ancient spot. One chased a rabbit into the dark. A girl got drunk and balled the dead. And I gave empty sermons to my head. Cemetery cool and quiet. Hate to leave your sacred lay. Dread the milky coming of the day.

While listening to the disturbing song and the few that followed Simon did his best to make her appear as if she was still alive. Renee's corpse looked quite impressive when he was finished. Perhaps he was in the wrong business and should consider a career as a mortician? Now that she was looking her best, Simon was ready to get drunk and dance the night away. He put all his mother's beauty supplies back where he found them and quickly returned to the living-room to spend the evening with the young girl he murdered in cold blood.

She almost looked real enough to pass as a living, breathing woman. Switching through the radio-stations in search of something a bit livelier he came across a much more soothing type of music. There was a song from Buddy Knox playing on the radio and the lyrics snatched Simon's attention immediately. He sang, come along and be my party doll. Come along and be my party doll. Come along and be my party doll and I'll make love to you. To you. Ill, make love to you. The four-eyed maniac imagined Renee Price was his party doll.

He wanted to run his fingers through her long yellow hair. After all, every man needs a party doll when their feeling wild. He turned to look at her as nasty thoughts charged through his skull like a stampede of

Rhinos at full steam. Even the way the woman in the song was described matched his victim perfectly. He turned and walked over to Renee who was dressed to kill, even though she was already dead. Lifting her off the couch, Simon held her tight and started dancing around the living room. After only a few footsteps, Simon was no longer staring at a corpse, but the angelic, vibrant young woman he became fatally obsessed with. Her baby blue eyes staring back at him, just as the song said. Renee looked even more stunning than when she was alive. Her hair glowed and her skin was soft to the touch, as they moved gracefully across the living room floor, twirling and spinning until they were dizzy, as the song played on. Simon pulled Renee in closer and the two of them started to kiss.

The experience seemed so vivid Simon was convinced it was happening. He couldn't believe how amazing she looked in that red, dress and wanted to dance the entire night away. By the look on her face, it appeared Renee was enjoying herself as well. He stared into her eyes and swore to his dead queen that he has waited for this moment his entire life. Renee smiled at him as if she felt the same way. Simon knew god was never going to forgive him for what he has done, and he planned to smother himself in pleasure before his final judgment arrives.

He continued dancing around the living room, his deceased lover in his arms. In reality, she had no rhythm or interest in being his dance partner. Renee simply dragged her toes across the floor, as Simon glided around like a true gentleman, her corpse held tightly in his arms, as he briefly turned his attention to the snow falling outside. Simon imagined it made the evening even more romantic for the two of them. He pulled Renee in even closer, as the next song started to play. Dream, Dream, dream, dream, Dream, Dream, Dream, dream.

When I want you in my arms when I want you and all your charms Whenever I want you all I have to do is dream, dream, dream, dream. When I feel blue in the night. And I need you to hold me tight. Whenever I want you all I have to do is a dream, I can make you mine, taste your lips of wine. Anytime night or day. Only trouble is, gee whiz I'm dreaming my life away. I need you so that I could die. I love you so and that is why whenever I want you all I have to do is a dream. As the song came to an end Simon realized it was all in his head. Renee wasn't dancing with him and he was moving around the room with her corpse in his arms.

Once again, she was lifeless and cold to the touch, her pale white eyes staring back at him. He gently placed Renee back on the couch and kissed her, leaving a disgusting taste in his mouth. Simon then noticed the bottle of vodka resting nearby, trying to understand why god has chosen this despicable path for him. It was pathetic and pitiful in his mind. He took a sip from the liquor bottle to help rinse the bad breath out of his mouth, after sucking face with a stiff. Simon Fletcher wondered if he could ever show his face in church again after what he's done. Not only did he take a life which is the ultimate sin, but now he was desecrating his victims remains in the most ghoulish of ways. He knew to give Renee a proper burial somewhere and letting her rest in peace was the right thing to do. Instead, Simon lugged Renee down into the basement and placed her back in the freezer when he was through with her. He wanted to invite her into his bed again, but Renee had been gradually defrosting while dancing around the house with him. If he leaves her out any longer, the odor of death would seep out and invade every square inch of the family home. He had no choice, but to get Renee back on ice. That is if he wanted the morbid companionship to continue. What was he going to do at the end of the week when his folks return from vacation?

For now, all Simon had to do is get Renee back in her icy coffin without falling down the basement stairs and killing himself as well. Drunk as he was, it seemed quite reasonable he might take a nasty spill. As he did his best to move across the house with the corpse clutched against him, Simon still couldn't shake the eerie feeling that all his mother's statues were watching him somehow? It was as if he wasn't alone, but had guardians spying on his every move. Ignoring the troubling vibes, Simon made his way down to the basement and placed Renee back inside the freezer. Leaving her dressed, he leaned over and gave her another kiss before sealing her up for the night. He then went back for the wedding photo he stole from Renee's house. Before retiring to his room, Simon wanted to cut the picture in two, so he didn't have to stare at Paul's annoying face anymore. He wanted to keep Renee's half forever to remind him of her beautiful face. Walking into the kitchen he went into the junk-draw to retrieve a pair of scissors. Cutting the picture in half, Simon turned on the stove burner and dropped his fallen enemy to melt into ashes. He watched as bright flames shot from Paul's eyes and scorched his face into nothing. When he was through, he turned off the stove-top and staggered to his room, so he could try and get some sleep.

Simon was frustrated to find himself alone again. His dead queen safely stored away in the family icebox down in the basement. Simon finally had what he always wanted but not in the way he expected. He lay there believing it was all for nothing. She already expired when it came to having sex with her. The meat may appear fresh, but Simon was convinced it was spoiled. He was becoming more concerned with what to do with her bodily remains when the time comes to dispose of her. He stared up at the ceiling as the snowstorm continued its assault outside his cozy walls. Simon couldn't stop thinking about what Renee told him just before she died. She vowed to get even from beyond the grave. He wondered if she meant it, he also contemplated the notion that it was even possible for someone to travel back from the other side and attack the living. Simon kept Renee's picture at his bedside as he closed his eyes and prayed, she doesn't come back from the dead to haunt or even more terrifying kill him.

Eventually, Simon closed his eyes and drifted off, but he was soon awakened by a soft voice calling out his name in the night. It was the sexiest and most angelic voice he had ever heard. Simon wake-up. She softly whispered in his ear. He could feel her warm naked body beginning to drape over him, as Renee snuggled up closer. He could feel her breath in his face, and most of all her soft, sensual touch. Gently, she started playing between his legs, softly gliding her fingers against his balls and stroking his penis as if she was inviting him to a night of extraordinary sexual pleasures. It felt really- good and Simon couldn't move a muscle, he just laid there allowing Renee to pleasure him, as her long yellow hair slid across the sides of his face. Renee was smothering her killer with affection, and he was completely falling prey to the woman he savagely murdered. Simon was enjoying himself and instructed his deceased dream-girl to continue what she was doing. Does that feel good baby? She questioned in a soft sensual voice. Simon didn't care that she was dead, he was allowing his demons to take control since her touch felt so amazing. Do you want to fuck me? Renee whispered in his ear while in the middle of nibbling on its soft tissue exterior. Simon turned over, so Renee could jump on top of him, promising the sex would be better than ever before. Simon couldn't resist and soon the two of them were at it, kissing passionately as Renee lay on top of him, moving around on his penis. He also couldn't resist touching her soft skin and playing with her perfect breast. Simon could tell Renee was on the verge of climaxing by the look on her face and the sounds she was making, as she placed her hands around his throat and started to strangle him, asking why he ended her life. Simon could see the rage growing in her heavenly eyes as if dark, menacing storm clouds were rapidly moving in. Renee reminded him that she had her entire life before her and that he was responsible for snuffing it out before her time. How can you do this to someone you love? Renee asked while squeezing her hands harder around her neck, her filthy ridged nails digging into his flesh. Simon imagined he was going to die the same way he ended his victim's life He fought for air, as blood dripped from the open gashes in his throat. I'm going to kill you for what you did to me, Simon. He struggled to scream out but couldn't as Renee dig her fingernails deeper into his flesh. He was forced to watch as her features drastically began to change, from the beautiful and sexy young goddess to a decrepit corpse before his eyes.

Simon was torn away from the vicious nightmare by the sound of his mother's pipe organ being played downstairs. When he opened his eyes and had a look around, Simon saw no sign of Renee and the house was silent, even though he was sure to have heard the creepy instrument playing a sad tune from below. He scratched his head wondering where the fuck Renee could have gone, she seemed to vanish into thin air. Simon wasn't sure what the graphic nightmare meant? He refused to believe the gorgeous woman of peace he murdered was going to come back to seek revenge upon him. Simon did his best to ignore it, but it was something he wouldn't soon forget. Simon didn't know if he could fall back to sleep after that, nor that he wanted to. He wasn't sure if Renee would attack him again? Knowing she wanted to get even with him, made Simon even more fearful of the vivid nightmare. He was almost expecting Renee's corpse to be lying by his side when he surveyed the room. In truth, her lifeless body was still resting on ice without so much as a shiver. She remained immobile in her chilly casket. Simon did his best to get some sleep with one eye open. He remained restless and on edge all night long. Impatiently waiting for the bright sun to rise the following morning. It seemed impossible the way the snow was coming down. Simon was praying that her body would be right where he left it the night before. If her corpse had in-fact become animated? Perhaps she would see her way out the front door never to return? Or just maybe she would creep up into Simon Fletcher's bedroom and murder him in his sleep. It was enough for Simon to think twice about what he has done.

For the first time, Simon couldn't wait to go to his mother's store the next day, foolish enough to believe the sunlight could save him. Terrified as Simon may have been, he waited anxiously for his victim to show herself again. The next day it was still cloudy outside, but the snowfall wasn't as bad as it seemed. Simon could still make it to work without a whole lot of grief. He decided to open- up the flower-shop since he would be off the next day anyway. The whole time he was there, Simon thought about Renee and the bone-chilling nightmare he suffered from her seeking revenge from beyond the grave. Simon tried convincing himself that it was just a dream, fearing guilt was slowly finding a way to trickle inside and destroy him. He didn't want to grow too frightened of the woman he had viciously slain. After all, he still possessed her remains, hidden in the freezer in the creepy old basement. He was hesitant to even remove her from the coffin when he returned.

Luckily, he was bombarded by distractions. It was the holiday season, and everyone wanted to pick up their groomed vegetation before church the next day. Simon did his best to pretend like nothing was wrong. He didn't want anyone to know he committed the most heinous crime this fine little town has ever known. When the work day finally ended, and Simon was heading home, he wondered if it was a good idea to remove Renee from her temporary resting place and spend some time with her. He was curious to see what? If anything would happen if he violated her sacred flesh again this evening. Simon wanted to know if he would encounter another nightmare, or if perhaps this time Renee would show herself in the real world? Proving to him that she is still angry over her untimely death. There was only one way to prove it.

When Simon gets home, he was going to indulge in some of the remaining vodkas and remove Renee from her chilly resting place. He wanted to see if it would provoke a reaction. As of now, Simon was still quite convinced, he was growing worried about nothing more than a stupid dream. He knew Renee was dead and that she was no threat to him. When he finally returned home, Simon heard the phone ringing. He raced to answer it and see who was at the other end. It was his mother calling to check in again. He assumed she would continue calling every night until she and his father were back in Jersey. She wanted to make sure everything was alright, especially after the storm they had the night before. Simon swore it was no big deal. He even managed to open the flower-shop on time this morning. Eleanor was proud of him for taking charge of things while she and Stanley were away. She explained that she missed him very much and would be back before he knew it. Simon told her they left just in time. The weather had taken a turn for the worst since they had gone. He thought he was very convinced that everything was going according to plan. After speaking to his mother and father about their wonderful time in the sun, Simon finally hung up the phone and quickly retrieved the bottle of vodka from the freezer in the kitchen. He wanted the drink nice and cold, so it would go down smoother. He took one generous sip and placed it back in the freezer for the moment. His thoughts went right back to his murder victim down in the basement. Simon wondered how long he could keep up this morbid ordeal. more importantly how long could the corpse remain fresh under the constant process of thawing and refreezing?

Eventually, Renee is going to smell up the entire house if he doesn't dispose of her soon. Simon kept wondering how long it would be before the tiny insects were feasting on her flesh and crawling through her eye-sockets. When Renee's beauty is gone and she is eventually resolved to nothing more than dry bones, would Simon still want to possess her? He was going to have to take great care of her if he wanted to keep her looking at life, like. For now, he was unsure if he wanted to lug her out of the basement or leave her be for the rest of the night. If he wasn't going to spend time with Renee, there was no reason to keep her around. At the very least Simon wanted to say hello to his frozen corpse in the icy tomb. His sanity was draining like the sands in an hourglass. Simon didn't seem to care as he took another generous swig out of the bottle and listened carefully for a sign from the woman, he brutally murdered. If she was going to seek vengeance from the great-beyond? Where the hell was, she? Simon imagined it was all in his head. Just like the feeling of someone watching as he danced around the house and even engaged in a sexual encounter with the corpse. He couldn't explain it and knew it was impossible, still whenever he was around Renee's remains, he felt as though he wasn't alone. He tried convincing himself it was self, planted in his mind to see her. Simon wasn't sure if he could still make love to her now that she had been dead for days and was frozen stiff. Still, he could use the company while sitting around the house watching tv or diving into one of his morbid portraits. He even considered sketching a new image of his beauty-queen now that she's dead. He went into the basement to retrieve her frozen remains. When he opened the freezer, Renee looked beautiful.

She still appeared to be at peace. Unfortunately, her spirit was suffering in a restless state, and couldn't move on, until unfinished business is put to rest. She was so cold to the touch. It was ludicrous that

Simon was even capable of manifesting such as convoluted imaginings. He smiled and said hello to Renee. He even leaned in to give her a wet-one. His warm flesh against her ice-sickle tongue instantly proved to be a match made in hell. As Simon tried to back away, he nervously found his tongue glued to hers. He did his best to yank them apart, but it wasn't working. Renee just stared at him. Her pale dead eyes blankly gazing into his. He felt his tongue stretching and pulling itself apart. Her breath was foul as Simon was forced to continue breathing right against her face. He could feel the warm-blood pooling in his mouth. As Simon did his best to scream and remove himself from the frozen corpse, Renee's eyes shifted. They pointed right at him as she reached out for his throat. She wanted to strangle him to death as he did to her. A look of hatred and rage enveloped her pretty face as Simon struggled to getaway. Renee sat up and proceeded to come after him, as the terrified murderer cried and pronounced his love for her. As her icy fingers wrapped around his throat and began squeezing, Simon snapped back to reality.

He screamed out in terror, convinced what he just experienced was real. He quickly noticed Renee was still very much dead and lying stiff in her frozen casket. Looking around the eerie, dark basement there was no sign of an angry ghost lurking in the shadows. Again, Simon convinced himself it was all inside his head. This time he was wide -awake when the vision occurred. He thought about leaving her where she is for the night, but she looked so sexy in that blood-colored dress. Simon muscled his paranoia aside for the moment, so he could get drunk and stare at the gorgeous carcass he was holding prisoner. Even if she was too far gone to actually- have sex with? Simon could still use her to turn himself on. Not only did the attractive physical features remain frozen on her face, but most importantly the insane fact that he did kill her, and she was true with him, inside his house.

It was the ultimate trophy. There was a dark, malevolent satisfaction about it that Simon couldn't explain. He could never possess her in life but managed to own her in death. It was a bitter-sweet victory, but still a victory in his mind. Now he knew Renee Price wouldn't be with anyone else either. She was so heavy, and Simon didn't know how many more times he wanted to lug her up and down the old basement stairs. The grueling task would soon prove his devotion. How dedicated would he be to drag her around the house night after night? He was starting to get really, cold himself as he went up the basement steps with Renee's frozen body pressed against his. This wasn't turning out as Simon imagined it at all. He could keep her looking fresh, but she was too cold to touch.

This was the biggest mistake of his life and he was going to rot in hell for it. Simon was considering changing Renee out of that sexy dress and into the hot pink lingerie he stole from her bottom drawer? It would certainly make her more eye-popping to stare at, especially since he planned on sipping more of that vodka when he gets Renee settled on the family sofa. As he continued lugging her up the stairs one step at a time, Simon heard -the sound of someone pounding on the front door. His heart started to race as sweat began forming on his forehead. Simon wondered who the hell it could be showing up unexpected at his door.

He was almost at the top of the stairs when the uninvited guest arrived. As he panicked Simon slipped and as he caught his balance, he let go of Renee and watched her tumble down the stairs, hoping it didn't fuck up her image too badly. He stood there for a second trying to decide if he should place Renee back in the freezer or leave her where she lies for -the moment. The loud knocking continued, making it even harder for him to think straight. Praying it wasn't the police, Simon imagined no one else would need to go searching the basement. He assumed Renee was safe right where she was for now. He turned and hurried up the stairs. closing the door behind him. Simon took a moment to calm down and regain his composure, before opening the front door to greet the uninvited visitor.

When he finally did, Simon was surprised and relieved to see it was only the faithful priest from his family, church. He apologized for the bother and explained he was just checking in as his parents asked him to. His visit angered Simon, but he knew it wasn't the old Irishman's fault. It was his smothering parents who refused to let him spread his wings and fly. Knowing they were right about him, pissed the paranoid killer off even more.

Simon did his best to act as if there was nothing to hide. He stepped aside with a smile on his face, inviting Father Fitzpatrick to enter and have a look around if he must. He kept his fingers crossed the old man wouldn't get too nosy. If he ventures into the underground lair where Renee is lying dead on the floor, he will be forced to send the holy man to his maker. Simon was trying to remember if he put the vodka away. He was also concerned about the smell of his breath. He didn't want the priest to know he was getting drunk and kissing dead girls while his folks were gone. As you can see Father, no wild parties, and no crazy business.

The old man gave him an uncertain grin as he walked around the house. I understand why You don't want me coming to spy on you Simon. You are in-fact a grown man. You don't need to be looked after. I just wanted to come over when you least expected it because that's what I told your mother and father I would do. Simon felt his heart dodging beats, as Father Fitzpatrick continued to lecture him while reaching for the handle of the door leading to the basement where Renee's body lie completely exposed. Simon watched carefully to see if his hand turns the knob. Once that door opens there's no turning back.

The love, sick killer would have to find the courage to murder again, this time it would be a man of god making his sins even more wicked. Simon did his best to hide his fear, but the priest was beginning to see signs of stress on his face. Only when Father Fitzpatrick removed his hand from the knob and walked away could Simon breathe normally again.

He started walking to the front door to let himself out. Well, Simon, I'm sorry to bother you, it looks as if everything is as it should be. I see no reason to invade your space any longer I should be on my way. If you don't mind me asking? What exactly are you planning to do for the rest of the evening? You're finally alone on a Saturday night, the whole house to yourself? I don't know Father. I'm kind of tired from working all day.

Since you must know I am in the middle of one of my finest drawings. It's going to be splendid when I'm finished.

It is of the virgin Mary and the infant Christ. Sounds lovely I'd like to see it sometime. Yes, you will Father. I promise, but not until it's finished. No one looks at my work before it's completed. Of course not. A true artist never reveals his unfinished masterpieces, do they? I suppose not, well I'm going to get back to work on my delightful portrait and I'm sure you want to be heading home yourself? It is getting late Father. He walked the priest to the front-door praying silently he didn't grow suspicious of him during the brief visit. Father Fitzpatrick told Simon he would see him again soon. Simon lied through his teeth insisting he was looking forward to it. Father Fitzpatrick then reminded him of the church the following morning. God bless you son. Said the old Irish priest before exiting Fletcher's home. That was a close one. Simon feared he might not be so lucky next time.

One thing was for sure, he would be back before the week was through. Simon just didn't know when. He was going to have to remain vigilant around the clock, especially if he wants to take his corpse out and play with it. He had a bad feeling about removing her from the icy tomb and spending time with the slow decaying carcass. Making his way into the kitchen for a much, needed drink, Simon opened the freezer and snatched the bottle. He twisted the cap and tilted his head back. He was very jumpy and needed something to help him relax. It felt as if his entire nervous system was vibrating, Simon almost feared being electrocuted by the current of his very own soul. With the bottle in his hand, he went over to the front window and watched as the old priest walked off, back to the town church. He enjoyed his exercise and rarely drove his car. Simon hoped that might be a good thing he was slow-moving. It would be easy to see him coming if he was paying attention.

As he faded out of sight, Simon took one more sip and put the bottle of booze back on ice. With his head starting to spin, he headed back into the basement almost losing his footing again and taking a faster than an anticipated trip to the bottom. Even with the dim light on the basement was still a pretty -spooky place. He continued forward his eyes on Renee's body as she lay there face down. Simon always feared if the devil was ever going to come for him it would be in the basement. It was the only place in Fletcher's home not heavily guarded by religious symbols. The godliest representative down there was probably Santa Clause. Soon even he will be taking a vacation from its gloomy existence, to be placed on the front lawn for all to see. Simon assumed his nerves were still twitching from the uninvited guest showing up to remind him of his controlling parents. If he wanted to murder the pretty young neighbor and store her in the freezer downstairs, why the fuck couldn't he? Simon was trying to hang onto the false vision that this is all still part of his fate. It was a dangerous illusion that could get him in big trouble if he's found out. Ultimately, it may even lead to his very own death.

As he neared the bottom of the stairs Simon continued to gawk at the most beautiful corpse anyone has ever laid eyes on. He couldn't explain why he was still so sexually attracted to her. Too shaken up to enjoy Renee's company tonight, he felt it wasn't meant to be, Simon would rather put her away and try to forget about her for a while, he bent down to turn Renee over and noticed she was in pretty good shape considering the thrashing she just endured falling down the old flight of stairs, he wasted no time lifting her off the floor and placing her back in the frigid coffin. This time for some reason he didn't kiss, her goodbye, maybe it was because he had such an uneasy feeling lingering deep in the pit of his stomach. Instead, he closed the lid and turned to walk away.

As he staggered slightly up the stairs Simon heard Renee calling out his name in a soft sexy voice. He nervously called out to her while turning to see if she truly had returned from the dead, I hear you, Renee, where are you? I can't see you he cried out. Curious and afraid Simon focused his attention on where the voice was coming from. He imagined she would appear before him as a radiant ghost.

The dark eerie cellar remained silent and there was no sign of Renee's restless spirit until suddenly he heard- the sound of someone gasping desperately for air. It was an awful sound and Simon remembered it well.

It was exactly what Renee sounded like in her final moments when he choked the life out of her. Until this moment Simon imagined he was looking over his dead queen as if she was a divine pharaoh from a time long past. She somehow managed to remain exotic even as the transformation of death crept across her frozen flesh like a hurdling avalanche devouring anything in its path. Doing his best to leave her behind, Simon was quick to flee the basement. As he reached the top step, he felt someone blowing cold air on the back of his neck.

He turned his head preparing for the worst, but there was no one there. He knew it was someone's breath, not even the damp moldy basement smelled that ungodly. Simon expected to see Renee's corpse dragging its feet across the cellar floor when he turned his head toward the place where her body lies. He wasted no time getting out of there and slamming the door behind him. Simon believed he could trap her angry spirit with an old wooden door.

He wasn't comprehending the seriousness of the situation. It wasn't Renee's physical corpse that was coming for him, it was her enraged soul, so utterly scorned she came back from the other side to seek revenge. Again, Simon found himself wide awake during the blood-curdling experience. There was no questioning whether, or not this was all in his head. This time the experience was real, he heard her and even smelled her repulsive breath. He was frantically looking around the house waiting for his murdered victim to show herself.

Drunk and extremely angry he dared Renee to appear before him as if he could control her spirit as easily as the vehicle, he banished her from. Why are you doing this to me? I love you, Renee. Can't you see now how much I fucking love you? If you are with me right now do something, please. The house stood silent and he continued losing his patients. If Renee was there, he demanded to see her. Simon noticed the blood-red roses he brought home for her the night before. Now he was growing terrified of the beautiful young woman he coldly snuffed out. For some reason, he felt compelled to glance at the statues displayed all around the house.

It was almost as if he expected them to come alive before his eyes and drag him to hell kicking and screaming for his actions. Simon saw no signs of anything wicked, but he couldn't deny the eerie vibe spreading its invisible presence throughout the entire house. His heart continued beating fast as he anticipated something to happen. Simon wanted to see if their fixed eyes would shift position as he moved around the house. He was a little disappointed when there was nothing. As he went back to the kitchen for another round of vodka, Simon tried convincing himself none of this madness was real. He didn't have a choice the young man already felt his parents treated him like a child. What was he going to tell them? I killed Renee next, door and now her ghost won't leave me alone? He would be locked in a padded cell at the bottom of the church with an exorcist preparing to drive the demons from his body with prayer. Simon was going to have to find a way to survive for the next few days until they return from paradise.

His vacation was not going so well. Simon thought he was going to have the greatest week of his life while his folks were away. Instead, his dead princess was returning from the grave to seek revenge. As he opened the freezer and reached for the bottle, Simon heard the horrible gasping sound again. This time it was even worse than before. It was so close Simon could feel the rushing current of cold air sweeping through the tiny hairs inside his eardrum. He turned around trembling, expecting to find Renee standing right behind him. Again, there was nothing. He was growing weary of this madness and wanted her to go away.

Nervously he reached for the vodka again, taking a sip from the bottle, his hand shaking while waiting for another sign. Simon hated that sound, it sent chills up his spine. He would never forget the terrifying look on Renee's face as he squeezed all the air out of her lungs. The wind was whistling loudly as Simon put the bottle away and turned to walk toward the radio, imagining it might make him feel safer, as he did Simon was confronted by Renee standing only feet away as if she had truly returned from the grave. She didn't look frightened, but angry. Why did you kill me? Renee asked as she came walking slowly toward him, wearing the same clothes she was murdered in, he could even see his hand-marks around her throat.

Frozen stiff with fear, Simon listened as Renee warned him to remove her body from the basement freezer at once. She demanded a proper burial, or the hauntings would intensify. Renee pointed to the cellar door leading to wear her remains lie, frozen in a glacial tomb. Horrified as he was at the vision standing before him, Simon wasn't sure he could part with her remains, even if it meant losing his own life, he had grown so morbidly attached to them. He couldn't believe for the first time, he wanted her to go away. Simon no longer wanted to see the beauty queen he demolished in a jealous fit of rage. He just wanted her gone especially when the stench of rotting flesh hit his nostrils. It was nauseating and sent Simon to his knees, the vengeful spirit standing over him. You killed me, Simon, Renee coldly reminded him.

The perverted killer started crying, afraid of what she was going to do. He did his best to convince Renee that he killed her because he was so in love with her. She knew it was due to a sick and twisted obsession and wanted to see him pay for what he had done. Suddenly the odor went away as quickly as it appeared, Simon slowly got back to his feet, he walked toward the image of Renee standing before him, doing his best to appear brave, he walked right through her down into the basement where her body lies. It was the last place he wanted to be at the moment.

He was thinking about placing her in the back of his car and dumping her off in the woods, someplace remote where no one will ever think to look. As he went down the basement steps, Simon felt his entire body trembling from the smothering fear. After seeing her ghost standing in the living room, Simon didn't want to open the icebox and place his eyes upon her. He didn't know if he could face her again.

This morbid situation was getting out of hand and Simon had no idea how to stop it. Renee was right about one thing. He had to remove her dead body from the property before someone notices she is missing. Simon knew he would be the first person everyone would point their finger at if the law gets involved. He was so busy swimming around in his troubling thoughts he didn't even notice the minuscule sphere of light hovering in the darkest corner of the dungeon.

It was bouncing gracefully on a thin pocket of air, watching and waiting with sinister intent from a disembodied conscience state as Simon Fletcher stood near her chilly casket. Renee wished she was powerful enough to open the lid and reenter her body, so she could use it to murder him. The tiny orb moved around the dark basement desperate for Simon to take notice. His murder victim wanted to become something more tangible since she had a score to settle.

There seemed to be no true guilt in Simon's heart for what he had done. It was as if he only wished she was still alive, so he could enjoy her warm, soft skin. Simon was standing there about to open the freezer and remove her when he felt an ice-cold chill go by. It also sounded as if someone was exhaling in a suffocating sort of way, as the orb rushed, passed.

He stopped for a moment and turned around. Hello. Is anybody there? Only the gust of the arctic winds could be heard whipping past his eerie den of terror. Searching the basement for any sign of Renee, Simon saw nothing but the lonely darkness that surrounded him. He then opened the icy tomb to have a look at the frosty blue carcass frozen solid inside. His method of preservation was destroying her beauty in an entirely different way. He thought he was being helpful, or perhaps even merciful by keeping her away from fly larvae buffets.

Once she warmed up everything would rapidly breakdown and the putrid odor would give away his secret. Gone were his fantasies of sitting beside the burning fire with Renee in his arms. That would bring on the process of decay even faster. Simon continued to hesitate and ignore the warnings to give his victim a proper burial someplace peaceful. He felt as if he was effortlessly soaring toward a treacherous descent into hells gullet head-first. The terrified killer convinced himself that he was already damned. He even imagined if he so much as touched the family bible it would burst into white-hot flames. Melting the flesh from his hand in the process. The more he thought about his terrible future, the more Simon wanted to empty the liquor bottle down his throat.

Standing there staring at Renee's cold, dead remains Simon suddenly noticed a dark shadow slip passed him. There were no features and no words were said. He just watched it move across the wall in front of him and then it was gone. Growing up loved and protected, the four-eyed maniac didn't know much about fear. Renee was going to change all that. She was not going to stop until Simon Fletcher was truly sorry for what he did. She wanted him to beg for forgiveness knowing there would be none.

The increasing fright jingling his nerves was gaining momentum as angels and demons remained hidden under the cover of darkness tallying up all the unspeakable sins he was willfully committing., Simon didn't think it was going to be possible to bury her someplace decent tonight, it was far too cold and the ground would be difficult to breakthrough. He would have to wait until the snow melts and the ground softens a bit if he intended on burying her in the earth. Simon decided to close the freezer and ignore his victim's wishes for the evening. Before he could turn around, Simon felt two ice-cold hands resting on his shoulders.

They pushed harder and dug their nails deep into his skin. It hurt like a son of a bitch and as Simon screamed out in pain, he found himself alone once again. Turning around as fast as he could, Simon was shocked to find no one standing there. With that, he hurried out of the basement and into the living room where he noticed the snow had lightly begun falling again. Now he knew for sure Renee's frozen corpse would have to stay with him for another night.

He hoped that by leaving her alone, Renee would grant him the same respect. She had no intention of keeping the peace. She wanted to torment him slowly for a while, before driving him completely insane. As he escaped the creepy under-ground lair where his victim lied dead, Simon heard the phone ringing. He answered it thankful to have a connection to the outside world until he discovered who was on the other line. It was his mother calling again to make sure he was alright. She confessed that she had been watching the weather channel and that another snowstorm would soon be arriving in his part of New Jersey. Simon did his best to insure, his mother that everything would be alright. I know sweetheart, but your father and I want you to know you can call us if you need anything. We love you and please be careful.

This new storm is supposed to stick around until sometime tomorrow night. Don't go anywhere. Please Simon just stays home and relax until this storm passes over. I don't want to have to worry about you any more than I already am. You do this to yourself mother. You don't have to trouble yourself so relentlessly over me. I'm a big boy. I can take care of myself. You and dad are supposed to be having a great time. Go live it up. On the inside, Simon was frightened to be home all by himself with a corpse and an angry ghost haunting him. He was not going to tell his mother that. He knew she and his father would be on the first flight back to Jersey even in the blistery storm. Then what would he do with Renee's frozen remains? When he hangs up the phone, Simon planned to find something good on tv and try to forget about the dead woman for the rest of the night. He let Renee down but planned to dispose of her as soon as possible.

Deep in his drink, Simon stumbled to the window leading to the backyard. He watched as the snow fell heavily over his perfect little town. Simon stared at his treehouse high above the ground. It was the very place he claimed her life. It seemed a bit creepier to him now, even uninviting, he was afraid Renee's angry spirit might prove more aggressive in the location where she died? He was giving great thought to leaving her in the icebox until he decides what to do with her frozen remains. He knew it was only a matter of time before Mrs. Anderson or someone else notices her jeep hasn't moved in days. He imagined the snow depending on how bad it gets might buy him a few extra days. Who wants to go out in weather like this? Even if you do own a jeep renegade. As he turned away from the view of the treehouse, Simon was startled by the radio playing on full blast. It was even freakier since the Beatles were saying they saw her standing there. As Simon rotated his eyes in every direction there was no sign of Renee. He turned off the music to see if she was going to turn it back on.

The house seemed edgier now that it was silent again. Is that all you got? He Hollard, challenging Renee to show herself again. Simon stood there listening to the frenzy of the storm, convinced he was going to hear Renee's voice somewhere faintly trapped inside it. Plans to sleep with the lights on were definitely -in the cards for the frightened killer. He was almost too terrified to even sleep in his own home. Simon hated himself and didn't want Renee to see him as a coward. It was bad enough he took her life and raped her dead body.

If Simon had any intentions of sleeping tonight, he was going to need more liquor to help knock him out cold. He started heading to the kitchen when the television came on by itself this time. Simon almost leaped out of his skin. He couldn't believe she was able to fuck with him like this, he told her to knock it off and that it wasn't funny or amusing anymore. Simon soon noticed that the channel was airing an emergency broadcast. Something about a missing girl. His heart skipped a beat, thinking Renee was the person of discussion. It was impossible no one even knew she was missing yet. Unless her friends in California already alerted the authorities of her disappearance.

His eyes were drawn to the television set as they flashed the victim's face before him. Simon couldn't believe it. The face staring back at him was none other than his beloved Renee Price. The man broadcasting the news said she had gone missing a few days earlier. He added they have a strong suspect in mind. Simon was unable to breathe as he waited for his name to be announced on live tv. As he paid closer attention to the background, Simon noticed the news crew was standing right outside Renee's front door.

There was a large crowd of police and concerned citizens demanding answers. As Simon stared into her beautiful blue eyes, her picture was replaced by his. They even said his name. Simon Fletcher is wanted for questioning in regards to the missing beauty queen. Mrs. Anderson was speaking into a microphone announcing to the world what a pervert he was and how she caught him spying on the pretty young girl while she pranced around her house half-naked most of the time. Now everyone knew he was a sex addict and a cold-blooded killer. He never wanted to leave the house and show his face in public again. What if his parents were watching this? He was nervously waiting for the phone to ring. Knowing they were on to him and filming right next-door at Renee's house. Simon was also waiting for the cops to bust in and take him away in shackles. With all these thoughts running through his head, Simon continued to sit there watching the broadcast.

He soon became fixated on this one woman separating herself from the angry mob gathered outside his house. As she stepped closer, Simon noticed it was Renee Price with the Devil in her eyes. She marched her way right up to the camera never blinking or taking her eyes off of him. Simon was frozen with fear as she came closer and there was a loud pounding on the front door. He looked away from the tv and toward the front door expecting it to be kicked in. He didn't want to open it and face the music, but when he turned back to the tv, Simon noticed Renee was standing right behind him in the living room. He could see her reflection through the glass and feel her ice-cold fingers scratching down his back. They dug in and blood poured from the open gashes. When he finally got away from the phantom attacker Simon hurried to the front door. He would rather be taken to jail then killed by Renee's ghost. When he opened it, Simon expected to see bright lights flashing and a bunch of police and reporters in his face demanding answers.

The loud pounding on the door continued until Simon opened it and found there was no one there. He saw no police nor reporters eager to arrest and interview him for the sinister crime. Instead, the street was completely deserted. Only the falling snow and hollering wind could be seen and heard. As Simon tried to accept this bizarre situation, he heard the television shut off and the house went silent again as well. His blood ran cold from the fear that rattled his bones. How could she do something so elaborate? Simon wondered to himself.

The fake newsgathering for her missing body seemed so real. In truth, he knew no one was yet aware of Renee Price's death. Simon took it as another warning to give her remains a proper burial. He didn't know his victim was interested in far more from her perverted killer. She planned to slowly torment him until he keels over from fright. A home full of the holy spirit was being invaded by a troublesome spirit back from the dead for revenge. She would not rest in peace until she resolved all her unfinished business here on earth first. Simon was convinced Renee would not stop until he pays the ultimate price.

He started to shiver as he stood in the doorway shocked at what just happened. He closed the door and reluctantly stayed in the house with the vengeful ghost. He wanted to get out of the cold, even though he keeps poor Renee frozen in the icebox all day long. Once back inside, Simon found himself under attack by one of his mother's porcelain angels. She was flying right at him as if someone picked her up off the shelf and threw the heavy angel his way. Simon watched as it came toward him, getting out of the way just before being struck by the flying angel statue.

He assumed Renee was responsible for giving it lift-off. The fragile piece hit the wall and exploded into pieces. He wasn't sure how he was going to explain that one to his folks when they returned. Just when Simon didn't think things could get any worse? The lights started to flicker on and off. He wasn't sure if he was actually- losing power due to the storm? Or if it was Renee fucking with him again. He was drunk and frightened, but there was no place to go. He had no choice, but to sleep in the empty house with the angry spirit all by himself. Again, Simon lost his faith in God and started blaming him for everything he had done wrong. As if god told him to murder his attractive neighbor and store her in the family freezer. He couldn't see her, but there it was again, that sensation of someone gently breathing on the back of his neck.

The wind continued to whistle loudly as the snow piled up outside. Simon wanted to hop in his car and get as far away as he can from Renee's body and spirit, now that they had become two separate entities. He soon realized it didn't matter where he went. The house wasn't haunted.

Renee was going to come for him where-ever he went. With the lights momentarily off, Simon carefully made his way to the bathroom to piss out some of the vodkas he had been enjoying. When the lights came back on, Simon saw Renee's reflection sharing the mirror with him.

This time the beauty-queen abandoned all her pretty looks. She was decrepit, her flesh decaying and hanging loosely from the bones. Insects were crawling around her face and in and out of the black, bottomless pits where her sky-blue eyes once were. Why did you do this to me? She asked causing Simon to tremble and cry out to her. I'm going to get you for this. She warned while reaching through the glass without shattering it to attack him. Simon noticed her fingernails were long and blackened from decomposition, he closed his eyes and started to pray. He begged the lord to remove the horrible image from his sight. Renee was planning to bury her sharp animal-like claws deep into his flesh. Borrowing through his ribcage and piercing his ice-cold heart. Leave me alone please! he screamed out hoping Renee would go away, but he could still feel her presence in the room with him. When he opened his eyes, she appeared to be nowhere in sight.

He wanted to get out of the bathroom as quickly as possible. It was foolish since there was no safe place to hide from the angry ghost. He did his best to apologize to the thin air sharing the space around him, swearing to Renee that he never meant to kill her and that he loved her with all his heart. Turning his attention to the tv again, Simon noticed Renee's reflection on the picture tube. Bizarre since he couldn't see her standing only inches away. With tears in his eyes, Simon told her again how much he adored her. I know you do. She said when he turned around and found her standing nose to nose with him. Simon screamed as Renee attacked him. Using her sharp claws to cut and slice away at his face and chest mercilessly. Simon tried defending himself, but she was too strong, tearing and carving slices out of his face and smiling as she did it. When she finally relented, Simon hurried back into the bathroom to check on his injuries. He knew it was bad since his face wouldn't stop leaking blood. When he looked in the mirror, Simon noticed the gashes were quite deep, and he had to find a way to stop the bleeding. Simon would also have to explain to everyone where the bruises came from. There was no way to hide the nasty craters dug into his face. He was going to have to get rid of the body if he wanted this horror to end.

After doing his best to clean himself up, Simon went back to the living-room to have a seat on the couch and try to calm down. He watched as the snow fell, assuring him, he wouldn't have to attend church the following morning. He was not willing to shovel the driveway to visit a vengeful god who despised him. Simon heard his name being called again in the middle of the frigid wind blowing passed. Leave me alone! he screamed out, with no one in sight to hear him. He looked like a crazy person yelling at himself. While sitting on the couch Simon noticed the tiny orb floating around the room. It was just like the one that flew passed him in the basement.

This time he couldn't take his eyes off -of it as it danced around in front of the tv, eager for his undivided attention. While Simon watched the ball of light drift with eyes wide -open, he paid close attention as it drifted closer. He could feel this strange pocket of cool air coming his way as the tiny ball of light approached. When it was inches away, Simon noticed there was a face inside the minuscule ball of dancing light, he was expecting it to look like Renee, but the face staring back at him had dark pulsating eyes and a scaly type of covering. It was the face of a man, but the most -evil-looking man Simon had ever seen. He imagined it was the Devil himself coming to claim his tortured soul.

He was frightened but couldn't look away from the demonic beam of light in the glowing form of Lucifer the famous falling angel. When it finally disappeared, Simon heard Renee whispering that she was coming for him. He spun his head around, but there was no one there. When he turned back toward the tv, he saw Renee standing there completely naked. She looked as beautiful as the day they first met. She slowly walked closer and was soon sitting on his lap. Her gorgeous breast against his face, as she tried helping him out of his pants.

Simon wanted to get away from her, but he couldn't move. Renee had a spell on her killer, seducing him with her beauty, his body was frozen, but not quite like hers. Renee started kissing him and riding up and down on his penis. Only this time it didn't feel soft and wet. Her expired body was cold and dry as the red desert of mars. Does that feel good? She asked softly as Simon struggled to getaway. I thought you liked it rough, Renee asked with a pussy similar to a piece of extra gritty sandpaper. What's the matter Simon don't you love me anymore? I thought you wanted to be together forever. With that Renee leaned closer, biting into his throat and forcing blood to squirt out at high velocity. It was like a raging river flowing from his veins. He awoke screaming in the living room. Frantically looking- around, Renee was nowhere to be seen.

The television was on playing the three stooges. Simon assumed he must have dozed off while watching it and getting completely shit faced. The nightmares were so vivid, he couldn't believe they weren't real. Simon immediately got off the couch and ran for the bathroom to have a look at himself in the mirror. His nerves were still twitching as he saw all the gashes and claw marks were still there. Simon started touching them to see how deep they went. He screamed out in agony as his fingers started to slip further into the open wound.

Doing his best to clean them out and avoid infection, Simon used iodine which was very painful. He wanted to get even with Renee for terrorizing his dreams. He had to sleep, and she was making that impossible. Once he was through patching himself up, Simon went to his bedroom to try and calm down. He was going to leave the lights on and the tv with the volume up, if he has- to. As he neared the top of the stairs, Simon noticed a pungent odor coming from the top floor. It grew stronger with every step forward.

When he finally got to his bedroom it was almost enough to knock him off his feet. He opened the door and inside was Renee's rotting corpse. She looked worse than a zombie from that George Romero film and was staring right at him with those blank pale white eyes. Simon had no idea how she got out of the freezer? Or how she managed to walk from the basement to his room? She was awful to look at and the stench had Simon bending over to vomit up all the liquor he consumed earlier, as she started coming towards him.

His beauty queen was now a walking carcass out for blood. I want you to come with me to the other side. You're going to like hell Simon I promise. I know you like things hot, don't you? He screamed and tried backing away, but soon Renee had her icy hands wrapped around his throat again. He could feel the life being drained from him as Renee stared into his eyes.

When she finally let go Simon did his best to breathe again. Renee reached between his legs and squeezed as hard as she could, driving her nails into his testicles. Simon Hollard in agony as he leaped from yet another nightmare. His heart was beating like a marathon sprinter and he couldn't stop shaking. It seemed Renee might finally get her to wish.

CHAPTER 13

S imon was too frightened to leave her frozen corpse inside the house with him. His heavy drinking and constant paranoia were going to lead to one of the most foolish ideas any man has ever had. Simon thought he was showing the dead woman who's in charge. He would seriously regret his bone-headed decision the following morning. He saw that the snow showed no signs of stopping. There would be no church the following morning. It was to be called off by mother-nature.

The town of Renee Falls would remain still for the next twenty-four hours. Everyone was going to be buried up to their necks in the snow with nothing to do. At least that's what he imagined. Once Simon managed to calm himself enough to function properly, he bundled up to face the weather and hurried down into the basement where her frozen body resided. He was going to get even with Renee and create a little more separation between himself and his deceased princess. Simon didn't feel safe with her remaining under the same roof as him any longer.

He had a brazen idea that could easily bring more harm than good. Simon was going to leave Renee out in the frigid storm for the rest of the night. It was a preposterous idea that sprang from his intoxicated mind. If something should go wrong, it will certainly lead to his undoing. What a bold and maniacal plan it was. Simon didn't care, the deranged killer was coming apart at the seams and needed some relief from the angry spirit tormenting him both awake and asleep. Leaving the dead woman out on his front-lawn was announcing his guilt to the entire world or at the very least the few residents who call this quiet little place home. Simon was planning on hiding his beautifully preserved corpse in plain sight. He was going to disguise her frozen remains as a big, jolly snowman.

Making his way into the basement, Simon was ready to disturb her from her eternal nap in a bed of ice, so he can display her like a mannequin in a clothing store. He felt the eyes of all the religious figures watching him as he walked by with wicked intentions. When he opened the freezer and saw her blankly staring up at him, Simon felt a nasty chill slithering slowly up his spine. It was still hard to accept the fact that she was, dead, killed mercilessly by his hands. It was driving him mad and Simon feared it wouldn't be long before he joined her in death.

The scared young murderer wasn't sure if he could live with what he's done. He wanted to hurry and finish the ghoulish task awaiting him. Simon knew Renee had to be disposed of, but he didn't have the heart to part with her. Once he no longer possessed her remains, he would truly realize Renee's death was all for nothing. There was no escaping this selfish need to keep them as- long as possible. Simon swiftly went to work removing her dress, he wanted her to be completely naked beneath the man of snow who was nowhere near as cold as he turned out to be. Simon heard the stereo come on upstairs while stripping her naked, he ignored it thinking it was either a thank you for getting her out of that icy tomb? Or a warning for furthering his wretched abuse on her cold, dead body. Simon hoisted her out of Fletcher's family freezer while the music played loudly throughout the house.

He wrapped Renee up in an old blanket, imitating a cocoon, and proceeded to drag her up the basement steps. Her face exposed, Renee was blankly staring at the ceiling as he traveled through the house. Nearing the top of the stairs, Simon noticed the music fell silent again. He wanted to hurry and build a snowman shell around his victim, before someone notices.

He didn't want anyone to know what was buried at the center of old Frosty. Simon left her on the front porch while he hurried to the garage to retrieve one of his father's heavy-duty hand-trucks. He planned to strap

Renee to it and leave his heavenly angel standing there under the cover of pure white snow. Once she was securely placed on the dolly, Simon lifted her and began covering her in snow. It didn't take very long as the blizzard continued, unknowingly assisting the madman in his ludicrous act against humanity.

The blustery winds made it a little challenging and were beginning to affect Simon as he couldn't stop shivering. He could only imagine what the old bag across the street would think if she caught him out there in the dead of night burying the missing neighbor beneath a large man of snow. If she was to come outside and confront him for his actions? Simon imagined he would have a matching pair of snowmen standing on his property the next morning.

You're going to be the prettiest snowman the world has ever seen Renee, Simon promised while confessing his love and remorse to her for the millionth time. He buried the corpse as fast as he could to cover the violated carcass underneath. Stacking snow, Simon couldn't help but glance into her emotionless eyes. He felt as though they can still see him somehow. Almost finished my love, he stated as he began dumping snow on top of her head making her momentarily disappear. Simon knew when he was finished, he would have to go the extra step and give her a carrot nose and some black deceitful eyes. He imagined two black olives would do the trick. Perhaps a small handful for the carefree, smiling mouth as well.

When he was about done, Simon heard that eerie voice in the wind again. She was calling his name and warning that she would never stop until he was dead or locked in a padded room, further cutting him off from the rest of the world he has yet to see and experience. Looking around quickly, Simon noticed there was no one there. He told the disembodied voices he wasn't afraid. Renee knew that was a lie, he was going to be terrified of what her angry ghost had in-store for him. Your dead and I'm still alive. Do you hear me, sweetheart? I won. You belong to me forever. Simon warned. He continued burying Renee in her very temporary, vertical grave.

When he was finally done, Simon took a couple of steps back to marvel at his newest creation. It might just prove to be his finest work yet. It was impossible to notice there was a dead woman buried in the very center of the gigantic ice-being. Always taking great delight in his work, Simon drunkenly imagined he would receive plenty of compliments for the fine specimen standing at attention in his front yard. He ignorantly thought it was a funny way to insult the entire town, as they bragged about how lovely his morbid creation was. Under the fat layer of snow was Renee's frozen, corpse blankly staring back at everyone who stops to take a gander at it. It made the twisted psychopath smile inside and out. He couldn't wait to get back in the warm house and pass-out for the rest of the night. In the morning he would discover what people think of his morbid snowman. That is if he even remembers what he did with her when he wakes-up. Wasted as Simon was, he may forget about the foolish act he committed while drinking heavily. He didn't think about what would happen when the snow finally started to melt.

Attracting attention was the last thing the killer wanted or needed. This could prove to be his undoing.? Perhaps when he awakens the following morning, he will have deep regrets for his drunken actions. For now, all he wanted to do is get out of the storm. He put the shovel away and noticed an extra set of footprints in the snow. Simon's eyes widened with excitement when he realized they were not in human form, but those of a rabbit. Simon also noticed there were small amounts of blood in them. He decided to follow the tiny footprints, praying ignorantly that no one was watching his movements at the moment. Running for its life and eventually collapsing on Simon Fletcher's lawn was an injured and dying rabbit.

Simon approached slowly before going back inside to get warm. Seeing that the poor creature was suffering and, on a collision course with death, his sadistic side sprung back to life. Simon suddenly remembered the rodent devouring serpent starving right next door. It was the best day of his life, Renee Price looked at him differently that day, she got him high and even gave herself to him. It gave Lennon a sort of symbolic meaning.

Simon was overdosing on a toxic potion of anger mixed with fear. He bent down to introduce himself to the rabbit with a crude demeanor, before carrying it into his first victim's house where a hungry predator was trapped and waiting to be fed. Simon warmed himself with excitement, as he hurried into Renee's house, to feed the suffering rodent to Lennon like he always wanted to. Carrying the injured and helpless animal to its gruesome demise, Simon remembered the joints Renee had stashed. Playing Russian roulette, Simon decided to venture to her bedroom, the rabbit in his right hand. Quickly finding what he was looking for, Simon offered to share the weed with the rodent he was moments from putting to death. "You ready little buddy?". Said Simon, as he headed downstairs toward the kitchen, using the stove burner to ignite the priceless joint rolled by his worst enemy. Simon didn't even realize he was spilling animal blood all over his victim's house while moving around freely., The deranged killer lit the joint and began to feel carefree, it was almost an out of body experience, compared to the life he was used to.

With cannabis clouds filling the house, Simon made his way to the living room with the next innocent victim in his hands. Dislodged from the reality the strictly raised Christian was used to, Simon enjoyed being bad. Eternity couldn't stretch any further than it already was, and he was going to make it worth it. He could feel the rabbit starting to move harder and faster giving all, it's got, as he slowly approached the snake's tank. Simon knew the prey was fully aware of the sudden danger it was being placed in. The poor white rabbit with red eyes was purposely dropped as dinner for the slithering serpent. Simon sat in a lazy boy recliner nearby, as he continued smoking the pot and keeping a close eye on the live meal being used as a ghoulish sacrifice. Not to mention a ghastly form of entertainment for the twisted young lunatic. He began to feel different as the weed crept in and the hungry snake settled into position immediately after the dying meal had arrived. Simon didn't know where to focus his attention as the event slowly unfolded at first. He scoped out the meal he curiously offered to Satan's pet and watched the fear manifest from an electronic pulse inside a brainwave to a tangible reaction within the preys anatomical, structure. Simon found it fascinating, especially as he continued hitting the joint and fogging up Renee's house. This might very well be Lennon's last supper, depending on how long it takes to discover the bodies, at least he would be fattened up for a while when he was through. The temperature in the room plummeted, sending a cold front through Simon's bones. Renee's image appeared to him just before the famished predator moved in for the kill. The snake quickly coiled around the rabbit squeezing most of the life out of it, before painfully and horrifyingly swallowing it down. The rabbit stared at Simon with misery in its red glowing eyes, as if intelligent enough to hold him accountable, perhaps the marijuana was to blame for the entire thing. Simon watched ever so carefully as the childlike screaming stopped and the snake grew fatter as the hefty meal was gradually passed along its guts. It was as gross as it was fascinating to Simon as he remembered it wasn't safe to remain there.

With the joint still in his grip, Simon took a drag and absorbed the gruesome scene he just witnessed while stoned on weed. It was a vicious murder animal kingdom style and Simon couldn't help but smirk, as he remembered it was time to go.

From now on Lennon would have to fend for himself. Simon hurried home and started removing all the heavy, wet clothes meant to keep him warm. He slipped into his pajamas, removed his glasses, and collapsed onto his bed. He didn't even see the ghostly reflection of Renee's angry spirit staring at him from the mirror across the room. She looked furious as if she was going to walk through the glass without shattering it and wrap her hands around his throat. He viciously took her life and was now sleeping like a baby, while she remained traumatized in the afterlife. One way or another Simon Fletcher was going to get what he deserves. Turning her remains into a spectacle for the whole town to witness was beyond ludicrous. He was humiliating his victim in a very discrete way. For now, all Renee could do is watch over her killer, until she figures out a way to get even.

Early the next-morning Simon was abruptly awakened by the sound of someone knocking on the front door and ringing the bell. His mind began to race with the dreadful possibilities of who could be paying him such an early visit on a Sunday morning. Whoever it was? Was pushing Simon's buttons as well as the annoying singing bell, ringing out through the entire house. Vaguely remembering his idiotic actions, the night before, Simon imagined the snowman melted and the police were standing on his porch looking to take him away in shackles and a stray-jacket. What if a kid from town noticed Renee's body standing beneath the mound of snow? Strapped crudely to a hand-truck. His eyes were wide open as panic invaded his entire body. Reaching for his glasses, Simon's biggest fear was that his nosy neighbor Mrs. Anderson was somehow awake in the middle of the night watching him bury a corpse in the upright position during the awful blizzard. It appeared to be cold and gray outside as he looked through the window. Simon saw no sign of police cars or the bright flashing lights below him. He still feared someone discovered what he has done and now it was time to pay the piper. Nervously, Simon made his way down-stairs in his pajamas. He knew as, long as the snow stuck around, he could essentially leave Renee out there buried beneath a beautiful white blanket of frozen moisture.

In- reality, he knew when the sun goes down and darkness returns later that evening, he would have no choice but to dismantle his creation and relocate the frozen corpse back in the family icebox. Coming down the stairs, Simon took a quick look around and realized in his carelessness, he had left the depleted bottle of vodka out for all to see. He tossed it in the trash and buried it with the other garbage it was sharing a bag with. He then made his way to the front door. When he opened it, Simon found Mrs. Anderson from across the street standing there looking her finest for the church., only she couldn't get her car out of the driveway. She came to see if the stalker across the street would do her this enormous favor. Simon usually shared this duty with his father when storms like this blew into town. He was not so eager to bundle up and dig out the elderly woman's driveway this morning. She was determined to spend her weekly time with the lord, and nothing was going to get in her way. She begged the troubled young man if he would do her this huge favor? Simon knew he would hear all about it when his parents returned if he slammed the door in her face. They would be incredibly upset with him for his selfishness. "Please Simon I have- to get to church this morning or god will never forgive me." Simon smiled and assured Mrs. Anderson he would gladly come to her rescue. Sarcastically he commented, "if the lord was expecting us all to visit him this morning? He should have held off the wintery blizzard a little longer". Mrs. Anderson didn't care for his humor. She didn't laugh or smile at his foolish words. A good Christian woman, she bit her tongue, unwilling to say what she wanted to. Mrs. Anderson didn't want to cause any friction with the one person who could see to it that she makes it to church on such a challenging morning. She unwillingly placed her time with Christ in the hands of the devil.

Simon knew he hit a nerve with his nosy old neighbor. Doing her best to keep the peace, Mrs. Anderson changed the subject to something much more subtle. The fragile woman didn't want to piss him off ruining her chance to sing praises and feel the holy spirit invade her body. She didn't know her conversation was going to rattle the young man to his very core. Chilling his temperature to minus what Renee was feeling while essentially trapped under ice. That's an incredible snowman Simon. I have to say I've never seen anything like it. Then again? You've always been quite the artist, haven't you? Not even when you were a boy did you go to such great length to construct such a marvelous man of snow. I don't understand why he is so sad though, Mrs. Anderson asked. Because he too knows that life is short. Very short in his case. Chuckling slightly, Simon responded as he grew even more paranoid that the old lady was on to him. Why did she have to bring up the snowman? Did she know what lied beneath the thin covering? Or was she simply sucking up to make it to church on time? Again Mrs. Anderson found his answer to be a bit cold and disturbing. She did her best to hide her true feelings about him. Well, he's wonderful Simon. I'm sure the kids in town will surely take a liking to him as well. Who knows kiddo? Frosty here might be the most famous snowmen of all-time? My only question is when in the world did you find time to build such a spectacular piece? The more she spoke, the more frightened the young killer became. Mrs. Anderson was right. What if Renee's inviting display becomes a hit with all the children from town? How would he destroy the famous man of snow? If the folks from town are continuously showing up to take pictures with it? Simon instantly regretted what he had done. Now he would have to find a way to make not only Renee's cold-dead body disappear? He would also have to secretly do away with Mr. Frosty. Simon knew even with the cloud-shielded, the sun coming out, it would be impossible to take her down.

Even while most people would be in church, there were always the few stragglers remaining behind including the police who patrol the town day and night. Don't worry Mrs. Anderson. I'll have your car out before the service begins. The elderly woman almost felt bad for putting the young man through all the trouble. Especially now that she knew he spent most of the night erecting a remarkably big snowman for the kids in town. He told her he couldn't sleep, and it was good enough for her. At least he wasn't spying on Renee all night long. Simon was just glad the nosy old broad didn't dig deeper into the inspiration for the time-consuming monument he created under the cover of darkness. His biggest fear now was the passing children who he had no control over. How could he kick them off his lawn for admiring his work? It seemed to have sprouted up from nowhere and folks would surely take notice. Her kind, innocent words sent tingling sensations through Simon's vertebrae, which forced him to shiver harshly. Lucky for him he could blame it on the early winter weather they were enduring. Mrs. Anderson jokingly reminded Simon that his folks picked a good time to flee this tundra for beaches and sunshine. Simon returned a fake laugh and lied by saying they deserved it. In the back of his mind, he felt he needed a permanent vacation from them. He might get a permanent one if someone ever discovers what he has done. Only it won't be white-sands and palm-trees. It'll be concrete rooms and murderous neighbors anxious to end your suffering, even more brutally than the way Renee's life was snuffed out. Simon did his best to pretend he wasn't infected head to toe with fear and anxiety, while engaged in conversation with the nosiest woman on the planet. Simon kept imagining what would happen to him if he was caught and sentenced for his horrific crime. He knew he deserved anything awful coming his way, he just wasn't man enough to face it. He couldn't stop thinking about the neighborhood kids gathering around the gnarly snowman.

What if they start playing and rough-housing around the abominable- snowman knocking it over and exposing the frozen, naked woman hiding inside. He saw all their faces paralyzed with fright as they turn to run away screaming. Others are too terrified to move or even breathe. The last thing Simon needed was a fucking tourist attraction. He prayed silently that the kids would simply mosey on by ignoring the tall man of ice watching over his home. It was an act Simon experienced all too often in his miserable life, particularly when it came to women. He knew all it took was one smart ass to destroy it for a crowd's laughter to bring him down. Everyone standing around would see the dead beauty-queen freed from her cocooned pillar of ice. They would also know exactly who the spineless killer was. He had to get dressed in a hurry, so he could clean off Mrs. Anderson's driveway before church-bells ring out. He was exhausted and didn't care to perform this act of kindness for the elderly woman. Simon always had the feeling she was going to be the one who causes the lawmen to decent onto his property and discover what he has done. It made it even harder to want to help in her time of need. Simon could see that she was shivering. He told her to go home and get warm. I will be there in a couple of minutes Mrs. Anderson.

Give me some time to get dressed. She thanked him again for his generosity and kindness, before turning to hurry home and out of the cold. Simon felt like an idiot for not inviting her in during the friendly little chat, but he wasn't entirely sure all the evidence of his evil-doing was out of sight, especially the very slight hint of death floating around invisibly, but not completely un-tangible to the human senses. Frozen or not? Some decomposition was inevitable in the freezer Renee was stored in. He would need much lower temperature and some sort of mummification procedure performed, removing blood and organs if he wanted to make her appear life-like forever. With the slight discoloration of her flesh, Renee's face was already changing on him. That was the hardest part of the entire thing. Without her sexy looks, what good was having her body around? The place smelled fine to him, but he had been there breathing it in day after day. He wouldn't even notice if it was really- subtle, but a person from outside may pick-up on it in a jiffy.

Simon wasn't taking any chances. He was lucky last time when the priest showed up after dark and neglected to notice the negative scent. Simon was going to make sure he was prepared when the man of god decided to return. If he had to? Simon would simply spend lots of time in the kitchen. Cooking delicious, meals was the best way to make the place smell wonderful without alerting any suspicion. Continuing to regret his mindless, drunken decision, Simon went inside to get dressed and retrieve his shovel from the garage.

Once Mrs. Anderson was back in her house all toasty and warm, she looked out at the magnificent snow-giant guarding Fletcher's property. As astonishing as it was, there was something off about the whole thing. She vindicated her troubling thoughts when she shifted her attention to Simon's driveway. It was still completely covered beneath inches of snow, while he erected a bigfoot in ice on his lawn instead. She wondered why he would stay up all night and go through all that trouble to build a snowman? Mrs. Anderson was mostly ticked at his complete disrespect for their lord and savior. It seemed he didn't care much of Jesus's day and had no intentions on paying his respects to the mortal man who martyred himself for the very sins Simon Fletcher was doing his worst to hide. He actually- left Renee standing out there waving at all who pass screaming out for their undivided attention. It wasn't Mrs. Anderson's business in the end.

She knew he was doing her a big favor by allowing her to make it to church to celebrate and praise his name. While watching out the window and waiting for the odd young man to shovel her path to the road, Mrs. Anderson also noticed that the house next door was also buried in snow. She wondered how Renee was going to fair under these harsh conditions. Being a California native, she has probably never even seen snow like this before. In a silly way, the old woman was expecting to find the cheerful young blonde happily shoveling away the snow since it was so alien to her. It never took long for out of towner' to hate the heavy magical slush as much as the locals. She had a jeep which was the best possible vehicle to own during weather like this. It's been in the same place since at least Thursday? Far as she can recall. Sometimes Mrs. Anderson would question her own, memory, as we are all destined to do as we slide effortlessly into ripe-old age. Mrs. Anderson still had her wits and it was the beginning of her concern for the widowed young woman. She would be sure to keep an eye on her.

The seed Simon was so petrified of taking shape had in-fact been planted and soon it would blossom into chaos, unlike anything he could have imagined. The question now was, How, long before it germinates and bears fruit? If Mrs. Anderson didn't witness some movement soon proving the pretty young woman was alright? The police would be notified of her possible, disappearance. Without yet linking the two together, Mrs. Anderson shifted her eyes and attention back to the grotesque snowman standing vigilant and staring back at her. She knew Simon was no saint. The old woman just didn't know how dark and demented he could truly be? Simon was trying to pledge the same empty promise we all make to ourselves at one point or another. He swore he was never going to drink again. Not after all the stupid things he decided to do while under its wicked influence. Stanley and Eleanor were right all along. Liquor is Satan's manifestation in a bottle. It can possess your mind, and make you do the most, crazy things. He soon found it helpful for his safety to stand outside and clean off Mrs. Anderson's driveway. At least that way he could keep an eye on the snowman and monitor who is walking or playing around it. Digging away at the mass-gathering of frozen raindrops, Simon was heating up fast. It wasn't long before he found himself sweating. It would soon freeze and send chills throughout his entire body.

Looking across the road at the huge snowman standing on his parent's holy lawn brought joy to his inner being. Or was it the frozen man's inner being that had him feeling all jolly as he shoveled away what felt like an entire mountain of snow. There was a particular- arrogance about being the only person in the world that knew what was actually-standing there, staring out at the religious little town Renee Price came to die in. Perfectly concealed beneath the severely chilled liquid costume he placed her in. It was a very delicate balance that separated Simon's freedom and captivity.

A sudden shift in temperature could melt her mask and show everyone in town what a monster Simon Fletcher truly was. He would soon after find, himself seated in the electric chair for his heinous crime. After two whole hours, Simon finally had the runway cleared and ready for take-off. While lifting his head with a shovel blade full of snow, Simon noticed that the rest of the town was waking up as well. Henrietta and her husband Peter drove passed honking the horn. They to seemed delighted by the festive ice-giant Simon worked so hard on. Trying to catch his breath as the frigid air invaded his lungs, he quickly noticed a couple of midget wise guys.

On any other day, they would appear as nothing more than a couple of defenseless kids. Today they were like Godzilla stomping down on Mount Fiji. He was afraid one would feel the sudden urge to amuse the other by smashing the big friendly snowman. He stood in Mrs. Anderson's driveway staring at the young boys, carefully observing their every move. Anticipating the worst and praying to an empty sky for the best. It wasn't long before they ran right up on his lawn and stood face to face with the sad, intimidatingly tall and wide snowman. Simon felt his blood begin to kirtle as they began pointing and mocking his disturbing work of art. He wanted to chase them away but feared it may bring instant repercussions. If he angered the little brats? All they had to do is kick the flimsy disguise and down will come to Renee in all her putrid glory. Every frantic second was getting harder to watch. His heartfelt as if it were stabbing him in the chest. Like there were miniature daggers implanted deep inside the blood-pumping muscle meant to ward off an attack by painfully terminating its host. It was just as the ancient bat predicted.

The children began running around the carelessly hidden corpse, yelling for it to come alive, like Frosty the snowman. Simon watched helplessly, hoping neither of them falls and knocks over his gorgeous, yellow-haired victim. He wanted to turn away in fear, but something unexplainable kept him watching. What could he say? Leave the giant snowman alone, my dead Princess is hidden underneath? Even saying it to himself, it sounded wrong. Simon was so stressed he could feel that thick vital vein in his neck vibrating rapidly. He had no choice, but to allow fate to play its mercilessly unstable hand. The two young boys ran around orbiting the large man-made snow with the stagnated corpse of a dead woman tucked neatly inside. The rowdy children circled the snowman a few more times before one of them dared the other to jump up and knock his head off. Simon could do nothing, knowing his future lies in the balance. While standing, close to the slow decaying body, one of the boys noticed a horrendous odor, silently lurking nearby. Could it be the jolly fat man made of snow? Soon the other boy smelled it too. He jokingly suggested that the snowman had gas and must have farted.

They felt sick to their stomach as they assumed a dog, or something took a dump nearby and it was barely covered under the snow beneath their feet. Whatever it was? Caused the boys to suddenly not want to play there anymore. Yet they both remained curious about the foul odor seeping invisibly into the air. Each daring the other to knock down the man made of snow and figure out what was causing that god-awful smell. Neither of them in their wildest dreams could imagine that there was a real-life corpse buried beneath the saddened man made of heaven's frozen teardrops. Simon was saved by Mrs. Anderson who saw what the boys were doing and swiftly put a stop to it. He couldn't believe she somehow came to his rescue. It was as if she suddenly paid him in full for breaking his back to get her driveway clean. Simon never cared for the elderly woman more than he did at that very moment. She may have saved his life. Just as the older boy was getting ready to pummel the stinky corpse with the ice-shield around it. Mrs. Anderson told them to leave the snowman alone and take a hike. She threatened to tell their parents what they were up to. It was enough to send the brats scurrying away.

They stared at the old woman for a couple of seconds, before high-tailing it out of there. Simon didn't know how to thank her, that was a close one. Brats. Mrs. Anderson mumbled under her breath. She and Simon smiled as they made eye contact. Thank you so much for saving my snowman. I guess I owe you one, I should have told them to scram myself, but I guess I just lost my nerve. I worked so hard on it. I'd hate to see some young punk dismantle it, especially before the rest of the folks in town get a look at it. Don't mention it, Simon. I know how to deal with little deviants like that. You do need to learn how to stand up for yourself. This world can be an evil place. It is why we are all in need of god's protection. You have already paid your debt by cleaning off my driveway. So, then we're even? Yes, Simon, we are even now. They both shared a laugh, while Simon breathes a giant sigh of relief. His secret was safe for now. Simon stood there watching Mrs. Anderson get in her black Ford Fairlane and drive away. He waved with a fake smile on his face, and a ton of paranoia on his mind.

Mainly figuring out a way to keep the town's people from discovering what's hidden beneath the mammoth snowman. Simon also had to find a way to make it vanish under the cover of darkness without any witnesses. He was already so close to being caught and the day had only just begun. Simon made his way across the street and stood right in front of the plump snowman. He wanted to make sure there was nothing visible showing through a possible thin spot in the fragile texture. He did a pretty good job, especially as drunk as he was and in the dark. It was still really- cold- outside and the skies were very gray. It looked as though it could start snowing again any minute. Tired as he was, Simon couldn't afford to go back to bed now. His drunken mistake was going to force him to guard the frozen corpse dressed up as a holiday ornament. He was used to sitting around and spying on her for hours anyway. Only now there would be nothing sexy or exciting about it. He went up to his room and sat on the bed, looking down at Renee's corpse hidden in plain sight. His street was pretty -desolate during church hours.

The whole town was temporarily abandoned until the worshiping was finished. Simon felt his heart soaring toward his throat when he noticed a Renee Falls police car cruising slowly up the street. He knew the policeman was scoping out the impressive abominable snowman he constructed. He was praying he would keep on driving. If he pulled into Renee's driveway for a check-up? It will be the beginning of the end for the perverted killer. It felt as if time was standing still as the police-car sluggishly rolled up the street. Simon couldn't blink an eye or even breathe as he watched and prepared for the worst.

When the car finally passed his house and Renee's, he felt a rush of adrenalin and excitement like never- before. Convinced he was not in any immediate danger of being caught, Simon couldn't believe the cop drove by and looked right at the soon to be the missing girl. His blood was pumping so fast and hard, he feared it was going to come spilling out of his ears, nose, and mouth, causing him to burst at the seams. He continued watching over the corpse standing there ready to greet anyone friendly enough to say how do you do. So much for a quiet relaxing day off. It was bad enough people were probably already gossiping about his absence in the church that morning.

He was sure to hear about it when his folks returned. Simon wanted to crawl back in bed and skip over this troubling Sunday. He began to realize he couldn't sleep soundly even if he wanted to. Every time he closed his eyes now the only thing, he could see is Renee's beautiful face staring back at him. Sometimes she appeared happy flashing that radiant smile of hers.

Other times she looked as though she was going to tear his heart from his chest and take a bite out of it. Simon was afraid Father Fitzpatrick might feel the need to stop by, even if only to ask why he didn't attend this morning's service. He hoped maybe Mrs. Anderson would stand up for him after the huge favor he had done for her earlier. Sitting around and staring out the window to guard a corpse was not how Simon planned to spend his day, but there was no other option now that he made such a ridiculous mistake. He heard the phone start to ring and hopped off the bed to hurry downstairs and see who was calling? He soon discovered it was his mother once again checking in to see how her only son was doing. He as usual told her everything was fine and that she didn't have to worry about him so much. Nothing could be further from the truth. Simon was secretly wondering if he would already be locked in a cage or a padded room by the time, she and his father returned in five days. While talking to his mother, Simon was sure to focus his attention on the living-room window leading to the snowman with the corpse at its center. He didn't want to let his mother know how troubled he was. After the brief conversation he had with both parents, Simon hung up the phone and started walking to the window to stare out at the frozen corpse in disguise. He was soon interrupted by the sound of the phone ringing again. He assumed it was his mother calling back to tell him she loves him for the hundredth time. When he answered and said hello? All he got in return was the sound of a woman screaming. Screaming as if she was being violently murdered. Simon held the phone away from his ear. He was about to hang up, when a soft threatening voice spoke out, saying I'm going to get you for what you did to me, Simon. He quickly hung up the phone and had a seat on the couch. He was growing tired of the relentless hauntings. He began imagining maybe he should have simply let her go back to California to live her life. Now that it was taken away from her, his life was also collapsing into ruins. Simon wondered if she was going to keep it up, even after his folks returned from their vacation. How was he going to explain the strange occurrences to them? Angry as Renee seemed, the young killer wasn't entirely sure his mother and father could protect him from her wrath. One thing was now certain, there was an after-life and Renee was doing all she can to reach back and even the score. Simon turned on the tv hoping it would help him pass the time and calm his fears a little. Anxiously flipping through the channels, he found nothing of interest playing, what did he expect on a Sunday morning? While surfing the limited channels available, Simon could have sworn he heard- the sound of soft footsteps walking up behind him. When he turned his head, there was no one there.

He quickly turned back to the tv trying to ignore the restless spirit taunting him. With nothing to take his mind of the madness, Simon decided to turn off the picture tube and create another one of his sick and twisted portraits. He knew that always relaxed him and made him feel better. The wind was beginning to pick up outside, distracting Simon from his mission momentarily. He felt chilly just listening to it. Before going for his art-supplies, Simon decided to get a fire going. He wanted to make the place warm and cozy, before attempting another one of his barbaric creations. Simon soon had his supplies and the warm crackling fire to inspire him.

He quickly went to work on something hideously remarkable. Surprisingly it wasn't another one of his lude depictions of Renee in a sexy or violent situation. Nor was it anything to do with recreating her death. This morning he was going back to his hatred and disappointment in god. While concentrating on the sac-religious painting, Simon often glanced out the window to check on his devilish snowman, making sure no one tries to destroy it. He painted a bright silver flying -saucer in a clear blue sky over a lush garden. Standing in the center was a tall scaly, green-skinned humanoid holding the infant Christ.

The strange-looking being appeared to have an angelic glow illuminating from it. The lizard-like creature he first envisioned while wasted on the pot and L. S. D. was holding the infant messiah high above his head for all to see and worship. People were standing around with shock and amazement carefully sculpted on their faces. Some had fallen to their knees and were bowing their heads, or looking up, with their hands pointed at the sky. Simon couldn't believe the magnificence he created. It may be his most powerful painting yet. When he was through, he stared at it in ah for several fleeting seconds. When he finally looked away, Simon was disturbed by the sight of Father Fitzpatrick walking down the road and onto his property. He assumed the priest was coming to scold him for not showing up to his service this morning. Simon was a bit frantic watching helplessly as the old priest stood there for a while staring at the friendly man of snow on the front lawn. Father Fitzpatrick found the snowman to be quite interesting, he thought it would be even grander, however, if he made a couple of snow-angels instead. The old man also assumed that was the reason Simon Fletcher didn't make it to church this morning.

The longer he stood there admiring the impressive work of art, the more frightened and agitated Simon became. Why was he standing there for so long? Did the priest notice something strange about the giant man-made snow? Was he even unlucky enough to smell the putrid stench of death slowly seeping through the frozen water? It felt like an eternity for the killer as the man of god stood before his victim buried beneath a clever disguise. What could he possibly be looking at for so long? It wasn't until the priest smiled and started walking toward the house, that Simon could breathe again. He was almost expecting the old Irishman to start running for the hills. He felt reassured in his work, now that another person witnessed the morbid display and remained clueless to what was underneath. After working construction with his father for years, he imagined he better be capable of building a sturdy snowman. Simon watched the holy man approach the front door, allowing him to knock a few times so the priest wouldn't know he was being watched. After the third knock, Simon opened the door with a smile on his face, as if he was happy to find the priest standing on his porch for no good reason. Good afternoon to you Father. What can I do for you? That is one amazing snowman you got there. Must have taken a long time to build, but very impressive. Yes well, you know who my father is, I can pretty much do anything with these hands.

The priest chuckled slightly at his response. He felt the young man should have been in church, even though his folks were away. The old man knew where-ever they were in the world? They would be sure to find a temple to praise their loving, lord, and savior. I didn't come here to judge you for not attending my service this morning, although we are all disappointed that you missed it. Especially this time of year. Christ's birthday is fast approaching, it's the most important time of year to get close to our lord. I know what you did for Mrs. Anderson this morning and I commend you for that. Father Fitzpatrick could see the heavy baggage hanging like ice-sickles from his eyes. He knew something was troubling the young fella, but it wasn't his place to dig deeper.

He simply used his savior to invoke peace and light to this tortured soul. If only he knew about the disembodied soul suffering in another dimension parallel with his own. If only he knew of the unrest for the woman who was so violently killed. Remember Simon our loving and caring god is omnipresent and can see everything at once. No good deed goes unnoticed. neither do the bad ones. Simon humorously added. Yes. Well, I won't take up any more of your time son. I promised your folks I would check in on you and that is what I intend to do. I will keep your absence in my church this morning a secret from your parents since you were so kind to Mrs. Anderson earlier. Thank you- Father. I promise it won't happen again Simon swore while confessing he thought the service would be canceled due to the storm. Don't mention it. Said Father Fitzpatrick as he turned to leave. Simon couldn't control the overwhelming thrill of getting away with it again.

The man of god was standing face to face with the woman he killed days earlier and didn't even know it. If he so much as spit blessed saliva in her face? It would probably singe the ice, causing her frosty mask to effortlessly drip away. His good luck was not going to last forever. Mrs. Anderson had already taken notice that Renee hadn't been seen in days. How long before she sends the police to check on her? His romantic week with a dead woman was turning out to be hell. He watched as the priest walked down the street in the cold as if he was enjoying a stroll on the beach. Simon could never comprehend how someone could be so filled with the holy spirit? He knew the old man liked his walking and exercise. It's good for the old ticker, he often said. As soon as his heart started to slow down and return to its normal pace, Simon noticed a small group of kids walking toward his house. He realized the streets would soon be full of them. Running around and trying to take advantage of the fallen snow. He knew very well the corpse-sickle could be toppled over any minute. To Simon's horror, the three young boys walked right up to the big, fat snowman and started pointing at it. This time he knew Mrs. Anderson wasn't there to come to his rescue.

He was preparing to stand up for himself and chase the little bastards of his lawn for making fun of the amazing iceman he built to entomb his beloved Renee. The three boys walked around getting a good look at the sad-faced man. Just as Simon was about to come outside and chase them away, the three boys took off running. Leaving Renee, the snow-queen in one piece. Simon wondered why the children took off so quickly. Did they smell the pungent odor coming from beneath the thin mountain of snow? Once they were gone, Simon retrieved the new painting he just finished. He wanted to hang it on the refrigerator for his folks to see when they returned. It would be a nice welcome home present boldly awaiting them. He was abruptly struck down by that same horrific stench of death, he began gagging from the phantom odor. It was the worst smell Simon had ever experienced. He began blaming Renee for the foul fragrance and screaming out for her to please stop.

It began to dissipate as suddenly as it arrived, Simon started looking around and saw Renee's decaying body standing before him. More bone than flesh, the only thing that resembled his beauty was her long yellow hair. He screamed as she fell toward him with empty eye-sockets peering right through him. Simon was, hoping no one heard his desperate cries for help. Paul McCartney started playing loudly in the living room, causing him to freak out even more. While the music played on, Simon got himself off the floor and had another look at his most recent painting.

A loud wind whistled like threats being harmonized without the use of any distinguishable language. As Simon shifted his eyes toward the painting, he saw a completely different scene painted in its place. It was a sinister portrait of Simon dead and rotting on the floor of his treehouse.

Bloodstains splattered the walls and drenched his filthy gallery of sex and death. Vivid as it was frightening, the macabre masterpiece failed to show any signs of Renee or reveal how he died. It left him wondering and reeling in paranoia.

The inside of his head was soon pierced by deafening screams coming from within. It was as if Renee was somehow sitting in the lotus posture in the middle of his cranium and hollering as loud as she can. Simon felt as if a banshee was running loose in his brain and rattling his bony cage. When it finally stopped Simon noticed that he had dropped the shape-shifting painting on the ground facedown. He was almost too afraid to feed his curiosity and turn it over. When the screaming stopped, Simon noticed the music was still playing. It had been drowned out by the dreadful cries of his innocent victim. Trembling and breathing as if he just finished a rally race on foot, Simon tried to take a deep breath and turned the painting over to have a look. It was exactly how it should be. He smiled at Renee's fury and hung the morbid painting on the fridge as he planned. Inside he was terrified sooner, or later Renee was going to tear him to shreds. Simon began to imagine his folks walking into his room and finding him severely mutilated on his bed. He could only imagine how she wanted to repay him, after what he did to her. The music stopped playing and the house fell silent again. Simon went back to the living room while things seemed normal to have a look at the delicate coating he placed around his beloved Renee. He noticed a large hawk perched on top of her head. It started digging its sharp talons around in the shallow hill of snow. Simon grew even more nervous when it began pecking downward at Renee's frozen head. God forbid it penetrates her skull and sends a red slush bleeding toward the surface. His eyes widened as the wild bird pecked angrily at the top of the snowman. Did the flying creature know death was beneath the frozen man? The snow was falling quickly around Renee's face and she was becoming more displayed by the second. Simon could do nothing but watch in terror as the snowman's head began to turn red with his victim's blood. It was oozing out like an ice volcano on some distant rock formation far beyond the sun.

Soon the whole thing would be painted red with Renee's blood. Simon stood there fixated on the snowman as the hawk drilled deeper and deeper into Renee's skull for a meal. With her brains sticking out of her head, Renee turned around and looked right at Simon. Why did you do this to me? You said you loved me, Simon. Now you're going to rot in hell for eternity she warned, as the winged demon continued to dig its talons in and feast on her brains. Renee threatened Simon with death and eternal damnation, as the blood continued to pour from the defrosting corpse, it was racing down her face and melting all the snow away in the process, Simon could do nothing as Renee motioned that she was going to come for him. She broke free of the mound of snow and started walking toward the house, the giant hawk dining on her brains the whole time. As she slowly marched closer, the hawk dug its talons deep into her brains and leaned forward to poke out both of her eyes. They started bleeding, yet never took there gaze off -of him. Simon closed his eyes shut and prayed desperately to a god he no longer believed in. When he eventually opened them, Simon saw that the snowman was exactly the way he left it. A large hawk was standing there, minus the ice sickle brains in its beak. Simon eerily found himself locking eyes with the sky-born beast just before it flew away.

Relieved for the moment, Simon started giving more thought to the bizarre painting he witnessed under some sort of divine vision or something. It was either super-natural? Or he was losing his mind. Both scenarios seemed frightening to the twisted killer, he turned and headed to the window facing the treehouse in the backyard. He hadn't stepped foot in there since the murder occurred. Part of it was due to the unusually, cold weather they were having. Deep-down Simon knew he was too petrified to revisit the place where Renee's life was taken. For the first time, he was hesitant to enter his morbid house of sins. His attention was soon redirected back to the painting hanging on the fridge. It was as if it was calling out for his attention.

When Simon shifted his eyes and focused on the painting, he noticed it appeared to be coming alive. He was fascinated by his artistry as it started moving In- in front of him. The hovering saucer started spinning rapidly and creating a strange distortion to the space around it as if it were remixing the paint long dried. The tall lizard being started swinging his tail and pronouncing his sharp yellow fangs. Red eyes glowed from black holes in his cranium. Simon was sure he was standing face to face with Satan the dark reptilian prince himself. He must be trying to somehow enter the physical world through a hate-driven portrait to possess Simon Fletcher's angry, spirit. A large veiny set of wings sprouted from the creature's back and began flapping around aggressively. Simon could feel the gust of winds coming from the flying-saucer and the serpent's colossal wingspan. He was expecting the images to come flying off the page and step into the third dimension of spacetime. A long, forked tongue came forth and began flailing about obnoxiously, as Simon backed away careful not to kiss the devil. It felt like he was tripping on L-S-D again. There's no way this could be happening. Frightened as he was, the twisted killer couldn't remove his eyes from the Magnificent yet spinetingling vision. He felt as if he was one of the lost prophets mentioned in the bible. The first person to have a physical encounter with a demonic deity in almost two thousand years. A bright beam of light shined down from the sparkling craft, forcing Simon to turn his head for a moment. As it slowly dimed, Simon turned back to watch as it aimed for the infant messiah resting peacefully in the being's hands wrapped in a warm blanket. When the baby turned its head and locked eyes with Simon, he prepared to run for his life but instead stood locked in position over-powered by fear. The strange-looking infant had green glowing skin and dark infinite eyes that seemed like portals into a hidden dimension.

One of extreme cruelty and suffering. Even more alarming was the size and shape of the baby creature's skull. It was long, at least twice the height of what a normal head should look like. It stared at Simon while reaching out its webbed fingered hands determined to snatch him up and drag him into the wretched underworld to be tormented forever. It was a hideous Fate and Simon wanted to get far away from the false vision. There was no way he was going to give in and sacrifice himself to the demonic alien visitor that summoned itself through one of his very own portraits. Everything in the painting was animated and moving about in a hectic fashion. Simon kept his focus on the baby creature desperately calling out to him in a hypnotic sort of way. It felt like the evil life-force was- capable of re-arranging the properties in the chemicals that operated his mind and body. Taking full operation over his neurological functions, forcing him to stand still and allow himself to be lured into whatever punishment awaited on the other side. The beam of light from the hovering U F O lifted the satanic looking infant into the sky. It was fascinating and frightening, Simon couldn't look away. The mesmerizing gaze forced him to watch the terrifying event taking place in his kitchen. For a second Simon saw his own eyes in the head of the large lizard man. His flesh went from melting to freezing and back again. Simon didn't know if this was the work of the vengeful spirit torturing him, or his fractured mind coming unglued, showing remorse for what he did. He was ready to bury Renee in the backyard beneath the treehouse of sins, imagining it will make all of this madness disappear. Simon watched as he prepared to be taken aboard this hovering ship he painted in the sky.

The animated portrait continued to startle and amaze its creator until he heard the dreadful sound of Renee gasping for air in his ears again. He could feel her dreadful, presence in the room, but when he turned to have a look, she was nowhere in sight. When the disembodied gasps for air stopped, Simon turned his attention back to the portrait that came alive on his refrigerator. He was relieved to see that it was back to normal. He darted out of the kitchen and back into the living room where he was surrounded by the lord's saints and angels, hoping he wouldn't be attacked by the inanimate figures for his ghoulish betrayal. Simon wanted off this freakish thrill-ride, but there was no escape. He hadn't even noticed the house had fallen silent again with- the exception of the howling winds. Simon turned the tv back on hoping there would be something, anything to distract himself from the relentless terror. He found a football game getting ready to begin between the New York Giants and the Dallas Cowboys. He didn't care who won, but he was rooting for the Giants since they played in his home state. He just wanted to erase Renee from his mind for a little while, along with that vivid hallucination he just experienced. Always a great rivalry Simon was hoping to get lost in the game. He also wanted to be able to keep an eye on the macabre snowman outside. He had to make sure no one discovered what was lurking just beneath the pure white snow, covered flesh.

Things quieted down for a while as Simon shifted his attention from the football game to the corpse-covered snowman standing at attention for all to see. He noticed that it started snowing again, as the Giants intercepted the ball and ran it back for a touchdown. They needed it since they were down 10-0 at the end of the first half. It was a gridiron war, but Simon still managed to dose off for a little while during the game. He awakened harshly to the sound of children laughing. He sat up and looked out the window to find a small gathering of kids standing on his lawn, pointing and laughing like the ones earlier.

This time little girls and boys were mocking his macabre, ice sculpture. He had a bad -feeling things might get out of control, especially now that both sexes were involved. If there was, one thing little boys wanted to do more than impress one another, it was wanting to impress the young girls around them, whether, or not they knew one another. Simon could hear them screaming and laughing, insulting his cold dead hippie queen, even desecrating her by pulling off pieces of the snow mask and eating them. One kid even yanked off the carrot nose and was preparing to take a bite, until he got a good unwanted whiff of what was lurking inside. Quickly peering through the tiny hole, the young boy found the ghoulish remains of Renee Price, eerily staring back at him, her pale, white eyes blinking, as he backed away in horror.

The vile stench hit all the children's noses like a freight- train. It was coming from inside the biggest snowman any of them have ever seen. One brave young boy came forward eager to impress the pretty little blonde girl from his class. He wanted to get near the hole and have a look inside. They didn't know the man who was responsible for constructing the smelly snowman was keeping a watchful eye on them. All the other children told him he was chicken shit just like the rest of them. The stench alone was reason enough to keep their distance from the rotted anomaly. Thinking he would be labeled a coward if he didn't go through with it, the courage, stricken boy proved clever, holding his breath as he neared the tiny opening in the abominable snowman's face.

He assumed it would prevent him from inhaling the foul scent coming from within. Simon watched from the living-room window in terror as the young boy walked up and placed his eye right against the hole in the head. To his awful surprise, he saw a dead woman staring back at him. Suddenly the corpse beneath came to life and Renee's naked body began to shed her icy, costume terrifying the fleeing group of curious children. Her eyes opened wide as they trembled in terror. Simon could hear their screams, as could everyone else within a five-mile radius, or at least that's what he imagined anyway. It was an exaggeration stretched to its capacity from his overwhelming fear. He too was petrified as Renee broke free of the hand-truck straps and instead of giving chase to the fleeing children, turned her attention toward the man responsible for her death. Renee marched forward bleeding, as she warmed herself with hatred, leaving filthy footprints of mud and blood strewn across the pure white snow. It was a ghastly sight to behold, but Simon couldn't turn away. He stood there watching her inch closer even though his life was in danger. With all the children in town racing home to tell their mother's and father's what they just saw, Simon assumed his life would soon be over anyway. Before long men with badges and firearms will be knocking down the front door of his parent's sacred dwelling. In a single blink of the eye, the frightened killer saw that the naked zombie had vanished. He turned his attention to where the snowman ought to be and as he did the sensation of icy fingers slid down the back of his neck, and he heard the awful gasping again. Simon was convinced Renee was standing right behind him. He jumped abruptly, almost tossing himself off the couch and onto the living-room floor, as he awakened from another heart, pounding nightmare. He noticed the Giants had tied the game and were even up by a field-goal. A lot must have happened while he was away.

The first thing Simon wanted to do is look out the window and make sure his snowman was still in one piece. Simon was considering another trip to the liquor store for a new bottle of vodka, with balls of solid courage included. He imagined he might need it to help him remove Renee from her dangerous resting place and prepare for darkness when the house comes alive. This time, Simon was going to hit a different store for the booze. He thought about taking a ride to the next town, so the word doesn't get back to his folks that he's been hitting the bottle like a champion dart thrower stabbing the bullseye. Simon was planning to use the devil's urine like holy water to ward off the vengeful spirit that haunts him. He asked himself if perhaps he should have the old mick bless the mind, altering booze before taking a sip. Simon imagined if he flooded his body with enough of the blessed poison nothing could ever possess him. He feared things would get much worse before they got better, especially as long -as Renee's body is above ground. He committed the most condemning sin of them all and would suffer the fires of hell for his tremendous love. Tonight, when the sun goes down and everyone is fast-asleep, Simon planned to dismantle the snowman and invite Renee back into the house. In the end, New York defeated Dallas 24-21. When it was over Simon dressed warmly again, so he could shovel out his driveway. If he was going to head to the store, he would first have to clear a path. He also imagined it was a good way to keep the delinquents away from his dark-secret. He didn't think anyone would mess with the snowman while he was standing right there. Simon even considered leaving his glasses inside to appear more intimidating, then he wouldn't be able to see what he was doing very well. He turned off the tv and prepared for more shoveling. His body was already spent from cleaning out Mrs. Anderson's driveway earlier that morning. Not to mention he had been up all -night drinking and burying Renee beneath a sad giant.

It was the dumbest thing he ever did, yet he was planning another trip to the liquor store for more vodka. The thing that troubled him most for the moment was leaving Renee vulnerable to attack in his brief absence. Even Mrs. Anderson might be willing to explore the strange creation while he's away. Simon knew she would notice him cleaning out the driveway. She would surely watch him ride-off when he was through. There was no telling what shape he might find the snowman in when he returns. It was a risk he was willing to take. He wouldn't be gone long, and it's survived so far. As the hours began to pass and Simon could hardly move his arms from all the shoveling, he was encountered by a nice Christian family from town.

They were driving by when the remarkable snowman caught their eyes. They pulled over to have a better look at it. The pretty mother apologized for their sudden intrusion. One look at her and there was no need to say sorry. She was incredibly attractive, and Simon was soon wishing he could get in her pants. Renee was stone cold, dead and he wanted to lay with a warm functioning body again. She got a strange vibe off, of him as he seemed to be undressing her with his eyes. The way she played with her hair and the sound of her voice was driving Simon wild. She had two little girls and a boy, but no man with her. He was foolish enough to run off with another woman. She asked Simon if he would be so kind as to take a picture of them standing in front of the impressive snowman. Did you build it yourself? She kindly asked. Simon was proud to say yes and felt compelled to agree. How could he say no to such a beauty? Especially when she wants to stand so close to the other woman he couldn't resist. Simon silently wondered if her presence made Renee jealous, still, he dropped the shovel and took the camera from the pretty woman's hand, telling them all to line up in front of the frosty snowman. He was silently praying none of them to catch a whiff of what was buried beneath the friendly exterior.

The pretty mother smiled bright her children gathered around her. Simon couldn't help but wonder what Renee thought about the strange situation. The photo came out perfect and Simon couldn't wait until everyone was away from the morbid statue. The pretty woman thanked him again for letting them take the picture, the children did the same.

Simon insisted it was his pleasure. He jokingly told the kids now all he needed was a magical hat to place upon his head. Then he could come alive and dance the night away. Everyone got a good chuckle and Simon appeared to be on his best behavior. Still, something deep in his eyes didn't feel right with the woman.

She was ready to get back in the car and away from Simon. He waved goodbye with a smile on his face after everyone was rounded up in the backseat. Once they drove off, Simon felt a little better, but he couldn't get that sexy mother's face out of his head. For the first time, he found himself attracted to someone other than Renee Price. Perhaps this was the start of something new? The first steps in forgetting about his true-love and moving on. He turned back to the snowman attracting all the attention. It made Simon question himself again about leaving to get liquor while the corpse is still publicly displayed? It was unbelievable that of all the astonishing works of art he's created in his day, this fat, simple snowman was the grandest attraction. It was a difficult pill for Simon to swallow, but so far, he had been lucky, he was just glad no one noticed the frozen carcass beneath the mound of white snow shaped like a triple segmented man.

The reality of having folks from town standing so close to his frosty victim rattled Simon's bones to nearly the point of shattering them and stabbing him with sharp spears poking from the inside out. With nightfall quickly approaching, Simon pushed on to finish the driveway, so he could run to the store. There's no way he was staying in that house again without being completely drunk. He just hoped it wouldn't lead to something as foolish as displaying the woman he murdered on the front lawn. When he was shoveling, Simon headed to the garage to retrieve his ugly car. Mrs. Anderson happened to be walking back to the living room with a hot cup of tea in her hand when she noticed Simon pulling out of the garage. She watched as he drove off while sipping her tea, wondering where on earth he was heading? Driving down the road there was no music playing on the radio. Simon was far too busy with his menacing thoughts. He had to make that body disappear before the following morning. Once the snow begins to melt, his world will come crashing down.

Looking in his rearview mirror, Simon noticed a cop car behind him. His heart started beating faster as he grew paranoid that he was on to him for the murder of Renee Price. Simon waited for the bright flashers to come on, but they never did. The roads were icy and a bit dangerous to be driving on. Simon did his best to ignore the lawman on his bumper and admire how beautiful his hometown looked blanketed by the angelic white snow. He had to deal with the discomfort of the policeman on his ass until he hit the next town. He was lucky no one was aware of his horrific crime yet. Once inside the store, Simon did his best to remain discrete. He was almost completely covered under his wintery clothing and mostly walked with his head down. He was doing his best not to be recognized by anyone. Simon didn't care to humiliate his parents anymore, then he had already.

Snatching a fresh bottle of vodka off the shelf and making his way to the register all Simon could think about was getting home. He wanted to make sure nothing happened to Renee's hidden remains while he was gone. The ride felt like it was taking forever, the worry was crushing his mind from every angle. Simon didn't want to speed under the crappy weather-conditions and would have to take his time. Pulling up to the house, he was relieved to see the snowman was still in-tact. He was probably the only person in town who was a bit creeped out by the ominous ice statue. This time Mrs. Anderson was interrupted by Simon flashing his headlights toward her window while backing into the garage. With a new bottle in hand, Simon turned on the tv and saw there was another game on.

This one was between the Raiders and the Broncos. It was something to keep him busy until he can safely return Renee to her ice, coffin down in the basement. He placed the vodka in the freezer momentarily so it would get cold. All he could think about was removing Renee from the front-lawn before her true face emerges in front of dozens of witnesses. Even though it was dark outside the snow brightened the world enough for Simon to see his trophy standing at attention, just the way he left it. He started drinking the vodka in glasses of ice until the entire bottle was cold enough for consumption. It didn't require much for a buzz to take residence inside Simon Fletcher's head. He sat there drinking while watching the game and the corpse outside his window. It had been a long, stress-ridden day and Simon couldn't be happier to watch it wind down.

At last, there were fewer people out on the street. Most of the town's children were home playing in their rooms or getting ready for bed. Soon he would be able to make his daring move, once again under the thin cover of darkness and the influence of hard liquor. He didn't mean to, but at some point, during the game, he passed out again. Exhaustion claimed him, forcing his eyes closed and his chaotic mind to briefly shut down. When he awakened a few hours later, Simon jumped realizing what a terrible mistake he made. He had no concept of time, nor did he know if someone came along and violated his snowman. He instantly turned his attention to the carcass standing on the lawn dressed as frosty the sad man. Luckily it remained in place without him safeguarding it like he was supposed to. The game was long over, and the news was playing on the television set.

As Simon sat there, he couldn't help but wonder, how long it would be before his despicable story makes national headlines. Simon had to be certain the nosy old woman across the street was asleep, before he could tear down his most gruesome works of art. He knew if anybody was to catch him red-handed it would be her. Most of his buzz had evaporated while he was snoring wood on the couch. Still feeling a little funny from the effects, he planned to sip a little more from the new bottle. Simon looked out the window toward Mrs. Anderson's house. All the lights were off, and he was confident enough that she was sleeping. It was inching next to midnight, almost everyone in town should be in bed. All with- the exception of Simon Fletcher who just awakened from his long, needed nap. Simon knew removing the dead body from the front-lawn would be just as risky as placing it there.

The snowman had already gathered more than enough attention from the folks in town. Simon thought about building another one in its place. He knew no one would be fooled by the switch in the middle of the night. The last thing he wanted to be a large gathering standing around when her true face emerged, promising him a seat in the gas-chamber. Simon quickly bundled up again and headed out into the cold night to tear down the morbid iceman he created. It had a certain eeriness about it knowing what was just beneath the friendly ice figure staring out at the world. Simon approached and couldn't help, but stare at the horror he was responsible for.

After the way Renee has been haunting him, Simon was afraid to invite her back into his home. What choice did he have, the reckless killer felt his only options now were to be murdered by the angry ghost of his previous victim or the good old U. S. A. Careful not to reveal his evil secret, Simon did his best not to remove the cloak of snow from around his victim, until she was safely inside the garage. He slowly walked around to the back of the snowman and tried finding the handles to the hand truck below. He wanted to disassemble her in private. Simon quickly found what he was looking for, but as he started to pull her away snow began collapsing from the frozen carcass underneath, exposing the deceased beauty queen hidden inside. He further defaced the snowman, placing the carrot and olives in his pocket, while looking around to make sure no one was watching. He was terrified someone would catch him in the act. Luckily there wasn't a soul around. The snow was gently falling, and it was cold outside. Once out of the view of prying eyes, Simon did his best to knock as much snow off the frozen corpse as possible flooding the garage floor with melting snow. He noticed Renee was slowly changing, Simon already felt she hardly resembled the gorgeous young woman he once fell in love with. He also noticed the vile stench seeping out of the snow-mound as he brushed her clean. He had to make sure she's placed back on ice right away.

The pathetic murderer was going to have plenty of explaining to do when his folks returned, like where the wretched smell in the family-freezer was coming from? He wasn't sure if it could simply be scrubbed away. The thought of putting food back in there that they were actually, going to eat after the dead woman rested within its walls grossed Simon out. The smell grew stronger as he continued removing snow from the slow rotting carcass. Simon worked as fast as he could to get the wretched deed over with. He just wanted to relax, so far, he had dug out two driveways and a very unusual burial. After cleaning away all the snow, Simon removed Renee from the dolly and dragged her back in the house and down into the basement where she would remain, until he figures out what to do with her. Simon was relieved to finally have her out of the sight of prying eyes. He never wanted anyone else to be that close to her remains again. It was a disturbing and nasty task, but the young lunatic brought it on himself. It was part of his punishment for killing and then continually violating his victim's corpse. Once she was resting cozily in her crypt, Simon closed the lid and prepared to crash for the night. He assumed he would get an earful for destroying the one of a kind, snowman the next day. Simon didn't care what people said as- long as he was out of the house and away from Renee for a while. If he stayed alone with the corpse for another whole day? Simon feared he would go completely mad.

He was desperately searching for a distraction from himself, before his brain tormented him to death, even if it meant dealing with a bunch of grumpy old women and handsome young lovers. His negative presence made most people feel uncomfortable around him. It wasn't that he liked or even gave a shit about any of the customers who came walking through the door. For Simon, it was about trying to be normal. What he's been doing since his parents went away has been anything but ordinary. Everyone knows women are interested in men who appear exciting and mysterious, but his behavior was in a raunchy cage all by itself. How could he end Renee's life so coldly and then keep her dead body like some sort of trophy? Simon closed his eyes with hopes of passing out soon, still nervous about all the crazy shit taking place, he even wished his doting mother was there to comfort him, though he complained about it all the time. Simon could feel the room spinning from the careless, liquor consumption as he closed his eyes and imagined Renee opening the freezer down in the basement. With rage loudly pronounced on her face, Renee got out of the icebox and headed up the basement stairs toward him. She looked decrepit as she slowly made her way up the old wooden stairs. A cold mist lingered as she pressed forward. Her naked body was frozen but not shivering. He opened his eyes and quickly observed the room. For the first time, Simon felt as helpless as his victim. He could do nothing to stop her from tormenting him.

No gun or knife could fend off his otherworldly enemy. She was already dead. Simon got out of bed to piss out the rest of the vodka he drowned himself in that evening. He soon found himself trembling for no good reason. There seemed to be a cold spot in the bathroom right where he was standing in front of the sink, washing his hands after a long piss. Looking up at the mirror and away from his family jewels. Simon saw Renee's reflection staring back at him. She had the evilest expression on her face, as she reached out of the fragile glass without cracking it. Simon jumped and gasped with fear. He shut his eyes and when he opened them, she was gone. It didn't mean he felt safe, or alone. He knew she was watching him always.

It was payback for the way he stalked her and invaded her privacy in life. Simon was too tired and intoxicated to give it any further thought. He turned off the light and headed back to bed. He didn't notice the reflection turning its head in the mirror as darkness swallowed the light in an instant. Renee's eyes boiled with fury, she was never going to rest in peace until justice was brutally served. He passed out rather quickly once his head hit the pillow. Evil spirit or not? His body couldn't stay awake any longer.

CHAPTER 14

✦ ✦ ✦ ✦ ✦ ✦ ✦

The next morning came around quick as usual. Only this time Simon was awake ahead of time. He couldn't wait to get out of the house and surround himself with the living. A whole week alone was not proving to be as desirable as he had hoped. It turned out to be lonely and frightening. He hardly even got to use the gorgeous corpse, before it got too cold and stiff. Simon was starting to realize that he not only took her life but destroyed his own as well. Starving with time to spare, Simon fixed himself a delicious breakfast. He had been doing his best to consume as much of the meat as he could, so it wouldn't go bad from not being frozen. He decided to mix a little steak in with his eggs this morning. He could feel his belly reacting to the careless night he had.

As the food grew hot in the pan, Simon walked over to the living-room window and was thrilled to see there was no giant snowman standing on the lawn. He was so lucky to have gotten away with that ridiculous mistake. In his mind, though he saw the hourglass of time tipped against him and it was running out at a relentless pace. Someone was going to realize that Renee Price was missing. Simon was glad to see that at the very least the sun was shining again. He had enough of the dreary weather, as did everyone else in town.

The jolly Christ-followers could never get enough of being in the light. With the dead body safely tucked away and his belly full, Simon got in his car and headed to work. He looked at Renee's house as he drove by slowly, thinking about everything that's happened over the past

281

several months. He knew in his heart Renee didn't deserve what she got. He was sure she had no idea things would turn out this way when she and her husband chose this perfect little place to start over. Chillingly he knew sooner or later there would be a police car parked in that driveway. For all Simon knew someone had already reported the pretty blonde missing. When he arrived at the florist a few minutes later, he felt as if he was actually- safe from her angry spirit. His confidence wouldn't last very long. As soon as Simon opened the door and stepped inside, he noticed the smell of cannabis burning in the air. He recognized the smell from spending time with Renee. Hello? He called out to see if someone was hiding in the store someplace. He soon realized there was no smoke floating around the room to prove someone had been burning grass inside his mother's plant store. It didn't take long to assume it was Renee screwing with him again.

He checked the entire place, but there wasn't a living soul around. Simon knew the store was empty. In a way, he wished it was some dirtbag who snuck into his mother's store for a safe place to light up and get stoned. He hurried to open all the windows naively hoping it would somehow get rid of the phantom stench. He felt fortunate to be the only person in the store at -the moment. If any of the customer's notice the lingering odor? They will blame him for getting high in his mother's place of business. Doing his best to open the windows and let some of the cold fresh air inside, Simon was soon dropped to his knees as the smell of marijuana was swiftly replaced by the putrid stench of death. It was extremely powerful. As if he tore open her sternum and poked his head inside for a good, strong whiff. Simon began gagging and sweating as the foul, odor launched a full-blown attack on his sense of smell. He was on the verge of vomiting up everything he ate for breakfast earlier that morning until finally, the horrendous odor disappeared as suddenly as it arrived.

It took a few moments, but Simon got back to his feet and prepared to go on with his day. He knew it was simply Renee's way of letting him know she was still around. Simon didn't want to be brutalized all day by his victim's ghost while he ran his mother's flower shop. He knew there was no place he could run and hide, not when it came to avoiding Renee's vengeful spirit. Until her body was properly laid to rest, Simon would be forced to suffer her wrath. He was growing angrier with every hair-raising confrontation. Simon didn't even want to think about going back to his house later that evening. He knew he would be all alone and that the restless spirit would be there waiting for him. He shouted out like a crazy man, warning Renee to leave him alone. He didn't want the hauntings to continue in front of paying customers. He thought he saw the shadow of someone walking by, but once again, there was no one there. As the day went on and customers came to have a look around and purchase their goodies, Simon remained on edge. He was just waiting for something out of the ordinary to happen. Even some of the folks wandering around the store could tell how jumpy he was. They wondered what it could be that had Simon so tense. He desperately wished he was working with his father's crew out of town. Scared for his life, Simon wouldn't mind being surrounded by big strong workmen. Not that any of them could defend him against the super-natural. There was nothing Simon Fletcher could do in order to feel safe. He took an innocent young woman's life and it was only a matter of time before karma balanced the tally with death.

Although people could see something was troubling him? No one bothered to dive into his problems and ask what was wrong? It was none of their business, and no one in town cared enough about Simon to dig deeper. His parents were a different story. Everyone loved and respected them. There was something about Simon that sent out a strange vibe. Negative energy no one could put their finger on. One kind of elderly man was paying for a dozen roses for his wife of 30 years. Simon was praying the hauntings of his dead lover wouldn't last that long. He assumed she would find a way to kill him long before three decades sailed by. The old husband warned Simon that there was another storm moving in tonight. It was the last thing Simon wanted to hear. He was frightened enough of his dead victim while the sun was still shining in the sky. It had been hiding behind a mask of clouds for days. Now Simon was hearing that the bad weather would be returning. He didn't want to be all alone with the raging ghost during another awful blizzard. Simon certainly didn't feel like shoveling out two driveways again either. He thought about his parents enjoying themselves with their feet in the sand. It pissed him off to imagine their happiness.

Why'd the weather, have, to take such shit as soon as they left? Simon knew he was in for another long, nail, biting night. As the old-timer continued to talk Simon's ear off, he noticed a beautiful blonde woman entering the store. As she walked closer and Simon got a really-good look at her, he noticed it was Renee Price standing before him in the flesh. He didn't understand how that could be? She appeared as real as everyone else wandering around the flower-shop. Simon just stared in disbelief, losing trust in his own eyes. There she was walking right toward him. Renee looked beautiful as if she was still alive. Simon couldn't believe it? How could she possibly be there? He knew perfectly well that she was dead and resting uneasily on ice down in his cellar.

He wondered if anyone else could see her standing there. One thing was certain, Simon saw the woman he was fated to be with forever, and he couldn't take his eyes off, of her. For the troubled murderer, it was as if they were the only two people in the store. Simon had no idea what the old man was saying. All of his attention was focused on the sexy blonde walking up to the counter with a wilted rose falling to pieces in her hand. This time Simon didn't see any anger on her face. She was happy and smiling, exactly the way she was before he savagely took her life. The elderly man could see the troubled look on Simon's face, especially as Renee's expression changed, and she became angrier looking as Simon stared into her eyes. Just before she reached him, the image vanished. There was no sign of Renee or any other woman for that matter. Are you alright son? You look like you've seen a ghost. The old man's words seemed cliché since Simon was convinced, he did see the ghost of Renee Price. All he could do is nod his head, yes, but the fear in his eyes was like nothing, the old man had ever witnessed before. Simon continued to insist it was nothing, but his customer knew otherwise. He respected the young man's privacy and didn't make too much of a fuss about it. He also noticed there were other- paying customers lining up behind him. The workday seemed to fly by as Simon stayed busy most of the time with lovers young and old. He imagined it was because he was too terrified to be back in his own house alone.

The weather outside deteriorated as the hours passed. By the time Simon was ready to lock up and head home the skies started to fall. At least it warmed up enough to bless them with some cold November rain instead of more snow. It still made driving home a hassle. The roads were wet and slippery, and the heavy rain was falling relentlessly. Even with the wipers on full blast, the glass was hard to see through. Simon almost jumped out of his seat when the radio turned on out of nowhere, a Beatles song playing in Renee's honor. He assumed it was her fucking with him again. He glanced down at the radio as he angrily turned it off.

When he looked back at the road, Simon was forced to slam on his brakes almost tossing himself through the windshield. Standing in the middle of the street was a zombie-like woman slowly approaching as if she was oblivious of his car coming right at her. Simon was frozen with fear as she stared into his eyes, then suddenly she was gone. Like always Mrs. Anderson noticed Simon pulling up to the house across the street. It was impossible to miss as he shined his headlights right into her living-room. Simon wasn't the only thing the nosy, old woman was watching. She had been paying close attention to Renee's house and saw that there have been no signs of life for days now. Mrs. Andersson hasn't seen a single light turn on or off in the house since Thursday.

She hadn't even been out to collect the mail that was slowly building up with every passing day. She had a feeling in her gut that something horrible happened to the pretty young girl. How could she be locked away for so long without so much as a peep? Her sticker, graffitied, Renegade was still in the same spot and only the heavy rain was cleaning the snow away. Renee hadn't lived there very long, but Mrs. Anderson knew she was no recluse. Nor did she seem like the type to neglect house chores.

All Spring and summer, she was out there trimming the hedges and cutting the grass. Mrs. Anderson assumed she was used to taking care of the house since her husband traveled so often. Now that he passed away so suddenly, god rest his soul, Renee must be feeling the full brunt of the situation. Mrs. Anderson was starting to think the worst. She prayed the grief wasn't so great that the pretty young girl decided to take her own life. If there was no activity the following day? She was going to go over there and knock on the door. Something wasn't right and she was going to get to the bottom of it. Poor thing. I hope she's alright, Said Mrs. Anderson to herself out loud. Mrs. Anderson was also paying attention to Fletcher's home across the road. She knew exactly how obsessed Simon was with Renee and how he always kept an eye on her from a hidden location. It gave the concerned woman an even greater reason to worry. If something did in-fact happen to that sweet young girl? She did not doubt that he was somehow involved. Mrs. Anderson planned on being the first to call him out for the slithery, creep he was. What the concerned neighbor didn't know, was that she wasn't the only person concerned for Renee's safety. Her friends back in California have also been reaching out to her from across the country.

The phone rang and rang with no answer. They too were growing concerned for their friend whom they all loved very much. Simon's luck was running out. Someone was going to alert the authorities very soon about the young woman's disappearance. Her friends in L A were extra worried because she was so far away. Not- to mention her true-love Paul was recently killed and right before the Holidays? They were also beginning to think it was too much for her and she may have done the unthinkable. The same group of friends who made the long journey to attend the funeral had all been inseparable since Renee seemed to have gone missing. Why didn't she answer the phone or attempt to call them back? The only thing on all their minds was their dear friend Renee Price. It's bad enough they just lost Paul. If something did happen to Renee it was going to be really, hard to deal with. Simon was sitting on the couch with the vodka in his hand, he wanted to sip it directly out of the bottle as he watched the heavy rains falling outside. His mind was on over-drive as paranoia spread like a disease through his brain. All he could think about was getting caught. He had a dead woman in his house. It was all the evidence the police would need when they arrive to have a look around.

The icebox wasn't exactly a clever hiding place. If someone comes searching for Renee? She would promptly be discovered. He felt even stranger about his unspeakable behavior while all the saints and angels surrounded him. One day he was going to have to face judgment for what he has done. That is if the god his parents prayed to existed at all. If not, he might just get away with it free and clear in the end? Doubtful as he might be? Simon was petrified of burning in hell. It didn't stop him from building a fire to keep warm on such a drafty night. Slamming the bottle down on the coffee-table he got to work. Soon he was going to be drinking warm vodka if he didn't get it back on the ice soon. He had no choice, but to figure out a way to rid himself from the body, before his folks returned. For now, he chose to sit around and drink heavily with the fire burning beside him. Watching Star-Trek repeats as he did so many times before, Simon wasn't really in the mood for Captain James T. Kirk and the crew, but there was no way his distorted mind could focus on anything else. He was anxiously waiting for something strange to happen. He felt Renee's energy all around him, watching with hatred making him very uncomfortable in his own home. Simon didn't feel like he was safe from Renee's angry spirit no matter where he was, or how many crosses and angelic beings he had present in the form of wood and glass. Even if he did as she asked and buried her bones someplace nice? Simon still wasn't guaranteed that Renee's ghost would go away and allow him to live in peace.

The warming liquor sliding down his throat with ease, Simon started to become even more unhinged. He was extremely tense knowing Renee would show herself to him again sooner or later. He began to feel as if the anticipation was even more heart-poundingly strenuous then the actual haunting. Simon kept sipping from the bottle, allowing the liquor to do him in. He soon noticed the tiny orb floating around the room again. He had seen it a few times before. Not wanting to admit it existed Simon swore it was simply a bright spot in his eye. As if a single photon of light was somehow trapped on his pupil. He couldn't help but follow it as it fluttered around the room. He noticed that it seemed to stop and hover right in front of the basement where her corpse is being held, prisoner. Simon clutched the bottle tight while taking another sip, as he pressed on. The room grew much colder as he neared the door where the orb was still dancing around. He was waiting for Renee to somehow spring from the tiny ball of frigid energy and show herself in human form. He began to tremble as Renee watched from the tiny pocket of energy that was the soul.

The faster it moved around, the colder the room became. What the fuck? Was the only phrase Simon could utter, as he took another sip of vodka hoping it would settle his frantic mind and warm his bones. He stepped closer to have a better look at the dancing ball of light, even though it terrified him. As he homed in on the tiny dancing speck, Simon noticed a face staring back. It sort of looked like Renee crying out to him, but the features were distorted. Horrified, he took a few steps back, hoping to get away from the angry ball of energy. It floated toward him with a great burst of speed. Renee wanted to tear him apart, or at least frighten him to his own grave. Simon ran around the room in a clumsy matter trying to avoid the menacing ball of light that was pursuing him until it vanished. He noticed that the room temperature started to climb again the moment she was out of sight. He was incredibly angry with Renee for behaving this way. With his vodka in hand, Simon opened the door leading to the basement where her corpse was stored. This time Renee was hoping he would do the right thing and offer her a proper burial. It didn't mean she could ever forgive him for ending her life so soon. Renee didn't want her killer gawking over her dead body anymore.

As he opened the door slowly, Simon felt as if he was entering the mouth of hell. It appeared even darker than the lost soul stalking him. Simon was starting to get cold feet as he marched further into the basement where Renee's frozen remains lie. He was deathly afraid of the power going out, while down in the crypt with the icy carcass. Simon turned tail for- a moment so he could retrieve a flashlight just in case.

Once he was armed with a reliable light source and his bottle of booze, Simon made his way into the basement where he feared Renee's nasty ghost would be waiting. He always mocked his folks for their extreme belief in the lord, especially for having so many saints, angels and crosses watching over them. Now he was heading to the one place that wasn't swarming with religious figures. Simon felt extremely vulnerable even unprotected down there alone with the dead body, Slowly, creeping down the steps, Simon cast light down into the dungeon to make sure there was nothing demonic waiting to jump out of the darkness and harm him. It appeared to be safe from evil spirits for the moment, but the air was still thick around him. Simon eventually shined the bright light on the pale-white icebox masquerading as a coffin. If he survived this nightmarish week? Simon knew he would never be able to look at the family freezer the same way again. He feared his parents would discover what he's been up to while they were away. He also knew they would be going shopping soon in-order to stock up on meats for the winter. How would he preserve his precious corpse then? It wasn't as if he could simply hide her under his bed or bury her under some clothes at the bottom of his closet. Simon was aware of the trouble he would be facing once someone discovers the terrible things he has done. He knew once the police receive word of the missing girl and begin the grueling search for her remains, it would be much harder to dispose of her someplace. Simon had to make- a decision and act on it fast if he planned on getting away with the heinous murder. It was a matter of time before the law comes knocking on his door.

At the very least because he lives so close to the victim. What was he going to say when they start asking questions? Difficult ones he'd rather not answer. There were all kinds of nightmarish scenarios spiraling around in his head. Simon even feared one of them might actually- break free and come spilling out of his ears, or even more horrifying it would exit with enough force to smash right through his forehead obliterating his frontal-lobe and killing him instantly. It almost seemed merciful compare to what poor Renee Price went through. Simon kept telling himself it was impossible for thoughts which were tiny volts of electricity soaring around a chunk of soft tissue to manifest themselves in some tangible way. But after witnessing the shit he has lately? He was feeling like anything was possible. Before he could open the lid and have a look inside, he saw a dark shadow moving across the far, left side of the eerie, cellar. He tried shining the flashlight in that direction but wasn't fast enough to catch a glimpse of the shadowy figure before if walked through the solid wall. He was shaking like a leaf, almost too afraid to open the freezer and look at her again.

The walls were closing in on Simon as his heart continued pounding. He couldn't decide if he was more afraid of the gas-chamber, or Renee's vengeful justice? Simon imagined Renee would be sure to administer much more pain and suffering than the gas, quickly putting him to sleep. He could hear the rain falling as he opened the freezer and grabbed an old wooden stool nearby. With the flashlight on the floor at his side, Simon had a seat next to the crudely, preserved corpse, his bottle of vodka in hand. Simon felt he owned Renee a sincere apology for what he's done, feeling the end was fast approaching him too, he didn't know if anything he said could make things right, but he had to give it a try. At the very least to prevent her vengeful, ghost from tearing him apart piece by bloody piece. Simon began expressing his love and doing his best to convince both Renee and himself that he didn't mean to end her life. It was a fatal obsession, which is one of the most selfish and motivating reasons for murder. I didn't want to kill you, Renee. You have- to believe me. Simon said as he became slightly teary-eyed. I didn't have a choice. I just couldn't bear the thought of losing you. You were so perfect. Kind, gorgeous, and carefree. I know you were never going to so much as think of me again, once you were back in your hometown thousands of miles away. I imagine you were planning to start over with Travis. I saw the energy between the two of you, even if you didn't want to admit it to yourself. Who can blame you? Why on earth would you want to be around me? I'm nothing but a worthless loser. A child in a man's body. Someone like you could never understand what it's like to be someone like me. How could you? Then you gave yourself to me and all I kept thinking was that it was a dream, it had to be. Truth is I've been fantasizing about you long before we even met. It's kind of gross I know, but sometimes I just can't help myself. I think of you and everything else fades away. It's like the rest of my brain can't function anymore. I never really meant to degrade or violate you. I did it for my own selfish, disgusting needs, and for that, I am truly sorry. I have behaved like an animal- Simon stopped talking when he heard a thud on the other side of the basement. When he turned his head in that direction, he saw nothing. He assumed it was Renee trying to communicate with him. Simon again turned his attention to the corpse resting uneasily in the freezer. You're the most attractive girl I 've ever laid eyes on and I willingly fell victim to temptation. When I first saw you standing there, I thought about the countless attempts I made to create you, even before you moved next-door to me. I was convinced that fate brought us together. It was impossible to let you go, once you materialized in my world. My best attempt was the monstrous playboy queen made of different models, fused like some side-show freak locked in a cage. I know you saw my filthy drawings. I can't even imagine what you must think of me. I tried justifying your death by considering your knowledge of my perversion as a dangerous form of blackmail, even though I know you were planning to move to the opposite end of the country to be rid of me.

It's clear to me now that I meant nothing in your perfect little world. I wanted us to be together forever and you ruined it. Simon assumed it was the liquor that caused him to confess his sorrow and possible regret for killing the beautiful young woman next door. Renee didn't believe a word of it. She wanted to see him pay for taking her life. There would be no forgiveness for his cruel and meaningless sins. He had to pay for what he did, and Renee's spirit would never rest until his body was lifeless as well. Simon bravely reached over and took her hand.

His warm teardrops made a sizzling sound as they hit the cold flesh, heating the ice and changing its physical composition. Renee's corpse suddenly sat up without warning and turned her attention to the drunk killer sitting beside her. She reached out grabbing Simon by the throat and strangling him as hard as she could. Simon could feel her cold, dead hands squeezing the life out of him, as he stared into her pale white, emotionless eyes.

They seemed to be peering into his soul as if they knew how it was all going to end. Simon struggled to defend himself from the animated corpse. The young killer was about to die from mysterious causes with phantom hand-marks around his throat in the creepy old basement. His dead queen at his side. What a sight to behold when his parents returned in a few days. The lights flickered on and off as a strong gust of wind hurled itself through town like a cannonball of cold air. Simon continued gasping realizing this is exactly what he deserved, he sounded just like Renee in her final moments of being alive. Fighting off the zombie in the freezer, Simon began seeing visions in his head, of the blonde beauty before he put an end to her days.

As he suffocated in the dingy cellar Simon relived memories like when she first moved into the Stones place and he witnessed her in the flesh for the first time. Simon also remembered the sex they had on the night she died with his hands around her throat, the fear in her eyes, as she suffered and died by his actions. Renee's grip weakened as the pipe organ began playing upstairs, pulling Simon out of the trance and back to his terrifying reality. He found himself screaming with his arms stretched out battling a threat that wasn't there. Renee was stiff and cold, lying peacefully in her tomb, yet the sound of his mother's organ could be heard playing throughout the house, only the notes being played were far from the familiar tunes they play in church on Sunday.

These notes were dark and satanic sending a powerfully penetrated volt of terror coursing through Simon Fletcher's body. Simon turned his attention to the ceiling, as the music played on. He nervously slammed the freezer lid shut and ran up the basement stairs to see who was playing the spooky song. He could feel this lingering vibe following close behind as he darted for the room where the pipe organ was continuing to play as if the mass was in session. Reaching the top of the stairs, Simon encountered Renee standing before him, dark bruises around her throat made with his hand, prints on them. The image was enough to frighten Simon off his feet, causing him to fall and bruise his face while climbing up the basement steps. He ignored the pain and wasted no time hurrying to the floor above.

There was no sign of Renee anywhere in the physical form as Simon ran through a cold spot on the way to where the music was coming from. He soon arrived at a scene of pure horror as Renee slammed on the keys with blood spewing from her finger, tips while playing the devilish music. Simon could feel the gaze of all the religious sculptures staring at him as the angelic ghost played her heart out, almost recreating her final moments on earth in the form of music. Renee's head slowly turned to look at Simon, he almost fell in love all over again staring into those sky, blue eyes, with blackened shadows moving catastrophically within them. It was as if a witch's brew of a storm was forming, leaving Simon Fletcher unable to look away.

The wooden crucifixes hanging around the house were drenched in blood as the carved image of Christ tried tearing himself off the cross, agonizingly plucking the rusty nails from his hands and feet. Simon could hear the porcelain shattering and the flapping of wings as the inanimate relics came to life to protect Renee from the evil in the room. Simon turned his attention to the heavy rainstorm outside, only to find the reflections of monsters coming for him in the dead of night. A dark, massless shadow slowly invaded the religious home. Giant claw marks remained from scratching at the walls as the terrifying organ music played on. Simon wondered if he was experiencing a taste of the hell to come. He found himself praying to the god he despised for all this mayhem to go away, proving he was losing his mind and couldn't live with what he's done. Simon knew even if he could keep her appearing as if she was still alive for centuries to come, it wouldn't be the same as having her soft-touch or hearing her groovy laugh.

Attractive as the vessel she traveled in was? It just wasn't the same without the essence of life operating it. Simon wanted her alive, so he could hear her moan and kiss her soft lips. He realized after it was too late to prevent the madness that she would only exist the way he wanted her in his memory. After, all, what did he plan to do in the end? Place her bones in a wedding dress and walk her down the aisle. It would make for one hell of a honeymoon, just me and my bag of bones here. Simon thought to himself while trying desperately to hang onto his sanity. He slowly reached for his throat and noticed it felt very tender as he gently squeezed it to see if it was indeed bruised from the savage attack. He would have to check himself in the mirror to be sure of the physical damage done to his flesh. He even assumed some of his skin was trapped in the frozen corpse's fingernails. Simon knew he wasn't completely honest with the ghost relentlessly haunting him. He knew damn well when the storm passed, and the sun came back to regulate the world again, he would most likely take his chances leaving the slow-decaying carcass right in the freezer where it lies. He was an ignorant fool waiting to find out what else Renee could throw at him from beyond the grave. His main objective was to make it through the night in one piece. What Simon didn't know, was that Renee had no intention of being merciful.

Sparing his life for the moment was no, an act of kindness, she simply wasn't through with him yet. Renee despised her waste of sperm, cell killer. She thought he still had some suffering to do before leaving this world. If all goes well his mother and father would find him dead somewhere in the house, another unfortunate- victim of suicide.

CHAPTER 15

+ + + + +

All Simon could hear is the pounding rain, as he considered his next-move beneath a raging-river of vodka. The rookie drinker was way passed drunk and rational thought was obsolete. He kept wondering if the hauntings would proceed even after his parents returned, he also wondered if they too would experience the wrath of the hippie woman he murdered over jealousy and intense sexual desires. Simon began giving lots of thought to adding to his multitude of sins by going next-door and murdering Mrs. Anderson in her sleep.

He was blindly convinced that she would be the one to bring him down. He didn't even have the logical mind-set to consider being undone by her good friends back in California. Simon Fletcher felt compelled to wipe his nosy, old neighbor off the face of the earth, to protect himself. It has long been said that the first kill is always the hardest. If that were true, and Simon was going to hell for eternity for his unforgivable sins? What was to stop the body count from rising? He was cracking up and wishing for all of this to simply go away.

There was nothing he could do to bring his beloved Renee back from the dead. For only a second or two, Simon considered doing what he promised and finding a nice, peaceful place to bury her remains. He knew he was too far gone to do anything constructive tonight, as he foolishly, staggered back into the basement to visit his restless victim, with all sorts of vulgar thoughts galloping through his mind. If he didn't go to bed soon, Simon might find himself waking up on the floor next to the corpse in the morning. That's when he 'll decide what fate lies in store for both- of them. Simon gently placed his right hand on Renee's cold, stiff face. It instantly sent a chill through his entire body. Looking her up and down with a severe case of blurry double-vision he took notice of her nippy little nipples and the slightly discolored breast they were attached to. Knowing she was watching from some other plane of existence he couldn't access in life he decided to violate her remains one final time. Driving her poor lingering spirit further into disarray. She stood beside him screaming, but this time Simon couldn't hear her desperate cries as he removed his hand from her face and relocated it on her blistery, breast.

The cold sensation was rattling his bones gingerly, as he continued touching the corpse to satisfy himself. He felt rejuvenated playing with her body to the point he swore she was alive and even enjoying it. Simon rubbed his warm hand against her cold remains as Renee moaned in pleasure. She looked at him, those bright blue-eyes twinkling with insatiable, lust. Her lips were as red as Arora's blood spraying from the rotating spindle. She was soft and real, yet a bit cold to the touch from resting in a bed of ice for almost a week. Simon couldn't wait until she was touching him. He couldn't believe it, it was as if somehow, she was raised from the dead. He felt bad for Renee and wanted to warm her up. She was shivering but trying her best to hide it from him. She didn't think he would find it attractive if she started shaking all over the place.

Once again Simon selfishly thought only of himself. Warming her up would mean covering her goddess-like body beneath clothing. Where's the fun in that? She would warm up from Simon's body heat as they became more intimate, or she would remain cold as ice, while he vulgarly played with her. Simon wanted to climb into the freezer with Renee and make love to her all night long. His passion was powerful enough to end lives, throw planets from their orbits, and turn the icebox into a sauna if his majesty so desired. Simon moved in to kiss her lips, praying to god they were soft and tasty. He pulled down his pants as he courageously went for it. Staring into her eyes it seemed she wanted it to.

Renee pulled him closer and placed her cold but living hand on his balls and his spine reacted like a prophet's staff activated by a divine source.

The bone-chilling sensation did nothing to disturb his hard-on. Simon couldn't wait to get inside her again. Renee softly pulled away and laid back on the frigid bed he provided her with. It was so kind of her to protect him from freezing to death. Renee insisted she was practically immune to the cold now. Simon got on top of her and she began kissing and nibbling on his right ear. Naked from the bottom down, Simon found himself in the freezer making love to the woman he murdered days earlier. Oddly it didn't seem to bother him much. It felt real and so he continued, on. I thought you were mad at me for, you know. I don't like to talk about it. Especially with you. Renee giggled as Simon went to work between her legs. It was just like the time they tripped together and had sex in her house. I realized you do love me more than anyone else ever had, including Paul, who I thought was my one true love? He foolishly crashed his car and left me behind. You couldn't part with me no matter what, huh lover boy.

Not even death itself could convince you to let me go. That's why I came back for you Simon. I love you too. Simon smiled bigger and brighter than he ever had before. Renee made herself comfortable and prepared to make love to her cold-blooded killer, right there in her frozen sarcophagus. It felt so good to be inside her again, he wanted this moment to last forever. His face was smooshed against hers as he sucked on her inviting lips. Not so smooth with his actions, Simon was like a slobbering k-9. He was so drunk and horny nothing else mattered at the moment. Renee defeated the grave itself and it was all for Simon. Do you truly love me, Simon, Renee asked as she lay in the icebox unphased by the punishing cold against her back? She sounded so sexy Simon could hardly answer the question? In a way, he didn't feel he had to. Wasn't killing her and preserving her remains proof enough? He started pulling on her hair and breathing through his nose to remember the way she used to smell before the savage tragedy. Simon wanted to enjoy this incredible moment while it lasted. Renee sat up and again started gently nibbling on his ear and moaning ever so gently to get him completely stimulated.

It was the greatest collaboration of sensations he's ever experienced. Simon's entire body was tingling with ecstasy until suddenly her insides felt different. Cold and dry as the Martian desert. Simon also noticed her sudden lack of enthusiasm and the unmistakable stench of decomposition penetrating his nose. He opened his eyes and had a look at his dream girl resting lifelessly in his arms. To his horror, Renee was back in her true form and the vision was over. She was as dead as can be. Simon was grossed out as he realized he was still inside her. She was stiff as a board and Simon wanted to get away from her as fast as humanly possible. He quickly pulled out scrapping his privates on the cold dry walls between her legs.

Once out of the corpse and freezer, Simon slammed the lid down and clumsily, put his pants on. He raced up the stairs leaving the bottle of booze and flashlight behind. He could hear- the sound of footsteps chasing after him. Simon felt weak in the knees and his heart was pounding so hard he thought it was going to shatter his ribcage, piercing his chest and killing him instantly. When he got to the top of the stairs, Simon found Renee standing there waiting for him. He froze terrified as he stared into her wicked eyes. She clawed at his face digging her nails in and causing him to bleed. Reaching for the open gashes across his face, Renee shoved her killer down the stairs. He went tumbling to the bottom and crashed on the hard cement floor. Simon was lucky to escape serious injury. He looked all around, but there was no sign of Renee. He called out to her in an angry tone but got no response. You bitch. He stated as he slowly moved around to make sure nothing was broken.

While scanning the dimly lit basement for the angry spirit that pushed him down the stairs, Simon noticed his bottle of vodka lying nearby. How could he have forgotten that? Once he regained his composure the drunken mad man grabbed the flashlight and the bottle before making another attempt to get away from the corpse in the basement. His body hurt all over from the vicious spill he just endured. Placing one foot in front of the other he carried on. Simon was no longer sleepy, and his heart and mind were set on a violent path. As he approached the dangerous summit of the basement stairs, Simon saw no hair, raising apparitions waiting for him. He started paying attention to all the religious knick-knacks displayed around the house.

It was as if he was waiting for them to come alive and retaliate. He noticed that whenever he moved so did the painted eyes on all the statues. It was very subtle and only visible in his peripheral vision. Doing his best to ignore it, Simon was angry, not to mention terrified at the way his night was going. He was fully convinced he was having sex with the woman of his dreams. The same woman he snuffed out in cold blood. Simon started daring his disembodied tormentor to kill him and get it over with. He couldn't take the suspense anymore. He just wanted to die putting an end to his misery. When nothing happened, Simon made his way over to the living-room window to have a peek at the rain as it continued to come down in buckets. He saw Mrs. Anderson's house in a blurry image and discovered a way to release his pent-up rage and eliminate the one person he was convinced would eventually bring him to justice. He took another sip of warm vodka, causing a goofy expression to streak across his face from the taste and the rough sensation it left as it crawled down his throat and into his belly.

There was only one way he could prevent the old bag from discovering what happened to the pretty girl-next-door. She was going to have to join her in death. Simon killed once before and knew he could do it again. He was going to sneak into her house in the dead of night while she slept and kill her before she has the chance to alert authorities of the missing girl. This time he didn't care what shape the body was in when he was finished. He had no desire to keep the corpse around after death. This time Simon would enjoy himself making the murder even more gruesome and painful.

The deranged killer didn't bring a weapon from home to end her with. He planned to find something when he arrives. Taking one more swig from the bottle of vodka, Simon put on his coat and shoes and made his way over to Mrs. Anderson's house while still in his pajamas. It was down-pouring as he went out into the night., making it harder to see as the water pounded against his glasses distorting his already damaged vision. Simon was drenched within seconds of stepping out into the storm. Placing the hood over his head, he stood on the front porch for a moment and stared at his next victim's house. He knew she would be sound asleep when he got there and wouldn't put up much of a fight. Eager to get out of the monsoon, Simon hurried across the street to Mrs. Anderson's house.

He imagined it wouldn't be difficult to get inside since everyone in Renee Falls usually left their doors and windows unlocked. As he stumbled onto her lawn, Simon's first choice was to waltz right through the front door as if he had been invited. To his surprise, it was locked. He couldn't understand why she would do that? Then he realized the grim truth that she might very well be on to him. Did Mrs. Anderson already know something happened to Renee Price? Simon truly felt it was his life or hers. The old woman would surely point her finger at him if the long arm of the law came to call. Simon was there to make sure that didn't happen. He started checking windows but found that they too had been locked from the inside. Simon was convinced he was the reason for the sudden urge for Mrs. Anderson to barricade herself inside while she slept. It gave him even more of a reason to find a way inside and silence her forever. With no easy point of entry, Simon decided to break the decorative glass build into the door. He just needed to knock out a piece big enough to get his hand through and unlock it from the inside. He was afraid the sound of breaking glass in the night would waken her from her sleep and alert the elderly woman that trouble was on its way. He didn't have much of a choice if he was going to go through with his hideous plans. Simon didn't realize by killing another person would make his sinful crimes much harder to forgive. None of that mattered now. He convinced himself he had a better chance of getting away with the first murder if the person most likely to turn him in was dead and gone as well.

He found a small rock lying on the ground and used it to smash in the decorative piece of glass in the front door. It shattered with ease but made a loud sound as breaking glass usually does. He was praying his victim didn't hear -the sound of a deadly intruder with homicidal intentions lurking beneath the cover of darkness. Mrs. Anderson did lift her head for a moment after the glass was broken. She thought she heard something but wasn't entirely sure. Her ears weren't what they used to be. She imagined she was hearing things. Still, she sat up and listened carefully for a couple of seconds to see if perhaps someone or something was stirring below her in the middle of the night. Dressed in her comfortable pajamas. Mrs. Anderson got up and headed to the bedroom door. She thought about calling the police but foolishly decided to check it out for herself. She didn't hear a peep, but as she opened the door and asked if anyone was there, the elderly woman got a strange feeling in her gut. Somehow, she just knew something was wrong. She didn't know her crazy neighbor Simon Fletcher was making his way through the house at that very moment. She threatened to have already called the police, hoping it would stave off the intruder before their diabolical plans are set in motion.

While Mrs. Anderson was barking false threats, Simon ventured into the kitchen in search of the biggest knife he could find. He was going to plunge it deep into her flesh over and over until she's dead. He quickly discovered a wooden block stocked with exactly what he needed. Simon could feel his heart racing with adrenaline as he prepared for another gruesome murder. He knew this time it was going to be much messier and violent. He always hated the nosy old bat and planned to fill his victim with holes until all her blood is spilled out on the floor, walls, and even the ceiling. Mrs. Anderson could also feel her heart beating harder than she wanted it to. At her age, she did her best not to get upset easily. As her terror escalated, she could feel sharp pains stabbing at her chest I'm warning you. If anybody's there? The police are on their way, get the hell out of here while you still have a chance. It's times like this she missed having a man around the house.

301

Since her husband passed away, she had no one to protect her. Mrs. Anderson made her way through the dark house, turning on lights along the way. She kept praying that no one would come leaping out of the darkness and take her life. The storm outside was still in full swing and she could hear the strong winds and heavy rain savagely attacking the town of Renee Falls, living up to its wet and wild name. She didn't know Simon was patiently waiting for her with a sharp, big knife in his hand. Hello is anybody there? She called out with hopes of receiving no response.

The house seemed quiet, but something was making her feel very threatened and she was determined to figure out what it was. Again, she threatened that the police were already on their way. Simon could hear his soon to be victim calling out to him while lying in wait. All Mrs. Anderson could hear was the falling rain and ferocious wind whistling loudly as it passed. Inside, the house remained silent. Simon was careful not to give himself away. He wanted to catch the elderly woman by surprise. Once she falls into his clutches the stabbing frenzy would begin. Standing at the top of the stairs, Mrs. Anderson looked down and saw the broken glass on the floor. Wide-eyed, she turned her attention to the front door and saw where it was broken in from.

She immediately turned to phone the police from her bedroom. As she did there was an ungodly gust of wind gushing by bringing a large bolt of lightning and even thunder along with it, knocking out the power and turning the house relatively pitch black. As she retreated to her bedroom to close and lock the door, Simon made his move staggering gracefully up the stairs in hopes of catching her before she is safely locked away. He was determined to kill her and would break down the door if necessary. Mrs. Anderson could hear him coming as she did her best to hurry through the dark house, with a cold, blooded killer in pursuit. She already knew exactly who was coming after her. As she neared the bedroom door and turned the knob, Mrs. Anderson came face to face with the four-eyed monster, he forced her inside with a blade to her throat.

There was a demented look in his eyes, almost as if the boy she'd known all his life had been possessed by the devil himself. Trembling,

Mrs. Anderson quietly uttered, you did something to Renee didn't you? That poor girl. I knew it. I saw the way you used to look at her. Watching from behind walls and finding every excuse to be outside whenever she was in the front yard. You're a weirdo and a creep Simon Fletcher. Wait until your mother and father find out what you've done. How could you hurt that poor girl? She never did anything to you. God will see to it that you are judged for your evil sins. You can't escape punishment for what you did. Simon stood there staring at her, allowing his rage to build. The elderly woman's words were spilling gasoline on an already stable inferno, almost antagonizing him to thrust the sharp blade into her throat, perplexing his sins when the angels and demons came to collect. What are you going to do with that knife, Simon? I think you have a pretty good idea, Mrs. Anderson. You've always been a nosy old bitch. Poking around in other people's business, because you have no life of your own. It's pretty, pathetic if you ask me. You label me a stalker, but we both know you're no different. Mrs. Anderson knew this would be her final night on earth, she was silently making her peace with Jesus and preparing to be welcomed into his kingdom. She tried convincing her killer he was merely doing her a favor.

Now she can be in heaven with God and all his angels. She asked Simon how his parents could create such an animal? Simon didn't feel like listening to her shit anymore. Who was she to challenge and judge him, while he was the, one wielding the knife? He moved it away from her throat and placed the sharp blade against her cheek, slowly carving into her face, causing the running river of blood to leak out of the opening wound. You know something bitch, I did murder Renee because she was going to move back to California and leave me behind. I couldn't let that happen. I'm certainly not going to allow you to get me caught. Said Simon, as he began stabbing her violently in a fit of uncontrollable, rage. Mrs. Anderson saw the blood spilling out as the sharp pain of the stab-wounds inflicted flooded her mind. All she could focus on was the pain.

She tried fighting back, clawing, and scratching at his face. Simon felt like Renee was attacking him from beyond the grave again. You're going to burn in hell Simon Fletcher! Burn in Hell! Mrs. Anderson did her best to fend him off, but it was no use. Simon started screaming out with rage and swinging the weapon with even more thrust, puncturing holes in Mrs. Anderson's old wrinkled bag of bones, sending her to the ground, and covering himself in her blood. He never noticed Renee's ghostly reflection in the mirror, watching in horror as another one of his innocent victims fell to the floor, this time from multiple stab-wounds. She was being murdered by the same sadistic menace that ended her life. Mrs. Anderson started making horrible sounds as she inched agonizingly closer to death on her bedroom floor. Simon was overcome by fury.

He continued stabbing his victim over and over, continuing to capture her warm blood as it splattered all over the place. Simon's rage was in full swing as he continued to plunge the sharp blade into her even after she was dead. It was the greatest feeling he had ever experienced, releasing years of pent up anger for the way his life turned out. Simon even imagined his mother and father's faces while poking holes in another one of his unfortunate neighbors. Perhaps when they return from their happy vacation, Stanley and Eleanor will suffer the same horrific fate. He only relented when Renee screamed on top of her lungs, shattering the mirror as her image slowly faded from the exploding glass.

Leaving the hole-ridden body on the bedroom floor, in a pool of blood. Simon was aware that Renee was with him, watching closely as he got to his feet and prepared to leave. Once again showing no signs of remorse. Simon screamed out in pain, as phantom, teeth bit into his neck. He hurried down the stairs holding the railing to prevent being pushed, never turning to see that there was no one physically there. The sound of footsteps pursued him out into the storm. Hell is waiting for you, Simon. You can run, but you can't hide. The devil will find you where-ever you go. Renee's words sent shockwaves through his brain tissue, cracking his spinal cord like a bull's whip, tossing all reason into a spiraling vortex of fragmented emotions chilling him so badly, Simon thought his brittle bones would soon shatter to pieces, stabbing him from the inside out, as he crumbled apart. He couldn't get away from her fast enough.

Once again out in the storm, Simon agonizingly realized If Renee was -capable of harming him from beyond the grave? No place would be safe from her unholy onslaught of terror. He was being pelted with freezing rain and hail as he hurried home. Simon fell face first in the middle of the street as if shoved by an unseen force. He was almost hit by a passing car in the night. The man sitting behind the wheel of the blood-red, 64 Plymouth Fury didn't even ask Simon if he was ok? He quickly looked him in the eyes and sped off. Kicking dirty ice-water in the murderer's face. It was so cold his face went numb in seconds. An arctic chill vibrated his entire body, before allowing him to get back to his feet. The flying puddle of liquids and solids cleaned most of the old woman's blood off her killer's face, but not all of it. He felt Renee could kill him whenever she so desired. Simon feared he was completely at her mercy. All this time he believed he was in control. He was living on borrowed time. Renee had the power to snuff him out whenever she wanted.

As Simon struggled to his feet, he got the eerie sensation of someone watching him. He turned his head and saw Renee standing there beneath the falling rain and ice, yet she somehow remained completely dry. It was miraculous and terrifying at the same time. She started walking toward him and after a couple of steps vanished into thin air. Simon started to tremble and almost lost his way crossing the street from the combination of fear and drink, not to mention his glasses were completely soaked and fogged up. He wondered, what could be more terrifying than to know your life is in the hands of your deceased enemy. Trapped in a defenseless situation. Renee planned to slowly frighten him to death, although she appeared to be losing her patients and viciously picking up the pace. Simon wasn't sure if it was more terrifying to see the ghost of the woman he couldn't live without? Or not knowing where she would appear next.

He moved slowly through the storm towards an unsafe sanctuary, stopping along the way and making a 360 degree turn to be aware of his surroundings. Simon listened for Renee's threats being muffled by the wolf, breathing winds. He was soon on his property but with no sense of security. Simon's home was protected by god's army, only he was the wicked one and the attacking spirit from the other, side was the hero. Simon was convinced his mother's creations wouldn't defend him but change sides and participate in his rightful execution, assisting Renee in smiting him for his savage behavior.

The entire house was practically full of them. Just feeling like he's being observed by the statues made Simon's skin crawl, he would soon be dead, but for now, Renee's spirit was enjoying the torment he was enduring. Once back in the warm, dry house Simon realized his power wasn't working either. Drunk out of his mind, Simon simply removed his glasses and passed out on the couch in his wet clothes, his victim's blood drying on his face like a morbid death, mask.

CHAPTER 16

⁕ ✦ ✦ ✦ ✦ ⁕

The next day when the sun came out and Simon Fletcher arose from his brief coma, he started having flashbacks of the night before. Images of a brief struggle between himself and the old lady across the street manifested in his head. Simon didn't want to believe it was possible, until he felt this annoying sensation of some unpredicted liquid practically, plastered to his face. Simon put on his glasses and nervously made his way to the bathroom mirror, with flashbacks of terror from the night before replaying in his head. He was petrified to discover he was stained in his latest victim's blood. Not to mention he was all scratched up and severely bruised, including visible bite marks left behind by the phantom teeth marks of Renee's ghost. Simon's body vibrated with fear knowing the attack was real and not taking place in his head.

The deranged killer found himself trapped in the house with the vengeful, spirit that wanted him dead. As much as he wanted his parents to return, with hopes that they can somehow save him from this disaster, Simon also knew it wouldn't be good for them to find him this way. Not to mention the cold hard, fact that he now had not only one deceased neighbor, but two. Simon strongly felt this version of hell would soon be over, but the world of fire and brimstone waiting on the other side was just heating up. He could smell that rotting flesh odor traveling invisibly through the air again, attacking his nostrils and churning his guts, it was awful, and he just wanted it to go away. Simon started gagging and was on the verge of vomiting when it finally disappeared. Renee wanted him to experience the same level of terror she and now poor Mrs. Anderson had to endure. Simon Fletcher dared to wonder how an angry spirit could attack the living while looking over his drunken battle scars. Renee Price was coming for him from beyond the grave like she promised and there was nothing Simon could do about it.

After carefully observing the damage inflicted on his face and gingerly poking at it to painfully discover it was real, Simon noticed that the storm had finally passed. With no intention of going to work that day, the paranoid killer instead planned on teaching Renee's ghost a serious lesson for fucking with his head and haunting him so severely. Feeling hung-over from all the drinking the night before, Simon decided to make himself something to eat. He imagined food would help soak up some of the poison he consumed while being terrorized by his sexy murder victim.

As Simon thought more about the madness that took place the night before he began to remember vivid flashbacks of Mrs. Andersons gruesome, murder. He was standing in the kitchen making sausage and eggs when he recalled exactly what happened. Simon vaguely remembered breaking into her house and violently stabbing her to death in a drunken rage. Her body was still lying on the floor soaked in her blood. His nerves started to twitch something fierce and his stomach contorted from the dark reality he was facing. He now had two dead bodies above ground waiting to be discovered. He would worry about the old woman's corpse later. First, he had to take care of Renee. She was far more important since she resided inside his home.

Time was running out and today was the day he would have to part with his deceased lover. Only he wouldn't rid himself of her completely. Simon had a ghoulish procedure in-store for her when he was through with breakfast. First, he was going to have to remove her from the freezer, so she can thaw out for a few hours. He wasn't even thinking of the putrid, stench that would escape into the air as soon as it feels any warmth. Drinking the rest of the vodka wasn't something he wanted to do, but there's no way he could perform the grizzly task sober. Once she is defrosted enough, he was going to de-flesh Renee in the bathtub. He wanted to retaliate for the way she attacked him the night before. It was a sick and twisted way to keep some of Renee with him.

He realized that if he strips Renee's corpse to the bone, there will be nothing to stink up the place and he won't have to keep her in the freezer anymore. Simon was out of his skull and desired to keep her bones hidden away in his house of sins. As if the police wouldn't go exploring there. He had no idea how grueling this monstrous task was going to be? Nor did Simon know if he had the guts to pull it off. How was he going to react when he has- to remove her intestines, heart, and liver? Simon tried not to think about that stuff right now as he sat at the family table before the last supper painting and enjoyed his breakfast. He was glad to see that the power was back on. In a way, Simon saw the power-outage as a favor from god or the devil? He couldn't be too sure at this point who was on his side. It went out just when his victim needed it most. It seemed strange that her god would allow such a thing. After all, Mrs. Anderson was such a faithful follower. Yet somehow, he let a lunatic invade her home and end her life horribly. Simon wasn't sure what to do about her body yet? He would have to make it disappear as well if he wanted to escape justice for her death.

As Simon finished eating while staring off into space, he was locked inside his chaotic mind imagining what it was going to be like to truly know Renee Price inside and out. He would soon know how big her heart was. That is if he can handle reaching into her chest and plucking it like an apple from her ribcage. He assumed he could simply wash all the blood down the drain, and no one would ever know what horror took place there while his folks were away. Simon placed his dirty dishes in the sink and prepared to enter the basement where the frozen stiff dwelled.

He was interrupted by the sound of the phone ringing. Simon sighed already assuming it was his smothering mother on the other end. He assumed she tried reaching him at the flower shop and got no answer. He could care less about the stupid business dedicated to lovers and cult followers. Simon felt he had more important things to do. He let the phone continue to ring off the wall as he ventured into the cold dark basement to retrieve the crude mummy from its icy, crypt. It wasn't as scary down there during the daytime, but Simon knew Renee was hiding in the shadows, waiting to attack him again.

There were, no weapons he could use to fight her off. If he tries stabbing her with a knife it will simply pass right through her. Yet she somehow has the power to make physical contact with the material world. So far, the house remained quiet and peaceful. Simon began to wonder as he made his way down the old stairs why Renee didn't kill him last night in his sleep. He imagined it was because she wanted him to experience the torment while he was aware of it. Dying in his sleep would have been too merciful for such a vicious animal. Simon fell in love with Renee for her beauty. He murdered her and even tried to preserve her body because she was so gorgeous. The thought of tarnishing that beauty by carving her up troubled him deeply. Simon didn't want to destroy her but felt there was no choice. She was already different than the young woman he originally fell in love with. Her skin lost its soft-texture and most importantly its color. He could never make his fantasy come true with a woman who is no longer living. In the end, it was all for nothing.

He opened the freezer lid and found Renee's naked corpse resting right where he left her. Simon apologized to his love for what he planned to do to her. If she was going to put him in his grave for it, so be it. Simon was going to commit one final act of disrespect for the girl, he swore to adore forever. He was anticipating an attack, but so far there was nothing. The only sound that could be heard was the frantic, irregular crescendo of his heart twitching nervously. He pulled her stiff, frozen remains from the icebox and carried her out of the basement and into the bathroom where the dissection would later occur. Simon gently laid her down in the bathtub. He ran the water with the plug sealed, hoping it would help speed up the process. It was obvious that he has completely lost his mind.

The anticipation was driving Simon up the wall, he just wanted the gruesome deed done so Renee could be with him always. Simon has yet to learn from his incredibly foolish mistakes while drowning himself in a bottle. First, he placed the corpse on the front-lawn for all to see. Then he murdered another one of his neighbors. This time right across the street. It wasn't very safe to live next to the four-eyed pervert with a taste for gore. Anyone who gets in his way now had it coming. Simon would slay the entire neighborhood if he had to and live in his religious house completely- surrounded by the dead. His beloved queen made of bones at his side. He knew it would take more than a few hours for the stiff to warm up enough to carve through.

He also knew he had to start drinking soon if he was going to flood himself with liquid courage. With Renee soaking in a hot bath, he made his way to the kitchen freezer to retrieve his bottle of vodka. Plopping on the couch, Simon turned on the tv and searched for something to watch. As he did, the phone started to ring again. He assumed it was his mother calling back to scold him for neglecting his duties. He refused to answer it and have his ear chewed out over something he could care less about. Simon's world was crashing all around him and there was nothing he could do about it. He felt Renee was waiting for nightfall to continue her escapade of relentless terror. With his liquor bottle in hand, Simon settled in and started watching old episodes of Alfred Hitchcock. The deranged killer felt as if he was a character in one of the troubled writer's morbid tales.

Possibly even the most- deranged of them all. He was already responsible for two deaths. Nothing was preventing him from adding to his body-count. The hours passed, and Simon continued drinking heavily and watching the popular series. He could smell the vile stench seeping out of the corpse and spreading through the rest of the house as the decaying corpse broke down, making lively noises in his bathtub, challenging the love, sick murderer to keep his liquor down. Simon had no idea how he was going to deal with the putrid stench and the gruesome sight of tearing apart Renee's beautiful body piece by piece. He did his best to swallow his drink blinding himself from the gruesome task he was about to take on. Simon ventured to the bathroom with the foul, smelling carcass resting in the tub. He had to piss out some of the vodka he had been pouring down his throat.

He dreaded having to be in the same room as Renee's remains as the stench continued its assault on his nostrils. Bringing the bottle along with him, Simon almost collapsed to the floor as the smell grew more potent the closer, he got to the corpse. When he entered the bathroom, he could see that she was already starting to fall apart at the seams. Simon placed the bottle down on the bathroom sink and handled his business. When he was finished, he headed to the kitchen to grab the sharpest blade he could find. As much as he tried postponing the nauseating task of stripping Renee to the bone, Simon knew he had to get started. It was a big job and he expected it would take several hours to complete. On his way back to the bathroom, Simon heard the phone ringing again.

He would be better off answering it and allowing his mother to vent. If not, she was going to freak out and try her hardest to get ahold of him. Eleanor knew he was avoiding her for not showing up to the flower-shop that morning. She and her husband where angry with him, but they were growing more concerned for his safety. They just wanted to know he was alright. After a bunch of rings, the phone finally fell silent and Simon continued with his ghoulish plans. He found himself throwing his life away for a love that never was, nor could ever be, now that he has stolen her life away out of selfishness. Before slicing into the body, Simon hurried to the kitchen and grabbed the box of black garbage bags from under the sink. He needed them to dispose of the dead meat and organs of the slain goddess in the name of love. He knew making the first incision would be the hardest. Simon took another sip from the bottle and stood there staring at his decomposing trophy as the smell continued its merciless assault on his unfortunate, nose. Simon seemed to keep finding excuses to delay the unspeakable act he was preparing to perform.

Perhaps he simply wasn't drunk enough yet? Still, he headed back to the bathroom determined to get started, knowing the clean up after the crude dissection of his beloved corpse would take several more hours to clean and make it appear as if nothing ever happened. Simon soon found himself standing over the body, sadly looking down at what used to be the most gorgeous face he ever laid eyes on. Now that the time had come, Simon was finding it difficult to vandalize her precious remains any further. He would have to if he planned on getting what he wanted. He would also have to eventually dispose of Mrs. Anderson's corpse as well. With the knife pressed tightly in his hand, Simon just couldn't bring himself to damage her anymore. He even started to weep as he stood there staring at her precious remains.

He felt sorrow for what he'd done, but not enough to come clean and turn himself in for the violent act he committed, nor would he give Renee a proper burial so her soul could finally rest in peace, which was what her short life was all about. Instead, he wanted to mutilate her even more for his own selfish needs. Simon deeply, wondered why she was still around? Her adoring husband was just as dead as she was. Why wasn't Renee spending the afterlife happily ever after with him?

After all their souls were reunited on the other side and should be joyous. The twisted killer imagined she was trapped in limbo until her job here was done. If that were true, Renee would continue haunting Simon Fletcher, until he joins her in death. Fitting the normal pattern of a creature's habits, Simon's intense rage over, powered his heavy, heart. He knew he had a job to do. He was also terrified of someone showing up on expected and catching him in the middle of the despicable act. Once he starts the disgusting, process of carving up the foul, smelling meat, there can be no stopping. He would have no choice but to see it through to the end. Simon exited the bathroom and paced back and forth for several minutes in front of a mirror in the hallway, drinking and casually, observing the life-altering scars etched painfully into his face by a vengeful, spirit. Fighting fiercely to preserve his sanity and blind his memory from the present, the hell, born sinner chose a Ketel one shield for his defense, mechanism. A toxic liquid armor dispensed throughout the bloodstream he suddenly found himself dependent on.

Eventually, Simon felt ready as he would ever be for the gruesome task at hand, ingesting a ginormous gulp of toxicity, serum, he prayed it would instantaneously take effect as he went to work on one of Renee's arms. He imagined it was a good warm-up since he wouldn't have to dig too deep, but there was no getting away from the stomach, twirling smell that was waiting to escape into the air he was breathing. It was as if Simon cracked open a poisonous, genie lamp with the mythical creature dead and decaying inside. Renee's remains were still cold and a bit difficult to slice through, but Simon was undeterred.

He went to work, carving her arms and legs down to the bone. There were chunks of muscle still frozen and almost impossible to strip away. Simon opened the drain and allowed all the cold blood and cooling, water to escape. He did his best not to make eye contact with his victim, but it was impossible not to glance at his princess's rotting face from time to time. Simon could feel his stomach spinning as he continued carving up the girl, he couldn't live without, her pale eyes staring off blankly into oblivion. The bright sunlight began to dimmer slightly, as Simon struggled to shift his attention in an imaginative direction. He was desperate for a distraction, as Renee's flesh was jaggedly carved and peeled from her bones.

Doing what came naturally to the pervert, he focused on sexy images of Renee Price stripping slowly and having sex with him while on L.S.D. It was enough to get him aroused, but he could still smell the repulsive odor and the sensation of his hand slicing through her remains, in an adjacent door in his mind. Simon had only scraped the surface and was finding his disgraceful mission harder than he imagined. The eerie silence was abruptly shattered by the lyrics of a song, causing Simon to practically leap out of his skin. "Imagine me and you, I do I think about you day and night, it's only right. To think about the girl, you love and hold her tight. So happy together. If I could call you up invest a dime. And you say you belong to me and ease my mind. Imagine how the world could be, so very fine. So happy together"

The music sent false visions of he and Renee drifting gently on cloud nine, forever young and in love. They danced and kissed passionately, as Simon ran his fingers through her long yellow hair. He stared at her naked body, consumed by all the things he wanted to do to her. She appeared radiant and Simon never wanted the moment to end as he stared into her heavenly eyes and listened to the song play. I can't see me loving anybody but you for all my life. When you're with me, baby the skies will be blue. For all my life. Me and you and you and me. No matter how they toss the dice, it had to be.

The only one for me is you, and you for me. So happy together. Simon could feel her breath in his face, they held each other tight in a moment of bliss, when suddenly, Renee's appearance changed into a zombie-like image reaching for his throat so she could choke all the air out of his lungs. Her eyes were black, and her rotten skin was cold to the touch. Simon did his best to fight her off when suddenly he was brought back to the gruesome reality of dismembering his true love in the bathtub. Simon cut his hand carving away at the frozen meat while not paying attention. Son of a bitch he screamed, as he began to focus on the macabre scene before him. He found himself leaned over the blood bath as if he was working at a slaughterhouse. Simon felt sick to his stomach and turned to vomit in the toilet, as Simon and Garfunkel's

The Sound of Silence started playing on the radio. He had a long way to go and was already feeling weak and sweaty. Simon wondered how on earth he was going to get through this, as he realized he was mixing his blood with Renee's, creating a whole new disgusting bond with the dead girl. Simon knew he couldn't ask the Lord for help this time. He finished losing most of his drink and turned his head toward the wooden crucifix hanging above the doorway. He wondered if it could actually-see through those wooden eyes and witness the catastrophe taking place before him? Simon was going to be in for a long night. Stale blood and rotting meat were torture enough, without the painful visits from her angry spirit. His hands were drenched in blood and dangling pieces of flesh.

The wretched scent swept through the air gagging Simon often as he did his best to skin the dead body. He continued letting hot water run to heat up the carcass, making it easier to slice through. It would have been much easier to have simply chopped her up with an ax. De fleshing her with a knife was pain-staking work. It was Simon's final attempt at proving his boundless love for her. He would be at it all night if he planned to save her skeleton in perfect condition. Simon would have to toughen up if he was to get what he wanted. The bathtub was overflowing red with blood as it leaked out of her body. Simon pressed on, skinning her arms and legs down to the bone, unsure what to do next. He should have started with her face, so she wouldn't have the ghoulish task of watching. Instead, he made her observe every gory detail, as he sliced stabbed and carved away at the deceased goddess-like body she died for. It was his way of getting back at her for assaulting him the night before, and for being so attractive and popular, which was something he could never be.

Simon was purposely saving her face for last. He turned to puke his guts up several times while working on the corpse. As usual, he didn't notice Renee's reflection in the mirror, watching him as he held the blade above his head, and heaved it down in the middle of her belly, just under the ribcage where it was soft enough to make a deep incision. The stench of rotting blood came racing out like a river. It was cold enough to bag and donate to the local hospital. Simon again began gagging and vomited right in the tub, as he moved the knife downward, inviting her vital organs to punish his sense of smell even more. Songs came and went, but Simon didn't even notice them anymore. It was nothing but blended background noise. He was too occupied to pay attention until Elvis's suspicions ended, and a new song started to play.

Dripping with sweat from the atrocious task, Simon noticed the temperature in the room drop significantly. He started shivering, as he searched the bathroom for a sign of his angry murder victim. He hadn't heard anything from the old woman he slew the night before and wondered why Renee couldn't just get over it and rest in peace too? He took notice of the song playing and stopped everything for a moment.

It startled him because it was from the Beatles. Simon knew Renee was communicating from beyond the grave and she was using her favorite musicians to do it.

The name of the track help and it was exactly what she needed, but never received. It was creepy, to say the least, but Simon knew he had to keep going, as he stood there with the knife in his hand. His victim's blood covering him to the point he reeked like he was one of the dead-himself. He could feel Renee's presence, but couldn't see her.

He still didn't care about the woman he destroyed for a sick obsession he mistook for love. His warm sweat now felt like thin islands of ice covering every inch of his body. Ignoring the song, Simon went back to work. He allowed his rage to push him forward, mindlessly mutilating the rest of her body. The tub ran red with blood as lumpy chunks of rotten meat sunk to the bottom. Simon continued cutting and slicing away.

He zoned out and went someplace else for a while as he remained nauseated and trembling from the supernatural presence in the room. Eventually, the eerie presence subsided, and Simon turned to lose more of his guts in the adjacent toilet. When he turned to get back to work, he noticed Renee was alive and as beautiful as she was before he ended her days. This time Simon was not falling for it, he knew very well that Renee was dead, and he was in the gruesome process of carving up her remains. The sex-crazed lunatic had no intention of making out with her, no matter how attractive she might seem.

He started backing away, but Renee reached forward grabbing him by the throat and pulling him in closer. She wanted him to join her in the tub, so they could make love. Simon tried to resist, but Renee was incredibly strong. He turned away for a moment to pray to the Christ statue watching over him from above the doorway. He noticed the eyes of the wooden carving were real and they were looking right at him. Simon begged for his forgiveness, but there was none to be had. The wooden figure started tearing itself from the cross as if he was going to prevent the horrific situation at hand. One of the wooden nails popped out of the cross and headed right for Simon's head. He was lucky enough to get out of the way, as the wooden statue reached for another one and launched it in his direction. Renee grabbed his head and pulled him under the water. Holding his breath, Simon fought for his life and tried desperately to reach the surface, while drowning in the dead girls decaying blood. He could smell the odor of death as it invaded his nose and even his mouth as he gasped and gagged at the same time. When Renee finally relented Simon pulled his head out of the water and vomited all over the bathroom floor and in the tub with the bloody, mutilated corpse. He had to take off his glasses and rinse the blood off- of them, so he could see. When he did, Simon saw Renee standing right in his face. She stared at him for a fleeting second or two and disappeared again. Instead of taking the hint and giving up on this disgusting mockery and vile abuse of a corpse, Simon allowed it to fuel his anger even further.

Now there would be no stopping him. After cleaning his glasses and the blood from around his face, Simon continued to savagely slice her body apart. Stabbing down viciously, like a butcher dismantling cattle. Renee's body was soon completely opened- up and her heart and lungs were almost visible beneath the small lake of blood in Simon Fletcher's bathroom. It was almost time to do away with that pretty face once and for all.

Then Simon would have the gross job of picking up all of her insides and tossing them in the trash-bag lying near his feet, all but her heart, he was considering hanging on to that as a repulsive souvenir, showing exactly how morbid his mind was. What Simon was completely unaware of was that the old Irish priest was on his way over to check up on him. He had been contacted after Eleanor tried phoning him several times with no response. She even tried calling Mrs. Anderson to see if she could go check up on Simon real- quick. Again, the phone just rang and rang. What in god's creation was going on in Renee Falls while she and her husband were away? The old priest drove his black 64 Chevy impala as quickly as he could to make sure young Simon Fletcher was safe and sound. He had no idea of the horror that awaited him there. When the sun is hiding, people will do things others could never even fathom, but this was broad daylight and the faithful man was about to walk into a scene of carnage on a scale beyond his wildest imaginings. Simon could hear the damn phone ringing again while removing Renee's, brains from the bottom her skull is missing.

He held them up wondering if there was any responsive activity left in the soft squishy tissue, as he gently squeezed it in his hands. He stared at it without blinking, until suddenly an Aura of electricity emulated around it for a trillionth of a second according to his perception. Simon was searching for tangible thoughts or even lingering, feelings trapped in the dead organ. He was so busy trying to connect with his victim using her brain as an antenna to beg her to leave him be, Simon didn't realize not answering the telephone would prove to be his undoing. His mother sent for reinforcements since he refused to respond.

Now a man of god and the holy church was on his way to the killer's house, while in the middle of performing a morbid unauthorized autopsy. Simon suddenly had this weird feeling sprouting deep in his bowels. He was beginning to regret his decision to ignore his mother's call. What if she panics and calls the police to come over and check- up on him, as he continued taking his victim's carcass apart piece by gruesome piece. Father Fitzpatrick could hear the music blasting as he walked up to the front door. Could Simon Fletcher actually- be throwing a party behind his parents back? The ugly truth was much more horrifying. As Father Fitzpatrick walked up the steps, a subtle whiff of an extremely foul odor grabbed his attention, he entered the residence without knocking, since the door was left unlocked and was immediately struck down by the awful stench dominating the air inside Fletcher's home. It smelled like someone had died in there.

The concerned priests first thought was that something terrible must have happened to Simon. He expected to find the young man decaying someplace in the house cold and stiff. Never in a million years did he imagine what was happening in the home surrounded by God's watchers that fateful night. He was calling out Simon's name but not screaming loud enough to be heard over the music. Rock and Roll music which was considered the devil's work and forbidden by the catholic church. At least according to the old Irishman. Simon had no idea he already had company and that they were coming his way. The priest started going room to room preparing for the worst as he felt sicker and sicker to his stomach from the hideous odor. Whatever died here must have been dead and decomposing for a long time. The stench grew stronger as he made his way toward the bathroom, where Simon was hard at work reaching into the bloodbath and feeling around for guts and flesh at the bottom. Simon had even peeled away all the skin on her face, leaving nothing but bone behind. The smell was enough to make the priest want to turn back and head for the front door. He pressed on as the music played, calling out Simon's name, even though he didn't expect to find the young man alive. With Father Fitzpatrick creeping closer, Simon heard the phone ringing again. This time he was going to answer it and give his annoying mother a filthy curse-worded earful.

He couldn't tolerate the constant phone-calls any longer. With the bloody, knife still in his hand, Simon got up and prepared to storm out of the bathroom, only to find himself face to face with Father Fitzpatrick. The two locked eyes startled to see one other. Simon wanted to know what the fuck he was doing in his house uninvited. The priest could do nothing but stand there and make the sign of the cross as Simon slowly came toward him, the knife still hanging on to some of Renee's remains in between the fang-like blades. One thing was for sure, Simon certainly wasn't the one who suffered a tragic fate. The question racing through the old Irish priest mind was who then was it? He was almost too terrified to move as he stared into the eyes of a cold-blooded killer. It was as if Simon was possessed by the devil. Do you want to see what I've done? Simon asked while standing there drenched in someone else's blood.

The old religious man feared he would never leave the Fletcher house alive while staring at the blood bath and trash bag full of body parts on the floor nearby. He began praying to god in his head, so Simon wouldn't hear him pleading for his life. On the outside, Father

Fitzpatrick appeared brave and ready to meet his maker. Simon already murdered two people what difference was one more? He assumed he was going to the lowest level of hell anyway for what he did. Killing a man with a direct connection to the almighty seemed magnified compared to a drug-using whore and an old woman with most of her days behind her anyhow. Simon had known the holy man since he was a child. He was one of the kindest people he'd ever met. Still, he felt compelled to kill the priest for witnessing the condemning sins he's committed and began waving the knife around, threatening to slice his face open if he made a move. The elderly Christ-follower was in no shape to take him on. Instead, he used god as a weapon, just as he'd always done. He raised his hands in submission and begged Simon not to make matters even worse by killing him. The priest was desperate to know who the mutilated victim was, although he had a pretty good idea. He did his best to convince Simon into confessing his sins promising they would be kept confidential, no matter how dark and disturbing. He swore to be a servant of god and that his words would be held in secrecy forever. Simon wasn't entirely sure he could believe the old man's words, but it made no difference since he planned on killing him anyway. Do you want to know what I did Father? Come with me I will show you. Simon reached out and grabbed the old priest by the wrist. Come on Father. I want to share my story with you. Not only will I confess to a brutal slaying. I will also present you with the body. The old man started trembling in fear. Simon dragged him into the bathroom where the butchered corpse was waiting. The smell was unbearable, and the priest lost his stomach as he entered the bathroom. Simon was growing used to the stench and explained that he murdered the girl-next-door because he lusted over her sexy, body. I just couldn't help myself. I had to have her. I've been keeping her on ice until today that is. That would explain the awful stench devouring your nasal-cavity, Father.

After a while you sort of getting used to it. I know, crazy right. Simon seemed completely detached from the horrendous crime he had committed. If Father Fitzpatrick survived the deadly ordeal? He was going to break tradition and turn him into the authorities. What he did was wrong. It didn't matter if Renee was saved or not. She was a person and didn't deserve such a cruel fate. Staring at the bloody knife as he was dragged into the bathroom, the priest prepared for the worst. He could see what was left of the innocent young girl, who recently moved to town. There was nothing but bone remaining, and her decaying scalp surrounded by flies as it remained attached to her beautiful blonde hair. The one part of Renee he couldn't live without. Professing his unwavering love for his victim, Simon Fletcher snatched Renee's heart off the blood, soaked floor, and showed it off to the priest standing before him. It's the most beautiful heart the world has ever seen, wouldn't you agree father? The old man tried taking a step backward to get away from the lunatic he was suddenly confronted with. Where do you think you're going Priest, I'm not through confessing all my sins yet? Simon was becoming consumed by rage and unable to control it any longer. He grabbed the priest and stuck him three times in the gut before shoving him to the floor covered in blood and guts. The old man shifted his eyes to look up at him, asking why he was doing this? Because I love her, and you want to take her away from me. No. Said Father Fitzpatrick as he raised his arms to cover his face. He was already bleeding pretty good and in great pain. I have to kill you, or you'll turn me in. I can't go to prison. I just can't. Simon pleaded. No one has- to know. I am a man of god. I have taken an oath to protect secrets. No matter how dark and sinful. Said Father Fitzpatrick with his strong Irish accent. I'm truly sorry Father. I just don't believe you anymore, then that bitch across the street. Mrs. Anderson, so I had to deal with her as well. Did you kill Mrs. Anderson? Simon, listen to me. If you kill me? You will go to hell. You should repent your sins before it's too late, and the devil claims your soul. I have no choice and no soul Father. Said Simon as he raised the bloody-blade and struck him in the chest. The priest gasped, as Simon looked into his eyes with wicked hatred incinerating the surface. It was

almost as if the deranged killer was proud of what he had done. Simon knew he was way beyond redemption. The old priest was just one more tragedy in the disruptive saga of his short and miserable existence. The priest could hear Jefferson's White Rabbit playing in the background, it was an even tripper version of Alice in wonderland, sending the paranoid killer into a darker cavern deep inside his disembodied mind, influenced by a malevolent instigator. Mr. Fitzpatrick noticed the bottle of poison on the bathroom sink and blamed its effects on possessing the young man's mind. The faithful priest then focused his attention on the wooden crucifix above the doorway. He started praying quietly as Simon continued plunging the knife into him over, and over again, mixing his blood with Renee's on the bathroom floor ceiling and walls. It even poured from the priest's mouth as he gasped his final breath. Simon Fletcher couldn't help but wonder if it was blessed like the water turned to wine in the desert, when his god visited earth in human form and his followers were most desperate. It was a down-right disgusting way to die for such a holy man. Father Fitzpatrick paid the ultimate price for his loyalty and concern. With the priest dead alongside one of his other victims, reality suddenly came back into focus.

Simon could smell the horrendous stench devastating the air he was inhaling, it stunk to high heaven inside the tiny room full of blood guts and even his vomit. Simon looked down at the dead priest laying on his bathroom floor, his entire, body trembling from a combination of adrenaline and fear. He knew eventually, someone would put the word out about Renee and Mrs. Anderson, but the priest was going to attract dangerous attention very shortly. Simon knew he was the most important and loved man in Renee Falls. His death would not go unnoticed for very long, therefore, cleaning the evidence was extremely urgent. Simon was planning to chop the priest up into several pieces and bag it with Renee's remains. He was not going to suffer the grueling task of stripping all the old meat from the bone again. It was another disgusting task, but Simon was up to the challenge. He was going to hack his latest victim into pieces and shove them in the same bag as whatever remained of his beloved Renee Price. With two dead bodies in his home and another right across the street, the demented killer briefly abandoned the carnage to retrieve the ax from the garage, where all sorts of tools were on display, capable of severing meat and bone with ease. Feeling angelic eyes upon him from illuminating objects as he moved through the holiest house in town, Simon could also feel Renee's hateful spirit nearby. Ignoring his fears and carefully looking at everyone, of the sharp biting tools over including hand and power saws, Simon felt an old fashion weapon calling out to him. Not even a full week without his folk's strict supervision and Simon Fletcher was already responsible for three incomprehensible murders.

The music on the radio turned off as Simon hurried back to the bathroom where he had another vulgar job to do. He watched for a moment as the record player began to slowly lift off and float in midair for a couple of fleeting seconds, before launching itself toward him. Simon was fortunate to get out of the way in time, or he might be joining his gorgeous and adored lover on the other side. Simon had no idea what she was capable of, or what she might do to him once he was concentrated back into a purely energetic state. Petrified of what the future holds, Simon quickly got to work dismembering the Saints corpse, angrily hacking off arms and legs with no remorse. While Slipping and sliding in his victim's blood, Simon almost fell a few times, chopping away at the lifeless, body.

The old Irish priest winked at him with a blank, uncertainty, just before having his head decapitated by a sharp blade sparkling in the dark. Standing in a lake of blood, Simon dropped the ax and began shoving more body parts into the trash bag along with Renee's organs. He unwillingly found himself focusing on the Christ statue peering back with eyes made of the very trees he was destined to be nailed to. There was a treacherous warning in them, but Simon chose to ignore it, knowing god was not only real but watching over him with every optical lens of his omnipresent view over the heavens and all things trapped within the walls of matter contained inside. Simon tried his best to ignore the hauntings and potential divine encounters with beings from someplace else, by scrubbing the bathroom clean and praying the lord and all his winged soldiers could be washed away as well, even as he imagined the reptilian being of a higher intelligence he painted coming to life in his most recent artistry hung on the fridge.

Either there was something truly eroding the killer's mind, such as guilt and regret, or, Simon was receiving vivid, warnings from another physical place of complex substance outside our own three dimensions of space and time. It was too frightening for the perverted murder to comprehend, as the gravity of the horrendous situation continued sinking in. A chill colder than autumn's death cooling the surrounding, air rattled its way up Simon's spinal cord and into his brain causing it to freeze momentarily from the inside out. Simon removed the crude, wig made from her original scalp so he could disinfect it and prevent the skeevy bugs from consuming the last remaining flesh of Renee Price, the goddess who traveled unreachable realms to present herself to him in this vast, yet minute universe among the countless others. Renee's hair was all Simon had left as far as something tangible enough to smell and bring him back to when the girl of his dreams was still alive.

He scrubbed her bones clean, boiling them in scolding, hot water, until they were immaculate, with twisted thoughts of dressing her in the pink lingerie he stole from her house, but never got the chance to use. Simon loved Renee even the way she looked at the moment but didn't want her bony figure showing off its true nakedness. Renee should look ravishing after all the unspeakable things he's done to her. Simon sat on the bathroom floor with the skeleton and the chopped, up flesh, drinking his vodka and reflecting on the situation at hand. He turned to look at the trash bag full of human remains, Father Fitzpatrick's head blankly staring back at him in the upside, down position. He wanted to pack the human remains in the back of his shit box and dump them off on the side of the road someplace ridding himself of the whole thing but was in no shape to do so. Sitting in the bathroom of gore staring at the mutilated priest and the skeletal remains of the woman he couldn't live without Simon focused his attention on the remaining buzzards falling to their delayed deaths while continuing to feast upon her rancidly decaying scalp. Simon found himself trapped within a scenery cast directly out of the bible's most menacing versions of hell.

It was in that desperate and most honest moment that Simon Fletcher realized with the bottle to his lips, that the real reason he despised his parents most of all was the simple fact that they discovered love so young and easily in life. He knew it would never happen the same way for him, as he glanced at the bones of the woman he swore to love unconditionally.

Simon even went as far as to consider slaying the lives of the very people who brought him into this harsh and frigidly, soulless world. When Stanley and Eleanor returned from their perfect little getaway together, their only child considered claiming their lives as well. The killing was not only getting easier, but it was also becoming a morbid obsession, as the bodies piled up, reminding Simon that he had a whole other mess across the street to clean up.

First, he had to make sure no evidence remained in his parent's home where he laid his head at night. There were blood and guts everywhere, from not only one victim, but two. He continued filling the trash bag with body parts, while doing his best not to slip in the pool of blood covering the bathroom floor, like a cold and powerful gust of phantom wind blew passed, almost tipping him over. Simon frantically looked around, but there was no one there. He heard the dreaded gasp for air, as he turned his attention to the dead woman resting uneasily in the bathtub. Her skeleton lunged forward, reaching out to pull Simon Fletcher back into the tub with her. All he could do is stare at the animated bag of bones for a moment or two, before turning to run for his life. Simon slipped in the blood and landed face-first on the bathroom floor, as the skeleton continued climbing out of the tub. As Simon struggled back to his feet, he heard his mother's pipe organ playing. It was the most dramatic tune ever composed in the form of notes possessing keys. Simon hurried in that direction only to find the unsettling tunes being played by the ghost of the woman he swore to adore

. There was blood staining the organ keys and Renee's heart was still beating while resting on top of the musical instrument. Renee turned slowly to look at him, as she continued to play while fading into nothingness. The house fell silent momentarily until the sound of laughter filled its walls. It sounded sinister, Simon turned and ran through the house, as all the religious artifacts came to life and began following him with their eyes, wondering why he would do the terrible things he did. When he came to the dining room, the infamous painting of the last super caught his attention. He quickly noticed there was blood splattered across it and that the figures looked like zombies feasting on his mutilated body, Simon watched as they tore him apart and fed on his flesh. He could also see not only Renee's reflection subtly staining the un, sainted portrait, but also the tall reptilian being peering back at him. It had the coldest eyes as if it was some sort of highly technical robot programed by something from another world. Simon turned to look away from the morbid portrait, only to find Renee standing right behind him. He screamed in fear, as she dug her filthy fingernails deep into his face scratching and clawing, leaving craters that flowed with blood like miniature volcanic eruptions. Simon pleaded with Renee, swearing he loved her and didn't mean for any of this to happen, but she wouldn't let up. Afraid for his life, Simon turned to run from the vengeful spirit who swore to get even with him for her untimely death. He found himself dodging his mother's porcelain angels as they flew through the air at him, forcefully guided by the young woman he savagely raped and murdered. One of them hit Simon in the back of the head, knocking him to the floor and tossing the glasses off his face. He could hardly see anything clearly without them. With a fresh head injury soaking his hair in blood, Simon did his best to search through the hazy world around him for his bifocals. He reached out to grab them when he was startled again by demonic tunes being played on the organ.

He turned to look up with the glasses in his right hand, as he noticed the sound of stomping feet smashing the ground as they, hurried toward him. Everything seemed foggy through his poor vision, but Simon could see a dark shadowy figure looming in the air. As it came closer with the power of a speeding freight, train, Simon prepared himself for another thrashing, clutching his hands into a fist and crushing his glasses. He heard the crunching as a rib splintering kick collided with his chest, temporarily knocking the wind out of his body. Simon lay on the floor for a few seconds struggling to breathe again, it felt like his chest was on fire, he was certain at least one of his ribs had been broken by the unseen force. The music was still being played on the pipe organ, as Simon did his best to try and regain his composure. He was desperate to get out of the house and away from the dead woman trying to kill him. Simon eventually made it to his feet and headed out the back door, as the telephone started ringing again. He had no interest in listening to his mother's bullshit while venturing into the backyard to be confronted by the treehouse where it all began. Stumbling and falling on the way since he could hardly see through the darkness, without his other set of eyes, Simon was creating even more agony for himself, further injuring the damage done to his bony chest and the gaping hole on the side of his head.

Simon could feel the warm blood drying on his face in the cold night air, as it was constantly being replaced by an endless leak. He felt drawn to his house of sins as if he would somehow be safe there. The sound of footsteps creeping behind him could be heard, but when Simon turned to have a look around, no one was there. He was in pitiful shape as a cold chill jangled his spine while staggering up the wooden steps leading to his old sanctuary in the sky. Nervously, Simon sat in his chair, staining it with blood, while trying to ignore the fact that he was being terrorized by an angry ghost eager to fore fill her deadly, promise. He had lots of incriminating evidence to clean up before people catch on to what he's done.

If Simon wanted to get away with three murders, he would have to man up and get the job done. He focused his blurry vision in the direction of Mrs. Anderson's house for a second or two, reminding himself of the other mess he had waiting across the street. Simon looked away from the grizzly crime scene and briefly focused his attention on the shallow ground beneath him. If Simon Fletcher was going to make sure all his dirty deeds were properly disposed of so no one would ever discover what a weirdo he was, the first thing the twisted pervert needed to do is get rid of his secret treasure of satanic and violently graphic portraits, as well as the Frankenstein model he created to so closely resemble the dream lover he brought to life. It would be difficult to part with, but after all the terrible things Simon had done, he knew there was no escaping some form of justice. God's wrath was coming in one form or another, it seemed impossible to get away with the atrocities he's caused the once perfect little town called Renee Falls. He was going to dig up and burn all his finest works of art, then get busy making the dead bodies disappear.

Opening the doorway to his secret stash, Simon found himself reliving his darkest moments from the past. He could see himself scribbling the most barbaric and hateful pictures ever created. He could also feel the heat coming from the burning, wooden crucifix melting the messiah nailed to it. Simon didn't know the darkest of his memories were yet to come. He soon found himself back at the beginning of Renee's tragic murder scene, smashing her head against the wall and floorboards, with his hands wrapped tightly around her neck, squeezing with all his might. Once again, he was staring into Renee's angelic blue eyes, as she continued fighting for air.

The vision was so vivid, he could even hear, the sound of her windpipe shattering, while sucking the life out of her body and penetrating her at the same time. Again, Simon watched the light fading from her eyes and a blank stare come over them as death settled in. With his hands still around her throat, Renee's body rapidly turned back to dust, leaving Simon Fletcher to make sense of what just happened. He was tremendously shaken by the experience but went forth with the task at hand as he continued losing blood while grabbing his collection of raunchy, photogenic evidence. Simon slowly stood up and prepared to head out of the treehouse with all his sinful works of art in hand, only to be confronted by the solid manifestation of Renee Price hovering in mid, air blocking his exit.

Simon couldn't believe his eyes. He stood motionless watching as she rapidly decayed in the same clothes he murdered her in, while slowly spilling his unholy portraits to the floor. Renee slowly walked toward him, her skeleton practically marching through the rotting flesh, with a ravenous sparkle in her eyes.

Suddenly they were no longer blue and inviting, instead, her windows to the soul were tinted black as onyx gemstones and infinitely deep in her skull, like gateways or blackholes into dimensions so terrifying they could be mistaken for portals to a hellish destination. Simon trembled as he watched Renee reach forward and open her hands to reveal a beating heart in the center. It was so romantic of his victim to offer her most loving organ to him. Horrified, Simon stepped back from the blurry image, as Renee lunged forward. Clumsily he lost his footing, smashing the back of his head on the wall behind him, as Renee's apparition slowly evaporated into thin air.

CHAPTER 17

⁘ ✦ ✦ ✦ ✦ ✦ ⁘

The next morning Simon's parents were frantic, unable to get ahold of their son, they were on the first flight they could catch, back to New Jersey. Eleanor called the store again first thing and got no response, nor was Simon answering the house phone. She felt the knots tightening even more in her gut when even the priest seemed to vanish after going to check on him. Eleanor also found it impossible to get ahold of Mrs. Anderson across the street. She is almost always home and answers the phone for anyone on the other line.

Something had to be wrong. Her husband Stanley was on the phone with the Renee Falls police early that morning as well. It was as if the devil himself came to the little holy-town in-order to destroy it. Showing his dominance to the false worshipper's. Worried as they may have been? It wasn't Simon's folks who first alerted the police that something wasn't right on Madison Avenue. Renee's friends in California tried several times to convince them that she was missing.

The lazy cops who often had nothing to do insisted maybe she just didn't want to talk to them anymore, she did move to the opposite end of the country after all. They eventually agreed to check it out on the third day, just to make sure everything was alright. Renee Price was a part of their town now. Her husband was even buried in the earth there. If something awful happened to the pretty young woman? They were going to get to the bottom of it. They had no way of knowing the worst day in the town's history was just getting started. On the way to Renee's place, they were informed to check up on Simon Fletcher who lived right next door. Soon more calls flooded the police station. Folks were also wondering where Father Fitzpatrick disappeared to. Everyone loved him and paid frequent visits to his church, which meant any day of the week not just on Sundays for mass. Some come to confess and others just to feel closer to god, as if the old, Irish immigrant was a direct conduit to their maker. When he couldn't be found in the church, people began to worry.

For years Renee Falls inhabitants jokingly called their town Saints-Ville. It was because nothing wicked ever occurs within its blessed boarders. Now it seems as if hells gates were bashed in unleashing Satan's fury upon them. What kind of monster would harm such a sweet old man? It was unthinkable for most residents to accept. They demanded justice for the old Irishman who stole their hearts and saved their souls. The peace would be shattered, and innocence destroyed if the police don't find the one responsible for the heinous crime, should he have met with some sort of foul play. If the priest didn't turn up soon, the tension would continue to escalate. Thinking the worst, some of the peaceful worshippers wanted the killer's head for what they 'd done. No one would know the gruesome, truth until the police start knocking on doors. Something very strange was going on in Renee Falls and its people were growing scared.

No one is as much as poor Eleanor and Stanley Fletcher. They had no idea what terrible things their son was responsible for while they were away. It was the longest, most dreadful flight they had ever been on. The hours felt like weeks trapped in a metal capsule thousands of feet in the air. All they could think about was their son Simon. He was their only child and they couldn't imagine losing him. Eleanor did her best to stay positive, keeping the lord's prayer in her head, but that ancient motherly instinct was relentlessly telling her otherwise. She had to get home and make sure her baby was alright. She gripped her husband's hand and for the very first time in her life dared to have a couple of stiff drinks to calm her nerves. The first squad car to arrive on the scene parked in-front of Renee's house. The officer started pounding on the front door loud enough to wake the dead but got no answer. Busting in before back-up arrives is always risky, but he felt confident there would be no one there to greet him. The young officer was preparing to find her dead body someplace inside the house. He noticed that lots of things were packed. It appeared she was planning to leave this quiet little town behind. He assumed she was heading back to California as her friends had insisted. When he got to her bedroom, he noticed it was a mess.

There were open drawers and clothes everywhere. Still, there was no sign of Renee Price. He used his radio to inform dispatch that the Price residence was empty. There was no sign of the young girl potentially missing. By that time a rookie officer had arrived at Mrs. Anderson's house. He was supposed to be across the street at Fletcher's place. It proved to be a significant mistake. Entering the home, it didn't take long to discover the tip of the bloody iceberg. It was all the proof needed that there was indeed a killer loose in the town of Renee Falls. When he entered Mrs. Anderson's bedroom, he found her on the floor full of stab wounds. There was a large dried-up puddle of blood surrounding her body. He nervously transferred the gut, wrenching information back to headquarters.

The police officers didn't know the real horror was waiting for them inside the Fletcher's home. That's where they would discover not only the missing bombshell but also the old, priest murdered, chopped up and placed in a trash bag on the bathroom floor. The smell of decaying flesh would get their attention as soon as they opened the front door and stepped inside. They had one hell of a mess on their hands. Finding Mrs. Anderson's dead body was completely unexpected. They were not even looking for her yet. By the time Stanley and Eleanor made it back home, the sun had gone down and the street was crawling with cops. Eleanor's heart sank when she saw the yellow caution tape blocking off three houses including her own and the priest car still parked out front. She hysterically got out of the family wagon and went running toward the crime scene.

Stanley did the same but was corralled by the sheriff, who started to explain what happened, while he and his wife were away. He could see the panic in the father's eyes.

Eleanor continued racing for the house desperate to find her son. I'm truly sorry to be the one to tell you this Mr. Fletcher, but your son Simon is dead. Stanley became weak in the knees and almost collapsed from the tragic news. The sheriff held him up while explaining that Mrs. Anderson, Renee Price, and Father Fitzpatrick were also dead. Overcome by grief, Stanley started shaking and broke down in tears. He couldn't imagine things getting any worse until the sheriff informed him that it was all his son's doing. What? Was the only word he could utter as shock transformed the look of his face? The sheriff explained that he found Mrs. Anderson brutally stabbed to death in her bedroom. He went on to say the priests' remains were hacked-up and placed in a trash-bag with whatever was left of Renee Price from next-door. Stanley was praying this was just a nightmare. He expected to wake-up on the airplane any second and everything would be fine. What he wanted to know is where his son was now? That's when he heard the blood-curdling screams of his wife coming from the backyard. She pushed her way passed police officers and entered the house of sins only to find her son, Simon lying dead on the floor. It was clear he was in some sort of violent struggle with someone, or something, judging by all the cuts and bruises covering his body. Soon her husband would join her, and they would discover the horrific truth of what their son was capable of. Killing not only Renee Price but Mrs. Anderson and even the holy man from their church, turning their neighborhood into a horror show. Inside the house of sins, Police discovered a bunch of disturbing portraits, including a very bizarre one made from a collage of Playboy models precisely placed together. Renee's bleeding heart in his right hand and her skeleton at his side like some sort of twisted Romeo and Juliet love story. Simon's house of sins was finally being exposed, filled with police officers demanding to know what in god's creation the young man was thinking. One even opened the hidden chamber, realizing it was where he must have kept his secret stash of the forbidden art, work he had squirreled away, until this moment. There were graphic depictions of murder and explicit sexual paintings of the dead woman resting nearby. Simon Fletcher confused his lust and possessiveness for love. It can be the greatest thing this finite existence has to offer. It can also be as dangerous as a hydrogen bomb detonating in a major city destroying everything in its path.

For Simon Fletcher, the toxicity was powerful enough to eliminate several lives including his own in the end. Love is the most potent of all emotions. It's worth far more than silver and gold and can cause inconceivable atrocities if misunderstood in a chaotic mind. Stanley stood there crying his eyes out as the police searched the treehouse, he built for his little boy so long ago.

The innocence it once possessed was gone forever. Eleanor couldn't stop screaming as she stared at her only child being removed from the treehouse he spent so much time in, Renee's skeleton and heart were also taken, along with the mutilated priest found in a trash bag on the bathroom floor, sharing the guts of the young girl he murdered to be with forever. In the end, the Sheriff couldn't determine exactly what it was that ultimately killed Simon Fletcher and put an end to his reign of terror. It was most likely the injuries to his head. His skull was cracked in more than one place, and he suffered a severe brain injury.

It could have also been the cold from lying there unconscious, even the enormous amount of liquor he consumed that night was a considerable possibility to the town Sheriff, causing him to perhaps bleed out faster. He even pushed his imagination to the bizarre scenario that just maybe, it was the vengeful spirit of his first victim Renee Price reaching out from beyond the grave and frightening him to death. The world might never know for sure what killed Simon Fletcher, but we can all agree he deserved what had come to him in the end.

THE END

LOVE YOU TO DEATH

I loved you so much I couldn't bear it. When you were gone for hours Your photos I would stare at. Obsession made me a bastard. Just can't grasp it. My descend into madness, a brutal murder with a hatchet, stay here with me you don't need a casket. Praying to god for magic rage and jealousy sunk to the deepest, of depravity pure insanity. See your reflection staring back from the vanity, such a casualty wishing you were back with me. Bloodcurdling screams of agony the guilt sinks in naturally. Perished so senselessly crying hysterically trying to tap into your super, natural energy how insensitive of me a psychotic rampage your last memory pacing nervously clean, up the murder scene I'm going to just lay here with you for a while and dream.

Woke up in cold sweats, you're looking fresh in your wedding dress dance with the dead. Lost my head. Sex after death. So horrendous I hate to mention it. If bad intensions breathe karma let it be. I'll forever deserve to grieve. I kissed your cold cheeks, laid you down on the sheets like everything was straight, close the drapes. Can't bear to bury you in the grave. Your body's the memory I most crave. Fear escalates of the damnation that awaits, I'm so sorry. Please forgive me, give me strength. Trying to come to grips, trying to comprehend what I just did. Should I turn myself in the walls are closing. Why my most cherished became my most brutal homicide. I'm dying inside, as you slowly decay attracting flies. I closed your eyes. Shivering chills signified that you were still by my side.

This is getting way to morbid I think I lost it. Makeup over rotting flesh, looking gorgeous. There's hell to pay for my actions. Looking at your credit cards, should I max them? Life goes on. I'll never forget you when I hear this song. Trying to be strong, terrified of your hauntings, more intense. The stench is getting unbearable, think it's time I finally buried you. Nothing but pictures are left now. The silence is deafening. Cops knocking, I've been expecting them with loaded guns if they enter. The negotiator said surrender. Love you to pieces, you should be with Jesus. I'm speechless. Heard strange noises in the attic last night. Saw you holding a bloody knife. Should I apologize for my life? It seems the only way to make things right. Maybe we can walk together towards the light.

Lightning Source UK Ltd.
Milton Keynes UK
UKHW012029300720
367452UK00005BA/125

9 781734 713244